Blueface Dreams

By:
C. C. Spicer

Cadmus Publishing
www.cadmuspublishing.com

Published by Cadmus Publishing
www.cadmuspublishing.com
Port Angeles, WA

ISBN: 978-1-63751-085-8

DEDICATION

Look Mom, I made this!! Can we put it on the fridge?

Author's Note

Be more concerned with your character than your reputation because your character is what you really are, while your reputation is merely what others think you are.

CONTENTS

Prologue 1
Chapter 1 3
Chapter 2 10
Chapter 3 15
Chapter 4 20
Chapter 5 23
Chapter 6 28
Chapter 7 34
Chapter 8 40
Chapter 9 44
Chapter 10 49
Chapter 11 55
Chapter 12 59
Chapter 13 63
Chapter 14 69
Chapter 15 74
Chapter 16 79
Chapter 17 83
Chapter 18 88
Chapter 19 93
Chapter 20 98
Chapter 21 102
Chapter 22 106
Chapter 23 113
Chapter 24 117
Chapter 25 122
Chapter 26 127
Chapter 27 130
Chapter 28 132
Chapter 29 137
Chapter 30 141
Chapter 31 144
Chapter 32 148
Chapter 33 157
Chapter 34 164
Chapter 35 170
Chapter 36 181

Chapter 37..185
Chapter 38..194
Chapter 39..209
Chapter 40..218
Chapter 41..226
Chapter 42..232
Chapter 43..239
Chapter 44..245
Chapter 45..250
Chapter 46..256
Chapter 47..262
Chapter 48..271
Chapter 49..279
Chapter 50..287
Chapter 51..293
Chapter 52..300
Chapter 53..306
Chapter 54..315
Chapter 55..327
Chapter 56..341
Chapter 57..348
Chapter 58..356
Chapter 59..368
Chapter 60..375
Chapter 61..382
Chapter 62..398
Chapter 63..427

PROLOGUE

The police lit 'em up with their lights. "What's up Dro?" Black asked. ". . . want me to take them on a ride?"

Dro inhaled a big breath then exhaled. "Pull over."

They looked at him like he was crazy. It was something in his eyes that made Black comply. Truck in park. The officers pulled behind them. "I ain't goin' to jail, Slim," Dro said looking forward. "Mask down."

Everyone in the truck pulled their mask down in compliance to Dro's orders. "Kill 'em."

The officers never seen it coming. The windows were tinted 5 percent. Four doors flew open. Dro was geeking, ready to put in work. It was all or nothing. He had a new STAG 8T, a draco.' He was trying to see what that gas-operated piston action was about.

He lifted the rifle, looked through the diamond head premium flip up, sight set and squeezed. TAT TAT TAT TAT . . . Dro fired the assault rifle in semi-automatic spurts connecting with the first officer's body. The officer's mid-section looked like a Picasso painting as his shirt oozed blood.

After the first shot was heard, Izzo dived on the ground. The bullets felt like they were flying too close for comfort.

"This nigga crazy!"

Dro was shooting, approaching the squad car as endless shells hit the pavement. BOC BOC BOC!!! Black fired at the other officer as he jumped over Jroc, who was laid out on the ground not used to the sound of choppa bullets.

The police never had a chance to draw their weapons as their bodies laid spread on the street. One slid down the car slowly.

Dro shot so many shots that the car began to flame. Slowly, Jroc and Izzo stood up and looked at each other through the truck's open doors with wild eyes. Black and Dro walked to the corpse for good measure and fired. BOC. TAT TAT.

"I'll drive this time," Dro stated with his hands out for the keys . . .

CHAPTER 1

"What's understood, don't need to be explained."
— Dro

It wasn't your average night in the city. Washington, D.C. that is. The only place in this country of ours that should be called the city, Our Nation's Capital.

Rain descended from the dark clouds as Black and Izzo crouched behind a car waiting on the right moment to strike.

Black didn't mind the wet pavement. It actually was to his advantage. Izzo, on the other hand, was beyond pissed as a car cruised, splashing water as it passed.

"Shit! My sneaks."

"Shhhh nigga." Black hushed him.

Moves and quick come ups was a daily routine for Black. Nothing he did was for fun. There was always a reason behind this wrath. Today he decided to bring along one of his best friends who didn't mind doing anything for the sake of a dollar.

It was closing time at the corner store the Arab owned. Salim, he was a young, but balding foreigner that was talking greasy and slick to Black earlier in the day disrespecting his sisters and all while hiding behind the protection of the thick window divider.

That action alone was what triggered Black to make him pay. In a high pitch tone of irritation Izzo complained, "Damn Slim, you got me out here in the fukin' rain messing up my fit and I just got my dreads retwisted."

"Shut up, nigga, nobody told you to look all sexy for a robbery."

"All you said was come on and I came."

"Shhhh . . ., there he go."

Coming out the creases Black sprung up to make his presence known. No mask or nothing. He wasn't worried about his face being exposed; this was personal.

Frozen in place, Salim raised his arms to the sky in surrender. In broken English and a heavy Arabian accent, he pleaded, "Please . . . no harm . . . all to take yours," he said trying to pass off some pocket change as he stared down the barrel of a loaded handgun that Black pointed.

Izzo was still behind a parked car a few cars back trying to get his ski mask out of his side pocket. The rain made his pants stick to his skin a little too close for comfort.

"Stupid ass skinny jeans," he cursed himself.

Finally getting the mask out of his side pocket and over his face he got up to assist Black but heard a siren in close vicinity. He ducked back sown, hiding from the sound, but looking around trying to locate its physical presence.

Salim heard the siren as well, as if he was a cartoon and a lightbulb shined bright over his head. He had an idea and wasn't going to let that opening he had close. "Oh Allah! Thank you, the police!!" In his native tongue he lied and to his surprise it worked.

Black turned around with lightening speed, nervous and scared he would get caught. Looking around he didn't see any sign of the police. Turning his attention back to his victim, he seen the Arab sprinting down the street as water splashed with every stride he took. "Shit! . . . bitch ass nigga," Black murmured as he began to give chase.

Izzo looked up and over the car he was ducked behind to see the Arab running his way. "Uh uh nigga, I got your ass." He tiptoed to the sidewalk and stuck his leg out in an attempt to clip Salim up.

The power from Salim's stride forced Izzo to fall as the Arab fell and rolled a few times a couple feet forward. Black was on Salim's heels until he ran into Izzo as Salim got back up continuing to run. "Move nigga! Get out the damn way!" Black said running over Izzo.

"Ahhhh shit! Get dat' nigga . . . damn, fucked up my whole leg," Izzo whined, getting back up trying to run through the pain.

Salim was pretty fast. He moved through the parked cars and traffic with ease and agility. Onlookers and passersby looked on in awe of the chase. No one really cared for the Arab, so no help was in his near future, at least not from the residents in the area. He was considered an asshole to most. He'd put tax on top of tax and basically robbed the lower class but catered to the high class.

The chase was intense. Zip-zagging block to block, Black kept up his pace, but couldn't gain on him. Izzo was tired. Newport's and good weed had him winded. His leg was pulsating with pain which was another deterrent slowing him down.

Izzo leaned on a light pole, trying to catch his breath. "I'm right behind you bruh,' get that nigga!" Looking left then right, Izzo spotted a motor scooter approaching. "Bingo." As if he was a Major League pitcher he whinnied back a hay-maker punch.

CRACK! That was the sound of the connection from fist to chin as the rider flew off the scooter. "Can I ride?" Izzo asked, picking the bike off the ground. Chucking the deuces to the fallen rider he rode down the street to catch up with Black.

Salim was running for his life determined not to get caught by Black. He knew Black was crazy. Now he was regretting all of them wolf tickets he been selling behind the safety of the

Plexiglas.

Black was getting exhausted. Out the corner of his eyes Izzo came flying past him. "Come on Slim, speed up," Izzo smirked.

Izzo was on the Arab's trail gaining on him by the second. Pulling on the right side of him he kept his hand on the throttle. "Hey buddy, you okay?"

"No!" Salim responded still running but pointing behind. "Call police! Mad man robe me."

Izzo cruised beside him. He tried to throw a left hook. In his mind he thought it was gonna be a for sure knockout punch. Swinging the punch he boasted, "They call me Floyd!" The hit connected with the back of Salim's head with little to no damage.

"Ahhhh!! Oh no." Salim reacted instantly turning off the street through an alley. Izzo tried to grab him but ran into the car in front of him that stopped for the red light.

Black caught up with Izzo as he was trying to get the scooter off himself. "Floyd my ass. What kind of punch was that?" he said as he cut through the same alley following Salim.

"Fuck . . . you . . . nigga!" Izzo cursed at Black's back. ". . . Black ass got me out here chasin' a nigga in da rain . . ., in skinnies."

Izzo cut through the same alley to see Salim done trapped himself off. "Okay, Slim," Izzo said to Black. "Looks like Obama ain't the only nigga to catch a Bin Ladin lookin' mutha-fucka, huh?"

Black was heaving with his hands on his thighs and his gun resting on his knee. "Like I was saying before you decided to think you were Usain Bolt, where dat' shit at?"

Salim looked around and noticed he was caught. "Here." He tossed a velvet Ziplock pouch with today's take.

Flipping through the content, a smile spread across Black's face, then tossed it to Izzo. Izzo fired up a stogy and looked himself over. He was disappointed at what he seen.

"Look . . . at . . . this . . . shit . . . here," he said referring to his outfit. Izzo reached for his gun that was tucked in front of his briefs. "I'ma kill 'em."

Black laughed as he watched Izzo struggle. "Nigga, you can't even get that mutha fucker out of them lil ass jeans." His gun still trained on Salim.

Dipping and squatting, Izzo was determined to free his weapon. "Hold on, Moe . . . I got his bad ass."

"Please don't kill me," Salim pleaded.

"I wouldn't be Black if I didn't, Slim."

BOC! BOC! BOC!

Black shot Salim all in his upper torso. Finally getting his gun from his waist Izzo pushed Black out the way. "Move fool, I got 'em."

POW!

"Thank you, come again." Salim was silenced with the final headshot.

"Really, lil' ass p-shooter," Black said clowning Izzo's gun as Izzo blew his smokin' barrel.

"Who's bad?" Izzo imitated Michael Jackson.

Running out of the alley the coast was clear. Sirens was nearing. The car Izzo hit with the scooter was bringing unwanted attention. The doors were wide open with no driver and a blaring horn. "We gotta dip!" Black stated.

They weren't too far from their neighborhood and that was the next location. The rainy weather turned into a storm as the traffic lights began to flicker yellow.

The neighborhood had a leery silence as if everyone knew a life had just been taken.

Making it to the courtyard of the housing projects, Izzo noticed his building was fogged out, nothing was visible from the outside.

Climbing the few steps to enter the building it had no locks or keypads. It was always broke. Izzo just opened it to a cloud of smoke attacking his nostrils.

"Damn, who got it?" Izzo asked as he noticed his two other comrades.

Dro and Jroc were sitting on the stairs smoking the building out. These four together were unstoppable. As kids they made a pact to remain loyal and always keep it 100 with each other. Friends from the sandbox, nothing or no one could come between them.

"I should have known it was you two niggas," Black said coming through the door behind Izzo.

Izzo tossed him the pouch from earlier and they split it down the middle. Fifteen hundred dollars a piece between Black and Izzo was what the lick brung.

"I see y'all on that bullshit, huh?" Dro asked.

"The grind don't stop baby," Black said fanning the crisp twenty-dollar bills in the air.

"What y'all doing in my building?" Izzo asked.

"We knocked on your door but looks like you niggas weren't home. Now where you? Next thing I know is that it started pouring down, so naturally your hallway became the layover."

Thunder roared. The sky was lightening up. It looked as if fireworks were in the clouds. Everyone was on their own level as the blunt circulated in the hallway of the building.

Laughs and loud conversations had the neighbors opening and closing their doors to make a statement. No one cared. As far as they were concerned, this was their building, their hood. Couldn't anybody tell them anything.

The night was still young in most eyes. It was only a quarter to nine. Everybody was smacked, meaning they were high out their mind as they exited the building.

"Next spot after a body drops, the mutha fuckin' liquor spot," Black said as Dro shook his head, reading in between the lines of what that statement meant.

"Don't be trippin' in shit when we get this bottle either," Dro told him.

"He a'ight, we a'ight, we got each other, right?" Izzo said grabbing Dro and Black into a huddle while Jroc laughed, rolling another spliff.

"What's understood, don't need to be explained," Dro stamped.

CHAPTER 2

Dro (Mr. Logic)

". . . like you dying or some shit."
— Dro

It was one of them days. The kind that had you mad as shit. I mean I'm laid back, but it seems if dudes take that shit as a damn weakness. Here I am in my hood and can't even sell a damn rock, shit. This the shit I don't like.

"Slim, I'm tired of these wild niggas," I stressed. "They got me fucked up, keep thinking they gonna keep steppin' on my toes like I'm anything out here."

"Chill bruh'." Jroc tried to reason. "All that shit gonna sell anyway. Them niggas 'bout to roll out. They been out here all morning."

That's the bullshit I be talkin' 'bout. Even my man think it's okay. He missing the whole logic of my irritation. "That's the shit you not even paying attention to. Fuck, they think I can't hustle til' they leave. I'm tryna eat too homes'," I said.

"I feel you bruh', but while you doin' all that venting in shit? Pass the blunt, damn."

"See fool, you not even listening to a nigga."

Jroc blew a sigh. "Bruh I am. On my mother I'm listening, so what you wanna do? I'm always on your side, right or wrong."

I shook my head, lost in my thoughts. "I'on know, but we gotta do something . . . I tired of this broke shit," I said looking down the street, noticing my men. "There go Black and Izzo right there . . ." Cough, cough. ". . . call them over here. My chest 'bout to bust. Fuck, you get this shit from. It's some pack moe, on everything," I said complimenting the potency of the weed.

Jroc looked at me and frowned. "Um, must be nice being tho' you still got the damn blunt, especially since you ain't put up on it mannnn, dayum'," Jrock emphasized as he snatched the blunt from my hand.

I didn't trip as my homies neared. "Sup' wit you two niggas?" Both of them made their own gestures in response.

Black was on it as he inhaled the secondhand smoke approaching Jroc. "Damn fool, ain't fun if the homie can't smoke none."

Pulling the blunt back out of reach, then taking a pull, Jroc replied, "Nah' bruh, that line only work for the bitches only . . ." I was hip to 'em. He was still tight from me sucking the blunt down. I laughed on the inside. ". . . here nigga, wit' your suck face ass," Jroc relented passing the blunt to Black.

Izzo laughed at the whole encounter. "Y'all niggas wild, but what's up wit' you Dro, mean mugging in shit?" he asked, still giggling.

Before I could answer Jroc decided to cut me off and give his answer. "Bruh maaaaddd . . . bcuuuuuzzz . . . he been out here tryna sell that buuuullshit, garbage ass coke aaaallll day . . . um um, and the ol' heads ain't showing him no love." He smiled, happy at the revelation he just gave.

Now I ain't gonna lie, that shit had me laughing on the low, especially how he said the shit in slow motion tryna clown a nigga. He got that shit off. ""Petty nigga. My shit butta,' it's your wild ass ol' heads all in the way. Still on the corner in shit," I defended, shaking my head. "When I get on, I'm damn sure ain't gonna be still trappin' on the block for profit, believe dat."

"Yeah, my nigga, talk that big boy shit, that's right Rayful Edmonds Big meechie and em'," Jroc said while Izzo and Black continued laughing.

"Yeah, yeah. Fuck yuh, but we gotta find a new spot to bang if we wanna get this shit off," I propositioned.

"Fool, I'on care where we go. You know I ain't got shit to sell but bullets . . .," Black said reached. ". . . all I got is this 38 special looking for my next delivery," he said kissing the barrel. "Only you and Izzo got work. Come to think about it I've been scoping out this move that would put us on top," Black remembered as he looked toward the sky.

I looked at Black. This nigga stay on some bullshit. Every since we was small tots in the sandbox all he knew was a quick come up. I remember one time when we were younger, like 6th grade and our teacher said something to Black. I couldn't remember or recall what it was, but it had him livid. At lunchtime he dragged me with him back to the classroom. We fucked the whole room up, tossed everything around and some mo' shit. When we were finished, he went in the teacher's desk and stole his wallet, a quick come-up.

"Hell nah!!" I told him. "I don't rob regular dudes. That shit aint' my cup of tea, Slim."

"Listen fool." Black pushed. "Always quick to shoot a nigga down. I know you so I thought of all that and I'm talking 'bout an establishment, and if the shit go right, we gonna be on."

"Yeah, I hear you, but look, my mom's blowing my horn up. I'll see you niggas later," I said tryna walk off.

"On some real shit fool, just think about it. This could be what put us on," Black said holding my arm.

"Yeah, right. I hear you," I said as Black released his grip and

I walked down the street.

I headed down the street, many thoughts invaded my mind. This was usual, but Black had me really thinking. I made it to my grandmother's house. It was a two-story brick house attached to other homes. I think they call them townhouses or row homes, some shit like that.

This the house I grew up in with my siblings. They all grown now and have their own. I'm the last one left to leave the next.

Opening the door, I seen my mother on the couch playing with her phone. A game she likes to play had her attention until the screen door slammed.

"Sup' Ma . . ." I spoke when we made eye contact. ". . . you blowing my line up like you in here 'bouta die or some shit."

"Lil boy!! Who you think you talking to like I won't pop you in your mouth," Momdukes said.

"You gotta catch me first ol' lady," I said laughing.

"Cordell Washington, I am young and loving it. You should be happy that you have a young mom." She struck a pose. "But back to the subject at hand. Did you bring me my cigarettes?"

"What cigarettes?" I was confused. "I ain't know what you was calling me for."

"If you would have answered the phone you would've known. So, go and get me some smokes, please."

Momdukes already knew that I wouldn't deny her. All that please mess was just animation. I wasn't really tryna go 'cause my stomach was touching my spine and I was chasing money, but mom's is always persistent. "Give me the money, Ma."

"Hmph." My mother looked at me with her hand on her hip, then came all the extra hand gestures and more animation. "Ooohhh, you need money, huh. All that Ma, I'm out here getting' these chips Ma. You blowing my spot up, fall back, Ma this, Ma that and you can't get me no cigarettes. Um um, snack hustler here boy." She gave me a dub. ". . . and bring my damn change back."

Looking at the twenty-dollar bill I wanted to not accept it, but my pockets didn't agree. I grabbed the money and walked outside the door and headed to the store.

Walking I had to swallow my pride. What my mom's just said was right. I'm broke. Broke and hustling for a re-up and pair of shoes. I'm white T fresh, with a pair of Old Navy faded jeans. This shit gotta change.

Now my mind roaming. The more I think about my nigga Black and whatever crazy mission he got up his sleeve, I'm hungry and ready for whatever.

I opened the door to the store and made it to the counter. "Aye James, let me get a pack of Newport's, short box."

CHAPTER 3

Jroc (Golden Boy)

"So let the games begin."
— Jroc

I watched Dro walk down the street. That's my man. If it wasn't for him, I probably wouldn't even be in this group of good men right now. Dro used to defend me in grade school before I had the heart to do it myself. I love dat' nigga.

"Y'all niggas got something on the tree?" I asked as Dro disappeared from eyesight.

"Nope," Izzo said. "I just got out here, Bob."

Black looked around rubbing his hands. "Shid, I could in 'bout five minutes. Let me spin the block right quick and see what's shakin'."

"No bruh, chill . . .," I told him shaking my head. ". . . always tryna rob a nigga. You need a damn job or some damn work to feed you habits."

That nigga didn't pay me any mind as he waved me off. "You be sounding real stupid James," Black said and Izzo laughed because he called me by a government name. He knew I hated that shit. My mother named me James Taylor, but I felt that was only for paperwork purposes only.

See, me I don't need to hustle. I'm kinda okay when it comes to money. I'm spoiled thanks to mother. I'm her only child and I always get my way. I sell a little bit of tree, but shid, who don't. Everybody seems to have tree at least by the gram.

My moms work downtown making good money and gets me whatever I want. Really, I just go outside and chill with my homies. We all we got, straight outta da sandbox. I don't need to beat the block. Some niggas be mad and say I'm in the way but fuck 'em."

"Fool!!" Black yelled, snapping me out of my train of thought. "You flying in or what?"

"Yeah bruh. I got some pack too," I told them reaching into my dip grabbing my stash.

Izzo chimed in, "I got a dutch, Bob."

"Well, you can keep that shit. I got sheets and fun-done. You know how we do uptown. Keep all that dutch shit on the southside, bruh."

Most people not hip to fun-done. It's what we used uptown to smoke our weed in. Well, apart of it, it's actually a tobacco leaf dried out, sprinkled over the weed wrapped in sheets.

"Awww shit!" I said grabbing everyone's attention. Something didn't look right. "That look like the people's bruh," I pointed.

"Where at?" Izzo asked following the direction of my finger. "Nigga that's Reds from down bottom. He just brought that hot ass Crown Vic, and it still got the crash bars on it."

That nigga could have fooled me. I was sure them folks was about to pull up on us.

"Aye Black . . ." I turned around to see him halfway down the block. ". . . oh shit! Izzo. Look at that nigga bruh, he fast as shit,"

I said as we watched the nigga hop the fence, never looking back.

I shrugged my shoulders. "Guess it's just you and me playing ping pong on this dooby," I said referring to the blunt.

"Shid cool wit' me, fire that shit up! I need a getaway. It's slow as shit out here and I need some bread like asap. Nigga pockets ain't right at all." Izzo grabbed the blunt and inhaled. "This lil allowance . . ." He exhaled. ". . . mom's be givin' a nigga ain't shit. It's crazy I'm broke and 'bout to be 19, Fool. These other niggas eatin', why can't we get on?" Izzo preached.

"Shid, you know I don't hustle like that shit, cuz. I'm 'bout to head to college next semester. This lil weed I push don't count. My moms would blow a gasket if she thought I jumped any-where near the game you niggas be playing in these streets, es-pecially Black. She hate that nigga for some reason," I said dead ass serious.

My moms didn't like me to be around him at all. She felt as if he was a bad bad influence, but shid, Black was my nigga even though we don't always get along.

"Yeah, nigga whatever. I know you ain't tryna really be out here in these streets. Don't try to blame it on your moms with your scary-ass," Izzo said as he started to shadowbox with me.

I swatted his punches down. "Whatever bruh, but if you that fucked up you might as well see what that nigga Black talking 'bout. You know he stay on a move for a come-up," I told him. "I'm 'bout to roll out, I got some pussy lined up, da dig, some-thing you might not never know nothing about." I popped my collar, laughing at my own joke.

"Whatever Bob. I'll see you later," Izzo said.

"Yup . . . later bruh."

I walked down the street; a horn beeped. I realized it was my moms pulling off. 'RIGHT ON TIME' I thought. I had plans, didn't need her asking a lot of questions.

"Bye sweetie, love you!!" she screamed, driving down the street.

I entered my crib, walked to my room and headed to my stash.

I had some good weed that I planned on rolling up for baby girl that was on her way. In the back of my mind, I was thinking about my homies, wishing they would get their shit together. This hood shit getting old.

I didn't want them to get caught up in the life. But later for that. My phone rang, snapping me out of my daze. "Yo, sup' shawty, where you at?"

"I'm out front Boo," she answered.

I smiled, geeked. "A'ight, come on in, the door open." I hung up.

When I came down the steps, 'oh my' my jaws damn near dropped at the sight of this woman. Remember the cartoons where your eyes pop out and your tongue roll down the floor— that was me.

Shawty was bad. I mean better than the last time I seen her at the party. She resembled Angelina Jolie in Tomb Raider. I'm still wondering how I bagged her, but fuck that, she here now.

"What's up hookah'?" I spoke with a Kool-Aid smile.

She looked at me like, 'NIGGA WHAT.' I had to laugh. After a second, she did the same. I fired up the blunt then gave her one of my mom's wine coolers. She said she didn't drink beer.

I popped a Corona, pushed a lime through it like I was at a bar. She was one of them "green" pitches, so if all it took was a blunt of kush and some wine that's all I was gonna give her ass.

I was thinking of the many possibilities and positions I was gonna fold her into when I glanced at her figure. 'DAMN' I thought, shit was sweet too soon. After about 2 or 3 gulps of her drink that shit was gone.

This bitch drank that shit like it was juice and asked for another. All I could say was, WOW! I had to go to my personal stash and give her some of my White Remy. That shit put her in the right mood.

After a few shots shawty was all over me. She was goin' with no intentions of slowing down. That's the type shit I like. You know I was all for it. She started goin' for my pants, playing with

the zipper. That was my green light.
"Let the games begin."

CHAPTER 4

Black (Work, No Play)

Look at what we got here."
— *Black*

I made it to the end of the block. I didn't hear any sirens, so I felt I was good. "Shid fuck dat,' I ain't goin' to jail, fuck dey' thought," I said to myself as I tried to catch my breath.

Getting my wind back I walked down the street rapping. 'TUESDAYS AND THURSDAYS THE HOTTEST DAYS OF THE WEEK.' A classic Hotboys song. It was so true about the life I live. I rapped wondering why my men didn't run when Jroc said them peoples was rolling through.

I had the dawg (gun) on me. I knew I had to take flight. Now me, let me introduce myself. My name is Hov . . . sike naw. I'm just your average hood nigga with dreams of getting rich, but in reality, I ain't got shit.

My moms be in and out the house, chasing the next nigga. So, all I have is my two little sisters, they twins. I always try my best to make sure they get anything I could get my hands on.

That kept me on my bullshit and the next move. Going broke or hungry wasn't an option. My phone range and I recognized the ringer. It was set only for this caller.

"Hey princess, what's up?" It was my lil sister and I wondered what she wanted.

"Nothing, we hungry. Ma said she was gonna get us some food, but that was at breakfast . . ." She wined. ". . . now it's lunchtime and we still didn't eat."

I listened as I walked down a side street. "Tsst." I was irritated and smacked my teeth at the thought of my mother. "Okay baby, I'm on my way. What y'all want to eat?" I asked as I watched this delivery man park his car in front of a resident.

"Ummmm . . ." she contemplated. ". . . some carry-out."

Naturally a smile crept across my face. "That's what I hoped you'd say. I'll be there in a minute."

Classic situation of wrong time wrong place. "Look at what we got here . . ." I spoke to my pistol. ". . . Mr. delivery man I was gonna let you live, but my babies hungry and you have the antidote." Geeking like shit I whipped out. "Nigga, you know what time it is?"

The China man was scared. He was goin' through the same pockets like it was gonna change or multiply. I knew he was used to this procedure. The whole time he kept his head down and eyes low. He wasn't tryna get murked.

He tried to pass off the money. I gave the screw face, but he couldn't see me. His head was still lowered. I smacked the cash out of his hand. "Jackie Chan, I 'on want your money . . . I want the food." I snatched the brown bags.

The expression on his face was priceless as he finally made eye contact. I guess the shit was funny when you think about it. The deliver man was confused and didn't want to make the wrong move.

"Pick your money up and get the fuck on before I change my mind and blow your fuckin' face off!"

He hauled ass, happy and shocked all at once. I ran down the street, hoping dude wouldn't call them folks. Shid, I didn't even take his money even though I wanted to, but that wasn't the lick. I always try to stick to the plan.

I laughed to myself. I just robbed a dude for some carry-out. I made it to my courtyard in the complex and headed for my building.

I opened my apartment door and my lil sisters ran to me with open arms, screaming in joy. "Miss you!!"

I made them wash their hands as I set the food up for them to eat. I grubbed too. That weed I had earlier had my shit on empty. As I watched my sisters eat, all I thought was getting them out this shit hole.

More thoughts of this move came rushing my mental. "I gotta call these niggas and see if they tryna eat or nah."

CHAPTER 5

Dro

"Be Careful."
— Madukes

Leaving the store, I sparked one of my mom's cigarettes and walked out onto the street. It was a nice sunshiny, summer day. The whole hood was outside. The bad ass little kids even brought a memory back when I walked past an open fire hydrant with them running back and forth through the water.

'I REMEMBER THE DAYS' I thought. 'NOT A CARE IN THE WORLD.'

The good ol' days seemed like a distant memory but wasn't really that far in the past.

"Aye nephew! You good?" a regular (customer) asked, bringing me out of my daze.

"Yeah, what's up?" I responded. From his gestures and the

way he was fidgeting I could tell he was about to be on some bullshit. I was prepared.

"Maaannn listen, you know I get my check on the first, right. I'm a lil short right now, but don't trip, just work wit' me. You know I got you baby," he anxiously asked.

"How much you got Slim?"

"Baby boy I got 15 bucks nephew. But you know I got you baby, it's nothing."

I acted like I was mad but shit, I wasn't letting that money go. I need that. I reached into my dip and dropped 2 big boulders of butta (crack) in his hand. Okay, maybe more like pebbles, but he was short, so we were even.

"Thanks nephew!!" Unc' smiled. "I got you on da first," he said, talking to my back. I was headed the other way.

"Damn, it's hot out here," I sighed, pulling off my shirt.

Bending the corner, out of my peripheral view I see my man Black running fast as shit with what look like carry-out bags. I laughed, knowing he had to be on some bullshit. "I'll holla at that fool in a minute." It looked like he was headed to his crib anyway.

My phone got to buzzing, it was moms. "Damn, she must be geeking like shit," I said to myself, then answered the phone. "Sup Ma?"

"Don't what's up me. Where you at?"

"I'm on my way now. I'm walking down the street, you good?"

"Yeah, I'm good, but your lil friend called. I was about to give her your cell number but figured she would have had it if you wanted her to," she said knowingly.

"Thanks for the lookout. She a good girl doe. I like her a lot. I told her I didn't pay my bill. I'll hit her later," I hipped my mother.

"Didn't ask for your love life. Where my damn cigarettes?"

I giggled. There it was, the truth behind the call finally revealed. "I'm coming."

I caught a couple more sales before I made it back to the crib. I walked in the house, gave my moms her cigs and pushed it upstairs. In my room I sat on my bed to collect my thoughts.

Thinking about my next move the house phone rang, but quickly stopped. My mother must have answered it. A second later she was yelling for me to pick it up.

"Yo!" I answered.

"Hey boo, I miss you. What you doing?" Charmine asked with excitement all in her voice.

"I ain't doin' shit, coolin', just came from the store. Just sitting in my room now, just thinking."

"What you thinking about?" she asked. I could tell she was smiling, thinking I'ma say her.

"A lot and nothing at all, but I know I need some bread, and a lot of it real quick. I'm tired of this broke shit," I confessed.

"Well, I get paid on Friday . . .," she said like that was the answer to my problem. ". . . you wanna flip my check again?"

"Awww shit! I'ma be on now. What you getting, like a whole 200 dollars?" I teased.

"Tsst." She smacked her teeth. "I was just tryna help, you ain't gotta do me like dat," she whined.

"Sike naw boo, I'm playing. I'm good thanks. Matter of fact tonight I'ma do something for you, okay?"

She was excited again. "What we gonna do?"

"Something but be ready around eight. You know I got you. I'll call you, so make sure you ready and don't have me waiting."

"Okay bye, Boo."

I hung up the phone and sat on my bed smiling. 'DAMN I LOVE SHAWTY.' I knew when my shit get straight, I was gonna treat her better. She deserved to have the spoils of life. But right now, I need cash, so I headed back downstairs. At the door I hear my moms yell from the kitchen. "Be careful."

"Always."

'BACK TO THE BRICKS, IT'S THE SAME OLD SHIT 2.50 A PIECE, GOIN HALF ON A NICK.'

I rapped as I diddy-bopped down the street looking for a cluc-ka (crack fine). My phone rang. It was Black and I wondered what was good? "Heeeeyyy Supa' ugly!"

"Fucka yooooou, you where at fool?" he asked.

"Just leaving the crib 'bout head up 9th Street on Tst. side to see what's shakin,' " I told 'em. "Ayo why was you running earlier. I seen you come through the old lump lump alley kickin' it."

"Nigga you know, caught me one slippin.' But that's nor here or there, fuck dat. I need to holla at you."

"Holla then nigga," I told him.

"Nah bruh, not on the horn. I'm talking 'bout that move you in or what?" The phone fell silent for a second or two. I had my suspicions, but I put that shit in the back of my mind. I know I need that money and it could be a start to a new beginning, so my answer was easy. "Fuck it let's do it."

Black gave me the instructions, told me to call Izzo and see what he was trying to do and for us to meet him at the old recreational center Shaw, and wait by the basketball courts.

I walked down the street finally stopping to post up on the fence down L.W., short for neighborhood complex, Lincoln Westmorland Projects, and chilled with my men from around da way. They already had a jay in rotation as I dapped everybody up. I chilled at the other end of the gate and decided to call Jroc's number. It was the last in my recent log.

He answered. "Yo yo what up Babyboy?"

"Shit coolin' fuck you doing, Slim."

"You know me, just got up outta some cheeks, jealous?" Jroc asked laughing.

"Not never. I get mines, but you do stay wit them bitches, Slim."

"And you know this maaannn!!" Jroc said in a Chris Tucker voice.

"Yeah, yeah bump dat doe. What you 'bout to do? I really need you to head up to the old rec so we could holla at Black about that lick."

I could tell by the pause that he really didn't want no part of this. If anybody knew this nigga it was me. Ever since we were younger it was like he would zone out, contemplating every possible outcome of every move.

"I'll roll but if that nigga talking crazy, you already know I ain't fuckin' with 'em," Jroc finally answered.

"A'ight be there at 4:30."

"Damn, it's already 4:20, bruh."

"Well, go ahead and wipe your dick and come on dirty ass," I said hanging up on him, not giving him a chance to respond.

CHAPTER 6

Izzo (Hustlers Ambition)

"Uh Uh boy. What you doing in my living room."

'NIGGAS KILL ME.' I shook my head. 'WONDERING WHY THEY CAN'T GET NO MONEY, SHID CAN'T NO-BODY STAY STILL LONG ENOUGH,' I thought as I leaned against the light pole smoking a stogy. See me, I'm your average street nigga looking for a come up. The only problem is the money I make. It falls through my hands like water.

My mother named me Isaih Miller, but the streets call me Izzo for short. We are what you would consider a lower middle-class family, if that makes any sense. Moms got a good job, driving the city bus which is cool. But when you have a few kids, that check be gone as fast as she cash it. So, anything extra I want I gotta get it how I live.

"Damn, it's slow as shit out here," I said to the air that surrounded me, waiting for the next sell to come.

I was still buzzed from that good pack Jroc fired up. I walked to the store down the street to get a bag of chips and maybe a soda. I had the munchies, and a vicious cotton mouth. Headed down the street I seen Dro leaving out the store. I was gonna call for him, but he was halfway up the block, so I let him continue to push.

When I made it to the store it was a few of my men in there playing Keno and the horseraces trying to get a quick come up. Other than them it was empty, so no line for me. I went straight to the front to the counter.

"Aye James, let me get a bag of plain UTZ and a bottle of water," I requested.

"Okay, that will be 1.75 please," James answered.

I looked around behind him. In the store everything was behind a thick plexy. When I was younger, I remember I used to be able to just grab what I wanted and bring it to the front of the store. Them days were long gone. Now I had to wait for him. "Matter fact, let me get a pack of smokes too, Newports."

"Okay that will be $8.00," he calculated.

"Damn!" I forgot how high this nigga store was on the tobacco products. I should have went to my man Sammy's store up the street. He sweet but fuck it I'm here now. I slid the money through the turnstile and in return I received my stuff.

As soon as I grabbed my bag, niggas in the store was already on my line. A nigga yelled could he get one of my cigarettes. I gave that nigga the screw face. He in here gambling and tryna mooch off me. He didn't want a square until he seen one. I looked at dude and fired one up. "Fuck no!" Then continued to walk out the store.

"Hey you . . . You! Show me your hands," an officer screamed.

"Fuck! Look at this shit here. My luck must be some shit on my mutha!" WHERE THE HELL YOU COME FROM, I thought.

"What you want?" I asked the police. "I ain't do shit, hands up don't shoot, Black Lives Matter," I shouted, raising my hand tryna grab somebody's attention, just in case.

The officer was white, and he chuckled. "Yeah, okay smart guy. Get on wall and keep your hands up then," he said as he made an attempt to check my person.

I glanced at the squad car that he got out of and seen the clucka (crackhead) I just served up the street. He was pointing in my direction and that shit had me nervous. I knew I was hit. It was a bold move on my part, but while his partner went into the store to check if I dropped a stash or anything in there, the officer went to grab my arm. I'm pretty quick and I spun around, then pushed the officer into the wall, then broke.

I hauled ass. All I heard was radio chatter in the distance. I never looked back until I hit the corner. I continued to run until I reached the courtyard. The courtyard was the chill area in the hood. It had a playground in the middle of the apartments that surrounded it with two ways to enter.

I seen one of the neighborhood girls chillin' on her porch. Tiara. She was a bad lil redbone that I had an eye for, but didn't really entertain the thought too much, thinking she had a nigga 'cause ain't nobody 'round here hit.

I ran right in her apartment. The door was wide open. She didn't care, she was hip to what goes on 'round here. Sirens were loud. Tiara acted like nothing happened as the jump outs ran through the courtyard behind me. I was scared, no lie. My heart was beating out my chest. I wasn't tryna go to jail. I was in her living room pacing the floor, tryna catch my breath. 'I THINK I SERVED AN EGG' I thought, meaning an undercover. To make matters worst, them fools blew my damn high.

"Uh uh boy . . ." Tiara's moms popped up outta nowhere with her hand on her hips. ". . . what you doing in my living room looking all suspect?" she quizzed.

"Go ahead Ma, I ain't doin' nuthin' but chillin' with T.T.," I said trying to throw her off.

"Well, you need to go in her damn room. I'm 'bout to have company and I don't need you scaring him off, so be gone," she said walking to the screen door to call Tiara.

That's all I needed to hear. She gave me the green light. I went straight in Shawty's room, sat on her bed and turned on her TV. You would have thought this was my spot.

Tiara cool. She a around the way girl. She always speak and flirt time to time, but always keep it moving. Ain't never gave a nigga no cheeks. Maybe 'cause I never tried.

She is sexy and definitely worth the time.

"Boooooyy!" she sang walking into her room. I laughed. "Something funny?" She paused. "You all laying in my shit like it's yours," she said with her hand on her hips.

I shot my shot. "Won't you come lay with me," I said just fuckin' with her, but she came and laid beside me.

"Fire up nigga!" she said after crossing her legs. She ain't say nothing but a word. I didn't mind. I was like why not? I couldn't go outside right now, might as well get high.

We didn't have no roll up, so I sent her to the store. I wasn't goin' nowhere. 'Bout 10 minutes later she came back with 3 backwoods and a fif' of Goose.

We smoked and drank while she retwisted my dreads. I was in my zone. It always felt good when females played or did my hair for me. "Izzo, why you always playing with me?" Tiara asked from behind me.

I was lost for a second. I looked at her face and seen her eyes and demeanor, then knew what she meant. She was choosin.' I smiled inside, geeked. I been waiting for her to give a nigga a chance and I hope she wasn't just talking. So, me being the flyest nigga of them all, I played it off like it was nothing.

"Girl, don't nobody be playing wit your big head ass." She walked to her lil iPod setup with the surround sound and decided to play some music. She act like I wasn't even watching TV. It was cool doe, I just kept sippin' my drink.

She rolled the last backwood, then licked it super slow and sexy. 'SHE TRYNA GO' I thought to myself. A throwback Beenie Siegal song came on, Feel it in the Air. That joint had my shit in a zone. I laid back with my eyes closed rapping the words.

"Damn this one of the realest joints he ever wrote," I said out loud as I opened my eyes to Tiara passing me the blunt.

She was sitting on the bed Indian style. I noticed she didn't have any panties on under her skirt. She caught me looking and smiled. In the back of my head, I was like, 'I'MA FUCK HER.' I'm smoking, she shuffling through songs and stopped on Wale's song, The Body featuring Jeremiah and got to slow winding to the beat.

The way she moved her body had my man brick. The Goose didn't help, it made it worst. Had me ready to go balls deep. She was twisted now, having the time of her life. It seemed like she would just grab this joint and get to it the way she was looking.

Walking to me slowly, but still dancing she decided to give me a lap dance. When she sat down on me, she hopped right back up and looked at me, then my print through my cargo's. I looked at my print as well, then back to her. "What?" I asked sarcastically.

She smiled, stepped right back in front of me and dropped to her knees. I was happy as shit in the inside, but I couldn't show my excitement. Tiara had the prettiest lips, and they were so soft looking. I couldn't wait as I helped her take my dick out. I licked my lips in anticipation. She looked at it and smiled.

If she could read minds or even look into my head right now, she would be tripping out. The thoughts that ran through my mind, crazy. I guess she was satisfied with my length, she kissed it, licked it, and then devoured the whole thing.

"Yes!"

Her eyes were trained on me. I didn't know if I screamed that out loud or in my head. Drake and Nikki Minaj song, Make Me Proud came on. Here I am thinking to myself, 'YES, HOW PROUD OF YOU I AM,' as she did her thing. She was sucking like it was no tomorrow.

I was about to blow my top, then logic came to mind. I decided to let her know. I didn't want to fuck up my chances of getting in them guts. If the head game was this good, the box had to be torch. She was looking at me the whole time while she was sucking and didn't stop when I told her. So, naturally everything I had, became hers as I came in her mouth.

I fell back on the bed, my phone started ringing. It was Black. I didn't want to answer, but I didn't want Tiara to think it was another broad I was ducking or some shit, so I answered it on speaker. "Yeah Bob."

"Sup creep, we all meeting at Shaw at 4:30 to talk about what I said earlier."

I looked at my watch. It was already 4:05. I peeked at Tiara who was listening attentively as she sat up, taking a sip of her drink. Eyeing me knowingly, she knew I was about to skate.

Really, I didn't want to. Shid, I was tryna smash. Luckily, she stood up and kissed me on my cheek then told me, "Handle your business and come back tonight so we could finish what you started."

With that confirmation I told Black, "I'll be there."

Black being nosey he asked, "Yo, who dat, moe?"

I didn't say nothing except, "I'll see you later, Bob," and ended the call laughing.

I sparked a jack (cigarette) and headed out the door. Tiara was on my heels. She gave me a hug at the door with the promise of a good time later when I returned.

I left her apartment looking around making sure the coast was clear from the incident earlier. It was 4:20 now. I knew the shift has changed and hopefully the officer that chased me was on his way home.

Walking through the courtyard, I chucked the deuces as I spoke to people in the area. I decided to head up to the rec' center and see what was up with the homies. Hopefully, money was the conversation. I was just hoping Black had a good plan. I'm tryna get on. Not like that bullshit he did with the Arab, that shit was anything.

CHAPTER 7

The Meeting

"Do we gotta send somebody to the moon?"
— Izzo

The weather was humid. This time of the day was its peak. It wasn't getting any hotter, but it was hours from it getting any cooler. "Okay, so what's this master plan you got up your sleeve?" Dro asked Black.

He didn't even get a change to answer before Izzo added his frustrations. "Yeah nigga, fuck you got me at this hot ass b-ball court with no shade, and I was 'bout to be knee deep in some pussy, damn!"

That comment by itself, pussy, that alerted Jroc's senses, and he had to ask. "Oh yeah bruh, who was you 'bout to hit?"

This made the conversation go left and off track for a couple of minutes as Izzo explained. "Moe, shit was crazy. I was getting chased by them people's earlier. I think I served an egg, so I ran in Tiara's house and—"

"Who's house?" Jroc cut him off.

"Tiara nigga! The lil joint that live in da courtyard . . ." Izzo hipped him then continued, ". . . so I flew her in (got her high) with some pack and some Goose to pass the time. Next thing I knew she was sucking the skin off my dick, on my mutha'." He looked to the sky smiling, in remembrance. "Um um."

The story drew Black in as well. He was listening as Dro looked around scoping the area out just to be on point.

"Damn, why you ain't crush?" Black asked.

Izzo gave him the dumb face. "Um, I wonder . . ." He scratched his chin. ". . . maybe because you called my damn phone about this shit right here, stupid," he stated sarcastically.

Dro's mind was somewhere else. Out of that whole conversation all he heard was the police chase. "I was wondering why them peoples kept circling the block and riding like that," he said, but no one was listening because he was barely audible.

"Aye, back to business though, listen," Black said getting everyone's attention. Jroc fired up a jay (blunt) as Black began to talk and put it into rotation. "Okay, I've been checking out this nigga that live around my girl way and—"

"Whoa whoa whoa Slim. Pump your brakes," Dro said. He didn't even let Black finish. He didn't like the way this conversation was goin.' "I told you I'm not with that robbing nigga shit. If I rob a nigga I'ma smoke 'em. Not tryna body (kill) a nigga for no petty shit. I leave that up to you."

"Oh, okay den, tell me why mad." Black laughed. "You didn't even let me finish. I was gonna say the nigga got a sweet ass job—"

"Hold up, Bob, phone off the hook," Izzo stated, letting them know a few dudes was rolling up on bikes.

It was a few dudes from surrounding neighborhood. The basketball court was like neutral grounds. You're liable to see anybody there. Friends of friends, friends of enemies. It could go down on the court. The leader of the bike posse spoke. In response, all he received was head nods. That was sufficient enough.

The air was loud. It was full of funk which led to the basis of their pull up. "Where dat shit at? Polluting the air in shit, we tryna get our shit dirty too."

Jroc made his presence known. He is the weed man. "What y'all tryna get?"

Another spoke. "Shid, we tryna get a 7' (grams)." Jroc got excited to make a few dollars and forgot the whole reason they were up there in the first place. "Bet!" he said as he asked to see one of their bikes so he could make it happen faster.

Jroc rode off and Black cursed him out as he pedaled away. Now he had to wait for Jroc to return for him to be able to continue. "Chill Slim, he'll be right back." Dro tried to relax him.

Black wasn't tryna hear that. Really, he didn't even want to include Jroc because really, he didn't need the bread and in his own opinion, he didn't think he was built Ford tuff. "I know, but damn, he ain't even got a big part in this shit. You know the nigga scary anyway," Black barked.

"Yeah, this is true," Izzo interjected. "But he still our man doe."

"No bullshit Slim. Chill." Dro agreed.

They debated amongst themselves about different shit, but didn't get into any particulars, then it happened. "Fuck y'all niggas talking 'bout?" one of the biker boys asked.

Black's face turned into a mean mug. If looks could kill, dude would have been on the pavement. "None of your damn business, ain't nobody talking to you, wild nigga!"

Shocked, surprised, and a little bit nervous with bubbled eyes he responded, "My bad, damn Slim." He tried to save face.

Everybody knew Black didn't play. He was a loose cannon at any given moment. That made niggas try to stay on his good side, or out his way.

While chilling, boredom started to circulate. It was decided to shoot the basketball around to pass the time since they were on the court. What started off as a free rec' game turned into a physical game of '33.' Playing that seemed to draw a crowd as it got pretty deep. The game changed into a full court 5 on 5. Everybody was balling hard and actually having fun.

The game was close. Dro came down court and shouted, "steph Curry!!" and shot the 3 pointer that won the game for his team. Sitting down everyone drank water and talked smack to each other about the game.

Jroc rolled up in the midst of the conversation. He served the guys who had patiently waited while the ones that balled, put their clothes back on. After they got the tree, they gave everybody dap and rolled on about their day.

Black looked at Jroc. "Damn, fool, fuck took you so long?"

Jroc smirked. Everybody knew what he meant. He had a story behind it and couldn't wait to tell them. "Moe, it was an emergency—" Dro could see right through him and cut him off.

"Wellin,' " he said, meaning Jroc was lying.

Jroc bust out laughing. "A'ight, you got me. I saw this bad ass Nubian Queen by Howard. She looked like one of the women off the movie Coming 2 America 2. I had to shoot my shot," Jroc responded, smiling, flashing them her number and picture on his phone. He sat down and started to roll a jay and asked, "So what's up?"

Black's phone buzzed. He stood, frozen in time, just staring at the phone with death in his eyes. It had to be something bad. His face was screwed up, looking crazy.

"Black, what's up Slim?" Dro asked.

Black clenched his teeth and fist. "We gonna have to cancel this shit, this nigga got me fucked up." He was livid. Dro knew something was up and knew Black was stubborn. He knew he wouldn't say shit until he was ready, but still he tried.

"What's goodie, Slim. Somebody want smoke?" Dro asked.

Izzo felt the same way. He ready to ride or die for the team. "No bullshit. Do we gotta send somebody to the moon . . ." Izzo was geeking, hyped. ". . . you know my shit stay geeking to let go."

"Nah, I'm good. I got it. I'll see you niggas later 'bout that other situation," Black said, then jogged off not waiting for a response.

They all watched Black jog off, wondering what was on his phone that made him take off so abruptly. Lost in their own thoughts, no one noticed how empty the court became.

"Damn bruh, that nigga was mad as shit. Think we should follow him?" Jroc asked.

Dro and Izzo looked at him with a wild expression. Izzo laughed. "You serious? If anybody could handle their own, it'll be that nigga."

"Tsst damn." Dro was blown. "I was hoping to find out the details of that move. I'm ready for whatever."

"Shid you too. I was praying that shit was asap. I got plans, Bob. If this move big as Black sayin' it's gonna change our statics in the hood," Izzo stated, smiling like he already had the money.

"Whatever it is I just hope we ain't gotta do nothing illegal, ya know," Jroc said.

Dro looked to the sky and shook his head. Izzo glared at Jroc and said, "Nigga! Shut da fuck up wit your scary ass. Of course, we gonna break the law. If it was that sweet everybody would have done it and been on, you stupid dumb nigga," Izzo said, frustrated.

"Fuck you bruh. Fuck you think you talking too?" Jroc defended, jumping forward.

"You!! Wild nigga," Izzo said, walking to his face, not ducking, nothing. "What's up?"

Dro intervened. "Both y'all chill out." He stepped in between them, instantly squashing their small beef from brewing. "I'm 'bout to head back up top to see if I can make a couple of dollars til Black hit me to tell us what' up. Fuck y'all 'bout to do?"

"Shid, I'm 'bout to go up there wit you. I got like an ounce of tree left I'm tryna sell before I smoke dis shit up," Jroc said.

Izzo had different plans. All he was thinking 'bout was Tiara.

She had his mind going crazy. Determination to make her his own was his new mission. "I'm 'bout to go back down bottom to see what baby girl doing. Maybe she will show a nigga some love." He was cheesing. Dro laughed. "A'ight Slim. See you later. Me and Jroc gone up."

"Yup, that's a bet." They parted ways . . .

CHAPTER 8

———⋘∘⋙———

Black

"Did he touch you . . ."
— Black

This nigga done lost his damn mind. I ran through the court-yard headed to my apartment. I was tight. I received a text from my sister saying that my mom's friend put his hand on her. How she said it, I knew it wasn't in the right way. My head was spinning with a bunch of wild thoughts of the worst.

I didn't know what I was gonna do when I got to the crib, but it wasn't gonna be a good scene. I made it to my apartment. Moving fast, I couldn't even find my damn keys.

BANG! BANG!

I kicked the door. It rattled with each connection. Careless could describe the blunt force of my foot, almost taking it off the hinges. "Boy! Have you lost your damn mind?" Moms asked as she snatched the door ajar.

I didn't even bother to answer. My mind was elsewhere. It wasn't on the courtesy of how I knocked. "Where Shaniyah and Shanae at?" I brushed past her, almost knocking her rover.

She was on my heels as I walked toward my sisters' room. She was talking to my back, I had tunnel vision. "I don't know what them girls told you, but you need to calm your ass the hell down!!"

This the shit I didn't understand. Moms so quick to curse me out but be so oblivious to the hardships and pain my lil sisters go through. It's been times when I wanted to treat my moms how she treat us—second and third to her needs. I held my tongue as my sisters entered the room. They heard my voice.

"Hey Donte!" My sisters jumped from the floor trying to catch my neck with hugs.

I put my emotions to the side as I greeted my sisters. "Hey lil uglies!!" I said, smiling as if all was good.

I love my sisters; they are my mission. I made myself a promise to give them the best of what I never had. I didn't have kids, but I took care of both of them as if they were my daughters. I looked behind myself to see my mother still lingering. "What you want?" I asked her.

"This my damn house." She stated the obvious, tryna pull her trump card. "Don't be askin' me no question," she snared.

I waved her off and turned my attention back to my sisters. "Which one of y'all texted my phone earlier?" I asked. They both fell quiet but looked at my moms.

"That's a good question. I'on know what they told you but now I wanna know," my mother said talking to me, but looking at them.

"They didn't say shit 'bout you. Mind yo' business." I scowled her and mugged. I could tell she wasn't gonna move. She was gonna be nosey and gather as much information that she could. I wasn't gonna make it easy for her as I heard the all familiar sound. "Come on, I'ma take y'all to the ice cream truck."

From the window I could hear its jingle. This was my way to get the girls out of the apartment and out of moms' face so I could get some answers. All I knew was that my trigger finger was itching. Somebody was gonna pay for it soon. I just had to find the person to let go of this wrath I had boiling.

"What y'all want?"

Shaniyah's face lit up. It was like stars was in her eyes. "Ummm, I want a vanilla cone with sprinkles."

Shanae frowned. I knew she didn't want the same thing. They were twins, but complete opposites. "Ugh, I hate sprinkles. I want the uhhh . . . chocolate e-thingy."

"Eclair," I corrected. I grabbed the ice creams and passed it to them. "So, what's up?"

"Nothing," Shaniyah said looking down, twisting one of her toes in the dirt beneath the ground.

I knew she was lying, but Shanae confirmed it. "Tell him!" Now I was eyeing Shaniyah. "Tell me what?"

"I don't want to get mommy mad, so I didn't tell her," Shaniyah said, now kicking woodchips off the playground floor.

All types of thoughts was running through my mental. I was getting mad playing the waiting game. I grabbed my sister by the shoulders, picking her up so we could be eye to eye and told her to spill it. She started crying, still tryna talk.

"Mommy . . . 'sniff sniff' . . . boyfriend touched my . . . 'sniff sniff . . . private with his finger . . . and it hurt but he didn't stop."

My head hung low. I felt like my heart just broke. It skipped a beat or stopped working for a moment because I couldn't breathe. I hugged my sister. "Is he in there now?" I asked 'cause I didn't get to check my mom's room before I left out.

"No, he'll be back tonight. That's what I heard him say to mommy." Shaniyah sniffed. I turned my attention to my other sister.

"Did he touch you too?" I dreaded the answer.

"Oh no! He know I'll tell on him quick fast and in a hurry," she proclaimed, firmly.

I told them to stay outside and play for a while and to hit me before they go in the house. I let them know not to tell moms what we talked about and not to worry. I'll take care of it. I also grabbed their phones and erased our texts in case my moms wanna get nosey.

I hugged them again as they kissed my cheek. 'DAMN,' I thought. 'THIS NIGGA MUST DON'T KNOW WHO DA FUCK I AM.'

CHAPTER 9

Izzo

"Bout time."
— *Izzo*

'MAN, I HOPE THIS GIRL AIN'T PLAYING GAMES,' I thought as I walked back down the street trying to run into Tiara. She got a nigga chasin' after what she did to me earlier.

Entering the courtyard, I seen Black. He had the look of murder on his face. I really wasn't tryna say nothing to him. I had pussy on my mind, not murder, but we were in each others path. "Pick ya' head up, bob," I said to him as we got close.

He gave me a look that said he didn't want to be bothered. I was like me either as I kept it pushing, laughing to myself. That nigga crazy, no telling what's goin' on in his head, but whatever. I had plans, better plans ahead, hopefully. I looked at my watch and it read 7:30. In the summer it was still hot, even as the sun began its descent.

I noticed Shanae and Shaniyah playing on the playground. They were getting big right before my eyes. I knew Black would be fucking up somebody's sons in the near future. His sisters were gorgeous. They seen me and waved. I called them over. When they came, I gave them both a dollar. They looked at each other and then toward me. "This it . . . a dollar?" Shanae asked.

I smiled and gave them a ten-dollar bill. "That's more like it," Shanae said and stepped off. "Thanx'."

I shook my head because Shaniyah stood there with her hand out. I had meant for them to split that ten, but I see that wasn't happening. I peeled off another ten and gave it to her. "Now, go back and play you lil con artist." She smiled and jogged off.

I just got swindled and I knew it. They were just like their damn brother, always on moves. I looked across the way and there she was. Tiara. 'I FOUND YA ASS.' A smile crept on my face. "Hey Izzo!" she spoke.

"Hey hey, how may I help you today?" I asked and spread my arms wide and low as if I was presenting myself as her favorite dish. She giggled. That's all I needed to see. She had a sense of humor, always a plus. Stuck up broads might have been turned off by that gesture. "Sike nah. What's up?" I asked as I got closer.

"Nothing, just chilling. I just came from the store, you?"

"Same shit I do every night Pinky, try to take over the world," I said smiling. She started laughing. I was winning, she understood the joke.

"Okay, Mr. Pinky and The Brain."

That was an old cartoon that we grew up on. I don't even think it still come on anymore. The stuff on TV for kids now are corny to me. I miss the throwbacks. "That was my shit, but we still on for tonight?" I tried to slide that in there because I'm geekin' like shit.

"Boy . . ." She stood there in a bow-legged, pigeon-toed stance. ". . . you actin' like it's a date or some shit. What you doing now?"

I love this girl and she don't even know it yet. She ain't with the bullshit. I guess I took too long to answer 'cause she stood there now putting all her weight on one leg and placed a hand on her hip.

"You got anymore of that jet fuel you had earlier?"

Jet fuel. I didn't even know she was hipped to the lingo. Every time I say that shit to other broads, they think I'm talking 'bout some PCP or some shit like dat. I forgot she was from uptown and that's all we blow, high quality weed. "Do I, hell yeah. Want me to go get us some drink?"

"Nah boy, what you think I'm a wino'? I still got that Goose from earlier I saved for us."

"Bet. Let's get it den," I said, already cheesing, happy as shit, but hiding it well.

We walked into her apartment. I rolled another jay', jet fuel. I was high as shit already. I been smokin' all day. She poured herself and me a drink. I seen she had a loose wrist and pouring my cup to the top. "Hol' up Shawty, put some cranberry in mines."

She frowned. "What?" looking at me sideways. "When you start chain' your drink?"

I sighed. "Shid, I've been drinking and getting lifted all damn day, just change the color a lil for me."

"Whatever punk." She tilted the juice and mixed it well, then brung it to me. I took a sip. This shit was still strong as fuck. I heard her open the room door. "Hey y'all," Tiara spoke as two of her friends walked through the door. 'GEESH' They had a bottle too.

They didn't waste any time as their nose adjusted to the aroma in the air. "Where that shit at, girly?" one of the girls asked. Tiara looked at me with a head nod.

"Izzo, you got anymore on you?" I wanted to well and say no, but her eyes was pleading. "I only got 7 grams on me."

Her friend was excited like I said she could have it for free or some shit. She must have read my expression. "Sell me an 8-ball of it, then we could match the rest."

That was her proposition. Once again, I wanted to well, but I wanted to stay in Tiara's good graces. I didn't think I could smoke another 7 grams, but fuck it, I agreed. I didn't even think this through. "A'ight bet." Their faces lit up from excitement. I shook my head. "It's gonna be a long night.

Jay after jay was in rotation. It was a hellava cycle goin' on. All types of conversations was being talked about as I sat in the middle of it. I was glad Tiara was a tomboy and had a PlayStation 5 and games to occupy my time. I knew they were asking Tiara questions about me. I could see how they kept looking, but I paid them no mind as I continued to play the game with my mind on my own mission.

Nicotine was calling. I decided to go out front to hit a jack' (cigarettes). It was smoked out in her apartment but didn't want cigarette smoke in there. I didn't get it, but whatever, I needed some air anyway. I was sweating bullets and needed to mellow out.

"Izzo booooo!" Tiara screamed from her window.

"Yeah!" I looked up.

"We need the lighter, comere'," Tiara said hanging out the window, smiling hard.

Looking at her I could tell she was feeling good. I couldn't wait to be inside her guts. A smile was on my face at the thought of that. Back in the house all the girls done changed their clothes and was in their nightclothes. Legs was everywhere. "Here." I passed the lighter to the friend.

The other friend passed me the bottle and I poured another cup. I was feeling good, to the point I was on wobble statics.

"Boo . . ." Tiara called me, and I looked at her. "Go lay yo' ass down in my bed." I didn't reply. All I did was try to make it to her room. 'BOUT TIME,' I thought as I stumbled to her bed. I kicked off my shoes, fell face first and waited for Tiara to come.

❖   ❖   ❖

Tiara and the girls was chilling in the living room and thoughts of Izzo came to mind. "Let me go check on my new boo," Tiara said.

Her friends gave her a look as one of them spoke. "You betta' stop playing with dat man and go ahead and break him off."

Tiara playfully pushed her friend. "Shut up slut! I'll be back," she said, throwing a pillow.

She walked into her room to see Izzo passed out on her bed. She took off his clothes but left his shorts and boxers on. For a moment, she just stared, admiring his body as he rolled over trying to get comfortable. She wanted to wake him but decided to let him sleep. 'SUCKS FOR YOU' Tiara thought as she kissed his cheek, then turned to head back to the living room with her friends to enjoy the rest of the weed and drinks. Izzo slept.

CHAPTER 10

Dro

"Tuh', not in that joint, I'll find another way."
— Dro

Finally made it up top. It was live, everybody was outside. The walk from the rec' center was long and exhausting when it's this hot out here and I'm high. We walked up on a few of the ol' heads. They were just chillin', smokin' and drinking. The usual type shit they do all day.

Jroc leaned on a parked car and posted up. "So, what's up? This where we at?"

My mind was still on Black. "Ion' know, Slim, but I know I'm tryna see what's up with Black. He left mad as shit; I don't want him to start trippin'."

"Yeah, you right. That nigga be wilding out sometimes," Jroc agreed. "I'm 'bout to go in the store for a minute. My shit on E, hungry as shit, bob."

While Jroc went to the store I shuffled through my phone. I decided to call Black and make sure he was good and wasn't on no bullshit. All his screws wasn't always tight. Loose cannon would be a good description of him. I dialed his number, well, scrolled to his name.

"Yoooooo!" he answered.

"You a'ight, slim?" There was a pause and a sigh before he answered.

"Yeah, I'm cool, just chillin' round da way."

I could tell he was holding something back. He wasn't gonna tell me on his own, I had to ask. "You good? You looked mad as shit when you left. You gonna tell me about that message you got?"

That's all it took for Black to spill it. "Madukes' lil friend violated," Black said fuming. "He touched my sister and I'm trying to see that nigga 'bout that." He was mad. By the tone of his voice, I could imagine his demeanor, clutching the phone and all. "The nigga ain't here, but I'ma lay on his ass til he get back."

"Chill bruh. Meet me at the 7-Eleven, unless you want to come up here with me and Jroc. It would be better if me and you do this shit together. You know you; you be sloppy wit yours. I don't want you getting locked up over that wild nigga," I reasoned.

"Come down here, that would be better. I don't want everybody knowing what happened or what's 'bout to happen," Black countered.

"Bet, I'm walking down now."

Jroc came out of the store smacking on some hot fries. You could tell he high. He was eating really fast. The nigga didn't even offer me none. "Damn, slow down, slim."

He looked at me wit a mouth full, chomping. "These my joints, bruh."

I shook my head, thinking of the lie I could tell so I could step off and holla at Black. 'BINGO.' "Slim, I'm 'bout to catch a sale down bottom. I'll be right back." I told him a lil white lite as my grandmother would call them.

Sipping his big burst squeeze juice, he nodded, then replied, "Go ahead. I'll be up here getting' money, holdin' it down."

I walked down the block headed to meet Black. I had to get to him before he started to thinking with his gun instead of his head. I felt my stomach growling, it was speaking to me. I decided to stop at the crib before I made it down the street.

"Hey, young lady." That's my greeting to my grandma. I love grams, she always made sure we had what we needed. Shoes, clothes, food, and a roof over our heads. The love came easy. As far as material things, they were limited.

"Hey Cordell," she spoke smiling.

The fragrance in the house smacked my nostrils. "What you in there cooking? I smelt it down the block," I asked, wishing it was already done and ready to eat. It was a slight meal, a quick fix. Hamburger Helper, but when she make it, it look like something from The Olive Garden, restaurant ready.

I grabbed one of the throwaway bowls that was in the pantry and filled it up. "I'm 'bout to go to 7-Eleven. You want anything?" I asked, stuffing the last couple of spoonsful of food in my mouth.

"Slow down baby." Grams noticed me eating all crazy. "But no, I don't want anything."

I was halfway down the block before I seen Black walking toward the store. "Black!!" I yelled, tryna get his attention. He looked back and began coming toward me. We approached each other and embraced each other with dap and a half hug. "So, what's goin' on slim?" I asked.

Silence.

He gave me a screw face, then answered, "I done already told you, bruh."

This nigga Black, he always had to be difficult. When he mad, all he see is revenge. "I'm hip, but we gotta come up with a better plan than that shit you saying earlier," I told him.

"Okay, I'm listening."

"Do the nigga drive, walk, get off the train or what?" He scratched his chin in thought, then spoke, "Matter fact, I think that nigga drive that blue Roadmaster with the white walls."

"I got a plan, bruh." It was coming together. "We gonna lamp on this nigga."

Looking at my watch, it read 9:30. The sun been down for about 20 minutes. We chilled and I laid out my plan as we smoked a blunt and blew smoke.

❖   ❖   ❖

About 10:00 workcall was in effect. The car that they were waiting on finally pulled up. They were alias how they hid behind a conversion van as their victim to be parked without a worry or care in the world. "Man, I hope lil punk ass son ain't in the house. He gonna make me fuck him up," Fred mumbled as he was checking himself out in the mirror.

Fred got out of the car and went to lock his door until Black popped up in front of him. Dro appeared behind him. Fred was in the middle of them with cars parked on his other side.

"What's up, baby boy?" Fred spoke with his ol' head swag. "Yo momma still up?" he asked as he turned, tryna walk past Black, but to no avail. Black didn't move. "You gonna let me pass youngin'?"

They looked at each other. Silence. The answer to his question was answered with the butt of the gun Dro smacked him with. It knocked him out cold. "Damn fool, you musta' did that before," Black said and started kicking Fred in the face with fury. Dro grabbed him, tryna calm him down. "Grab his legs fool, you kickin' dat nigga like he Rodney King or some shit," he said after popping the trunk.

They tossed him in his own trunk. Dro got in the driver seat while Black got in the passenger. Firing up a jack' they drove under 3rd Street tunnel, headed to the southside, the dirty.

Dro pulled up at the Anacostia skating rink. It had been there for years, a landmark. "Pop the trunk, fool," Dro said.

Black was geeking, pacing and everything. He wanted to get something off his chest. His sisters, they are his world and he had to make an example out of him. Soon enough, the trunk opened. Fred hopped up, looking crazy, scared and confused as he stared down the barrel of the gun pointed at him.

"Wha-wha-what's goin' on Donte?" he asked with bubbled eyes.

Black punched him all in the face with the body of the gun and his free hand. "Shut the fuck up, nigga," he spat. "You think you can just touch my lil sisters and I wouldn't find out. You thought she was too scared of your sucka' ass to tell me. Your dumbass musta' thought I was a bitch!" Black screamed. Slob left his mouth with each word.

Black pointed his sidekick, a 38 special and was ready about to blow Fred's head off and send it to the moon until Dro grabbed him. "What's up, nigga?" Black asked. "What's da hold up?" He was agitated.

Dro looked at Black and smiled. He reached for his waistline, giving him a two-tone Glock. "Here, use this." Dro grabbed the pistol when he stopped off at gram's house.

"Where da fuck you get a silencer from, fool?" Black looked at the gun he was holding then waved Dro off. "Matter fact, Ion' even care, you stay wit some exclusive shit."

Black pointed the gun to Fred's temple. "Night night." 'PST PST' Fred's body dropped and was now twitching. Black stood over his body and emptied the 30-round extended clip in his head, only. His head exploded as the multiple shots disconnected it from his neck. They both dragged the body to the river nearby and rolled him over in it. Anacostia River was known to have a body or two floating most mornings once upon a time.

Black picked up what was left of Fred's head, did a crossover move and shot it like a jumper in the river. "Now what?" Black asked, vindicated.

"Nigga, I'm gone home. What 'bout you?" Dro asked.

"I'm talkin' 'bout the car."

"Torch it, leave it, I don't give a fuck. I already wiped it down," Dro said. "We can catch the train."

"Train, for what? We could drive it back. It ain't like it been reported stolen or nothing yet," Black suggested.

"Whatever nigga, keep it for all I care, but Ion' think it's a good look. Drop me off back up 9th Street."

"I thought you were goin' home."

"Tuh, not in that joint. I'll find another way."

They got back in the whip and peeled off.

CHAPTER 11

Jroc

"Oh yeah, you bangin' good, huh?"
— Dro

It finally started to pick up. It was pumping, but I didn't have the product which most folks came through for. Then a possible weed head approached. 'IT'S ABOUT TIME SOME MONEY STARTED COMING THROUGH THIS BITCH,' I thought. "What's up, bruh?" I looked the dude up and down as he neared.

"Hey hey, nephew! Tell me something good and I'll make your day," he said smiling with one gold tooth in his mouth.

By the looks of this guy, I might not even have what he wants, but it's never good to assume, so I asked, "What you got?" Ready for the game it looked like he was about to kick.

"Look here baby, I'm tryna get 7 for 50." It sounded like a crack sale to me, but he continued as I looked at him sideways.

"or wait . . ." He put a finger up. ". . . there's more. You can give me 7 for 35 and get this sixty-dollar food stamp card."

He definitely sounded like a potential crackhead. "You know I got tree, right?" I asked, to make sure.

"Yeah nephew, Ion' fuck around. That's all I smoke youngin' pack," he said referring to high-quality weed.

'YEAH RIGHT,' I thought. "Oh a'ight. I only asked, 'cause you sitting here tryna negotiate like you was clucka' chasing a dream, but I got 8 dimes for it all."

His face told it all. He was tryna add it up a few times, but lost count. Giving up, he agreed. "Fuck it, here, but I need the card back, nephew."

"I got you tomorrow."

Noticing the time, I realized I've been out here for over an hour now since Dro stepped off. I was wondering what he was doing. I was almost finished all the tree I had. It was almost time to re-up. I decided to call Dro to see where he was at. He answered. "Wut' up, slim?"

"Damn bruh, fuck you at?"

"I'm right here with Black. We ain't doin' shit, but chilling for a minute. I'm 'bout to be back up there," Dro said.

"A'ight but uh, that shit I had almost gone. I'ma need you to call your folks for me," I told him.

"I'll be there in a minute, like 10, hol' fast."

I was wondering why it sounded like he was in a car but didn't dwell on it too long. I was just hugging the block with many thoughts on my mind.

Me and Dro was in the 12th grad about to graduate in a few days, then real life would begin. My mother was hoping I go to college out the city, but I had street dreams. Growing up with my homies I was already living the fast life. Only thing was I didn't have the money to splurge. I was just playing like I had it, but in all actuality my moms looked out for me. I played this role so long I felt like I belonged in the streets. Shid, I am a hood nigga.

I had feeling that only time would tell if I was really ready for these mean streets of the nation's capital. D.C. that is.

BEEP BEEP. I heard a horn from a car pulling up on me. The car looked familiar, but I couldn't place where I remembered it from. Then it stopped right in front of me. I reached under my shirt for what I knew wasn't there and turned to the side, bluffin,' as if I had the dawg' (gun) on my side.

The window came down, I stood my ground but really, I was scared and ready to break if shit got ugly.

"Nigga, you faking like shit wit your scary ass!" Black said as the window came down and his face was visible.

"Whew." I blew a sigh of relief. "Y'all niggas play too much. I was 'bout to fuck dat joint up, on my mova,' bruh," I said wellin like shit.

It's crazy, my homies laughed me out. They could see right through the façade. "Nigga, you wasn't 'bout to do shit!" Dro said laughing as he got out of the car.

Still eyeing the car, I asked, "Where you get that whip from, bruh? It look familiar."

SKRRRRRRR. Black's answer was simple. He peeled off, leaving tire smoke in my face.

I didn't think much of it. I looked at Dro who was fanning the smoke. "Y'all was together the whole time?" He nodded and I continued, "Fuck y'all was doing?"

"Damn 21 questions. We wasn't doin' shit, but chillin', but never mind that, what's goin' on out here?" Dro asked. "Any money?"

"Yeah, it's cool. I made a few dollars on my end, but you know what I got, well had. I wasn't really checkin' for that other shit."

"Is that right?" Dro looked me over. "You looking like you was out here getting high off your own supply."

"Jealous." I smiled. "But I need you to call your folks for me. My man ain't answering the phone."

Dro dialed his man's number while I waited. It was getting late, and the night was just about to livin' up. I knew I was gonna be outside tonight. The vibe felt good, and I was gonna soak it up.

"He said he'll be 'round here in 20 minutes, so what you tryna get?" Dro asked.

"Tell 'em I'm tryna get a QP'." (Quarter ounce) Dro's face lit up. I didn't understand why that would be a surprise to him. "Oh yeah, you bangin' (hustling) good, huh?" Dro asked. Then I realized why it was such a shocker what I had asked him for.

"Reggie bruh, not pack," I told him letting him know I wanted regular weed not exotic.

"Reggie!!" His smile disappeared. he held his hand over the receiver of the phone. "Niggas still smoke dat shit?"

"Fuck you nigga." I know he was tryna clown me, but it was all good. "Just tell 'em, slim."

"Whatever nigga," Dro said getting back on the phone. "He said he on his way wit dat dirt you ordered."

That was music to my ears. I needed it. I wasn't gonna keep pinching off my personal stash for these niggas. Shid, I had my own habit to supply.

CHAPTER 12

Izzo

"This nigga here, a natural Casanova."
— Black

I felt like I was still passed out as I stared at the back of my eyelids. Didn't know where I was at, at the moment. Then I felt it, a presence. I hopped up, rolled over and jumped out of the bed.

Tiara was laying in the bed with nothing but a T-shirt on. I looked myself over to see I only had on boxers. Her eyes opened slowly; smiling was her first expression. "Hey sleepy head," she spoke in a sexy voice.

"Sup' baby girl, what happened?" I asked. Lost, confused and in a state of shock would briefly describe what I was feeling in this moment. I didn't remember shit. From the looks of the scenery, I had a good night.

"I wore dat ass out boy. Told you you couldn't fuck wit me,

boy," she boasted.

"What!?" I was confused. "Anything, damn."

Leaning up on the bed with a screw face she asked, "Who anything, boy?" She was livid. I could tell all in her voice.

"Nah, boo, not you. I'm talking 'bout me. I'm just a lil mad guh' (embarrassed) that I don't remember it," I told her looking into her eyes.

Her face lightens up. "Oh, that's good to know." She leaned in for a kiss but stopped. "We ain't do shit anyway. Your ass was too drunk and high. You passed out, now that's anything," Tiara said laughing and getting up and heading to the shower. She looked over her shoulder. "Plus, it's no way you wouldn't remember this gushy. Like y'all say, I got torch'."

"Oh yeah!" I think my dick jumped. "That ain't funny," I told her back because she kept it pushing as I tried to get a few free feels in my attempt to grab her.

"Uh uh boy. Don't start nothing you can't finish."

"You ain't saying nothing but a word, believe that, I'm well rested," I defended.

Her body was soft, and it smelled like candy. We wrestled for a second before she had enough as I caught up with her. "No, boy, I have to go to work tonight, so stop it," she said giggling, tryna pull away and head to the shower again.

I let her go. It was cool. I needed to head back outside. I told her to hit me tomorrow when she got off. After smacking her ass, I headed for the door.

I walked outside her apartment door and seen a bunch of young niggas smoking weed in the hallway. Noticing me, they tried to cuff their jay' like my nose don't work and can't smell. I laughed. 'I REMEMBER THEM DAYS.'

Hiding from certain neighbors, tryna not get caught. It used to be a thrill. I could relate to the young boys in this moment. But shid, we used to go at least 6 to 10 blocks away from the hood, not the next floor down or up. Everybody knew everybody.

Nowadays the respect level is at an all-time low. These

youngins' gonna blow wherever the jay' got rolled up at.

Leaving out the building, I decided to head up 9th Street to get some of this work' (drugs) off. Going up the street I seen Black coming off of S Street, headed up top as well, I assumed. He was in front of me. I called out to him. After finally hearing from a couple shouts, I yelled, he turned around and stopped.

I jogged the rest of the way to catch up. "Sup', big boy!!" I greeted him.

He embraced me. "Shit, 'bouta head up top to chop it up with Dro and Jroc. They up there on T Street," Black said. "So, what happened with you and shawty earlier. I know that's where you were goin when I seen you."

I didn't wanna really tell him. I knew if I told him the truth, he was gonna clown me, but fuck it. "You ain't gonna believe this shit, moe." I shook my head, dreaded telling him the rest. "We smoked and drank, then two of her friends came over." I started to smile 'cause I was about to well'. Black stopped walking. He was getting interested. "Oh yeah, bruh!"

I told him to chill and let me finish. I continued, "Yeah fool, you already know how I do," I hyped.

"So, what happened?" Black asked. "Did you at least hit one of them?"

Black was too interested. I couldn't help myself. I had to mess with his head and put a 10 on a 2, meaning exaggerate the situation. "Did I?" I asked like he insulted me. I had the mug on and everything. "You know me bruh. I gave them what they wanted. They was gay too but loved the dick, so you know I had fun all night long, ping pongin' the pussy. It was a big ass orgy."

"On who nigga?" Black was smiling like it was him in my shoes last night. "Put that shit on something, fool."

"Bruh, I put that shit on . . . sike naw, slim. I was so bent that I passed out on her bed with no happy ending to talk about," I said shaking my head again.

Black bust out laughing, clowning me, but I guess I deserved it. Dro approached us with a puzzled face. He was oblivious to

Black's outburst of giggles.

"Fuck that nigga laughing at?" he asked me, but Black decided to answer as he tried to stop laughin'.

"This nigga here," Black pointed at me, "he a natural Casanova, slim. He got got for his tree and his drink."

I let him talk and get his lil rocks off (jokes), but soon enough Jroc wanted answers as well and decided to ask what happened. He wanted to hear my version.

All eyes was on me. I told them the story from the best of my abilities with Black adding his punchlines throughout it. I ended up turning myself into the joke of the night. It was cool though. It wasn't gonna happen again. Next time, I get the chance to smash, believe me when I tell you I'ma crush.

Everybody was out tonight, most just coolin.' Dro sparked a jay' and asked Black about the move since we all were together again. That question put a silence in the air and all eyes on Black. He made the decision. "Let's walk to the bar."

CHAPTER 13

The Move

"We gonna smoke 'em . . ."
— Izzo

"Let's walk to the bar," Black requested. Things needed to be explained and planned out. Too many eyes and ears were on the block to discuss the matter.

"Which one?" Jroc asked. "It's like 100 bars around this bitch now." Which was true, a lot had changed in the surrounding neighborhoods. Streets were cleaner than they had ever been. Trash cans were on every corner. Drop something on the ground, you might get an evil stare, maybe even confronted. U street was now gentrified.

"It don't matter, any one of them so we could talk about this shit, I'm geekin' on da low," Black admitted.

Walking to the bar, they chose the one that was popular with the college kids. Howard University was right up the street. They talked and walked, nothing was the topic of conversation, just the day-to-day bullshit about the hood.

Anxious could be a way to describe the anxiety they were goin' through. They were all fucked up, money wise. Black held the meal ticket to get the ball rolling.

Izzo's phone rang. He looked to see it was a text. Reading it, he grinned at the photo of light shaven pussy. The owner, Tiara, with a message:

'STAY WET 4U'

"What you smiling at, bruh?" Jroc asked, noticing him. Izzo remained cool and downplayed it. "Nothing, my lil joint sent me a message."

Dro was already hip and made a slick comment, "Oh, she your joint now, huh?"

Quickly turning his neck, Izzo faced Dro. "Damn Moe, you don't even know who it is."

Dro waved him off. "You know I know."

Izzo knew Dro was hipped to him, but he wouldn't stamp' (confirm) it, not yet. He definitely had plans on trying to get Tiara on the team. Izzo wasn't the handcuffing type, but it was something about Tiara that had him gone. "She ain't my joint yet, but I'ma make her mines and when I do, I'll let you nosey niggas know, okay?" Izzo said confidently.

Black looked at Izzo and seen it all in his eyes. "Ol' sucka for love ass nigga."

"Nigga you mad. Only bitch you got is huggin' your hip right now wit your virgin ass," Izzo said, laughing and referring to Black's gun.

"I got bitches. I just don't bring them around your pretty red ass, nigga," Black defended. "Plus, I punish the pussy, you save 'em, you Captain Kurt ass nigga."

Arriving at the bar, they headed straight to the back and tried to get a booth in the cut. They wanted to see everything and want the people in front of them. After cracking jokes on each other for about 5 minutes, a waitress came over.

"Hey guys! What can I get for you?" She was gorgeous and an instant silence was at the table.

Jroc was on her line first and broke the quiet spell. "Hey beautiful, let me get 2 shots of Patrón and a Corona with lime." He just knew he was the smoothest of them all.

She looked at him, squinted her eyes, staring at his baby-like face. Thoughts of his age came. Realizing the possibility of a nice payout, she looked him over and went to the next order. "And the rest of you guys?"

The orders was given. They ranged from Heinekens, Remy Martin and a Long Island Iced Tea. The vibe was set, and it was laid back.

The waitress sashayed away. "Um um, shawty bad." Jroc admired, watching her walk away.

"Yeah, yeah yeah, back to business," Black said. "Remember what I said earlier. I know a nigga, his bitch live next door to my bitch on the Maryland side of Wheeler Road. He work for an Armor car type of service, but they sweet, well he is."

Dro wasn't convinced. "And so what." Black took a breath and focused on Dro. "Listen fool, they heavy. He be having weekend routes and always stop by his girl's house before he drop the last package off. Him and the dude riding with him stop by, go in and do whatever. The bamma be in there like 15-20 minutes, every time. I think he be fucking her some shit then roll out," Black explained.

Still not convinced, Dro asked, "How you know whatever he carrying still be in the truck when he get to his folk's house?"

"I knew you was gonna ask that. I was thinking the same thing, so I followed him for 3 weekends straight. After he leave his girl's house, it's off to the bank on Southern Avenue by Eastover shopping center. He drop 'bout 4 bags off, heavy, then return to the truck headed to another bitch's house," Black confirmed.

Jroc joked. "Damn James Bond, you like dat."

Dro was contemplating. "So, what's the catch?"

"Nothing, just get up on him when he make dat pit stop. Easy."

"We gonna mask up or straight up smoke 'em?" Izzo asked, ready for whatever the lick bring. Black rubbed his hands together. Thoughts of counting money ran through his head. "Nigga, you know either way I don't give a damn."

They sat and drank for the rest of their stay at the bar discussing the details of the plan. Everybody was on board but Jroc. He was a little leery. This was his chance to put in work. In the back of his mind, he was scared but hid it well. "Earth to Jroc." Dro was waving his hands in Jroc's face, tryna bring him out of his daze.

"Yeah bruh."

"Nothing, slim, just making sure you good," Dro said, patting his friend's back.

"I'm gucci. Maybe a lil twisted, but I'm a'ight," Jroc welled.

Getting ready to leave. all the tab was paid. The bill accumulated to about eighty dollars. A single blue face was left for the waitress.

Heading out the bar Dro looked back to see Jroc still sitting. After a few seconds he went back to see what was up.

"Jroc!!" He was now talking to the waitress. "You coming, slim."

"Go ahead bruh. I'll see you later," Jroc replied and gave him the eye, telling him he was working on something.

Dro chucked the deuces and rolled out. Black and Izzo was halfway down the block. He had to jog to catch up. Black turned around quickly and on point, "Fuck you running for?" he asked, reaching for his waistline.

" 'Cause you niggas left me, dumbass."

Izzo exhaled a jack'. "What's up wit pretty boy?" Dro waved the question off. "He good, tryna push up on the waitress. you know he be tryna fuck everything." They all agreed on that with light laughs and giggles.

"Speaking on that . . ." Izzo started. "I'm 'bout to roll and see if Tiara tryna get a nigga out the way while I'm feeling sexy."

That started a domino effect as Black spoke. "A'ight niggets' I'm 'bout to head on the southside and holla at my baby." He fished for his keys. "I'll see you niggas tomar.' "Need a ride Dro?" he asked, dangling the keys.

"Negative!" Dro replied, giving him a look telling him he needed to get rid of that car. Black smiled and walked off with Izzo headed down L.W. Dro pulled out his phone and place a call to his girl.

With much attitude, Charmine answered, "Hello!"

"Sup' Bae. Where you at?"

"Who the fuck is this?"

"Boo it's me." Recognizing the voice, she quizzed. "Who phone you on?" Silence. Dro forgot Charmine never had his number. Now he had to decide if he would lie now and deal with it later, or just give her the digits.

It's not that Dro didn't want to give it to her. It was the fact that she will blow it up non-stop, for dumb shit.

"This my new phone number, so save it, boo," Dro said tryna play it off.

"Oh, so now you got a new numbah' at 1:30 in da morning." Sarcasm could be felt through her voice. "Um um, and what happened to you coming to see me and us goin' out, huh?" she asked with much attitude.

All the mess and bullshit of today's events Dro forgot his date that he set up. "My bad, boo. I'm sorry," he apologized. "Too much was goin' on, and it slipped my mind," Dro said, regretting his choice of words as soon as it was spoken. Charmine could be so literal at times.

"Oh, so I slipped your mind?"

"Not like that. You know what I mean. Let me make it up to you."

"Whatever, you get on my damn nerves, ugh." She sucked her teeth out of irritation. She was guh.'

"Can you come get me?"

"Bye," was her response as she hung up the phone.

That could have been a yes or a no, so he decided to wait for a minute before he left. Dro was still at the top of 9th Street coolin' with a few good men from around his way. Dudes were doing their own thing. Some was drinking, others high in another world. it was typical everyday all-day shit.

Jroc came staggering down the street making it to Dro. He stopped and slurred, "Wuh zup, brah, wuh you doin' still out here in shit?" Dro laughed.

"Slim, I could ask you the same thing. I guess shawty wasn't fucking with you, huh?"

"Wuh! You know I got them dizits' on-my-muhva'." Jroc flashed his phone. "I'm twisted. I'm 'bout to hit da rack (bed). I got class in the a.m."

"Yeah okay, big boy. I'll see you."

They dapped each other up. Jroc only lived a half a block down the street. Dro watched him walk, swerving side to side, but he made it safely. Dro posted up for about a half hour and sparked a jack'. 'LAST MAN STANDING,' he thought to himself as he exhaled a cloud of smoke.

CHAPTER 14

Black

"Hey you! Looking for a good time?"
— Another

Izzo walked down the street with me headed for L.W. He cut through the courtyard. I guess he was tryna see what was up with baby girl from earlier. I was on the way to my moms' crib, really, I just wanted to check on my lil sisters.

Walking down the street, 8th Street side of the block, I noticed a few of my young boys outside up to no good. They flagged me down and I stopped to see what was good.

"Aye big homie! You got the joint (gun) on you?" That opened my eyes and put me on high alert.

"Why, what's up, lil nigga?"

He got to looking around, then pointed, "That nigga at the station faking like shit. He tried to take my jacket, so we jumped his ass, then he started chasing us with a knife, so we ran."

I wasn't 'bout to give my baby' to these lil niggas for no bull-shit. If they decided to smoke dude, I really didn't trust them to hold water when it came crashing down. I decided to solve the problem myself. "Where he at now?" They pointed to the station, and we began walking toward it.

Making it to where the dude was posted, I approached. "What's up ol timer?" He looked at me with disdain and pulled his knife out. I smiled. 'SILLY RABBIT TRICKS ARE FOR KIDS.'

"You think something funny bitch?" he asked as he advanced toward me. "Give me yo money punk!"

I let him get close before I whipped out and smacked fire out him with the pistol I had tucked in my waist. He fell on his face, instant knockout. I kicked him and he didn't budge.

The young boy that called me, ran over and started kicking him as well. I offered the gun to the kid, and he smiled. Pointing the cannon, he aimed at the guy's head.

I walked beside the kid. "Squeeze." He looked at me and then at the unconscious ol timer and did just that.

BOC!

A shot was fired, followed by a loud scream. The young boy shot him in the ass. Ol' timer woke up screaming with bugged out eyes. I grabbed my gun as the rest of the crew of young boys stomped him out, knocking him out again.

I chuckled but kept it moving. Making it to my moms' apart-ment I opened the door to see her on the couch. She jumped at the sound of the door. "Oh, it's you," she said as the smile left her face.

"What!? Expecting somebody else?" I smiled, walking to my sister's room, enjoying the fact that dude would never step foot in this house again. 'FUCK 'EM.'

I opened their door to see them asleep. Walking to the bed, I kissed both of them on the cheek and pulled the covers over them and made my exit. "A'ight Ma, I'm gone. I'll see ya tomar'."

"Where you think you going this time of night?"

"I'm goin' to my girl's house if that's okay with you," I responded with sarcasm.

"Yeah okay, smart ass. Leave me some cigarettes."

I gave her the rest of the pack I had, then bounced. I walked outside, went to the 7th Street side of the block. It used to be a patio there, but now it's some new condos. Cell block was this section of the hood. That's where I had the car parked.

Getting in the car I made my exit. Cruising, I stopped at the gas station to get some jacks' and condoms. I was still a little saucy (twisted) and had a pint in the backseat. Back in the car after my purchase, I rode down New Jersey Avenue headed for the 3rd Street tunnel. I got off the exit on Malcom X.

I was gonna stay on the highway and get off on South Capital, but I wanted to cruise through a couple hoods, might find a sweet vick, who knows.

Driving down MLK Avenue, I hit Wheeler Road and passed Wahler Place. At the light was Southern Avenue, a hood called Geraldines. I seen a phat ass broad tryna flag me down from the Shell gas station across the street.

Shawty's body was crazy out of this world. I checked my pockets. I didn't mind tricking, tempted I was. As she got closer, I noticed she wasn't real, it was a nigga! I was furious. Mad at myself for not recognizing. From the back that nigga would've fooled anybody, at least that's what I keep telling myself. The nigga made it to my window. He was quick. I looked up and he was in my front seat. Sounding like a bitch, he spoke, "Hey you!"

Anger took over, but my body language and expressions didn't tell the same story. I pulled out a wad of money. "Tryna roll?" The nigga thought he came up on a lick' (sweet money), but whole time his faggot ass was my lick. I don't have any problems with the LGB . . . whatever the letters are. I'm not homophobic, but when you try to trick a real nigga, that shit don't sit well wit me.

He sat in the passenger seat. "So, what you tryna do?" he asked. I looked at him. "How much for that pussy?" I asked fishing, seeing if he could save his own life.

I done crossed over to the Maryland side of Wheeler Road. Nothing to my left or right but woods for a nice small stretch.

"Uhhh, I'm on my period, but I got 2 other options for you," he said, smiling like I'ma damn fool, but I played the role.

"Oh yeah!" I acted geeked as I smiled hard. "Look in the side panel and hand me dat condom," I told him as I faked unbuttoning my pants.

The nigga leaned over tryna find something that wasn't there in the first place. In that quick second, instead of pulling out my dick, in my hand held my pistol.

BOC! BOC! BOC!

I crushed (killed) 'em, all head shots then pulled over. I looked in the dude's purse. He was heavy' (got money). I pulled him out of the car, dragged his body to the woods off the road and pulled off. Not one car passed, clean getaway!

Pulling up in my girl's neighborhood, which was only a mile away from where I just left that body, I rode past my girl's house first. I was about to pull in the driveway, but I seen the nigga I planned on robbing on his girl's porch chillin' with a few niggas. I decided to park on a side street down the block form her house and walk up.

Coming up the driveway, they all looked in my direction. "Sup' homie?" one of the dudes spoke. I looked at everybody in their face, then spoke to the dude that said something to me. The rest of them got a head nod.

I knocked on my girl's door while smoking the butt of a jack.' She opened the door with a sleepy face. "Why you coming here so late, boo? You could have called. Where you been at? Who was you with? You smell like cheap perfume. How did you get here?"

"Damn Ms. 100 questions. Can I get through the door? You act like you don't miss your boo or sumthin'." I reached for a hug. She caught my embrace. "Give me a kiss."

MUAH, she complied.

We kissed the whole way to her room as I convinced her I ain't been doing nothing but missing her. The way she was taking the kisses greedily, I could tell she was ready. She grabbed my lil pint that I been sippin' on and started to drink it straight. I fired up a jay', and smoked while we both sipped. I listened to her talk about her whole day. Once the drink kicked in, she got to just rambling. She was wide awake now.

She had nothing on but one of my oversized T-shirts that I kept on feeling on. I knew what she had on under it, nothing. My buzz came back strong and in blast. I covered her face with my whole hand, then pushed her back, forcing her to fall on the bed.

When she fell back the shirt flew up, all pussy was exposed. I seen that and jumped on top of her before she tried to pull the shirt down. I started from her neck and made my way down her body. My stopping point was her love button. As I ate the box, she moaned in ecstasy, orgasms repeated constantly. She was begging for me to enter her tunnel, but I refused. She tasted too good right now.

I kept pleasuring her clit. I was working my tongue knowing that she was puddy in my hand when she was on her back. I was the law and in control.

I was sexing her something serious. She got to shaking un-controllably and I stopped to look. This was a first reaction I was witnessing. I musta' hit dat G-spot. She looked back at me and smiled. Then in that same moment she damn near tackled me and got to riding me hard and crazy. I was in a zone.

I knew she was feeling herself 'cause the condoms I brought was still in my pocket. She never fuck without condoms, but shid, if she ain't say shit, I damn sure wasn't gonna speak a word 'bout it. I been geeking to get this "real" pussy latex free. We sexed for the better part of the morning, then passed out.

CHAPTER 15

Dro

"Ashley, right?"
— Dro

'DAMN SHE REALLY GONNA LEAVE A NIGGA OUT HERE.' I was still on 9th Street coolin,' waiting to see if my girl was gonna come through and get me. I been waiting for a little while and if she would've left when I called, it would have taken like 20 minutes tops. 'FUCK IT.' I decided to walk to grandma's crib and crash.

Really, I didn't want to do that. I hated to have to wake her up just to let me sleep on the couch. It was that or stay out here all night until she get up in the a.m. Niggas was still outside and shit, but I was ready to roll and call it a night. So grams, here I come.

I walked toward the crib. When I made it to the door it was like my intuition told me to look and check my surroundings.

There she was, my wife, sitting in the car parked in front of the house asleep.

Naturally, a smile crept across my face. I tapped the window after I made an attempt to open the door but failed. She jumped up and looked at me crazy. After noticing it was me, she unlocked the door so I could get in. She was stretching as I spoke. "Why you ain't call me and tell me you were here, boo?"

"Tsst." She smacked her teeth. "I accidentally erased your number, but you knew I was coming."

I went to get in the car, and she put her hand up as if to say, halt. "Uh uh nigga, you driving," Charmine said, sliding to the passenger seat. I smiled. She was funny at times, but I loved that about her lil stand attitude. "So, what's up lil evil?" I asked as I pulled into traffic.

She got to telling me her whole day part by part like it was a movie. When she finally finished and asked me about my day, we was pulling into the parking lot. I ignored her question with my own. "Do you work tomar'?"

"Yeah, I got to be there at 3:00 and get off at 11:00. You gonna take me to work?"

"I'll let you know." I didn't want to make any promises. She think she got all the sense, and I don't. The only reason she offer the car is so that she know where I am, and she can keep tabs on my day.

"Whatever," she said closing the door, walking to the apartment.

She walked straight to my room. I went to check on my moms. Seeing that she was asleep, I kissed her cheek and went back to my room. Charmine was laying down in nothing but panties. I loved to see her like that and couldn't wait until we had our own spot. She rarely wore clothes in the crib, and it turned me on instantly. When moms was at work, she would walk around butt ass naked as the day she was born.

Seeing her in just her thong was a regular thing now, but not an invitation. Knowing this, I pulled my clothes off and laid beside her. We cuddled, then eventually went to sleep.

The buzzing of my phone woke me up. I looked at the phone to see that it was 8:00 a.m. "Rise and shine, nigga!" Jroc shouted in my ear, loud as shit.

"Moe . . . You geekin' like shit. Fuck you want? It's early as fuck."

In a calm manner he responded, "Shit. Nothing at all. I'm just your wake-up call. I'm 'bout to head to class. I know you got a class at 10, so get that ass up!" he said, raising his voice slightly, then lowering it again. "It's the end of the year, ain't no time for bullshitting."

"A'ight . . . damn, I'm up." I banged on him. (Hung up without notice.)

Carmine was still asleep. I watched her sleep for a second. It was like she felt the rays from my eyes 'cause she opened one eye and smiled. "Creep."

"So what and," I said, rolling out of the bed to get ready for my day. Soon as I finished, I went back in the room to get my girls' keys. "Aye boo, I gone to class. I'll be finished by 12:00 p.m."

"Take the car and come back to take me to work later. You ain't gotta come straight back, okay."

'YOU GOT ALL THE SENSE.' She think I'm not hipped to her.

In the car all I was thinking about was the move that was coming up in a couple days. I needed the money and was willing to do whatever I needed to make sure it worked.

I entered the building they called school, not really wanting to be there, but glad it was almost over. I couldn't wait to graduate in a couple of weeks. As I walked through the hallway waiting for the bell to ring for class to start, I ran into Jroc. He had his hand extended. "Hey bruh, I see you made it," he said smiling.

"Yeah, slim, I'm here and ready to leave already," I told him as I checked the scenery.

"What's the move after class?"

I shrugged my shoulders. I didn't really have any plans for real.

I was still asleep in the mind. "Probably go around the way, make a couple of plays." That was the first thing that came to mind, but the I said, "Really I am anticipating this weekend."

"Yeah, I feel you, but ain't that shit a lil wild. Don't act like you ain't nervous about it at all," Jroc quizzed.

"Hell nah, I'm ready. On the low I'm geeking," I confirmed.

My man be throwing me off sometimes. He be wit it then he be undecided. We chopped it up for a minute until the bell rang. I headed to class and sat in a chair. This was the last credit I needed to get my diploma, then fuck school, I'm out.

Class was nearing an end. This girl that was on my line all year started flirting with me, like she always do. She was a pretty girl, but I was gone off of older woman. These lil girls can't do shit for me.

"Hey you, what you doin' after class, boy?"

I looked at her and smiled. She knew I had a girl. I told her on multiple occasions, but it didn't stop here. I started to say something but ignoring here was more fun.

"Oh, so you gonna ig' me?" she asked sliding her desk closer to mines.

"Girl, you better stop playing before you get what you asking for," I said in a playful voice. She reached under the desk, grabbing for the love below. 'OH SHIT' I shouldn't have called her bluff knowing she was geeking anyway. She started playing with the outside of my jeans, quickly in the same motion she snatched my phone and got up, leaving me with a semi-erection.

"If you want your phone back, come get it." She walked out of class.

I wasn't gonna follow her until I remembered all my freaky shit that was in the phone, and it wasn't locked. I jumped up outta my seat and did what she told me, I followed. We ended up in the bathroom. "Damn, you go hard," I said barely above a whisper. I entered behind her. She sat in a stall with the door wide open along with her legs, smiling as she twirled my phone. I walked up on her. She grabbed me by my belt buckle and pulled me into the stall.

She didn't say a word as she undid my pants and went straight for my dick. She acted like it was actually hers and started sucking the skin off of it. She definitely knew her way around in that area.

It didn't take long before I came. She swallowed every drop and made me fall in love with her instantly . . . with her mouth that is. She put her number in my phone. Told me to use it and don't forget about her. "Ashley, right?" I asked.

She smiled. "The one and only."

She ain't have to worry about me forgetting. Her mouth was very special to me. I wish I would've been sampled that. Leaving out of the bathroom she was grinning, looking phat to death as she walked away.

I didn't even go back to class. I left out the side door and headed to my whip. I decided to pull up around the way and maybe make a few dollars.

Parking, it was chill outside, no noise. I looked at my watch. It was early, only 11:30 a.m., so I posted on the gate to see if I could catch a few sales and let the day unfold.

CHAPTER 16

Izzo's Night

"You spending the night with me?"
— Another

As I walked into the courtyard, I was hoping Tiara was still up. Coming up on her building I seen her moms on the porch with an older guy. I'm guessing that was her friend she was talkin' 'bout earlier. "What you doing out here this late?" I asked.

"Nothing, enjoying my company." She smiled. "And you?"

"Oh me, this my shift. You know I'm a nightcrawler, enjoying the nightly breeze."

"Oh, okay, well enjoy," she said, turning her attention back to her date. I felt like she was shooing me away.

"Tiara woke?" I asked.

She looked at me like I was crazy. I didn't understand why she gave me that look. Ain't like you really tryna do nothing for real, you still outside. "Yea, she woke, but she ain't up in here. You know damn well she at work."

'DAMN.' Now it made sense. How did I forget that. Shit, I just left up outta here a few hours ago and she told me she was gone to work. "Thanks dukes.' I'll see you, don't be out here past your curfew, okay young lady?" I smirked and she waved me off.

I stepped off and decided to call Tiara. All I received was her voicemail. I put my phone back in my pocket and it vibrated. There was a text:

"HEY BOO IM@ WORK, WHATS UP"

"SHIT COOLIN THINKING OF U"

"COME C ME DEN ILL TELL DA DOORMAN"

"SHID BET, ON DEE WAY!"

Walking down the street, looking through my phone for a contact, I found it. It was an Uber driver five minutes away from me. The driver pulled up. His navigation system had the address I gave him in it, but it was reading Stadium Night Club.

I only been there on a couple occasions. I wasn't old enough on all nights to come and go as I please. It didn't matter tonight, because my boo worked there, and she say she got me. One thing I knew was that when niggas from the hood come to the club, she treat them like V.I.P. and I know I was one of them niggas, but a step further.

I pulled up at the club and it was wrapped around the corner. Lucky for Tiara put me in the fast lane. I walked straight to the front and name dropped. "Hold up big fella, the line back there," the bouncer pointed.

See, this the type nigga I don't like. This nigga 6'7, about 280 in weight, but he calling me big fella. That shit kills me. "Sup' lil guy, my girl performing and told me I'm good. She ain't hip you," I said, matching his sarcasm with the lil guy comment.

"And who might she be?" he asked with his arms now folded, looking big as shit.

"Her name Tiara, but her stage name Red Bottom."

He looked me up and down then let me through. He acted

like he wanted a tip or some shit, but dat was dead, not from I. I walked through the club and all the girls was bad. I was thinking where the fuck these bitches be in the world. I almost forgot I came to see Tiara when a dancer grabbed me and took me to a secluded section and damn near forced a dance on me. 'SHID WHY NOT.' I went with it.

She got to poppin her ass on me and I was in my zone. Out of what seemed like think air, Tiara popped up and told the dancer to roll without words as she tossed her a dub' (twenty dollars).

"Damn boo, you must gonna finish that dance. The song was still playin'." I smiled.

She mugged with her hand on her hips. "Why the fuck you ain't tell me you were here?" Tiara asked with nothing but a bra, thong and some red bottoms on.

"Damn, you look sexy," I told her as I pulled her on my lap. She turned around and started to kiss me. At first, I was shocked, then I just went with it I tend to do that a lot.

She stopped kissing me and looked me in my eyes for a second—well, more like a minute. I broke the stare and turned away. She grabbed my face to face hers. "I want you for myself. Is that possible? I was lost for words, so I just started kissing her as a reply to her question. This time she broke my kiss. "Don't make fuck no bitch up. You know my shit say bang'." I laughed and told her she good.

Tiara chilled with me for the rest of the night until she hit the main stage where the real money was at. She did things that made me anxious to see her later. I was feeling myself and was zoned out. As she danced, I ended up throwing about $450 in my soc. 'DAMN.' Pussy make you do the dumbest shit, I realized after her shift came to an end.

"So what's up boo?" Tiara asked.

"Shid, Ion' know what you 'bout to do but I'm 'bouta get up outta here, maybe catch some z's. I'm hit." I grabbed my pockets to show the lint.

"You spending the night wit me?"

In the inside I was cheesing like shit. "You tryna hold a nigga hostage, huh?"

"If you let me?" She licked her lips.

We got in her car, she had cool lil whip for a chick. It was a Chevrolet Volt. She was into that energy saving shit. The electric car was okay for the most part. It retailed at about $30,000 for a standard with promises of 200 miles of accommodations. Tiara decided to treat me to IHOP, since she had a good night. Cool with me. If it's free, it's me. My shit was hit. I couldn't wait for the weekend to come so my pockets wouldn't be beefin' with me no more.

We ordered food and talked, laughed and enjoyed each others company until about 6:00 a.m., then decided to roll. Parking in the complex we got out and she was in front of me pullin' my hand, leading the way. We went to her crib and enjoyed each others company a lil more this time. 'FINALLY.'

CHAPTER 17

Jroc

"If you know what I mean."
— Jroc

I was in class coolin'. A thousand thoughts invaded my mind. I was still straddling the fence. I wanted to do the right thing and stay away from the life of crime. The other side wanted to jump in headfirst with this street shit.

I was thinking of the conversation Dro, and I had a few minutes earlier before class. I sometimes wished I was suave and nonchalant like he has always been. I looked out the classroom window and saw Dro walking past. Waling with him was the baddest bitch in the school. It looked like she had his phone as he followed with his hand out. "That's the shit I'm talkin' 'bout," I said louder than I expected.

People in the class looked back. I started writing in my book looking busy. I sat in class until the bell rang, then it was off to the next one. I had about 2 more hours and this school day was over.

I walked down the hall and seen Dro leaving out the side door. I bent the corner and seen the girl that was just with Dro walking toward me, her face in her phone.

"What's up lil mama?" I said to her, sounding too sweet. I know I got game and knew she was gonna bite.

"Lil Mama? Boy, do that shit ever work?"

'YEAH, BITCH IT DO.'

I can't lie that shit had me guh'. She tried to shine on me, so I replied, "Fuck your lil apple head ass then!" But it didn't even faze her 'cause I was talking to her back. She never stopped walking but sent one more shot at me.

"Never, not even in your dreams."

Now that shit hurt. I decided to skip the next class. Really, I had already passed. I just had to finish a few things for graduation. I tried to back track to catch up with Dro and see what he was 'bout to do.

By the time I made it outside, that nigga was pulling off, blasting the music. I tried to call him, but only got the voicemail. I already knew he wasn't gonna answer. That shit was loud as shit he was listening to, so the train was my next move.

Exiting the train, I was at Shaw Howard Station. I got off on the R Street side and looked around. First person I see was Dro, posted up on the gate, smoking.

I could tell it was pack.' The aroma was thick in the air. Before I got off the train, well the escalator, I could smell it. I walked across the street with open arms. "What's up, bruh?"

"Shit coolin, just came from class. Fuck you doin' out here?" Dro asked.

"Got bored. Shid I was tryna catch you at school, but you got ghost on me."

"My bad, Slim. I had to holla at my man to get the best thing smokin.' You know I only smoke dro, so I had to get an ounce of me." He laughed. "You get it . . . I had to get an ounce of me," he repeated to emphasize his rhyme.

"Yeah, I get it. Dro as in weed nigga, but if I would've known that we could've went half on it."

The day started to brighten up. People started coming outside to enjoy the weather. Today was Friday, a favorite day of the week for me. It was 1:00 and the block was dry of hustlers. That was a plus, only me and Dro had work. The best part was we had different shit so we couldn't step on each others' toes.

But like all good things, they come to an end. Izzo came around the corner looking like he had a long night. He had on cargos and a tank top. To complete his outfit was some pink bunny slippers with the big ears and all.

"Yo, what up?" Izzo spoke as he Diddy-bopped up on us. I looked at him and asked, "Where the fuck your shoes at nigga?"

"Damn." He looked down. "I'm still sleep bruh. I thought I could come out here and steal a few dollars before niggas woke up. I was in the courtyard for 'bout 45 minutes but I kept smellin' this nigga," Izzo said, pointing to Dro as he exhaled a cloud of smoke.

"Nigga you still ain't answer the question," Dro said, blowing smoke in Izzo's face. Izzo tried to reach for the jay'.

"Damn homes, let me hit that. I stayed at Tiara's house last night. She washing my shit for me. I didn't even plan on leaving the stoop."

Dro pulled the jay' back. Give me $10 and I'll give you a fat spliff for your face."

I giggled and shook my head. Izzo knew Dro was dead serious. One thing about Dro is that he 'bout that dollar. He gonna hustle. I was hip to Izzo; he was fucked up. The nigga told me how he tricked off a lot of his bread at the club and I had pictures that he sent to confirm it.

"Fuck it." Izzo peeled $10 from his pocket. "If all goes well tomar' we gonna be good anyway. Fuck dat change," he said, handing Dro the money.

As promised, Dro gave him a nice fat jay' and then stepped off. He didn't even say where he was goin', just left with the wind. That left me and Izzo chilling, watching the neighborhood go by as we hustled.

My phone range. "Talk." I sounded sweet. I always answer the phone like that when the number is unknown or unavailable. A sweet voice came through in response. "Hey, boy."

"Who dis?" Whoever this was had my attention.

"Janai."

I looked to the sky tryna search my brain and put a face on the name. It didn't even sound familiar, but she sounded sexy as shit. She must have sensed my uncertainty and decided to refresh my memory. "I met you by Howard the other day."

A lightbulb hit me. I remember when I was at the court and went to get some niggas some tree and met her on the way back. "Oh yea, I remember, but this ain't the number you gave me," I said, not really knowing if it was or not 'cause I didn't save her number.

"Yes, it is, but can I see you?" she asked.

"No secret, you sure can. Where you at?"

She told me she was at home and wanted me to come get her. I ain't got no damn car, but she don't know that. Thank goodness for Uber. That was gonna be her ride.

She texted me the address and I was excited. 'GOT ONE.' I forwarded the address to the driver. Izzo was right beside me shakin' his head. "Damn bruh, that's all you want to do is fuck all day. I'm surprised you ain't got no kids yet."

"Jealous . . . always hating the player and not the game. Matter fact . . ." I waved him off. "Don't bother me, I'm workin'," I said as I uncovered my phone, jokingly.

Izzo just laughed at me, then walked back to Tiara's house to get his clothes. he noticed people started coming outside and anything can happen in the hood. Nobody wanted to get caught slippin'.

That left me by my lonesome. I headed to the liquor store to get some drinks for shawty since she was on her way.

I was gonna make sure I had everything I needed so we wouldn't have to leave the crib once she got there. I even brought a couple of Mojo's (performance pills) to ensure I show up today. If you know what I mean. I was going to do something terrible to that box. She called me and asked can she see me, well I got something worth her while. It's go time.

CHAPTER 18

Black

*"If they find fingerprints in that
motherfucka' they like dat."*
— Black

I rolled outta bed to the smell of breakfast. I didn't know what it was, but it smelled real good. Putting on my slippers—they were a pair of Cartman from South Park with the head in front. It was for gangstas' only and was "like dat." Making my way to the kitchen there she was, my baby, Keisha in nothing but an apron dancing over the stove as she cooked.

She didn't even know I was behind her as she placed the food on plates. Looking at the food, I noticed it was my favorite—waffles with patty melt and hashbrowns.

I smiled, then snuck back to the room and waited for my meal to be delivered. I laid in the bed with my hands behind my head thinking of past days. The thoughts of the last few days flooded my mind. The door opened. 'SHE DID THAT.'

"Hey sleepyhead, good morning handsome," she said, breaking me out of my daze.

"Hey beautiful." I smiled. "That shit look good as a mutha fucka.' You know it's my favorite meal. What's the occasion?"

"Nothing baby, I just wanted to make my boo some breakfast. Why it gotta be an occasion?" she asked with a devilish grin. She was up to something. Her demeanor was obvious.

"Cut the act. What you want?" I asked, taking a bite of the waffle. She stopped in her tracks and folded her arms.

"I want to go out somewhere. All we do is stay in the house, sometimes go to a store or two, but we don't do shit together," she said, pouting.

I looked at her. She was so cute. It's like she was my kryptonite. I loved her 'cause she had her own. I took care of her and all that good shit, but when I'm fucked up, I can get bread from her too. Now that's a bad bitch. "Where you wanna go, boo?"

She whipped her head. "That's for you to decide, but it need to be soon. I need a getaway from all this stress."

"I got you boo. If all goes well tomorrow, we gonna be good. I mean like supa' straight. We could even get a crib to have our own space as a unit."

I cleaned my plate. That shit was on point. Now it was shower time. I had to wash off last night's fun. Keisha thought she had all the sense and took off running to the shower like that shit meant something. I jumped my ass right in there with her. "Move over!!" And got ready for my day.

Keisha was a student at Everest College tryna be a nurse or some shit like that in that field. Her graduation was near. She looked good in her little scrub outfit, and she was clappin' (thick in her clothes). "Boo, what time you leaving? I'm 'bout to leave," Keisha said.

'NONE OF YOUR DAMN BUSINESS.'

That's what I wanted to say. "Go ahead bae, call me when you get to class. I'ma get on the train."

She met me in the hallway, and I kissed her goodbye. She was out the door after that. I had a whip for the day. My sweet lick from the night before. I locked the crib up and walked across the street to where I parked the ol heads car, Fred's.

As I neared the car, I noticed a detective's car parked about 4 cars in front of it, so I kept it moving. 'DAMN.'

I should have listened to Dro and left that car alone. That nigga always right and I hate it sometimes, smart ass nigga. Now I had to get on the bus for real. I was mad because I didn't get a chance to sipe the car down. Then it hit me.

I turned around, walked back to the house 'cause I had a plan. I went to the fridge. I had a 6-pack of beer in the back. I grabbed them and walked to the shed. I emptied all the beers and filled it with gasoline.

I exited the crib and crept to the car. The DT (detective) was still there so I stayed low. Since it wasn't my car, the door was still unlocked. I entered through the back door and poured four bottles on the interior of the whip. The fifth bottle I poured on the hood, and it leaked into the engine and transmission. The final bottle I made a cocktail bomb and lit it.

After tossing my lighter inside the car, flames ignited. Well, that's what supposed to happen, so much for the movies. It laid on the seat unlit. I picked the light up and lit one of the rags that was on the floor and tried again.

This time it caught flames instantly. The detective was still unaware. That soon changed as I lit the cocktail bomb and tossed it as his Dodge Charger.

It was like slow motion. While the bottle was flying in the air making its way to its destination, I was running through the house's lawns in front of me, leading to the opposite street. Both cars was in flames.

I came out on the other side walking down the main road which was Wheeler Road. I stood at the bus stop. I looked to the sky and noticed the smoke clouds. I smiled. Now the bus had to hurry up so I could get the fuck from this side of town.

The bus finally came after about 20 minutes of waiting in the heat. Riding on the bus I seen the fire department out there doing their job trying to tame the fire as 10 police cars blocked off the streets.

I got off the bus at the transfer point—Southern Avenue and Wheeler Road. I crossed the street to go to the other side. I smoked a jack and waited for the next bus.

A car pulled up on me. Naturally, I reached for my gun. I let it go when I seen it was Dro and his ol lady. "What's up, Slim?" Dro asked from the passenger seat. "Where you going?"

"I'm headed uptown. Where y'all headed?"

" 'Bouta take my girl to work, then round da way."

I looked at Dro's girl and asked her could I get a ride. She didn't mind, everybody loves me. But before I got in, I told Dro with my eyes that I was strapped, and he was cool wit. If anything I'll just get out and kick it if I have to.

We drove to the beat of the music while Charmine sang every song. Arriving at her job we all got out. She kissed Dro and gave me a pound, then a straight jab to the chest after I puckered my lips for a kiss, playing with her.

She didn't leave right away. She laid down a bunch of rules for her car. I just laughed as Dro nodded his head like he was used to this spiel all the time. "Damn fool, she told you."

"Yeah Slim, she act like a nigga mother sometimes, but whatever, let's push before she come back."

Dro pulled off and I was skeptical about telling him what happened. I knew he was gonna curse me out, but I had to put him on point. There was a silence in the car and Dro turned the music down like he was a damn black version of Ms. Cleo. "What's up Black, you look guilty, spill it."

"Don't curse me out but listen." I paused. "You listening?"

He looked at me like I was dumb, so I continued. "Them peoples was stalking that whip I had from the other night. I was about to get in that joint and head uptown, but it was a DT sitting on that joint, lamping tryna see who was gonna get in. That's why I was at the bus stop. I'm guessin' they found ol boy."

"Stupid dumb nigga! I told you leave that joint!" Dro was heated but calmed down. "At least they didn't catch you in it. I hope you wiped it down though."

"Nope." I smiled.

"Fuck you smiling for. You retarded, on my motha.' "

'NOT RETARED.'

"If they find fingerprints in that motherfucker, they like dat," I said to Dro, not even telling him what I did. He'll watch the news and find out. he pulled onto the highway.

CHAPTER 19

24 Hours and Counting

Dro and Black parked on the backside of the neighborhood as they arrived uptown. Walking down the street they headed to the apartment complex, L.W., short for Lincoln Westmorland Projects.

It was still early and wasn't too deep outside, as it would usually be for a summer day. Most of the kids were at summer camp or summer jobs. Ol heads still asleep or hungover, not even tryna see the sun right now. A few people were out, it was never empty, you'll always find somebody lurking.

"Fuck urbody at?" Black asked.

"Don't care. I might get a few dollars before they decide to come out and step on toes," Dro stated.

"Well, you go ahead and do that. I'm 'bout to shoot to the crib to check on things."

"Yup, I'll be right here."

Dro posted up on the gate and seen Jroc walking up the street smoking and carrying what looked like a bottle in his eyes. 'THIS NIGGA START EARLY,' Dro thought, shaking his head.

"Hey bob!" Jroc happily spoke.

"Shit, coolin'. I just got out here," Dro said, pointing to the bottle. "I see you ain't waste no time gettin' your day started."

Jroc laughed at his assumption and shook his head right back at me. "Nah bruh, it ain't even like that. I got this lil broad coming over," he said, brushing his own shoulders. "You know the one from Howard I met the other day," Jroc said, tryna jog Dro's memory. "I showed you a picture of her at the court."

"Oh yea, I remember, but speaking on that day, you ready for this big money move, baby boy?"

"No doubt, Slim. You my shit say work," Jroc boasted. Dro started laughing, hunched over the gate. "Yeah okay, your shit say work huh, we gonna see." he continued laughing.

Dro and Jroc were callin', enjoying the beginning of a good day. It was 80 degrees with a slight breeze. It wasn't to hot, and the humidity was fine. The neighborhood girls had their finest attires on, looking like ghetto superstars.

Izzo was still in Tiara's house. He planned to get his shit and roll. Once he walked in her room, seen her in a wife beater, no bra, or no panties, his dick damn near jumped at attention as if it had a shock collar on it.

Tiara was bent over trying to grab something. Izzo could see her pussy print from the back. She didn't even know he was behind her as she shuffled through her dresser.

Izzo shit was brick. It had that morning wood feeling and wasn't goin' anywhere without a fight. She looked back at him when she finally felt his presence and smirked. He damn near busted one right there, the way she licked her lips at him.

Tiara stood up and walked to the bed backwards and laid back on it. Eagle wings are how her legs were spread. 'DAMN SHE GOT PHAT PUSSY.' She was now playing in her love tunnel just how Izzo liked it.

She had her head all the way back, looking at the ceiling using one hand to spread her lips apart, the other goin' in and out. Izzo couldn't take it no more. 'FUCK THAT< I GOTTA FEEL THIS PUSSY.'

Tiara had him open and he knew it. Izzo looked her up and down as she laid there watching him staring at the print in his pants. He walked over to her, and her legs were in the air, calling for him to enter.

Izzo walked up on her and wasted no time digging in that flooded canal. He must have had an energy boost from last night, she couldn't take it. She tried to put her hands on the bottom of his stomach to shorten his stroke and stop him from full penetration. "Hell, nah! All that shit you just did, ain't no running," Izzo said, pulling her close with long, deep strokes.

He grabbed the pillow from under her head and threw it at her face, never stoppin' his stroke. "Here, put your face in that!" She turned over. Now Izzo was slapping her ass, crushing her from the back. "Awwww shit!!" He came like a virgin and laid there as she shook from her orgasm. He smacked her ass again for good measure and asked her what she was doing today. She didn't even respond, she was drained. All she wanted to do was curl up and sleep, and that's what she did. Izzo cleaned up, headed outside. He had shit to to today.

Black was in the crib. His moms just came back in from wherever she was at, and he was mad. When he got there his sisters were there by themselves with no food in the house. To make matters worse, she returned empty-handed. "Why the fuck you ain't call to tell me you wasn't gonna be in here?" Black screamed on his moms.

She didn't even respond. She just started crying. "THEY KILLED HIM!" she screamed, then repeated it while she sobbed and sniffed.

"Killed who?" Black acted interested.

"Fred . . . they killed Fred. Oh my God!" she screamed hysterically.

Black had enough. There was no sympathy in his heart for a pedophile. He walked past her, leaving her at the door and went to the girls' room. "Girls! Go put y'all clothes on, we goin' outside," Black said as he put his cap on his head looking in their mirror.

Shanae and Shaniyah did as they were told. A few minutes later they exited the apartment. Black looked back at his mother who had her hands on her face, crying. he had no remorse as he closed the door.

'FUCK DAT NIGGA, FUCKIN' CREEP.'

Shanae and Shaniyah ran down the stairs of the apartment, pushing the door open, ready to go play. When Black made it outside, he noticed the weather got a little hotter, not brutally hot, but humid.

He started strolling through the hood, bent the corner and seen his homies. They was chillin', talking shit on the gate as he walked up. "Sup' niggets!"

Everyone looked in Black's direction, then dapped him up. Izzo started smiling extra as he greeted him. Black frowned his face up and looked at him. "Fuck you so jolly for, moe?" Izzo started singing a T-Pain song. "I'm in love wit a stripper . . ."

Dro shook his head, shocked at the revelation. "Love nigga? Go head' with that," Jroc interjected. "Damn, I knew I should have tried to get some of that if she got you like that. It must be torchy'!"

Izzo didn't like that. "Yeah, okay. Should have, could've, would've, but didn't, so you can't. She mines now so make sure your horny ass stay away from her wit dat too," he said, narrowing his eyes, dead serious.

"DAAAYUUMMM!!" They all said in unison the moment they seen her hop out of the Uber. You would have thought they were in the movie 'Friday' how they all leaned back.

She had on some tight jeans. Tight like how did she get in them. The seam between her legs was so thin you could see the outline of her clit. The outfit looked painted on.

In a sexy voice she said, "You just gonna stand there?" They all looked at each other, trying to see who she was talking to. Jroc stepped up, then looked back at Izzo. "I don't need Tiara nigga, I got bitches."

"Jeezus! I hear dat," Black said, taking shawty's glow in.

CHAPTER 20

Jroc

"Is your dick as good as your slick ass mouth?"
— Another

I just purped' out (stunted) sounding too sweet as I wrapped my arms around my Howard joint. Her name was Janai, I think. She was bad. I'm talking 'bout model-type. She looked at me and asked, "So what we 'bout to do?"

"You know, off to the bat cave." I smirked.

I walked the long way to the crib. I wanted everybody to see this eye candy I had with me today. I craved the attention. The looks that Janai brung our way made me feel like dat nigga. She was bad.

Niggas didn't see girls like her walking through this side of town a lot—well, at least this neighborhood. It was like a show, and she was the main attraction. Right now I'm the ringleader.

We made it to my house, and she looked around. I could tell she was surprised, in a good way. She got comfortable. First thing she did was kick her heels off. I just sat on the couch as she looked around. 'DAMN YOU BAD.'

Pussy in my opinion is a gift and a curse, but all in all it's like one of the greatest wonders of the world. Niggas kill for it, die for it, and even go broke for it.

On everything, I could spot good box a mile away. It's a gift I have and right now I think I have a contestant. She looked at me. "What you over there thinking about, boo?"

I laughed and shook my head. Many thoughts ran through my head. She asked another question, "What's so funny?"

"Listen, when I met you, I didn't think you would call a nigga. Really, I thought you gave me a wrong number and was just tryna be nice, ya know. That's why I didn't call you, but damn you fine as shit."

"Why would you—"

I put my finger up, cutting her off. "Hold up boo." I winked at her, but really I was gambling with my next choice of words, but continued, "If you got a man, that's cool. I ain't looking to marry right now or disrupt what you got goin' on. As you could see I'ma dope boy," I said with my arms wide, presenting my house like it was mines and not moms. "And you a college girl. I'll treat you good and all that, but what I really want right now . . ." I licked my lips. "Is to watch you jump up and down like a pogo stick on this dick."

She damn near choked to death from the Goose goin' down the wrong pipe as she sipped. I guess I was a little too blunt with her in my approach, but hey, I like what I like.

I jumped to her aid and started patting her back. "Shit, you a'ight sweets?"

Silence.

She patted her own chest and looked at me, not saying a word, so I spoke. "I didn't mean to offend you or sound crazy, but we grown. We make our own decisions, so I decided to keep it 100."

"Is your dick as good as your slick ass mouth?" she eyed me. 'BITCH I'M KING KONG. FUCK YOU THOUGHT.'

"Is that pussy wet?" I asked. She nods. "Good."

I grabbed her hand and walked to my room. She could see the tent growing through my pants. She dropped to her knees and took my boxers down, looked at me and began to suck while never breaking eye contact. "Damn girl." I grabbed a handful of hair, pulling her up.

"Ummm," she moaned. She like the aggressive shit.

I grabbed her, throwing her on the bed. I slapped her ass, and another moan escaped her mouth. She arched her back and pushed her legs under her. Now that position put her ass high in the air.

I drove deep and deeper in her tunnel after each thrust. "I'm 'bout to blow my top!"

I swear shawty was a freak how she was taking the dick. If I wouldn't have kept it 100 with her, she the type you might wife up and blow a bag on. She that gorgeous. But me, like I told you, I could see the freak inside. Worse that could happen is she say no, but she didn't.

❖   ❖   ❖

Later that night everyone reunited naturally. All personal ventures were complete. The whole crew was in the hood just relaxing, kicking it. Kids ran around, girls in their own groups mingling in different areas of the hood helping the light poles and gates hold up and get put to use as they leaned on them. The vibe was ordinary.

Everyone was lost in their own thoughts. The silence was deafening. Dro decided to break that. "Shit, somebody fly in, damn." Jroc was quick to pass the ball and decided to throw Dro under the bus. "Nigga, you got it. You the only one that ain't been nowhere, so I know you up."

That made sense to Izzo as he co-signed. "No bullshit, fool, it's like 7:30. We all dipped out and left the block to you. I know you heavy." Dro wasn't tryna hear all that as he made his point clear.

"Y'all right, I guess I'm the only nigga hustling in the hood, huh. Can't nobody move til I'm finished." Sarcasm all in his voice. "Get the fuck outta here, but it's cool doe'. I'll fly in. It has been a decent day. Matter fact a great day." He smiled.

After the conversation went in the right direction of Jroc's liking, he changed the subject. "Bruh, I wish I would've thought to record shawty, she was bad. I was geeked and had to hurry up and get in them cheeks, asap," he boasted.

Black rolled the tree up. Dro gave him some lemon haze. It was exotic with a hint of citrus. Blazing the blunt, they got high and on their level. Just another day in the hood. The time was ticking as the day slowly turned into night.

Thoughts of the come-up that Black talked so highly about, invaded everyone's mind. They all was ready, making plans for the money before it was even in their possession, or knew how much to expect. Only thing they thought was that life was going to get so much better and become real easy from that day forward, or so they thought.

CHAPTER 21

Gameday

"Let's roll then, Mr on time."
— Black

The sky was blue, not a cloud in sight. The air was dry with the sun high at its peak. Inside the apartment everybody was in the air conditioning getting the plan together.

Dro's house was about 10 minutes away from Keisha's house. Black's girl next door to the victim to be. Black and Izzo was playing 'Call of Duty' smoking trying to get themselves in the mood. Dro on the other hand was in his room placing all the semi-automatic weapons he borrowed on his bed to show the others. He wanted to give them options.

He loaded and cleaned everyone's weapon. He didn't want any mistakes, no jammed pistols or other defaults to alter the outcome of this mission. High points and Stars were not among the selection of guns. Dro was determined for this to go off incident free. Jail was not an option for him. He did all he could to insure everybody was on the same page.

Dro called everyone to his room. They all entered with bubble eyes upon seeing the tools laid out for today's mission. He introduced each gun one by one.

"Listen, moe, I owe a nigga for these so have your pick. This right here is a Glock G33 wit a 3dot fixed sight and could hold .357 sig caliber bullets. You get nine rounds."

Izzo smiled, grabbing the gun. "Let me get that bitch." Dro grabbed the next one. "This right here, um um, it's a Heckler and Koch HK45 autoloader with polymer finger grooves on the grip. It hold .45acp caliber bullets with 10 rounds. Who want her?"

Jroc stepped from the back. "Here I go, let me get her." Dro smiled.

Dro turned his attention to Black. "Big boy, I got something special for you," he said picking up the gun. "This right here nigga. I feel it was made just for you. It's a AF2011-A1 double barrel pistol.

"That's a pistol?" Black asked in awe.

"Yeah, it's a semi-automatic double barrel with a double clip. It hold .45acp and .38 super autos with 18 rounds at the same damn time.

"Give it here."

Dro had a big grin on his face as he walked to the end of his bed. He lifted it up. "This is mines. It's a Stag Arms Model 8T." Izzo damn near broke his neck to get a peek at it. "It's a what? Mutha fucka look like a choppa,' "he said amazed.

"Yeah, a choppa' that hold 30 rounds standard. This if shit get crazy. Dro stamped.

Black was on the porch smoking a jack', sippin' on a 211 Reserved Steel. For some reason he felt better and at his best when he was under the influence. Plucking the jack' and taking his last gulp of the beer he walked back to the apartment.

Everybody was in the living room playing the game. Black

called next on the game as he sat down. Dro questioned him. "Ayo Black, your girl gone yet?"

"Yeah moe."

"We need to be heading over there to start lamping and getting our mind right. Slim gonna be there in a few. I rather be early than late," Dro stated.

"Let's roll then, Mr on time." Black chuckled, turning off the TV in the middle of Jroc and Izzo's game.

Grabbing all that was needed, they exited the apartment. Dro left his door unlocked. He didn't know if they were going to be 'coming in hot' or what. That made him think of the easy option. A black Yukon truck was their transit. Black stole it the night before at a gas station uptown.

Whoever truck it belonged to had to be furious. It was decked out with rims, TVs and a nice system. Izzo jumped in the ride. "Oh shit, this bitch sexy!" He smiled. "It even got a PlayStation 5."

The truck was a dopeboys dream car. They cruised to their own thoughts for the short commute. Everybody was ready pulling up as the truck parked directly across the street from the house.

Black led the way to Keisha's house. It was next door to where the planned caper was to take place. Sitting in living room, discussions of the plan was rehearsed to make sure they all were on point. It was game day. Now the waiting begins until kickoff . . .

FUCK
COVID

CHAPTER 22

Workcall

"Get the fuck on the floor!"
— Jroc

There it was the answer to every ghetto prayer. It was pulling up, guarded by two men oblivious to the power they had in the cab of the truck they drove. So comfortable and relaxed, he did the same routine for a month straight. The wrong guy noticed. The driver of the Armor truck parked.

'WHAT THE FUCK? THAT'S DIFFERENT,' Black noticed peeking through the blinds. The driver exited the truck, opened the back cab where another dude got out. They walked to the front of the girl's house like they usually do, holstering guns on their sides. They carried .357 magnums but looked like mall security but packing.

"Y'all see that?" Dro asked. "Them niggas got them dooky

shooters on 'em, no loafin.'"

Jroc was sweating bullets. He was scared, to say the least. You could see it written on his face. he had the easiest job, but at the same time an important one. he left the house through the back door and was now walking toward the girl's front door. He wore a worn out, greasy overall with oil stains all through it. He was in character, looking the part.

'KNOCK KNOCK'

A sexy voice answered as she peeked through the door. "Who is it?" She had one of them doors that had a curtain on it that exposed the outside when you slid it to the side. She opened the door. "Hi, can I help you?" She looked Jroc up and down. 'DAMN HE SEXY BUT DIRTY AS SHIT.'

Black knew she was a sucker for a pretty boy and Jroc played the roll well. Dro and Izzo was creeping around the corner of the house. Jroc's heart started to beat fast. He was getting nervous but tried to swallow it. "Hello Ms. lady, my car broke down and I was wondering if I could use your phone to call a tow, mines dead." He flashed his phone.

"Yo! Who at da door?" one of the truck drivers asked, coming from the back in his boxers.

Jroc seen he had the up on the guy. The driver was close enough to grab, so he shipped out his gun. This was the first change of plans that Jroc did. He was supposed to get the girl to come outside and talk on the porch so Izzo and Dro could bum rush the front while Black come through the back. He was supposed to play victim but nope, he wanted a bigger role. Now he got one. "Get the fuck on da ground!" Jroc yelled.

The girl screamed which made Jroc panic. He swung the HK45 toward the sound of her voice, accidentally smacking her in the temple, knocking her out instantly. "Shit!" Jroc said as he went other aid.

In the midst of all that, he must have forgot about the other guy 'cause he came around the corner, gun drawn, pointing it at Jroc. 'BOC' Dude fired, he missed.

Jroc, being quick, mainly scared but quick on his toes, he grabbed the other guy with the boxers on, hid behind him covering his own body, pointing at the shooter.

"What do you want?" the shooter asked. They were now in a standoff.

"Fuck you! Drop your gun or your man's head gonna be everywhere in this room," Jroc threatened.

The standoff was really intense. It was 15 second which felt like forever to them as neither man budged. The shooter knew the invader wasn't about this life. The eyes never lie. His face was readable. The shooter taunted him by moving closer.

If Jroc was by himself that might have worked, but as the shooter inched closer, he was about to clear the door that led to the hallway to the front door where Jroc stood his ground.

'SMACK!'

Black came from around the corner of the dining room, hitting the driver with the butt of his A-1 double barrel pistol. The shooter dropped like a fly.

The other guy, who Jroc still had yoked up, started crying. He was scared and taste his possible fate. Dro came through the door, gun drawn, cautious with a puzzled expression when he seen the scene before him. "What da fuck Jroc!" Dro screamed. "Fucks the point in a plan if you gonna come up in here and start freestyling. Stupid dumb nigga!"

Jroc stood still, in shock from the standoff. he glanced at the girl who was still clearly unconscious. Izzo came through the door. "Okay den, remix this shit den'," he joked, looking at Jroc. "Fuck your mask at boy, since you doin' you."

Silence.

"Get this nigga up outta here!" Dro yelled, irritated. Izzo grabbed Jroc and walked out. Black picked up the driver, took his keys, then tied his legs up. Black walked out to the truck and backed it into the garage, taking it off the street.

Dro was still in the house watching all three of the victims. Izzo came back in the house, looked at Dro for direction. "Get the rope and tape."

Black came back in the house through the garage and helped to tape and tie everybody up. They were back-to-back in a triangle.

"Moe, we gotta hurry up. Dude should still be on delivery," Dro said. Izzo co-signed. "Yeah, no secret, time to bounce." Black was on board. "You niggas ain't saying nothing. Let's get whatever up in dat truck."

Entering the garage, the back of the cab was the reason behind all this drama. The doors were ajar. Big smiles spread across all their faces when they saw a case of gold bars and four duffle bags, straight cash.

"Jackpot!" Black smiled a rare smile.

They grabbed the good, loaded it in their SUV where Jroc sat in the backseat, quiet.

"A'ight, let's go!" Dro said, jumping in the passenger seat.

Black closed the trunk, looked at Jroc and had a thought that wouldn't leave his mind. "Hold up," he said. "I left something in there." He jogged back to the house. The crew sat in the truck wondering what he could have left worth running back in there when the sounds of sirens were faint.

'BOC! BOC! BOC!'

Black came running out of the house and hopped in the truck. "I got it." Dro shook his head as Black pulled off. Everyone sat back as he drove. No words were exchanged. Sirens could be heard in the area, getting real close.

Black was geeking to get back, not realizing he was speeding doing 50 mph in a 25 zone. Turning the corner of the victim's block a police cruiser was driving past and then made a U-turn to get behind them. "Shit!" Black said looking through his rearview mirror. "Them peoples are right behind us."

Slowing down he drove at a moderate speed trying to see what the move was. The police was riding behind them on their bumper. "They running the tags, moe," Izzo suggested.

Dro was calm. He was thinking of the best outcome. Here

they were about 2-3 minutes away from the house. The mother load in the truck, 3 bodies dead in a house, and car full of pistols. And only 2 cops.

The police lit 'em up with their lights. "What's up Dro?" Black asked. "Wand me buss 'em?" Dro took a big breath, then exhaled. "Pull over."

'THIS NIGGA MUST BE CRAZY' Black thought as he looked at him, but something in his eyes made Black comply.

Truck in park, the officers pulled behind them. "I ain't goin' to jail, Slim," Dro said. "Mask down." Everybody pulled their mask down in compliance to Dro's orders. "Kill 'em."

The officers never seen it coming. The windows was tinted 5%, four doors flew open. Dro was geeking. It was all or nothing. he had that new Stag 8T, draco. He was trying to see what that gas-operated piston action was about. He lifted the rifle, looked through the diamond head premium flip up sight set and squeezed.

'TAT TAT TAT TAT TAT TAT!' . . .

After the first shot was fired, Izzo heard the automatic flow of the bullets. it felt close, too close. He dived on the ground, out of the way. 'THIS NIGGA CRAZY FOR REAL.'

Dro was shooting approaching the squad car as endless shells fell. 'BOC! BOC!' Black fired his cannon. He wanted some of the action.

The police never had a chance to draw their weapons as their bodies spread on the street and over the car. Dro shot so many shots that the squad car started to flame. Jroc and Izzo stood up and looked at each other through the truck's window as Black and Dro walked to the corpse and fired a couple more rounds into the bodies of the officers for good measure.

"I'll drive this time," Dro stated with his hands out for the keys.

"No problem, playa'," Black dropping the keys in his palm.

Everyone looked around and the coast was clear and oddly silent. This was the sign to get up outta there and get to the house.

Dro got in the truck, and everyone followed suit.

"Let's dip," Dro said turning the engine over, bringing the car to life.

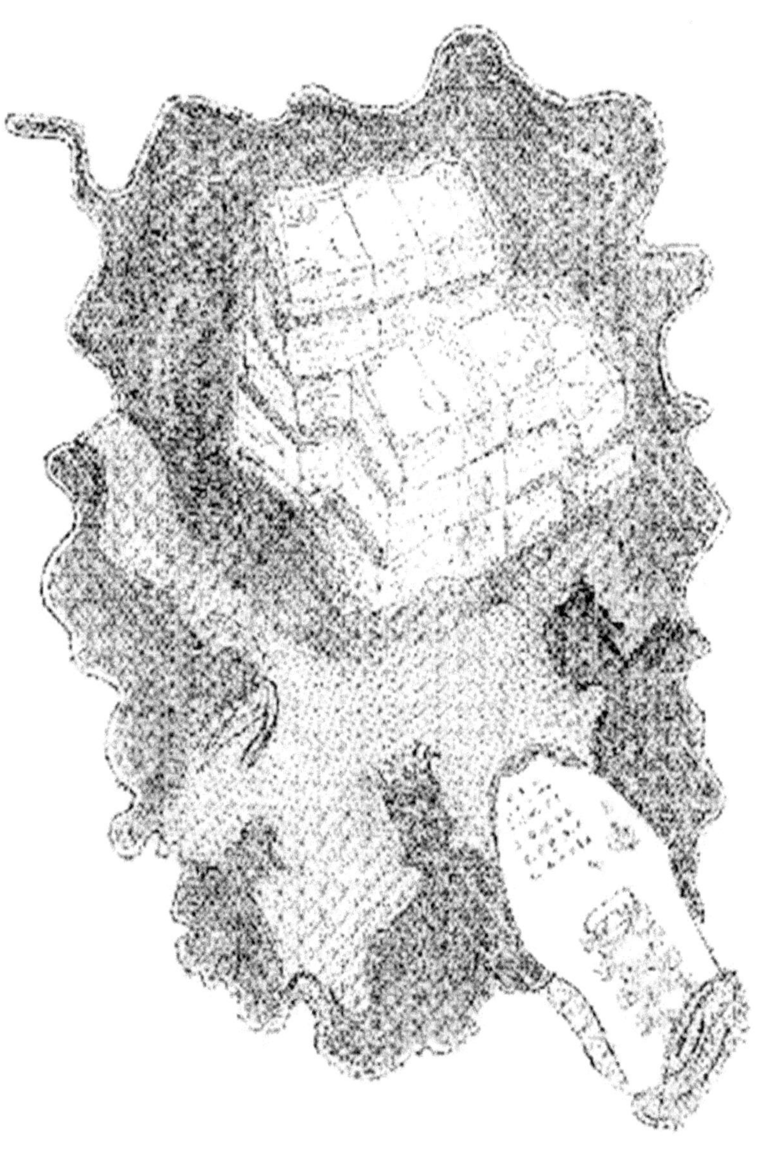

CHAPTER 23

Mission Complete

"Black, get that truck from 'round here."
— *Dro*

Dro drove the truck down the back streets slowly, like they just didn't break in a house, held victims hostage at gunpoint while robbing them, killing them and knocking off two cops. He cruised.

Driving to-his own thoughts, he listened to oldies music with the window down smoking a cigarette. Black was on the phone talking tohis girl letting her know he left the house and was up-town chilling so she wouldn't worry when the shit hit the fan.

He didn't have a conscience, just like that his conversation went left as he started talking freaky shit like he just didn't com-mit a homicide heartlessly.

Izzo was sexting Tiara, making plans to see her later as he

watched the street pass him by. Even Jroc was beginning to come around. All that action in one day woke him up, even though his clip was still full. He was talking to his latest girl, Janai, trying to get his mind off things.

Dro pulled up at his house and they unloaded the truck. After the last bag was safe Dro looked at Black. "Black, get that truck from 'round here." He nodded and left.

The money and all the gold bars were counted from the duffle. They were tired, Izzo blew a sign of relief. "What we gonna do wit' these gold bars, Slim?"

"Shid' Ion' know yet. I don't even know how much them shits is worth," Dro responded.

Surprisingly, Jroc had a solution. "I might could get them joints off."

They looked at each other but Dro responded, "Yeah okay, nigga, but the transaction goes through me. You ain't taking shit with you, wit your scary ass," Dro concluded.

"Lets finish counting this money," Izzo said, rubbing his hands together.

It was time to get paid. All the hard work they put in together, especially today was payment enough. Today wasn't incident free, but freedom was the main variable.

Penitentiary chances were taken, and they beat the odds. It was time to finally start living the life and to begin having more than just enough. "We on baby!" Dro said, smiling like an only child in a rich child's home on Christmas. He was genuinely happy.

Black drove the Denali around the city. He was still high off the move they just finished. Many thoughts ran through his head. He decided that this side of town was the best option to try to get the car off. Southeast, home to some of the most ruthless project housing communities.

He pulled up around Woodland Terrace, a ghetto housing complex. He had a few good men that he knew in that hood. He parked and could see the halfway house and shook his head. 'NO HOPE VILLAGE.' That's what it should be called. It was the halfway house for convicts coming from the FEDS.

The hood was live, and everybody was out doing their own thing. Some young boys that knew Black, ran up on him when they noticed it was him. "Sup' Black!!"

He gave out dap and leaned on the truck. "What's up lil' niggas?"

"That whip like dat big homie," a young boy acknowledged. Black smiled.

"You like that?" he nodded at the truck. "I got a little business proposition for y'all. Give me a meatball ($100) and y'all could have this sexy bitch, PlayStation and all."

"Is it stolen?" asked another.

"What da fuck you think, stupid dumb nigga!" Black was irritated by the dumb question, but continued, "To make you feel better, even though it's dirt cheap, I'll let you rest easy. It wasn't no carjacking type shit so y'all a'ight. I know y'all gonna stunt in it for a minute, then sell the parts."

"Shid okay!" They started putting their money together like they were putting up on some weed.

Black smiled to himself. Looking at the young crew getting their funds together reminded him of his past, just a few years back that was him and his men. He knew that all them lil' niggas was gonna do was act like it's their car, get a few girls and stunt. The money was given to Black as he dropped the key in one of the young in's hands. That was his cue to dip.

Black was walking down the street and ran into one of his childhood delinquents he met at Oak Hill, a juvenile detention center and that was a while back. "Fuck you doing 'round here, big boy!" his friend asked with excitement.

"Shit, 'bouta head uptown. I had to drop my man off something in the halfway house. Give a nigga a ride, I'll fly in (get you high)."

"Say no more."

They drove, smoked and caught up on bullshit. Black decided to go to his crib and see what's up with his sisters. Getting out of the car, he dapped his man up and gave him 20 dollars and 3.5 grams of the O.G. Kush he had.

Going through the courtyard, Black bent the corner and seen his little sisters on the playground. He walked and sat on the bench to finish his blunt. The smell of the smoke forced Shanae and Shaniyah to turn around and notice him. They ran to him, giving him hugs and kisses. He smiled his rare smile. "I miss y'all."

Shanae eyed him. "Where you been at?" Shaniyah co-sighed with a hand on her hip.

Black shook his head. 'YOU LITTLE CHICKS NOSEY.'

"I been at my girl's house. Why you all in my beeswax?" he asked, teasing.

"Dooooonntteee!!" They sang in unison with their heads tilted to the side.

"Did y'all eat?" Black changed the subject.

"Yeah, we had cereal," Shanae answered.

Black looked at his watch and sighed. 'IT'S DAMN NEAR DINNER TIME.' He reached in his pocket and gave his sisters 15 dollars a piece and told them to make sure they eat tonight. He wasn't planning on being home later.

He walked off after he received an alert from his phone letting him know his Uber was pulling up. Black reached the car and got in. He was getting chauffeured, now on his way back to Dro's house to hear the verdict of the move. 'I COULD SMELL THE MONEY.' Black smiled at the thought, letting smoke leave his nostrils, blowing it out the passenger window as they cruised.

CHAPTER 24

"Oh shit! We on da' news."

Blacks' Uber arrived. He stood at the door of Dro's house, geeking. He couldn't stop smiling. He knocked on the screen door and Jroc was there to open the door and let him in. "You look much better," Black said sarcastically, sliding past him as he headed to Dro's room where everybody else should've been at.

Dro felt a presence, turning around he seen Black. "Moe, you get rid of that truck?"

"Yup, sold it to some young boys around Woodland. You know they gonna ride till the wheels fall off then sell the parts," Black said matter-of-factly. "So what's the take fellas?"

"Well money wise we got 400,000 out the duffels and about—"

"What, a piece?" Black asked, cutting him off.

"No nigga, to split. As far as the gold bars, Jroc talked to a nigga tryna buy 'em for 1,500 a piece. We got 50 bars so that's 75,000 to split nigga," Dro emphasized, looking at Black. "So that put us at or about 118,750 a piece."

"Now that's what the fuck I'm talking 'bout!!" Black was excited.

Everybody dapped each other up, they was on now. Black was so happy to see all the money that he ran to the stacked piles and started throwing it all in the air.

Dro was vexed. "Slim, you geeking like shit," he said. "Now we gotta put that shit back into stacks. You ever count $400,000, nigga?"

Black looked at Dro then everybody else. Dro raised his eyebrow, waiting for a response. After not received it, he concluded, "I didn't think so, nigga."

The day was a success, everybody made it out alive and well. Couldn't say the same for the victims. This was a new beginning for them. It was about to be on and popping in the hood . . .

BREAKING NEWS

'Good evening, folks. This is Pat Reigal. Today a tragedy has struck us with more gun violence on the city streets. We have Lindsey Waters on the scene with an update. Lindsey are you with us . . .'

'Yes Pat, I'm here. I'm in front of the gruesome scene where a couple days ago a police vehicle was torched, along with the vehicle of a homicide victim found floating in the Anacostia River. But today the scene is no better. It's worst. A burglary, home invasion and murder has taken place. What looks like a robbery gone wrong in this quiet Prince George's county residence, a second time there has been a tragedy. The police have a few leads and are requesting the help of the public. The department feels that the two incidents are related. If you have any information, call the police hotline. There is a $20,000 reward for the arrest and conviction of the perps. Back to you at the studio, Pat.'

'Thank you Lindsey, but just in . . . a few blocks around the corner from that same location, another torched car with the bodies of two officers was found with multiple assault rifle bullet wounds to the face and body. This also may be related as the officers were responding to gunshots in the area. The vehicle was stolen when the tags were ran through the system. Violence is at an all time high. Any information call the tip line.'

❖　　　　❖　　　　❖

Jroc turned the channel after watching the news broadcast and nervously shook his head. Izzo raised his hand in an attempt to slap high five's. "Oh shit! We on da news." Black and Dro shared a knowing look.

Dro was a little upset to the fact that Black kept that car and now the police was tryna link everything to one move. This wasn't part of the plan. Nobody was supposed to get hurt, but shit happens, and it all went left.

"Damn Black, fuck made you do them people's dirty like dat?" Izzo asked really wondering. "I mean we was in the air, gone, 'bout to roll. That shit just not making sense to me." Izzo shrugged his shoulders. "Guess you just that fucked up."

Black didn't like that. "Naw nigga, I was saving all you niggas, while thinking 'bout the future." Now Dro had the screw face. "Fuck you mean, saving our asses . . . nigga that shit you did and probably do again is because you wanted to. You get a rush outta that shit and grown addicted to it," Dro countered.

"Whatever Rambo." Black waved him off. "Nigga you maxed out too, like you said, I ain't goin' to jail either, especially not for that scary ass nigga." Black pointed at Jroc. "That dumb nigga having a face off with the nigga without a mask. I'm surprised the nigga ain't smoke his ass, shakin' in shit. I was watching that fool. His face told the whole story. He was scared, Slim, so no face no case." Black was goin' non-stop. "And look, this nigga ain't shoot one shot. Clip still full like the moon in the sky. If I would've left them alive, they would have told. It's their job, remember."

"What the fuck you calling me hot?" Jroc jumped up.

"Nah, but you got potential. You ain't no jail nigga, they would fuck you up in many ways imaginable and yes, I believe you would talk if it comes down to it," Black said, standing up as well. "Now, what up!!"

"What's up then?" Jroc responded.

Black waved him off, yet again. "Nigga please, aye Dro get your man before he be on that TV screen too," he said, sparking a jay'.

The room was tense. The blueberry Kush circled a few times and vibe loosened all the way up. "So what y'all gonna do with the bread?" Black asked.

"Shid' I'm 'bout to—"

"Whoa," Dro said, cutting Izzo off. "Whatever you niggas plan on doin', don't go crazy and draw no heat. It ain't a milly'."

That was wishful thinking. Everybody had a plan, but when the money touch your hand, it's a whole other story. They wanted the fast life, now they had the funds to start. Nothing or nobody could have told them anything different. They were on.

CHAPTER 25

"Lil' Piece? I'm his wife . . ."
— Charmine

Charmine got off work early. She thought about calling her boo Dro but decided again it. She went to her mom's house to grab a few things because she planned on spending the night at his house anyway.

She had 2 hours to burn before she was due to be off. 'DECISIONS DECISIONS.' She decided to go to the mall and buy herself something special to wear tonight. Funds was a little tight, but she knew how she could cheer her man up. She had a vision of pleasing him while he returned the favor.

Charmine was strolling through the mall and found the store she was looking for. 'VICKY DON'T TELL NOBODY,' was right in front of her. Victoria Secret. She entered with all smiles.

She was browsing the different looks. She felt someone looking at her and followed the heat of the stare. She came eye to eye with a female. The female didn't break her stare, neither did Charmine. 'UM MUST BE ONE OF THIS NIGGAS LIL' BITCHES' Charmine thought. "Can I help you?" Charmine asked with much attitude.

"Ion' think you work here," Tiara said, returning her sas. "But actually you looked familiar that's all, but all that you doing, girl," Tiara said with her hand on her hip. "Ain't you Dro's lil piece or something?" she said, smacking her gum.

"Lil piece? I'm his wife, get it straight and who might you be?" Tiara laughed. "Oh, I'm nobody, just the neighborhood friend, no worries. I talk to Izzo anyway. That's my boo, so like I said, all that you doing."

Charmine looked at Tiara for a second and decided to apologize. From that moment they had a connection and would later become the best of friends. They continued to shop for a while. Tiara was spending like she didn't have a limit in Charmine's

eyes. "Girl, where you work at? Maybe I need to be putting in an application," Charmine asked.

"Oh I'm sure you'll get hired on the spot with a body like dat. I work on Bladenburg Road at the Stadium Night Club. I work tonight. Want me to introduce you?"

"Oh no, no, no, never mind, that's a negative. Dro would kill me," Charmine said, picking up different outfits.

Talking came easy for them. Charmine realized the time and decided to wrap the mini shopping spree up. Tiara and Charmine was undecided on their next destination until Tiara asked her for a ride round the way.

Charmine didn't mind, anything to get uptown to be around her boo. They drove listening to the radio. 'Money Set,' by Shy Glizzy came through the speakers. Both of them got to rapping the song as if they were in the video, swinging their necks and snapping their fingers. They were getting it as Charmine weaved in and out of traffic. "Girl, you know he from the city."

"Oh yeah, he doin' that," Charmine said.

Tiara was on her phone sliding through Instagram as Charmine drove. Tiara decided to post a few pictures of them in the car. Almost instantly, she started getting likes and comments. "Damn bitch! Niggas on your line."

Charmine blushed. "Girl, you gonna get me in trouble, especially how I been on Dro's line about that IG shit."

"What's your IG?"

"Same as my boo, Lady Dropak."

"Oh, okay. I sent you a request. You better follow me back too."

Charmine pulled up by the metro station and parked. They both got out as Tiara called Izzo but didn't get an answer. Charmine did the same thing and got the same result. They looked at each other and said the same thing. "They together."

They decided to text. Their assumption was correct as they read the responses. Tiara got another text: 'I'M AT DRO HOUSE BOUTA HEAD UP.' Tiara showed Charmine the text.

Charmine smiled and showed her phone too: 'GONE UPT B DER IN A MIN.' They both laughed.

Charmine thought about just staying up there until Dro got there. She could go to Dro's grandmother's house, or chill with Tiara, but thought to ask him first. 'HE BE TRIPPIN WHEN I JUST POP UP.'

"What you 'bout to do?" Tiara asked. "Tryna sip with me until they get here?"

"Sure," Charmine answered. 'HE JUST GONNA BE MAD CAUSE I GOT ME A NEW FRIEND ROUND' DA WAY.'

❖   ❖   ❖

Everyone was in the Uber XL, four deep, cruising down the city streets. Multiple thoughts was goin' through all their minds. "We on now!" Izzo said, to break the silence in the truck. Dro looked at him telling him to shut the fuck up without saying a word. Izzo caught the gesture and changed the subject. "What's the move for tonight then, damn."

Izzo was geeked to go out and stunt for real. He always used to stunt, but now he had the funds to actually do it and not be broke in the morning.

Jroc was always down for a party. he was throwing out random spots that actually they couldn't get in, but with the money, things were different. No need for an ID. Ben Franklin was the answer.

Black was cool with whatever, even though it wasn't his scene. He could chill for a while and not worry about money, so his schedule was free, and he didn't mind that at all.

Only Dro was the quiet one. He was in deep thought. He wasn't trying to blow his money, he was trying to be up' and stay up,' never looking back was the plan.

It was a lot of traffic outside for a weekend and the truck wasn't even moving. Bumper to bumper was the flow of traffic. They were anxious to get out. First stop was Black's crib. He was 5 minutes away, but as they neared they seen why traffic was crazy. Police was everywhere. His girl's house was hot right now for obvious reasons that they so quickly forgot about.

That changed the destination, now everyone was headed uptown to the hood. Dro's phone rang. He seen it was his girl again. 'SHE MUST BE OFF WORK.' He didn't answer, but replied through a text:

'SUP BOO, N U.BER, BEATS LOUD WHATS GOODIE.'
'NOTHING MISSING YOU DATS ALL.'

Dro looked and smiled but didn't reply, he decided to call her back when he got out of the car. Jroc was back to his normal self. He just got off the phone with a female of his that agreed to rent him a car for a week. He told her that he would rent her one as well and she bit.

That call changed Jroc's destination, which made him the first drop off. "A'ight fools, I'm gone," Jroc said as a redboned came out of a house to greet him as they got into another waiting Uber and peeled off.

Everybody else was going uptown and was about 15 minutes away. They pulled up and got out with North Face backpacks full of cash, all but Dro. It was the final destination where everyone dapped up and went their own way.

CHAPTER 26

Izzo

"Damn, that shit look good."

"That's what's the fuck I'm talking 'bout!" I said, walking down the street heading to the courtyard. Nobody couldn't tell me shit now. I'm that nigga and these niggas gonna start showing me some respect around here."

I approached Tiara's house, might as well see what's up with her. It almost seem like I had to check in with baby girl anytime I was around. People in the hood even noticed us and was sneak dissin' (talkin' trash). The hood buggers was the funniest. They hated and threw shade at Tiara—that was to be expected. The crazy part was how them same bitches was the ones throwing me pussy just so they could have something to tell her. 'WHATEVER.'

I go up the steps that led to my boo's apartment and was

shocked to see who was leaving up outta that joint. "Excuse me, you act like you seen a ghost," Charmine said with her hand on her hip like nigga move. But I didn't, not until I get to the bottom of this. I didn't even know they knew each other.

"Girl, what the hell you doing up in my spot?" I asked. Before Charmine could answer, Tiara came around the corner.

"Your spot?"

'YEAH BITCH, MY SPOT,' is what I wanted to say.

"You know what I mean." I smelt some pack' in the air. "Let me hit da jay,' but lil Dro, what's up?"

"Boy you ain't my daddy and Dro ain't either. I'm grown," Charmine said, pushing me out of the way. "I'ma call you later girl, we gonna hook up."

I pulled my phone out in an attempt to call my man. I had to put him on point, but Tiara snatched it out of my hand and tossed it . . . 'BITCH IF YOU BROKE MY PHONE,' and started kissing me. "Hold up bae." I tried to stop her. The kisses was coming at rapid fire. She was feeling herself and her breathing was hard. "Boo . . . boo chill." I tried to reason with her, but nope, that shit fell on deaf ears.

Tiara was on a mission. I was pent on the wall against the closet, backpack and everything still on. 'FUCK IT.' I gave in and started kissing her back while feeling her up. That got her even hotter.

We was in the living room like it was our shit. "No the hell y'all not! Not in my living room. Take that shit in your room, hefa." I looked to see it was her moms talking to her like that. 'THEY TALK TO EACH OTHER LIKE FRIENDS.' I didn't even know she was in the house.

Looking me dead in my eyes I could tell moms was serious. The look she gave told me she wasn't playing. Tiara act like she didn't care but shid I wasn't her so yup' I stopped.

Tiara was tryna get her some. She was aggressively pulling me in the direction of her room, but I came to my senses. Thoughts of this money came to mind. 'DO I TRUST HER ENOUGH

TO LEAVE MY BREAD HERE WITH HER, UM, NOT YET,' I was thinking.

I decided not and killed her dreams of sex. Thinking fast, a lie came with ease. I told her I'll be back 'cause a money move was in my near future and I had to do something. She huffed and puffed, but in the end, she understood when I say I got shit to do. That's one of the reasons I fucks with her tough.

Headed to my house, I entered and wasn't a soul in there but the rodents that ran through the walls. Moms was probably at work. My lil brother and sister was probably outside. They were the same age as Black's sisters.

I went to my room and could tell that somebody was in here, but I didn't care, everything criminal and valuable was hidden well. Firing up a jack' I shuffled through my closet and found what I was looking for. My safe. I rarely use it. Shid it wasn't nothing worth putting in it except my pistol, but that stayed on me or close by.

Before I placed my newfound fortune away, I spread it all over the bed and just stared at it. 'DAMN THAT SHIT LOOK GOOD, IT'S BOUT TO CHANGE ROUND HERE.'

CHAPTER 27

Dro

"Damn, where the fuck you come from?"

Everybody went their separate ways while I walked to the store. It was a regular day for me, shit ain't change but the number of dollars in my kitty. The fact remain that coke still had to be sold and I had it ready to go.

Walking down the street I felt good on the inside. But in front of the world I wore my regular face, game face. I didn't need people all in my business.

My phone buzzed: 'HEY BABY, WYA.'

It was my girl coming through on a text. She does this constantly, just to know my whereabouts. 'I BETTER ANSWER OR SHE GONNA START MAXING.'

'IN DA HOOD,' I responded.

Putting my phone on my hip I entered the store as someone

was exiting. I looked up to catch the door. "Damn, where the fuck you come from?" I asked Charmine.

She was smiling like she had one up on me or some shit. Then, she walked right past me. 'WHAT THE FUCK?' And got in her car. I didn't even notice it was parked right in front of the store. 'I'M SLIPPIN.'

I followed her to the car but stood on the outside of the window. She rolled down the window. "You getting in?"

'HELL NAH, FOR WHAT I JUST GOT OUT HERE.'

"I'm gonna chill bae. You know. try to make a few dollars."

She wasn't tryna hear that. "Boy, come on," she basically told me. It's sad, who was I kidding, she knew that she was the law. I love her and her shit torch' (Good). She my kryptonite so home was where I headed . . . again.

CHAPTER 28

Black

"Nah, these rug rats my sisters."

'DAMN IT FEELS GOOD TO BE A GANGSTA.' I walked through the hood, my hood, headed to the crib. We pulled that shit off, now I could make some shit happen. Niggas thought my plan wasn't concrete. 'WHATS MY MOTHER FUCKIN NAME, JIGGA!' I crack myself up. I already was thinking of the possibilities, endless.

Um, let me see, I could get a couple . . . nah a few more guns. You could never have too many bangerz' (guns), believe that. I could get some new fits' (clothes) for my babies so they could shit on people with me. Gotta look out for my moms ratchet ass too. She is moms, but not like I'ma get my sisters.

Everybody outside was in their latest urban fashions, looking too sweet. A lot of niggas I would've been brung them a move but believe it or not I do have morals. Don't make the block hot, is one of them, if I could help it.

It be hard sometimes. These niggas be bitches and be testing my gangsta like I won't blow they face off without any remorse. A couple of these bitches could have got it too. Don't get it twisted. I don't have no type; anybody could get it.

Walking up the steps to my apartment I opened the door to see moms laying on the couch, no shit talk from her or nothing. Shit was weird.

Shocked would have to be an understatement. "What's up with you Ma, you a'ight?"

"Yeah, fine." She didn't even look my way. "The girls in the room."

"Did they eat?" I asked, walking back to their rooms. She gave me a look and ignored me. I heard her inhale a breath, tryna hold back whatever slick response she wanted to say but didn't. I smiled to myself as I opened the girls' door.

They were both sitting Indian style beside each other, watching a cartoon movie with the little yellow things that look like thumbs to me. I think they are called Minions. Matter fact the movie was called 'Despicable Me.'

So into the movie they were oblivious to me walking in. Sitting on the bed, I fired up a cigarette and watched it with them. It was kind of funny. I realized I smoked the whole jack' and neither one of them turned around, not once.

I had to fuck with them. Me being funny, I sparked a blunt of purple haze. The first exhale it was like the 'Matrix' how both of them turned around at the same damn time. I coughed. The expressions on their faces had me laughing after they noticed it was me.

They jumped up, always happy to see me, then came the hugs and kisses. "Sup' lil' uglies. Go get in the shower. Y'all stink. Put some clothes on, we goin' out."

I went to my room and put my bread up. I had a spot in the room in my vent that nobody could reach but me. I knew it was safe there. My moms yelled from the living room.

"Boy, I told you stop smoking that shit all over my damn house. It stink, open a damn window."

She only say that shit just to say it because she smoke weed too but say my shit different. 'DAMN RIGHT IT'S DIFFERENT, NOBODY SMOKE THAT REGULAR SHIT NO MORE, OLD PEOPLE.' And where you taking them girls to?" she asked just being nosey. I know she was listening to the conversation when I was in their room. She mighta' even been at the door.

"Outside," was all I said.

A lot has happened, and it wasn't even 4:00 yet. When Shanae and Shaniyah finished getting dressed, they came in my room unannounced, letting me know they were ready as I put ten racks in my pockets, all blue faces.

"Didn't I tell y'all don't just walk in my room like that without knocking." Shaniyah nodded, but Shanae had to be sarcastic and step a few steps back and knock on the now opened door.

'SMARTASS.'

She was gonna be a problem. She reminded me of myself in so many ways. When I looked at them, they looked wild. It didn't matter, the shit they had on wasn't gonna make it back home. My mind was made up. We was goin' to the mall and get fresh.

I told them to go watch TV for a minute while I take a shower and put some nice fits on. I felt like since I was goin' out, I needed to look a little better than usual. Plus, I didn't get in the water today.

In the shower it felt good washing the deeds of today and the last few days off me. After the shower I put on some cargos and a white V-neck t-shirt. I even put on my chain that I took from a nigga a few weeks ago. The 990 New Balance's finished my look, but it wasn't complete until I grabbed my pistol, right side hip was its location. Now I was ready. "Let's go!!" I yelled throughout the apartment.

My moms looked at me with pleading eyes. "You got any jacks'?" I didn't respond with words. I dug in my pockets, tossed her a yard ($100), while ushering my sisters out the door.

Walking through the hood I had a new pep in my step. I guess 10 racks ($10,000) in your pocket would do that. I was gonna call an Uber, but my sisters wanted to ride the train.

It excited them. I hate the train. 'BEING WITH THEM I SHOULDN'T HAVE ANY PROBLEMS.' Riding the train stop to stop I couldn't help noticing so many potential victims on this cart, loafin'. This shit was an instant high as I grabbed my pistol through my shirt, holding the grip.

"Donte, come on!" Shaniyah said, excitement all in her voice as she pushed me out the doors, killing my vibe. Thankfully snapping me out of my daze.

Exiting the train, we headed to the mall. Joy was seen on my sisters faces, happy just being away from the hood. They were holding hands, skipping down the parking lot toward the entrance.

First stop. 'FOLLOW YOUR NOSE.' The pretzel stand aroma smacked my nostrils. I was on my level and the smell hit me before I even entered the mall. I had to have one. The little ones got sugar cookies; they were happy with that.

Coming to the mall was like a field trip to them. It was a rare occasion. I planned on changing that. Everything they had was hand-me-downs or free in some type of way. Popping tags was a foreign feeling.

We went to damn near every store that sold children's clothing, looking for the new-new. I bought them everything they picked out; some shit I didn't like. I be forgetting they getting older and some stuff is form fitting and that's the shit I didn't like.

I bought a few outfits, totaling about $2,500 including shoes and a couple hats. My sisters hit me for real. It was well over $3,000. We had endless bags. I had to put them in a stroller for kids as we still shopped, the bags that is.

I looked at my sisters. They were cheesing and happy. I was good til I noticed their clothes. 'Y'ALL LOOKA HOT MESS.' Their hair was just as bad. Then an idea came to mind.

I took them to another store. The sales associate was on our heels. "Can I help you?"

Really, I didn't know what to get them. I looked left, then right and the display case was already put together. I asked the lady to give me what the manicans had on in their sizes, shoes and all. She brought the clothes back, smiling. "You treat our daughters good," she said, fishing I guessed.

"Naw, these rug rats my sisters," I responded, grabbing the clothes from her telling them to go put it on, but most of all throw that shit they got on in the trash.

They changed and looked so much better, but I wasn't done. I had to get something done to their hair. We walked to the beauty salon. As I entered all eyes were on me. I guess I looked out of place, that was until they noticed I wasn't by myself.

"Hello, you need anything?" a receptionist asked, sitting in her chair behind a counter.

"Nope, but you can help them." I pointed. She smiled and reached her hand out. "I got them. What you want done?"

'BITCH I DON'T KNOW.'

That's what I wanted to say. I don't know shit 'bout no damn hair. I just told her to hook them up and the price wasn't an issue. I began to walk off. Shaniyah ran back to me, grabbing my arm. "Where you going?" she pouted. "Don't leave."

"Nowhere baby, just to take a smoke break. I'll be back, you know I'll never leave you, okay!"

CHAPTER 29

Jroc

"Fuck what Dro talking 'bout, I'm 'bout to look sweet."

I was so excited as I pulled off in the backseat of my lil joints Uber. You couldn't tell me nothing. I was 'bout to get me a lil rental for the week. Renting a whip was the power play for today. Baby girl riding with me, I'm treating her to a car also, just for a couple of days, a token of my appreciation. It's the least I could do, ya know.

Me and shawty was cruising in the back enjoying the scenery as we crossed the bridge headed to Virginia. Really, I don't fuck with Virginia, well not the people, their fucking laws. That commonwealth shit fucked up. I wasn't tryna fall victim to their system. It's a saying in D.C. and I quote, "It takes 5 minutes to cross the bridge but 15 years to get back."

'NOT TRYNA BE A PART OF THAT STATISTIC.'

For a guy like me, this is way out of bounds, especially with all this money on me. After we get these whips, it's straight to the crib for me.

Pulling up to the lot, it was an average selection of cars, all this years and previous years brands. This lot was for her. I was going across the street, that's where the big boy whips was at. The chick decided to head toward the Dodge Charger ST-8, a smile etched her face. That was a cool ride, and the price wasn't too crazy. But me, I had bigger dreams. I walked across the street after I gave her the cash for her ride. She was in the trailer making the rental official.

I told her to meet me over at the other lot when she was done. The car I stood in front of, I done had wet dreams about this woman. She was so sexy. I had to have her, at least for a week.

'FUCK DA PRICE.'

"Oo weee!!" I said, rubbing my hands as I attempted to open the door of the new Porsche 918 Spyder. It retailed at $845,000.

I couldn't own it, but I could rent it. My lady friend went into the trailer, yet again, to do the transaction while I sat in the car talking dirty to it, telling her all the nasty things I was gonna do to her.

"All done." She came out of the trailer. "Why couldn't I get a car like that?"

I looked at her like she was crazy as she dropped the keys in my hands. I was excited and ready to roll out. I didn't know where I was going, but wherever it was I was gonna look good doing it. "Your ass better be happy you got that," I said as I mashed the gas, leaving smoke behind me.

"Booooo!" she screamed.

I almost didn't hear her. The engine was roaring, but I came to a stop and backed up. "What's up?"

She was smiling with her hand on her hip. "Damn, you just gonna pull off. I wanted to thank you," she said with a slight grin, letting me know what she really wanted to do.

"Follow me." I pulled off.

'FUCK WHAT DRO TALKING 'BOUT, I'M 'BOUT TO LOOK SWEET.'

I felt like the man, couldn't nobody say shit. I arrived in my neighborhood and all eyes was on me. I felt like a celebrity. Niggas was flagging me down, but all I did was hit the horn twice and kept rolling. Bitches was tryna get in, but my shawty for the day wasn't having it. She made sure that they knew she was fucking with me. I doubled parked in the middle of the block, just to stunt and holla at a few guys I knew. My phone rang, but it was a text: "BOY COME ON, I'M TRYNA FUCK."

I looked through the rearview to see baby girl with the "Let's go" expression on her face. 'AIN'T GOTTA TELL TWICE.' I told everybody that I was 'bout to roll, put the car in drive so I could park down the street in front of my house.

Cruising down the street, I rode past my house to see my moms on the porch. I didn't have time for the 21 questions, so I continued to drive, leaving her to talk to the neighbor.

I went through the back so I could access the back door. She was on my heels.

"Why we goin' through the back boo?" she asked, looking around nervously.

"Girl don't act like you ain't never been through no back doors. You probably done hopped fences before and some mo' shit." She sucked her teeth.

"Whatever," but still followed me in . . .

'FIRST THINGS FIRST.'

I told her to lay back and chill in the living room for a second while I put my Pitbull's away. I didn't have no damn dogs, but she didn't know that. I had to go stash my backpack full of cash.

Entering my room I headed straight for my closet. I have a walk-in and it had these removeable shelves inside of it that looked regular to the blind eye.

Going back downstairs, halfway down I called for shawty to come up. She came and off to the bedroom we went. I didn't know she looked this good—well, today she did. I felt like she knew it too. She had me gone with her 'fuck me' eyes.

We sat on the bed and talked for literally a minute, then out of thin air she surprised me. "Okay, so what's up? You tryna fuck or what. I got shit to do today," she said, standing up, sliding her pants down. I guess I was bullshitting. She did tell me from the jump what she was tryna do, but damn, I mean I never fucked her before and didn't want to seem like an asshole or a dick. but from the sound of things, that's what she wanted.

Instead of answering her, I whipped out and started rapping 'Lil Wayne's Lollipop.' As the lyrics left my mouth she started doing exactly as the song said, and ate the dick up.

'EAT EAT.'

CHAPTER 30

Dro

"Come here, it's important."
—Charmine

We made it to the crib and a random thought came to mind as I scrolled through my messages. I read one that was unopened.

'HEY BROVA, ION REMEMBER IF I GAVE YOUR FOLKS MY # BUT GIVE IT 2 HER 4 ME.'

"Huh?" I said to myself, but Charmine heard me and noticed my face and how confused I must have looked. She asked who was on my message.

'NOSEY ASS.'

I just looked at her, then showed her the message. She smiled. "Oh, I got it."

Now I'm looking at her with questioning eyes, seeing if she was gonna fill me in on what just happened, but nope. She started walking off like shit was cool and dandy. "Aye! How you know Tiara?" She kept walking. I wasn't goin' like that. She wasn't just gonna ignore me. I decided to be an asshole right along with her. I leaned on the car and fired up a jay' of sour diesel. "You ain't gotta act like you don't hear me. Let's see how you get in the house with no key," I said, dangling the house keys in my hand, the blunt in the other as I exhaled the jet smoke. She came to her senses and walked back to me.

'THAT'S WHAT THE FUCK I THOUGHT.'

She smacked her teeth and stopped in front of me. "Damn, I met her at the mall today, happy." She pouted. I wasn't satisfied. Me not moving let her know she had to say more than that if she was tryna get in the crib. "Hmph," she sighed, irritated, but eventually told me about her whole day.

By the time she gave me the play by play, my blunt was a roach and I was feeling good and wasn't really even paying attention as much. "So can we go in the damn house now? You wasn't even listening to me anyway wit your high ass," she said.

I snapped out of my daze and walked to the house. It was getting late and really, I wanted to be outside. I looked at my watch. 'IT'S ONLY 8:00.' We went in and the first thing I did was put on the game and started to play 'Call of Duty' online.

This was my shit. I could sit in front of the TV all day for hours talking shit to the TV and kill everything on the screen.

Charmine went straight to my room for a minute, then reappeared about two minutes later. She walked straight past me with nothing but panties on. I glanced. Really didn't pay any attention. That's a regular gesture, just chill attire for her. She walked back past but with a bottle of Chardonnay, her favorite wine. "I'm getting in the shower," she said, walking with an extra dirty roller strut.

I nodded, followed her with my eyes then went straight back to the game. My phone rang. I looked at it, Black was the caller. 'FUCK HE WANT.' I ignored the call knowing he'll text. I was deep into the game and the score was tight. I couldn't get caught slippin' so I continued to play as the text came through. It read:

"MOE IM INDA' MALL. GOT SUM FITS. WE STILL GOIN OUT."

I looked at the phone for a minute before I responded. 'BLACK AT DA MALL,' I thought to myself. I hit back: "WTF MADE U GO 2 DA MALL."

Another message came through as I sent mines. 'DAMN THIS NIGGA TYPE FASTER THAN MY GIRL,' I thought as his popped up:

"NIGGA YES OR NO, U KNO NIGGAS AIN'T GONNA MOVE UNLESS U DO."

"I GOTTA SEE, IMA HIT U BACK INA HOUR."

"YEAH OKAY, GO ASK CAN U COME OUT 2 PLAY," Black responded with all types of emoji and shit. 'WILD NIG-GA.' I laughed. I had to fire up another blunt of that diesel after that. I looked in the ashtray and seen a boney ass jay' in there. It must have been one of my moms' friends. It was too small. I like my shit healthy.

As I looked for my pack', I heard my name being called from another room. "Yeah girl, what's up?" I asked, looking for my sheets.

"Come here, it's important."

I walked to my room and jaws hit the ground. My bitch bad and she know it how she looked at me. Charmine noticed me noticing her and smiled. She walked over to me in some tall heels. Them joints had to be about six inches 'cause she was my height now. 'SO THIS THE REASON YOU WENT TO THE MALL.'

"Did you miss me?" she asked as the robe dropped.

'SHID, I DON'T KNOW IF IMA MAKE IT OUT TO-NIGHT,' I thought as I walked toward her taking off my shit as well.

CHAPTER 31

*"Niggas don't even look hungry, they
like bitches, they thirty."*
—Black

"What's the move, Slim?" Jroc asked while he was blowing some lemon haze. Everybody was outside that night, all but Dro and all eyes was on them.

Dro decided to stay in. That didn't stop the rest of them from going out. It was live in the hood. Jroc had the music blasting out of the Porsche. He wanted to be seen. After a few back-and-forth suggestions, Izzo had the best option. What better way to stunt than the Strip Club? Izzo had dropped Tiara off earlier and had her car.

Izzo knew he could get the hook up, but his men were oblivious to that fact. Everyone was dressed to impress, and their pockets were swollen.

They all had somebody's name on their back that cost more

than they used to spending. Black had the most expensive outfit. The attire he bought from the mall was just some urban wear for 'round the way, but the designer he had on tonight came from the source.

Gucci. The slacks cost eighteen hundred, a backpack with a tag that read nine hundred, some Privé Revaux glasses valued at eighty dollars and to finish the look was a pair of Charlotte Olympia leather loafers. The amount was seven hundred nine-ty-five dollars. Most thought it was a pair of girl shoes, but he didn't care, they looked sweet.

Izzo kept it regular but fashionable. He had on a Giorgio Armani suit and some Ralph Lauren loafers. It set him back about seventeen hundred.

Jroc looked too sweet too. He had on a Louis Vuitton top and bottom, all black but fucked 'em up with the gold bubble gum Foams, totaling about $2,000.

Black rode with Jroc. Izzo drove Tiara's car and they were on their way, ready to below some dough. Black pulled out his phone:

'AYO HOUSE NIGGA, U MISSIN OUT.

I'LL SEND YOU SOME ASS SHOTS,' and laughed at his own message as they cruised the city headed to the club.

Pulling up to the club, the looks the Porsche got, Jroc loved and enjoyed. It was like people knew when you had a couple dollars. The women were looking and anxious to get their attention. Even the fellas were looking with envy, some even hated.

"Niggas don't even look hungry, they like these bitches, thir-ty," Black said to nobody in particular, just peeping the vibe.

Izzo took the lead once they got to the front since he had the 'connect' in the club. The bouncer even remembered him, which made him look even better as he waved him in. But this time Izzo gave him a blue face ($100).

Entering the club, it was all the way turnt' up. Izzo flagged down a dancer. She smiled upon recognition and walked toward him. "Hey Izzo," she spoke as Black and Jroc looked at him, wondering how he knew her.

"Sup' boo. I need a VIP section for me and my men. Make sure you bring us 3 bottles of Ace of Spade and 3 fifths of Patron'," Izzo said, slapping her on the ass when she walked off.

Black rubbed his hand together. "Damn fool, youz'a hoe, you know deez bitches and they calling you by name." Izzo was brushing his shoulders off about to purp.'

"Yeah, you know I be—"

"Izzo! Tiara said come in the back for a minute." The waitress interrupted his bluff session.

"Tiara work here huh, that's how you got it like dat." Jroc put the pieces to the puzzle. Black's mind was on her body.

"Fuck dat, is gonna dance. I know that joint phat to def'," He licked his lips anticipating the sight to be seen.

Izzo didn't like what was being insinuated. "Nigga that's my girl now, so chill with all that fein shit."

The club was jumping, and the dancers were doing their thing. They was bad. You couldn't point out a stretch mark or blemish on any of these women. Black and Izzo was making it rain like crazy. Tiara made sure only the baddest dancers entered their section. Izzo made sure she didn't come over to their section or even dance until he was about to leave. He peeled off 5 blue faces, told her to chill and only give lap dances if she wanted. She was cool with that and didn't wanna make Izzo mad, so she complied.

They were acting a fool in VIP. The dancers were ass naked. Jroc was in the corner getting some head from one of them. She was like dat, after about a minute, she topped him off and was headed to the next guy. Jroc was wilding. He started kissing bitches and doing the most. Black and Izzo got twisted as they smoked a few blunts, enjoying the vibes in the building.

They were lit, but lucky for Jroc Tiara was there to get his keys as their night neared an end. Izzo was still able to drive her whip as Black sat shotgun.

Izzo was following Tiara as Black noticed somebody following them. The tail was behind them since they left the club parking lot. Pulling up at the Denny's on Bladensburg Road, the northeast side behind Trinidad, a notorious hood in the district, he parked. They met at the door together.

Eating and talking is how they all sobered up a bit quicker. Jroc looked at Tiara. "I ain't know you work in that joint." She gave him a screw face.

"You ain't suppose to know where I work, niggah."

Black decided to cut in the conversation. "Aye Tee, why you didn't dance for us? I know you seen us making it rain in that bitch," he said, noticing two guys enter the establishment, but sit in a back booth.

"Because . . ." she started as she smiled. "Daddy said I couldn't come out to play tonight." Tiara pointed at Izzo.

Izzo stuffed a pancake in his mouth and kept eating to avoid having to comment. It was a good night, and everybody was happy. The bill was paid and back to their whips they went. Jroc felt better and decided to drive. This time Black rode with him. Black noticed the same car still following them.

"Moe, I think these niggas tryna pull us a move." Jroc looked and seen them too. "I thought I was trippin'. I swear I saw them at the Denny's." Jroc agreed.

Pulling up on R Street, by the library that sat on the corner, they parked in the lot. They wanted to see if they turned into the lot with them. They didn't. The would-be victims in Black's mind kept going down the one-way street, never turning off.

"A'ight Bruh', make sure you watch dat car, Slim," Black said, getting out of the Porsche.

"I'm good," Jroc said, patting his hip, then pulled off headed down the street to go in the house.

CHAPTER 32

—∞C∽∞—

Dro

"Jet smoke nothing else but it, fuck you mean."

Woke up and stretched. It was one of the releases that felt so good that made you want to lay back down, but I knew I had to get up. My girl was already up cooking breakfast. I smelled it from the bed. I looked around the room and seen it was dirty, well not dirty as in filthy, but messy from the night before.

I don't know what got into my girl last night, but she did that. I headed to the bathroom and my shit was brick. I had that morning wood and had to piss. I got in the shower to wash last night off me. In the water I sparked a jack'. 'GHETTO,' I know. I even had an ashtray where the soap bar was supposed to be at.

A lot of thoughts ran through my head. A few of them was like—what's next? I got money to blow, but that's not what I'm gonna do. Most importantly, I know I needed some work, first and foremost. Getting out of the shower I went to my room and put some shorts on. By the time I pulled them over my ass, my boo was bringing me a plate.

Licking my lips hungrily, my mouth watered. "This shit look good bae," I said to Charmine as she put the food in front of me. It was turkey bacon, thick strips, four omelets with corn beef hash, A FAVORITE and buttered toast. "You did dat'!" I said, reaching for a kiss over the plate. That's when I noticed she had my phone in her other hand.

'AWWW SHIT.'

To my surprise she gave it to me. "Here, this shit been ringing off the damn hook," she said, still standing there after she gave it to me.

I grabbed my phone and slid it open nervously. Another surprise, I had 6 unopened text messages on my screen. I opened the message and started smiling. "Them nigga did it up last night," I said, showing Charmine the phone because she was still hovering over my shoulder tryna see it anyway.

"Boy, I don't want to see all that." She pushed it away.

'I CAN'T TELL.'

All the messages was from Black. Pictures of all the different girls they had in the club in various positions and poses. Then I noticed their fits.' They were on some grown man attire, tailored gang, looking too sweet. I know them niggas spent a couple stacks. I seen Jroc posing in a Porsche and shook my head. 'GO AHEAD AND STUNT.' I slid my phone closed and locked it.

The meal I just ate was like dat. I walked into the kitchen to see all the dishes from last night and this morning. The ones from the night before had to be moms. I started washing the dishes when my mom walked in. "Hey Baby," she greeted me kissing my cheek while adding another dish to the pile I was already washing. Everybody in the house knew that a sink full of dishes was a peeve of mines, so of course they let it stack on purpose, knowing I'll clean them up most of the time.

That's a reason I avoid the kitchen unless I'm smacked

(high), then I don't have a choice. I'm gonna feed my munchies. Charmine yelled from the other room, "Hurry up boo. I hope you ready. I gotta be to work in thirty."

I had my clothes on, but really didn't want to take her to work today, reason being I didn't want to pick her up. I had plans on copping a whip today. "Huh?!"

"Cordell, you heard me. Get the keys!!

"Fuck it. Let's go!" I said, leaving out the crib headed to the car.

Sitting in the car I listened to the iPod she had plugged up. Shuffling through songs I found a good track. 'D.N.A.' by Kendrick Lamar came through the speakers. I was vibing to the words, so high I could relate to the struggle, but oblivious to my surroundings. Just cranking out until I heard my girl.

"Boy, calm your ass down," she said, looking at me up and down like I was crazy. I was in my zone and thought I was in the video. She looked at my hand. "What the fuck in that blunt you smoking?" she asked with her hand on her hip, like it was crack or some shit.

"Jet smoke, nothing else, but it, fuck, you mean."

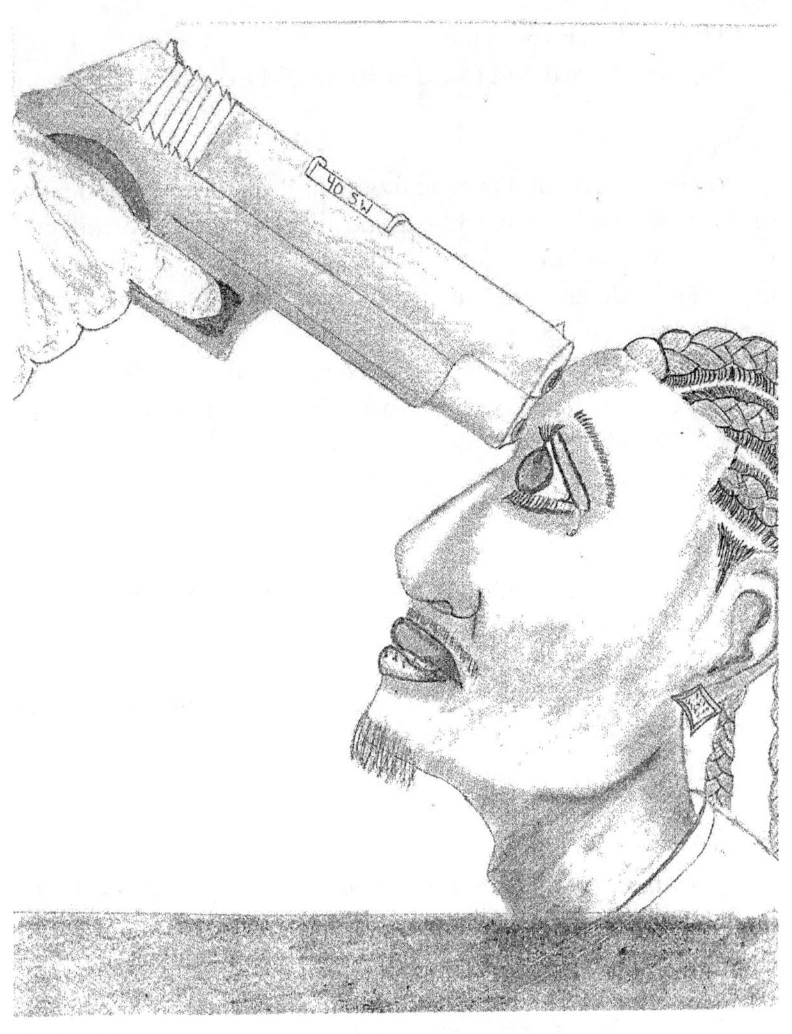
40 SW

Dro was headed uptown after he dropped his girl off to work. He decided to call Black. He made the decision to take Black with him to the appointment he had lined up with a dealer for the gold bars instead of Jroc.

"Hello?" Black answered.

"Big boy, I need you to ride with me," Dro said. "I'm on my way to get you."

"Yup."

Making it uptown, Dro could only find a parking spot in front of Jroc's house. The neighborhood blocks were filled today. It was a show goin' on at the famous Howard Theater. It's one of the city's landmarks that reopened a few years back and got remodeled for the better.

Parking his car, Dro went to see what Jroc was doing since he was right in front of his house where the Porsche was also parked. Approaching the door, he knocked.

"Hey sweeties," a sweet angelic voice spoke.

This is a voice that never changed or altered in any way since he was a toddler, Jroc's mom. She was best friends with Dro's mother since their childhood and was even pregnant around the same time as each other.

"Hey ma!" Dro spoke. "Is Jroc here?"

"Uh huh. Come on in baby. You know where he at. You hungry?"

Even though he just ate, Jroc's mom could burn (cook) so he wasn't gonna pass that up. "Only if you made it," Dro said smiling like a fat kid about to get some cake.

Dro made it to Jroc's room eating a philly style steak and cheese to find him on the webcam with some girl giving him a strip tease. Jroc turned the computer at an angle so Dro could see the screen as well. "Damn, shawty thick," Dro acknowledged.

"Nigga, I keeps bad bitches," Jroc said proudly with a smack of his own chest.

A squeaky childlike voice came through the computer. "What you say, daddy?"

"Nothing boo, don't stop til' daddy say so," Jroc said, trying to make the girl think they were alone.

Sitting on the bed, Dro grabbed a mini basketball and laid back on the bed. "You a'ight, bruh?" Jroc asked, noticing him.

Dro started tossing the ball up and down against the ceiling as he laid back. "Yes, Slim I'm cool. Just thinking."

"You always just thinking."

Dro's hip started to vibrate. It was a missed call from Black. Realization hit as he leaned to get up. "Where you going?" Jroc asked.

"Bouta go get our bread from dude for them bars," Dro said.

Closing the laptop while the girl was still on the screen Jroc got up. "A'ight I'm coming."

"Black goin' with me, chill. I'll bring yours back." With that being said Dro was headed down the street to meet Black.

It was a fair day. Weather was nice. It felt like a new beginning for all. Dro knew Black was probably still hungover from last night. He wished he was there after looking at all the pictures Black sent, but he was in some legs' last night, so he was still well taken care of.

As he walked down the street, surprisingly he seen Izzo come from around the corner. Izzo spoke. "Hey Bob!"

"Shit, waiting on Black."

"Fuck y'all bouta' do?"

"Get this bread from dat nigga for them bars."

"Shid, I'm tryna go, hold on," Izzo said, jogging off before Dro could respond but looking back to say, "Gotta get my joint'."

Dro laughed.

Izzo always think something is a move. That come up didn't mean nothing to the next and being around Black so much put fuel to his fire. To be fair, Dro had his gun as well. Birds of a feather flock together cause here came Black pulling his shirt over his head concealing the pistol on his waist.

"Ready?" Black asked.

"Yeah, Izzo coming too. He right there," Dro said, pointing to him as he ran up on them.

Jumping in the car they had a road trip ahead of them. Their destination was in Newark, New Jersey. Jroc set the meeting up through a friend of a friend. Dro drove with Izzo, and Black accompany him. Dro had plans and wanted to involve his men in the vision. He was gonna play the streets for a while, get his money up, then wash it up through the entertainment business. He wanted a record company.

Dro knew Izzo could rap, along with a few other dudes in his hood. Most of them were on YouTube trying to make a name for themselves. Black could be the muscle 'cause that's what he's good at in Dro's mind. These were the thoughts that he drove to up I-95 for the half hour drive.

The warehouse was off the grid. Quiet and leery. This location automatically put them on point. Each of them had a backpack on, evenly weighted full of gold. Looking around they made their way to the garage and gave the coded knock. Passing two guards, they noticed they holstered Smith and Wesson SD 9 milly's. Dro smiled as he tried to walk past.

The guards held up a hand. "Aye fellas, can you stand a search."

Black smiled. "Nigga we scrapped, just like you are, so keep your hands to your motherfuckin' self," he said, continuing to walk.

Walking up to an older Arab, looked to be in his mid-forties, maybe early fifties with all gold everything on, even his clothes. His factory was in full swing. Melting gold and making nice piec- es was all that was seen. They knew this was the right place.

Dro did some research on the gold bars and found out the value was triple what the guy told Jroc. This didn't sit well with Dro at all. Another reason he didn't want to bring Jroc, he was gullible.

With a thick Arabian accent the guy spoke. "Ello' mi friends, I'm Samir, come, come," he said with a wave of his hand, directing them to a long table. Approaching the table everybody dropped the backpacks on the table. Smiling at the bags Samir asked, "Yes,

yes, mi friend, we have pre-made arrangements, yes?" the Arab said as he placed his duffle on the table, full of cash.

"Change of plans," Dro said with venom. "You was tryna rob us with these prices and I don't appreciate that," Dro said as Black grabbed the duffle full of Samir's money but leaving the gold bars untouched on the table.

The two guards rushed to the side of Samir, reaching for their weapons. Dro anticipated this. He had his FNS-40 already pointed. It was a pretty gun, stainless steel with a black and silver finish, a polymer grip, making it feel like love in your hand with a striker fired autoloader. To top it off, it had 14 big dumb dumb .40 caliber bullets in the clip.

'BOC! BOC! BOC!'

Dro fired at one of the guards. Arm, leg, head, he fell and died before he hit the ground. Izzo raised his gun to the other guard, geeking. He had a compact Glock 19 with .40 caliber bullets. The guard didn't have the drop, so he threw his hands up in surrender. Izzo smiled. "Hope that's how you pray."

'BOC! BOC!'

Izzo walked and stood over top of him and blew him a kiss.

'BOC! BOC! BOC!'

Two bodies lay in front of Samir. He was scared shitless as he slightly released feces in his trousers. Dro wasn't nervous at all. He knew he was in the middle of nowhere. Pandemonium was inevitable in the factory.

Black dropped the duffle, whipping out his gun. "Damn, moe, why you ain't tell me, I was tryna get some. I didn't know you was gonna spark flames." Dro ignored his comment and told him to guard the door and if anybody try to leave, kill 'em.

Dro walked around the long table and put his arms around Samir. "Come on buddy, let's talk about these prices."

Black and Izzo held down the door. In about 10 minutes Dro came back out of Samir's office with more money. They were talking and smiling like it wasn't two bodies dead, and all his employees on the floor sitting on their own hands. "So I'll see you soon about what we talked about," Dro said, patting Samir's back. "Let's go!"

"What about them, we gonna smoke 'em now?" Black asked, mad his gun was still full.

"Nah, not this time," Dro said, walking to Black's arm, lowering his gun.

CHAPTER 33

"They bullshitting, for real."
— Izzo

Things were looking good. It's been over 3 weeks since the gold exchange. Dro and Black were headed to a jeweler in Maryland to pick up a few pieces Samir had delivered to the store. He refused to give it to them personally, for obvious reasons.

Making it there they had one doorman. Dro walked past, Black crossed the threshold, then stopped and stood on the opposite side of the security guard like he worked there as well. He wasn't letting nobody with a gun stand behind him or Dro. Dro walked straight to the counter and banged on the hotel type bell even though the guy was right in front of him.

With a big hand he covered the bell and slid it back, out of reach. There was a big Somalian standing before Dro. In a deep African voice and accent he asked, "Can I be of service?" giving full eye contact in his glare.

Dro looked back at Black who was mimicking the door security and laughed. 'NIGGA A FOOL'. Then answered the jeweler.

"Yeah, I'm here for a pickup from Samir," Dro said, returning the glare.

After hearing Samir's name, his big presence seemed to deflate as he started acting really fidgety and nice. "Oh yes, uh, hold on. I'll go grab it for you." He stuttered going to the back tripping on the corner of the display case.

He returned with a bag and emptied its contents on a soft mat on the glass table. It contained 5 chains, 8 rings, and 4 bracelets. All gold with diamonds all over it. The charm hanging from the chain was a big S and G interlocked with 'sameguy' written in diamonds beneath it. Dro would gift these to his men, a re minder to them to stay the same and not let money change them.

Calling Black to the counter, Black looked at the goon across from him. "Coma on nigga, you too!"

The goon looked at the owner who nodded. He didn't want to get these guys mad. The goon walked but went on the opposite side of the counter. Dro put the chain 'round Black's neck and gave him a spiel along with 2 pinky rings. Black grinned and thanked his friend for the gift.

Dro packed the rest of his gifts up in a separate bag and headed for the door. They hopped back in the car and peeled off. Driving down the street, he had to make a stop while on this side of town.

He arrived at an auction. His eyes were on a certain car. He was tired of driving his girls' car. After he watched several cars go by, not placing one bid, his car came up—a 1996 Chevy Impala. He loved this car. Dro smiled as Black commented, "Bout time, shit," he said, growing tired of waiting.

"Shut up nigga, patience get you a long way."

"Fuck dat. I don't plan on goin' far."

After a long bid that started at $7,000, Dro ended up paying $15,000 cash for it. He had it delivered to a shop uptown and was on his way.

Making it back around the way Izzo was posted up so they pulled in front of him and parked. "DAYUM!" Izzo said, waling up. "Y'all niggas icy as shit, Slim," he said, admiring the chains, bracelet and rings they had on.

"you like dat?" Dro asked, lifting his chain. "You like shiny things?!" he asked as he tossed the bag to Izzo.

Izzo opened it. His face showed it all as he started putting all the jewels on. "This what fuck I'm talkin' bout." Izzo dapped Dro up and thanked him. "Aye, y'all know that car?!" Izzo asked, pointing with his head.

"Moe, that's the same car with them niggas that followed us from the Stadium Club a couple weeks ago," Black said reaching, tired of the car and ready to fire at it.

Dro calmed him down, showing him all the people that was outside plus the kids. Black blew a sigh, then headed toward the courtyard about to check for his sisters. The car pulled off slowly. They bullshitting for real Izzo thought as he patted his waistline, tippin, letting them know he was ready.

"I'm bout to walk to Jroc's house and give him his shit, but I got plans for us. When I say let's go, be ready," Dro said walking off.

❖   ❖   ❖

"Ain't that Black girl's house?" – Charmine

Cruising the city streets, Charmine and Tiara was on a mission. These last few months was all love. Dro had been looking out for her in a big way. She was loving her new car. For her birthday he bought her an Infiniti Q60. It was candy apple red, her favorite color.

They were headed to see the weed man. Tiara didn't have any

cash on her. "Stop by my house right quick," Tiara asked.

"Girl, I got some coins. I can get it for us," Charmine offered.

"I know girl, but I gotta check on something too, please."

They smoked the last of the 'train wreck' they had. Charmine always took Dro's weed he left out, and that was everywhere. They felt good. Finally pulling up they made it to the apartment. When Charmine's high she drives like she tryna pass a road test.

"Bout time, bitch," Tiara said, getting out of the car.

"Shut up. You know I be flying down these streets," Charmine said lying like shit. "Don't act like you don't know how I drive when I'm slizzy."

Walking in the apartment Charmine sat on the couch and turned on the TV. Tiara went straight to her room. Watching TV, Charmine's eyes were bubble-eyed with surprise. Ain't that Black girl's house she thought as she tuned into the broadcast—

BREAKING NEWS!

> After 120 days in a coma, Victoria finally came to and is recovering. If you remember there was a robbery homicide at this residence a few months ago. Detectives are at the hospital, waiting for her to get well enough to talk. That was a tragic day that claimed the life of 2 armored truck drivers. It was a disclosed amount of money taken from the company, but it wasn't worth these guys lives. The gruesome scene where all these victims were duct-taped together and executed. Two guys were pronounced dead on the scene while Victoria fought for her life but slipped into a coma. Hopefully, she will have a full recovery and help get the person or persons involved. This is Pat Colins re-

porting. Back to you at the studio . . .

Charmine was wowed into silence for a second before she decided to call her man who didn't even answer the phone. Instead of calling back she sent a text:

"AYE BOO YOU NEED 2 WATCH DA NEWS ASAP"

Then continued to watch TV. Tiara came around the corner. "You ready girl?" she asked, noticing Charmine's expression. "Why you lookin' like that?"

"Girl, you remember that shit about that break in on the southside, Maryland side of Wheeler Road? That girl that was in a come woke up. She probably gonna tell on them niggas," Charmine said, oblivious to who did it.

Tiara turned off the TV. "Girl, fuck that, come on we got moves to make."

Leaving the apartment and heading to the car, they were on their way, but decided to get their lungs dirty first. Being the women in Dro's and Izzo's lives they picked up a vicious habit, blowing trees was the least of it.

❖   ❖   ❖

From the Projects straight to the pro's everybody was doing it big. Niggas had a lot of paper like they was working at Kinkos. Just a couple of months ago they used to be broke.

"I remember we ain't have nothing," Dro said.

"No bullshit. We stayed struggling tryna turn nothing into something. We good now," Izzo countered.

Jroc started to laugh. "I'm glad I don't got to be the only one buying all the pack' no more."

The money they had didn't really change them. The only one of the crew that was heavy' (had a lot) was Dro. He didn't blow any of his money on bullshit. His cash went straight to the street, and it paid off. It's been 4 months since the move and their life was changed. Dro was the Plug to a few people in the city. All them ol' heads that used to step on his toes a few months back was now calling his phone, asking for favors and deals.

Dro had a plan and was nearing the goal to achieve it. Jroc even jumped off the porch and stopped selling weed. He changed the game now. He was in college slanging molly and coke to the students and their associates. His pockets was fair, but not heavy'.

Izzo was a different story. He had cash and was considered hood rich. Dro had him in the studio making tracks and he could really rap. The internet loved him, and it brought him groupies and Instagram fame, but he was still a hustler at heart. He was just waiting on Dro to make it official as far as whatever Dro told the whole team to be ready for.

Meanwhile, he had enough work to be a'ight, but couldn't supply the hood on a large scale. Izzo had a crew of young, wild niggas ready for whatever and he was their boss.

Black on the other hand was on the same shit, back to the basic, square one. His kitty was under $10,000 and that's crazy. When you just spend money and don't flip, it just depletes.

That put him back on plot mode, looking for the next move. His girlfriend, Keisha was gone off him. He had her wrapped around his finger, so she was his Bonnie to her Clyde.

"Shit!" Black said as he rolled his last jay. Keisha looked at him and asked, "What's wrong, boo?"

Black was mad at nobody but himself. When he grabbed his last bit of weed, he noticed the space where his money used to be. Now it was in a small corner. Thoughts ran through his mind, and he expressed them to her. "I guess I didn't know what I had until it magically disappeared. It's time for me to put in some work."

"Well, whatever you need me to do, I got you baby," Keisha said, rubbing Black's shoulders. Black sat on the bed thinking.

"I'ma go get this rent. I'ma do what it takes to get this paper."

Black already had a move in motion that he wanted to do with his men, but he knew they weren't gonna want to roll. Why would they, they already up, only Izzo would go just cause.

"Boo, I'll be back."

Black walked through the parking lot to clear his head. He spotted his whip. It was this year's Challenger with smoked rims, mirror tints with the matte black paint. At night he was a ghost with a loudmouth. The engine roared. You could hear him but couldn't see him and that's how he liked it. He started his car. It growled as he took off.

'TIME TO PUT THIS SHIT IN EFFECT.'

CHAPTER 34

Izzo

"That bitch ain't crazy."

On . . . my . . . movah, shit was goin' good for me. I was winning. I had work and my pockets wasn't hurting. My nigga Dro made a nigga city famous when he pushed me to rap. I used to do that shit all the time back in the day but didn't think shit of it. Now he tryna get me to be his first artist when he open this studio. I ain't care, mo' money.

Me and boo Tiara was still goin' strong. 'THAT MY BITCH.' I even had my own lil trap house in the hood. I paid rent in a Section 8 apartment, but pumped crack out of it. I have a team of young, hungry niggas that move on command. Anytime I was there I had to keep a Draco by the door, .40 cals and all types of pistols in the sofa. I didn't play no games; my shit say work. A nigga won't catch me slippin' or any of my lil niggas.

I already knew it was niggas like my man Black, lurking in the tall grass of every hood, so I stayed strapped. All I did all day was beat the block. I had to feed the block. I was selling out crazy, my lil niggas stayed calling my phone for more which had me calling Dro cause he sold to me dirt cheap, and I taxed everybody else. 'SHID THEY WASN'T WITH ME SHOOTIN IN DA GYM.'

I had ice cream for the crack fiends and passed out ice cream for the children. If anybody owed me money, I was on dat ass like tight pants. I needs all mines and was gonna get it by any means. I had to go hard, or the streets will treat you like a pussy.

I was in the trap, coolin' how I cool. Usually I don't be in here for long, only to collect or drop off. Too many felonies in here. But today, the block was hot as shit on fire. Them peoples was rollin' like e- muthafucka.

'HEY BABYDADDY WYA' was the text that came through my phone. It was Tiara.

'IN DA TRAP.'

I was in the middle of a Madden game so I couldn't be dis-tracted. This game was for some money, but Tiara didn't care as another text came through:

'I NEED $500 IM OUT FRONT.'

I looked at my phone and paused the game in the middle of a play. My lil man was heated. I didn't give a fuck. I paid for this shit in here and the rent, a thought before I said, "Hold on nigga, I'll be back."

I went outside and Tiara was leaning on my car. "Girl, if you don't get your ass off my new paint job . . ."

"Boy, bang." She waved me off.

"Boy, shit! You scratch my paint. I'ma scratch your ass," I said, dead serious. I don't play with my whip. I had a Corvette that was my first love and I love her wholeheartedly, my whip that is.

"Um, I might just like a couple of scratches on me," Tiara said, licking her lips sexually. She walked up on me with the dirty roller walk with her hand out. Oh the money I gave her, the bread, and she quickly grabbed it, then kissed me while grabbing a handful of my nuts, and slightly squeezing them.

"Whoa," I said as she smiled walking back to a car. She hopped in the passenger's seat of the car. I didn't recognize it as it pulled off. What da fuck. I wondered who was driving, then shrugged it off, walking back to the trap. That bitch ain't crazy.

❖   ❖   ❖

Jroc
"Thank you, come again."

Grinding. Up this is me, out here getting this money. I've been attending U.D.C. (University of the District of Columbia). These white boys and girls love that molly and coke. I kept a few grams of crack for the neighborhood, but my money came from here, school. I had to stop tryna sell weed. I was smoking more than I was selling. As the saying goes: Don't get high off your own supply. So I quit, selling it that is.

I was in class; my major was accounting. I loved numbers. That is the reason that I chose it. My phone was jumping, and I knew I couldn't leave class, so I sent everybody a text letting them know I'll see them after. I kinda enjoyed class. I love anything dealing with number. Numbers didn't lie, they always made sense and could be proven. I knew I was gonna be good in this department. Checks and balances was nothing for me. That's why when it came to money, I won't get beat.

The period ended. I went to the bathroom, and it looked like a soup kitchen line. I mean like the line was outside the door, but me being me, I walked to the front. Come to find out damn near everybody was waiting on me. Shit, I'ma have to run to my car 'cause when these white people get high, they pop off like it's skittles.

I jogged down the hall headed to the parking garage. My car was the best thing in the lot, and I had it painted candy blue, so you know it was glistening. My moms co-signed on my brand-new BMW 650 Coupe. I made it to my car and grabbed a few bundles. I knew it was gonna sell asap and not make it back to the car.

Walking back to the bathroom, the line got right back long. The shit was crazy. It even had a few teachers in line, but I didn't care. Either they were buying or pissin, didn't matter to me. I need money, so I kept up with the hand and hand transactions. I was like the grocery store, but only cash, no credit, no checks.

"Thank you, come again," was all I said for the better of 10 minutes.

After the last person getting served, I left the bathroom. In the hallway I counted my money as I walked. $2,100 can't be mad at 10 minutes of work for this type pay off. I smiled.

"Hey Jroc!" a girl spoke, tryna grab my attention. I turned around to see who she was and spoke back.

"What's up, sweets?" Me having a lot of friends I really didn't remember anybody's name so all the females I gave them pet names. They didn't care so I damn sure didn't either.

"What you about to get into?" she asked.

"Shid, I don't know. I just let my day happen. What you tryna be a part of it?"

She smiled. "Only if you take me home first, then we could chill," she said.

I looked to the sky as if I was really thinking about my answer. Shawty looked good and I hoped she was ready for a nigga, plus she was white.

She gotta be a freak.

All I gotta do is give her a few mollies and have fun from there. "That's cool, I got you," I told her walking off as she followed.

Dro

"Change too!"

Life has made a turn for the best. I was finally close to where I needed to be. I moved out of mom's spot. Charmine and I lived together. She was my ride or die and was with me from day one, so I give her all the spoils of life. We are planning our first trip out of the country, but me being travel stupid, I didn't know I needed a passport, so we are waiting on them to be mailed. I thought you just buy a ticket and fly. So, from now on I let her do all the planning and give me the receipt.

I was about my dough, and everybody knew it. I'm da man. I just signed a lease on a building that I'm getting renovated to become my record label. "Same Guy Ent."

My first artist was gonna be my man Izzo.

Fuck da world, I would tell myself as an ego boost to go out there and get what's mine. I came into the game to get money. Now I'm flipping chickens and water whipping all over town. Niggas get to playing with my shit. "Click, bang," shit change over money.

I swear niggas used to love to see a nigga down bad, so when you come up, you better keep it on the low. I rode around in my '96 Impala with the factories on it. It wasn't complete without that king kong in my trunk. I tried to look average to the naked eye.

Behind closed doors when I break it down, it's 36 onions no less on the table. I'm not doin' bad at all and shit, still growing and progressing. I'm in the process of meeting a new nigga when them passports come through. I'ma make sure I stay on and ride this wave and hopefully never fall off.

All the work I put in I used to be a light pole when I stood on the block like an addict. That shit wasn't for fun. I had to. I ain't have shit, well shit to my liking. Them days over. A lot of my niggas envied a nigga's overnight come up, so I had to stay on the block with a Glock, cocked as always.

Often, I reminisce on the days of me on the block like a savage. I would take any and all money. Change too. It all spent the same. Twenty-four hours a day all I did was hustle. Either I was dropping off grams or setting up business moves, so I could get my men off the corner. I had to reach out to everybody and hit them with the deal I had for them.

My phone was always ringing. Sometimes I had to turn it off when I was out of work. I made good use of the Obama phone I had. It could be annoying at time. All in all niggas knew not to play with me. At least I felt confident to say they knew I wasn't a bitch. I play with that pistol like a toy, work call was definite.

I applied pressure when needed and supplied the streets. I had to feed it. My shit was ringing bells in the city—well, mostly uptown for now. I ain't have no Columbian connect or no shit like that, but I was planning a trip to meet a nigga in Miami and that's the next step. But for now, dude, I'm dealing with had good coke, but he couldn't keep up.

It was stepped on too. Couldn't really find no pure so me taking if off always cost me more money but made my shit top notch. I put the powder in da pot, kept whipping it til I was pulling off the lot. I'm out here, and the streets love me, and right now me and my men winning.

I ain't chill with my men in a while. I'm tryna go out tonight and let them know about my plans for us if they wit it.

I sent a group text:
"WHATS THE MOVE TONIGHT?"

CHAPTER 35

Black

"This the game you wanna play, really?"

I was on my mission and money was the motivation. I had to get my shit together. My phone was vibrating. It was a text from Dro. He was tryna get the good men together for a night on the town. Knowing this made me wanna get fly, I knew them niggas was gonna be showing off. The move was already stamped. All I had to do was put it into motion. Keisha was tryna get involved and I had the perfect roll for her to play.

The power of pussy was crazy, and I knew it. My girl is bad. To get under a nigga's skin was the easy part. Easy enough for me to slide in and take what I need and want. It was murkin' season, niggas betta act like they know and tighten the fuck up or Big Black coming through. If I have a mask all I want is the cash, but if you heavy and I come bare faced, you know what time it is. 'NIGHT NIGHT.'

Not gonna give you a chance to come see me about that bread. Nobody gonna live, definitely gonna get my blast on, all up in your crib, no question. All a nigga want is a piece of your pie, but if you get to faking with this big boy to your dome then it's "bye bye." I swear my shit say work and suckers and real niggas know what's up with me.

'SHIT!'

I realized I was behind schedule. "Aye boo, let's go!" I yelled to Keisha. She takes forever to get ready, but I guess all females do. Keisha had the easy job today. All the hard work had already been put in by her. This time around everything should go off nicely. Still, I gave her a KA P380. It was a nice lil pocket rocket that she could easily conceal. It held .380 shells with 7 rounds, and she already knew how to shoot from our many trips to the range.

We pulled up at Weaton Mall in Montgomery County, Maryland and parked in the lot. The lick was across the street in the residential neighborhood.

The nigga been pumpin' (hustling) real good in these parts all the way in the cut. I laid on him for two weeks and now it's time to get his ass. I was gonna ask Izzo to come with me, but I knew his trap' bumpin and he ain't hurting for nothing so, me and boo gonna get this money.

We crept up to the door. The neighborhood was quiet. I guess everybody was at work or whatever 'cause it wasn't no movement up or down the street. This was nothing like the city streets. I could scream and I'm sure the whole block would come to the windows looking. I made a mental note of that.

Keisha looked the part. She had on a small Dickies suit, and her clipboard in her hand. On her waist she had a meter gun.

Knock, knock.

"Can I help you?" a pretty girl asked, opening the door.

"Good afternoon. I work for Pepco, and I am checking the meters inside and outside of the house. Where are yours located?" Keisha asked, sounding real professional.

My baby was like a pro. It seemed like she did this type of shit before. As the girl came out of the house to show Keisha the side of the house, I came from this big ass rose bush the nigga had on the porch. WHACK! was the sound of the gun connecting with the side of the girls' head.

I know her shit was beatin' (hurting). I had a big boy gun. This was my baby. I had a Mark XIX Desert Eagle with a 10-inch barrel with autoloader action. The best part is that it held seven .50 AE caliber bullets. Dooky shooter. The girl fell into Keisha's arms, and she caught her, then laid her in the hallway.

I entered the house. "Watch her," I told Keisha as I looked around. "And take your gun out."

I heard the TV in the living room and followed the sound, tip toeing. "Let me see them hands big boy," I said to the dude's back as I pulled my mask down.

He turned around. After he seen the gun, he jumped up. "What the fuck man. How you get in here? Where my girl at? She okay?" Dude asked every question back-to-back.

"Shut da fuck up before she be at your funeral," I growled, so he would get the picture of what's goin on. "Where that shit at?" He looked confused.

"What shit?"

This nigga must think I was playing with his ass. Shit was bout to get real, real fast. "This the game you wanna play, really?" I asked with a smirk.

"I don't know what you talking bout," he said, nonchalantly.
BOOM!

"Ahhhhhhhhh!!!" He screamed.

"See, look what you made me do. Got me fuckin' up your nice carpet. This that plush shit too," I said, after I shot him in his arm. "Now listen, cause I think I got your attention now. If you wanna play this game we can, just let me know. But if I take this mask off, it's gonna be the last game you ever play."

In agonizing pain he held his arm from the ground. "Show me my girl and you could have everything," he said damn near crying.

'BITCH ASS.'

"Get up, nigga!"

Dude sniffed. "Aye homie, between me and you did my shawty have something to do with this?" he asked, talking about his girl as he got up.

"Nah, nigga. I don't know your bitch. If I know her, I wouldn't have smacked her with this pistol so hard. She still seeing stars right about now. Life is a bitch bruh, but if you keep asking me all these questions I'ma make her your ex."

"It's in the kids' room," he pointed.

"Lead the way, pussy."

He walked upstairs. The house was nice and well furbished. Ahead of me we walked into the last room in the hallway of this level. "It's over there." He pointed again. I tossed him some duct tape.

"Here, tape your wrist." Watching him finish, I grabbed him to add a few more layers to tighten the hold, for his safety.

I went straight to where he said the cash was at. It was in a baby basinet. I lifted the cloth and seen all blue face bricks laid on the floor of it. "Where the rest of it?" I yelled. "The fuckin' safe is what I'm here for."

"It's two keys of coke in the shoebox. That's all I got, bruh, shit. This ain't my house, this my folks' house. I got a job and all, look in the driveway cuz. I ain't ballin.' Please don't kill me," he pleaded.

I could tell he wasn't no street nigga, just another wild nigga in the way. To confirm it, I started lifting my mask, slowly. As soon as he seen what I was doing he closed his eyes and pleaded. "Please bruh, that's all I got, I swear."

'BOOM! BOOM!'

I shot him in his leg, then his ass for good measure. "Bitch ass, I should smoke yo ass out her purpin'," I said walking down the stairs. "Come on boo."

Keisha looked nervous. "I think she dead, baby."

'BOOM!'

I shot dude girl in her ass too. Her body slid across the floor, waking her up instantly, screaming. "No she not boo," I told my girl grabbing her arm and heading out the door.

The neighborhood was still quiet, even after the multiple shots from the cannon I had. We walked down the street like a couple that lived on the block.

We made it back to the mall and hopped in the whip. Driving, Keisha was talking a hundred words a minute and I was half listening as the music played as well. Cruising down the Georgia Avenue after she stopped talking for a while, she poked me to grab my attention. "I got to talk to you."

"Go ahead put a bug in my ear, but not on my phone." I smiled, joking as I quoted Lil Wayne's song.

"Boo for real."

"Talk then."

"I was thinking that we should move in a bigger spot," she said, looking deep in my eyes tryna read my thoughts.

'BITCH TRYNA CLAMP ME.'

"I gotta think about it. You know I have my lil sisters to consider." I came off the hip with that real quick.

Parking the car we arrived at the crib. She went straight to the shower like she put in some heavy work, but it gave me time to count this bread. I emptied the money on the bed.

'JACKPOT'

I counted the money while she was in the shower. $21,000 and 2 keys of coke wasn't bad for a days take.

'SHITTING ME TALKING BOUT YOU AIN'T BALLIN.'

❖   ❖   ❖

Jroc

"Well my name Heather."

— Heather

I just knew I was the man. Drugs was the reason behind my come up. Here I am riding down Connecticut Avenue with this bad ass white chick tryna roll. She didn't waste any time after we left her house, she was already sucking my dick as I switched lanes. She definitely knew her way around the dick, because I almost rear ended somebody twice being in a zone as she sucked. I came all in her mouth and she never missed a beat. "I think I'm in love," I said, smiling as she rose up.

She laughed. "Boy, you don't even know my name," she said, wiping her own mouth.

"You the one that skipped the introductions," I said, making a left down my street.

"I guess you right." She smiled brighter. "Well, my name Heather," she said all excited how white girls be. I looked at her.

Awwww, she sweet.

She looked at the house I parked in front of. "Who's house is this?"

"Mines."

Heather looked amazed as we walked through the door. She was talking but taking everything in for the first time.

'BITCH NOSEY.'

I had to redirect her interest to the bedroom. That's why we were here. For some reason she was observant to everything and asked a lot of questions. She was really ditzy too. I was feeling her though. I didn't want to treat her like a hoe. Yeah, she sucked my dick, but in school I've seen her carry endless niggas left and right, not giving them the time of day.

Matter of fact, she was always on my line, but I was moving and groovin' chasing the bag, but today she caught up with me on my exit and I had the time to actually rap to her and see what's up. It got really quiet, so I broke the ice. "Yo, so what's up? You tryna fuck or what?" I asked, really testing the water and feel her out and see how I was gonna treat her from this day forward.

She was livid. "Who you think you talking to with that smart ass mouth of yours?" Heather asked with much sass. "I knew I shouldn't have sucked your thing. Now you think I'm some type of hoe." I bust out laughing. I couldn't hold it in. She was looking at me like I was crazy with her face all balled up. She stood up. "I'm ready to go."

I looked at her but didn't say anything, but she did. "Oh, you think I cannot find my way," she said tryna get past me. "I'll call an Uber."

I grabbed her and pulled her into an embrace. Looking at her in her eyes, I could tell she was a little tight. I forced a kiss to her lips. She fought at first then gave in to kiss me back. After a few second of tongue fighting, she pulled away and looked down. I lifted her chin. "I'ma make you, my girl."

"What!" Boy who you think you talking bout?"

"You . . . You know I'm gonna hit that," I said nodding at her butt. "Then I'ma make you official mines, okay?"

"Whatever James. Matter of fact get your hands off me," she said playfully, pushing me away. I pulled her close.

I ain't got my hands on you, I got 'em wrapped around me," I smirked.

"Is that so? Well, you need to back up off me."

"You know you like it," I said as I rubbed her up.

"You real persistent," she said, acting like she ain't feel me playing with her zipper. This was my entrance. I spoke softly in her ear, "Let me touch you."

She couldn't fight it no more. The way she was feeling she couldn't hold it back. It was coming full force. "Oh my gosh, James." She moaned as I kissed her neck.

"It feel good, don't it?" I asked, now fingering her.

"Yesssss . . ." She came on my fingers, then pulled back. "Um . . . not like this boo, please."

I looked at her and stopped. She was eyeing me. I was satisfied that she wasn't a hoe. She just into a nigga and I know how that could be.

'I WAS CHOSEN.'

We chilled. I smoked as we started to get to know each other. She wanted to know everything. I was happy she was that interested in me. I even popped a molly and gave her one. I was rolling boots. I looked at her and she looked normal, like it didn't even faze her. 'WHITE CHICKS' I forgot they pop 'em like skittles. She might need more.

Time seemed to fly as we chilled. I almost forgot about us fellas getting together tonight. I had to take Heather home and get back to the crib to get ready. We coolin' tonight, so I gotta look sweet. It's been a while.

The agreement was set. Everyone planned to meet at the hotel on New York Avenue. It was around the corner a few blocks from the club they were planning on attending tonight. They were puzzled as to why everyone was meeting at the hotel. Only Dro knew, it was his idea.

The group text Dro sent to the fellas read:

'PARK YA WHIP IN GARAGE, COME TO ROOM 494.

One by one they arrived at the hotel to be greeted by a doorman. After a brief conversation, each of them were pointed to the direction of the room. Dro was already there when they arrived.

The guys looked like a million bucks and smelled like money. It was a runway in the hotel room. You would have thought they were competing—maybe they were.

Dro decided to do the stainless thing today. He rocked Gucci everything head to toe. All white was the colors except for the slight red and green to represent the brand.

Jroc was in a pair of Saint Laurent jeans and shades. His shirt was Purple Label, a V-neck.

Izzo had remixed trap boy apparel. He was gracing Lil Waynes, 'Truckfit' with a pair of Foams.

Black was matching his name in all black. Michael Kors top and bottom with a pair of Construction Timberlands completed his outfit. Everybody was Fly. Izzo looked around. "Why da fuck we in da telly? Where da bitches?" Dro passed Black a jay.

"Nigga, be easy and be cool, pass that nigga the jay' Black."

They smoked and chilled for the better of thirty minutes and was feeling mello. Dro looked at his phone and then to his friends. "Aye, listen up. I know I been telling y'all to just wait on me, but the wait is over. I just got the record company up and running. Everything is legit, so when this plug come through, we could wash this bread up through the music. My first artist is our very own Izzo—"

"Prophet," Izzo interrupted. "That's my rap name."

"Oh okay den. Y'all heard him. Prophet and we bout to get this industry money. I'm still working on that connect down south, but shit bouta start looking up, so Black I know you don't rap or nothing like that so you gonna be my right hand, my shooter for niggas I can't see. Izzo, I mean Prophet, you front and center and Jroc, you on the team, but I need you to finish that degree. We need somebody for these books be straight."

Izzo rubbed his hands together. "Cool wit me. Where do I sign and what's my bonus looking like?"

Dro shook his head and began to laugh. "Chill, that's for another day. Today is to celebrate, so let's go."

They all got up and headed to the door. On the elevator they were chopping it up. "I hope it's some bitches in this joint," Izzo said.

"Nigga you better tread water. Tiara would smoke yo ass," Dro said. Black looked at Dro with an expression.

"Nigga . . . I know you ain't talking like you safe."

Ding. The elevator sounded.

Jroc looked confused. "Moe, why you hit lobby? Our whips in the garage."

"Shut up and come on," Dro said.

Walking out of the hotel there was a stretch Hummer with the S&G (Same Guy) logo on it. It was jet black with the mirror tints. "This how we pulling up, big boy style," Dro said, smiling at his friends.

Black was hyped. "Nigga you never cease to amaze me."

The truck was decked out. They rode to Prophet's mixtape that Dro had made from their last recording session. On the way to the club, they continued to smoke and sip drinks from the bar. Pulling up, all eyes was on them. You would have thought they were famous. Walking to the bouncers, Dro peeled off $500 and he waved them in. They went straight to V.I.P. and ordered bottle after bottle. The spot was live, and the groupies were surrounding their section.

Dro pulled some strings and had Prophet's music playing in the club with multiple shot outs that put them on blast. You couldn't tell them shit. They haven't been out in months and was enjoying each other's company more than anything else. Instagram live was jumping giving them more of a fan base. "Make money, take money, but keep your head on a swivel," Dro said, toasting with his bottle held high. Everybody cheered, clinked bottles and took a big swig.

CHAPTER 36

30 Days Later . . .

Today was the neighborhood block party, everybody was outside around the way. Friends of friends came through to celebrate. The block was lit. Dro, Black, Izzo and Jroc all put up on the food and juices. Combined Izzo and Dro had about $1500 worth of food stamps. Jroc and Black put up some cash for the stuff and other materials needed.

Tiara, Charmine, and Keisha helped with the multiple industrial-style grills cooking all the food. Heather, the white girl, helped out as well. Girls was with the girls and the fellas followed suit.

Life was good on their end so showing the hood love was only right. Izzo had a single on the radio doing numbers, thanks to Dro pushing his music through local radio stations such as WPGC 95.5 and WKYS 93.9. Groupies was at an all-time high around the way, especially when Izzo got on the stage to perform as his alter ego Prophet.

They even had 4 different type of moon bounces for the kids

to enjoy with a few snow cone and popcorn makers, along with cotton candy and other treats. It was byob (bring your own bottle) affair. Niggas could drink without any limit, so they didn't even try to supply the hood.

"Yeah bruh, this living right here," Dro said, sitting on a portable beach chair on the middle of the block.

"No question, couldn't be better." Black exhaled some lime haze.

Meanwhile Jroc was ducked off in the cut with his lil' bun Heather. They became real close and she knew everything about him. It was crazy he couldn't say the same all he knew was she was his and that was cool with him. The two of them was inseparable. Izzo was still in work mode, even after his performance. Running in and out the trap he was still making moves. To him, this was like Christmas, fiends was everywhere throughout the crowd and was spending. Even as he was hustling, he still posed for pictures and selfies to promote his brand, just like his manager Dro had requested.

The ladies was by the grills talking and chilling. They became closer because they seemed to always be pushed together by the closeness of their men. They were brothers which made them sisters.

The day actually turned out to be a good one. S&G Entertainment was the host of the summer jam and couldn't ask for a better outcome. The day got crazy when the police pulled up and started stapling flyers on every other tree and light pole. Nobody paid attention to it because the party was still at a high level. Then a little kid ran up on Black and threw a balled-up flyer hitting him in his head then ran.

"Aye! Lil bad ass," Black yelled picking the flyer up to unravel it. He shook his head. "This the shit I be talking bout' slim," he said giving Dro the paper.

"What da fuck?! That look like Jroc don't it," Dro stated with a confused faced.

"Yup, and that bitch lived and now she talkin'."

"We gonna have to go pay her a visit and slid through that joint," Dro said folding the paper up. "Damn!" he yelled out loud as he opened his phone to text Jroc:

"COME HERE BOB,911."

Jroc felt his phone vibrate and seen he had a message. After reading it he walked over to where his girl a was to let her know he'll be back. Black was mad, soon as he seen Jroc he stepped off. Black was headed to check for his lil sisters who was flagging him down. Anger flooded his mind as he stepped off. First off, he gave the girl headshot, and he didn't die, secondly Jroc didn't follow the plan and he remembered his face. 'YOUR DUMBASS HAD TO FREESTYLE I'M NOT GOING TO JAIL FOR YOUR SCARY ASS,' Black thought as he picked up his sisters one by one giving them a kiss.

"Hey big bro," Shanae spoke.

"You having fun today?"

"Yes, but this man gave me this," Shanae said giving him a note. "He said give it to my big brother and that's you." Black grabbed the note fast. It read:

Keep thinking you untouchable keep stackin' I'll be too get it.

Black frowned. "Who gave you this?" Shanae pointed to the street to a parked car with smacks (tints). Black noticed it was the same car he kept seeing over the last few months. He' began walking toward it, reaching for his gun.

SKRRRRRRR. The car was gone.

Dro didn't say anything to Jroc when he walked up. The music was jumping as he two stepped and stopped in front of Dro. Before Jroc could say a word Dro had his hand extended, giving him the flyer as he shook his head. Izzo approached, bottle in hand. "Cheers nigget!" he said with a big ass smile that quickly disappeared when he peeped the vibe. "Fuck goin on?"

Dro just put his head down. Izzo looked at Jroc who just paused then passed the flyer. "Damn homie, we gotta shoot past that spot and see if shawty still staying there," Izzo said

"Sounds ·like a plan," Dro agreed. Jroc didn't say anything. He just kept staring at the flyer and walked off. "I'll be back."

❖   ❖   ❖

"What's wrong baby?" Heather asked Jroc as he came back from talking to the homies.

"Nothing boo, just some bullshit that I gotta handle."

"Oh okay," Heather responded, but knew something was up and was determined to find out.

In Heather's mind Jroc is a real cool dude who just started getting money. She was placed in his school to find out where all the drugs was coming from at the college. But when she looked at the flyer that he just balled up and threw, her heart dropped. She had true feelings for Jroc and didn't believe he was the one selling drugs at the college, but her job came first, and this intel could get her the promotion she been seeking.

If the picture hasn't been painted, Heather is D-E-A and there's a big case going on right now that's under investigation. She got an instant high from the thoughts of solving a multiple homicide as well. This could mean more money and respect from her peers on all levels of the department.

Now even though he has her heart somewhat, she was already putting the pieces to the puzzle of a lot of his conversations she had overheard but couldn't decipher. He was about to re-up soon and Heather would have a plan in place and just await the call to put it in action.

With this newfound information, Heather thinks his friends are involved, maybe not Dro and even Izzo but Black for sure. She knew Jroc didn't have the heart to carry out the violent murders and/or torture tactics that was used. That type of horror had Black name written all over that.

'I THINK THAT MAN CRAZY ANYWAY,' Heather thought to herself folding the picture of Jroc up putting it in her purse.

CHAPTER 37

Loose Ends

"My name is Shawn . . ."
— Black

The next day Black and Izzo went to pay the witness a visit. Black just dropped Dro off at the studio and told him he needed a personal day. Keisha had just moved about 3 weeks ago with Black, so he didn't have a house to lamp in no more. That didn't matter, anger consumed his mind and jail wasn't in his near future if he could help it.

When they pulled up, Izzo didn't expect for it to go down like this. "Aye where you goin'?" Izzo asked when Black opened the car door.

"To knock on the door."

"For what?"

"To see if anybody home. What else, nigga?"

"Nah, nigga you trippin'." Izzo said, grabbing Black's arm. "That wasn't a part of the plan."

"Nigga . . . if you don't get your hand off me. It wasn't no damn plan."

"You right, do you, slim."

KNOCK, KNOCK.

"Hello, may I help you?" an older lady asked.

She looked like she could have been the victim's moms or close relative. "Yes, how are you doing? I'm a friend of Victoria. I was coming to check on her. I just came from school, outta state and was informed that her health changed for the better," Black said, putting on his best educated proper talk.

"Oh, sweetie that's so nice, but she not here right now. If you want to you could come back tomorrow. She'll be here."

"Thank you so much momma. She just gonna die when she see me," Black said, waving and walking off. "See ya tomorrow."

"Hey, what's your name, sweetheart?"

Pausing, stopping dead in his tracks he turned around slowly smiling. "I'm sorry, how rude am I," Black said, walking back, extending his hand. "My name is Shawn, but please don't tell her. I want it to be a big surprise. She hasn't seen me in the flesh in a while."

"Sure, sure sweetie, nice to meet you."

Black got back in the car and pulled off. Izzo looked at him with a blank expression. "What happened?"

"Gotta come back tomar'."

"Jroc's scary ass should be the one out here doing all this stakin' out shit," Izzo said, frustrated.

"Nah, you know he ain't really 'bout this gun play shit, but after we cut this loose end, I'm not fuckin' with him on that tip anymore, on my mova," Black stamped.

Riding back uptown it was business as usual. Izzo checked his social media. He was trending from a freestyle he posted earlier. Black was in his own mind. 'SOMEWHERE SHIT DONE GOT CRAZY,' Black thought with one arm on the wheel and his eyes on the road. All he knew was he wasn't gonna trip, only deal with it.

"Moe, earth to Black. You didn't hear me?" Izzo asked, snapping Black out of his daze.

"Nah, what's up?"

"Nothing, fuck it," Izzo said as they pulled up on Rst. Izzo went to check his trap and Black went to his crib. He was walking and seen his sisters. They ran to embrace him.

"Hey Donte?" they sang together. "What's up?"

"Nothing's up lil gremlins. What's crackin'?"

"We bored."

"Come on. Y'all wanna go somewhere?" Black asked.

"Yayyy!!!" A loud scream of excitement was the answer.

"Okay, chill right here for a minute. Let me go check on y'all mother."

"That's your mom too," Shanae had to correct and include.

"Yeah, okay baby, be right back."

Black walked in the house to see his moms on the couch watching her soaps. He walked right past her and headed to his room so he could grab a few dollars but still asked, "You a'ight, Ol' lady?"

"Yeah, fine."

"Here." Black gave her $100 and some smokes. "I got girls with me. I'll bring 'em back tomar'." Black said, walking out the door entering the hallway.

❖ ❖ ❖

"What's up O.G.?" a young kid spoke to Black as he came down the flight of stairs.

"Sup' young niggas, y'all a'ight?"

"Yeah, we cool. Aye you got a dollar?"

Black tossed them $20. "Split that," he said, exiting the building. Making it to his sisters he waved them over, letting them know it was time to go. Going through the parking lot they got in the car and peeled off.

Meanwhile, Izzo was in his trap house. "How's my money?" was the first words as he entered the apartment. All his young boys looked up in shock, trying to act as if they were busy and started moving around. "Don't run now, like you niggas was working," Izzo said, laughing. His lieutenant came with a book bag from the back and gave it to him. Izzo grabbed it and asked, "Is it right?" With a nod confirmation he left to put the money in Tiara's house. When he made it there, he remembered she was outside, so he pulled his phone out:

'   W   Y   A   ?   "
'HEY BAE I'M WIT CHARMINE.'

'DAMN, GUESS I'LL PUT THIS BAG IN MY MOMS' JOINT,' Izzo thought, then another text came through:

'AYE BRUH TEM PEOPLES PULLING ME OVER. TELL DRO TO GET A LAWYER ON STANDBY IF I CALL BACK.'

"What the fuck?" Izzo said to himself as he reread the text again.

❖   ❖   ❖

Dro
"Seven again."

"The hottest nigga under the sun . . . Ain't nobody fuckin' wit me man," I rapped Lil Wayne's song as I got out of the shower. I had a lot on my mind, but the focus was still money and keeping my good men head on a swivel. Last night was good until that flyer started to circulate and fucked up the vibe between us. I got myself together and decided to head back out but didn't.

I remembered how when I was picking my money up through-out the hood, the flyer was in damn near every corner store and carry out with a $10,000 reward. I'm hoping a nigga didn't get thirsty and point my man out, but the chances of that are real small. Nigga's tellin' at an all time high. That could be problems for all of us and we don't need that. I put money up for lawyers and shit like that, but Ion' know if my men did, but guess since I got a retainer, we all good.

I walked down to the kitchen to get something to drink, my throat was dry. All I had was a jay' in my hand that was giving me cotton mouth. I had my clothes laid out but was yet to put them on. I was ass naked as the day I was born. This was one of the things I loved about our new spot. Me and Charmine would always be naked. Her ass and titties out and my man just swinging freely. Random fuck sessions was constant.

"Aye boo!!" I screamed coming down the stairs.

"Yeah boo, I'm in the kitchen."

Our kitchen was laid out with a bar style table with four chairs facing the stove with a walk around entrance from both sides. As I bent the corner, Tiara was right there in one of the circular spinning chairs and Charmine's back was facing me. Tiara's eyes got big, wasn't no shame in my game. I was blessed but not in that moment. "What!? It's cold in here," I said, walking to the fridge. Tiara giggled. Charmine looked at me like I was crazy as I asked, "Ain't no more beers?"

"Put some damn clothes on!" Charmine yelled. Me being an asshole and for the fun of it I took my time. Shit, I didn't know her friend was her. "Your dumbass should have told me you was having company, plus it ain't nobody but Tiara lil ugly ass," I said, opening the beer, turning to leave.

On the way out I noticed Charmine's face. Priceless. She was heated but hid it well in the presence of Tiara. "Hold on girl," I heard her say as I turned to go upstairs.

Charmine tried to catch up to me, but I heard her, so I ran up the stairs two at a time back to our room and hid. She burst through the door with authority ready to argue. "DRO!!" I jumped out on her, still ass naked and tackled her to the floor. I was aggressive. She liked shit like that. I had a pair of fluffy coated handcuffs. I put them on her as she tried to resist, but who was kidding. I was too strong for her. I ripped her bra along with her panties right off like it was some cheap shit, but it was expensive. Now she was naked right along with me. She had socks on.

Forcing my tongue in her pussy she tried to choke me with her legs. I didn't stop, only licked her button more rapidly in different rotations. Her grip loosened as she couldn't resist and started to enjoy the ride. I ate the shit out her juicebox, turned her over and fucked her doggystyle like I paid for it. No lovemaking straight crushed then came all in her tunnel.

She laid there shaking. I wiped off my man with her ripped panties and the baby wipes was kept on the dresser. I put some cargo shorts and a tank top, then threw on my S&G chain and looked back at her. She was still face down, ass up when she spoke. "Bae, take the cuffs off," she said, breathing heavy.

"Nope!" was all I said and ran out of the room, closing the door behind me. I came down the stairs and Tiara as right there, staring with narrowed eyes. "What you do to her?"

"Laid the law round here, go ask her about it," I said, running out the door headed to my car. I hopped in my car laughing, imaging Charmine tryna open the door with the cuffs on, then Tiara goin' in there seeing her in her b-day suit, sweating all over. 'THEY MIGHT FUCK . . .' I imagined. 'NAH!!'

Headed uptown was my next move. I had to holla at a few young boys that had been calling my phone, tryna cop' (buy). I was one foot in and one foot out the game. I had the label, but wasn't producing on a high level yet, so them white blocks was still my main income.

I called Jroc a few times. I know he played with that molly, and I had a few plays for him. 'FUCK IT,' I said, hanging up the phone, yet again. Driving down the street I was just sightseeing in my own city. So much has changed right before my eyes. It's been a lot of progress and gentrification and shit was expensive. One thing I could say is that I'ma always be from the original Chocolate City in my heart even though they kickin' us out.

I pulled up around the way and headed to grandma's house to check on her to see if she needed anything before I go make these drops and pick-ups. Walking through my section taking in the scenery, everybody was out coolin.' Since that block party, I've even been a lil hood celebrity and bitches was geekin.' I could only imagine how Izzo was dealin' with this shit. Well Prophet as he would say.

Really, I was just passing through to burn some time before I bust my move. I came up on a crap game and decided to shoot some dice. "What this shit hit for?"

"Oh, shit y'all! Sweet money here. Your shot $20 make your own bet," the fader responded.

"Bet, my kind of shit," I said, picking up the dice, tossing my bread on the ground.

I was looking sweet. I came in and stole 500 real quick off of one fader. Dude wouldn't stop. Once a nigga in your pockets, they don't be tryna leave til you break them so that's what I did and went to the next fader. I had the hot hand, then dude came up behind me. "Aye bruh,' you think you could show a nigga love. I'm fucked up." I looked at him and told him I had him. Shid, why not I did just get $1,200 off him real quick. Me being a good nigga I gave him $500 back.

Shooting the dice at my fader. "7 again," I said, picking up the pot.

Jroc

"Man, I'm tired as shit," I told myself, sitting in class. Last night that block party was lit. Niggas stayed out all night but had to get up early. First, I had to meet my connect, then off to class I went. Next period I'm supposed to meet my man in the parking lot. I was happy that he decided to get me out the way early. I had clients on standby.

I done turned this college out. My men thought I couldn't hustle but look at me now. "Class dismissed. See you guys tomorrow," the teacher said.

"Finally," I said, getting up from my seat in a hurry so I could go meet my man. I was speed balling down the hall and then out of thin air Heather popped up. "Slow down, boo before the hall monitor gives you a ticket," she said, kissing me. "Where you headed anyway?"

"I gotta go see my man about something. I'ma call you later." It was funny the look she had. It looked like a devilish grin like she was up to something, but I didn't pay it no mind. I had shit to do and getting this money was one of them. Damn near running to the parking lot I seen my folks in his car. I jumped in. "Sup' baby boy?" he greeted me.

"Shit, coolin'," I said, giving him the duffle bag, I was carrying. In return he gave me a similar bag and I got out of the car and headed to mines. I had another class but decided to skip it and take this home. Starting my car my phone rang.

"Yeah boo."

"I'm waiting in the hall for you, where you at?" Heather asked. I told her I was about to leave and drop some shit off. Then she got loud and panicked, repeating the same thing I just said to her. "Yeah, I'm 'bout to leave, why you a'ight?"

"Yeah, yeah . . . I'm good baby, drive safe. I'll see you later."

I hung up and pulled off with money on my mind. Cruising down the street listening to Problems by 6lack, the lyrics of the song spoke to me, and I was agreeing with what he was saying.

I'm bopping my head to the beat, then out of the rearview the potential for the worst was about to happen. The cherry and blue lights was behind me. I was nervous. First thing that came to mind was to text somebody. Izzo was my last message, so I texted him, then pulled over . . .

CHAPTER 38

Black

"We can't take you nowhere."
— Shaniyah

Pulling up at Chuckie Cheese in Bowie, Maryland I decided to surprise my lil sisters. They were happy as shit. "Yaaay!" they screamed when I parked, and they noticed the logo. "We gonna go in here for about an hour and a half then it's dinnertime, okay," I told them as they got out of the car and ran to the entrance. "Aye, don't be slammin' my damn doors!" I yelled to their backs because they damn sure wasn't paying me any mind as they continued to run down the parking lot.

SKRRRRRR.

"Get ya dumb asses out the street!" I heard a driver yell at my sisters.

'WHAT THE FUCK,' I thought as I ran to where my sisters

were froze in place. "Aye, fuck you, you bitch ass nigga!" I said to the driver who stopped. "Go inside," I told my sisters.

"No, Donte please don't," Shaniyah pleaded.

"What I say?" I scowled her. I was livid. She ran off behind my other sister who knew I didn't play when I'm mad. When you disrespect my sisters, I swear I'm cracking jaws and I'm always lit so you know it's fuck da law. Dude got out of his car. "What's up nigga?" he approached. He didn't even know he had the right one. That nigga was ugly, and I was gonna beat it right off him. I didn't hesitate. Soon as he got close enough, I took off on him. I'm not the talking type. He fell and I was determined to beat him to a pulp.

The parking lot is where it started so that's where it went down. He tried to put up a fight. Growing up in my hood all we did was fight. This was before everybody ran to go get pistols. I beat him to a coma, trashed him.

Picking up his body it was limp, and I threw him in his own backseat. I got in his car and pulled it into a parking spot, then headed to the front entrance of Chuckie Cheese.

Surprisingly, wasn't anybody right there with shocked faces or nothing. People actually mind their business in this neck of the woods, or they got on their phones, but kept it moving. I walked in like nothing ever happened.

"Hi sir, what can I do for you?" the cashier asked.

"Let me get $30 in tokens and one pizza," I said while my sisters sat looking at me like I was crazy. "Smile," I said them as they waited. But instead, they stood up and grabbed the tokens.

"We can't take you nowhere," Shaniyah said with a slight attitude.

"Thanks for the tokens, but you didn't give Shaniyah hers yet," Shanae said, walking off to the nearest game. "Oh yeah, you got that." Looking at Shaniyah I smiled. "Oh, you can't take me nowhere, huh." I turned to the cashier. "Let me get 30 more dollars' worth.

We enjoyed all the games and they even convinced me to get

on a couple of the rides with them. Time was up, tokens gone, and the pizza never came. After we left, I was about to get them a real meal from one of the restaurants around her but decided against it. Thoughts ran through my mind, and I knew after I did what I was about to do I couldn't stay around here much longer.

I walked the girls to the car and put their seatbelts on. "I'll be right back." I jogged to that punk's car which was still where I left it and opened his door to look around. He was still unconscious as I went through his pockets and took all his money, about $3,500 and jewelry plus his shoes. He looked dead, but I seen his body goin' up and down. Looking at his face made me mad all over again.

I had this new pistol I brought. This gun connect that Dro had had me gone off his multiple selections. This new joint I had now was a Walther PPX that held 14 .40 caliber Smith and Wesson bullets with a 3-dot adjustable low profile sight management with hammer fire action reloader—a bad mamajama'.

I whipped it out, geeking just to see what it could do. I aimed at his head, then lowered it to his ass. BOC! I shot him.

"Ahhhhh!!! Sheeit," he woke up, screaming.

Running back after I slammed his door, I made it to my car. My sisters was looking around but seen me then sat back down. I acted like nothing ever happened as I asked, "Wanna go to my house?"

"Yeeeeeessss!" they sang in unison, excited.

So that's what it was. We headed to my house for a sleepover. They had a room in my house, the new one, and while they were there, I was gonna get Keisha to do their hair and fix us some dinner. Looking through my rearview I seen them smiling and thought to myself, 'THAT'S HOW KIDS SUPPOSE TO BE GROWING UP, HAPPY, NO WORRIES.' I cruised with multiple thoughts and the witness came to mind and I made a self-note that tomorrow she had to get dealt with.

❖　　　❖　　　❖

Decisions
"Don't think too hard baby."
— Heather

As Jroc sat in the holding cell he wondered why they haven't booked him yet. He was pretty sure that the police found his stash. The money in his picket didn't help. "Fuck!" he said to himself as he sat handcuffed to a cement block wall.

Sitting there for about an hour, an officer finally came to check for him. "Hands!" the officer said, not realizing the was cuffed to the wall. "Oh, I'm sorry." He apologized, opening the door walking over to Jroc to escort him to an interrogation room. He was nervous. In the room they placed him in there was nothing but a desk and chair. 'THIS SHIT LOOK LIKE SOME LAW AND ORDER SHIT,' Jroc thought as he looked around the cold room. He noticed the glass mirror which meant others was on the other side, looking in.

The officer walked in. It was quiet. Jroc could feel the officer's footsteps as he approached. The officer was silent, no words were spoken. He slid the flyer in front of Jroc and sat across from him. Jroc put his head down in defeat. Thinking he had Jroc where he wanted, he asked, "So, are you going to help me and of course help yourself?" He smirked.

Lifting his head back up, Jroc felt a surge of confidence. "Why you showing me some artwork? Am I supposed to know the person or the artist?" he asked, sliding the picture back.

"I guess you don't know this guy either?" the officer spoke. "Or him, or him, huh?" He continued to place photos in front of Jroc.

'DAMN,' Jroc thought, but remained silent and blank faced.

The pictures was of all his men on different occasions. They were close shots like somebody snapped the photos that was in their close company. It was in the moment pictures. Jroc's mind was racing and began to get scared. Then it was a few homicide photos. The two guys in the house, the two officers and what to him looked like a woman, but was a transgender, all killed in the same area.

There was a knock on the glass. Walking to the door the officer met another officer with the contents of his car. Everything Jroc just purchased was in his face bagged and tagged.

"So, what you going to do?" the officer asked again.

"Slim, I got a name in deez streets. All them pictures don't mean shit to me. Plus, that shit on the table ain't mines. You didn't even have probable cause to pull me over. My shit legit and your officers planted that shit and first and foremost I don't do no snitchin'."

Not convinced the cop pressed, "I don't know a hustler yet that did this shit and won. You sure this the route you want to go?" He paused. "I mean, all that money you making just to give it all to the lawyer sounds like hustling backward to me, but if you help me . . ."

Jroc sat there shaking his head. "I don't know what to tell you."

"Give me the murderers and I'll throw this shit away." The officer threw his duffle on the floor. "Better yet, you can take that shit with you," he propositioned.

Self-talk, Jroc looked to the sky . . . 'I DON'T KNOW IF 25

YEARS' WORTH A FEW MONTHS OF BALLIN, SHID I COULD BEAT THIS SHIT, IF I LOSE, THAT'S A BIG PILL TO SWALLOW AND I DAMN SURE AIN'T TRYNA SWALLOW IT, THAT'S DEAD. I CAN'T DO JAIL, BUT FUCK DA POLICE DRO GONNA GET ME A LAWYER FOR THESE PUNK ASS DRUGS,' he thought as the door opened and another officer came in.

"Don't think too hard baby," Heather said, placing her hand on Jroc's shoulder.

"What da fuck you doin' here?" Jroc asked, turning around to face Heather as he recognized her voice. "Fuck, fuck, fuck!" Jroc screamed, kicking the chair.

"Hey baby," Heather said walking in front of the desk. "Calm down baby."

Jroc sat back in the chair when officer brought it back to him. He sat and thought of all the stuff she knew. He was kicking it with her a while. She sucked and fucked him like a pro. All this time he thought he had a ride or die he could trust. He put her all in his business. She even sat in the trap with him and Izzo while they bust down a couple bricks. This shit was over for him.

"After Heather write a confession, you goin' down unless you help put the pieces in the right places," the first officer asked. Jroc didn't say a word, only grabbed the pen as Heather smiled.

Izzo bent the corner and seen Dro shooting craps with niggas from round da' way. "Bet $50 on my man come out!" he yelled, trying to get a bet before the dice left his hand.

"You ain't sayin' nuffin' Prophet, bet nigga." The fader accepted. The dice left Dro's hand, click clack and the dice stopped on a four and three. "That's my nigga!" Izzo said, collecting his money.

Dro got up and said, "I'm gone, got shit to do."

"Come on, moe, that's wild as shit," the fader expressed. Dro followed the voice and dropped a blue face.

"$100 my shot, you got me?" It got quiet. Dro and Izzo stepped off, leaving the money on the ground. "Bottle on me," he said, never looking back. Dro looked at Izzo and told him to take a ride with him as he hit his car alarm.

"No doubt, what's the move?" Izzo wanted to know.

"I gotta go uptown to pick this bread up from this nigga. You know it's hot as shit up there and I ain't tryna get pressed in this whip in that neighborhood."

"Scared nigga," Izzo joked.

"As a mutha fucka, you better be too."

They got in Dro's recently purchased Mercedes CL 65 AMG Coupe, valued at $215,000 bands. To be alias Dro drove the back streets to avoid as many police as possible. Pulling up on a bunch of young niggas they didn't act crazy because they knew the car. It was one of the blocks that Dro supplied. "Psycho!" he called one of the young hustlers. The kid came out and dropped a duffle in the car and dapped up Dro, then looked to the passenger seat.

"Oh shit, it's Prophet!" he screamed, goin from gangsta to fan in a millisecond. "Bruh, let me get a pic with you, pussy rate gonna fly high," Psycho asked leaning in for a selfie. Izzo didn't mind as long as niggas didn't make a scene.

Headed back down the Ave, McDonald's was the pit stop. They had the munchies. Riding with that sour diesel in the air had their stomach on empty. "Wanna go in?" Dro asked, pulling in.

"Not really, not tryna be flooded ya know, by fans." Izzo looked at Dro and smirked. "But since I don't like Drive-Thru's I guess we could go in and enjoy a quick meal. Where Black ass at anyway, ain't he security?" Izzo said jokingly. Dro laughed.

Walking in the restaurant it wasn't that crowded. "Damn." Izzo licked his lips. "Them fries smell good as shit."

They made it to the front and ordered their food. Crush,

wouldn't even be justice to describe what they did to the food. After the meal they went back to the car. Dro noticed a foreign sight.

"Aye Slim, ain't that Jroc?" he said, pointing to the 4th district Police Station entrance.

Izzo squinted his eyes trying to focus them. "Hell . . . yeah that's that nigga. Fuck he doin' shaking that pig's hand?" Dro was shaking his head still in disbelief. "Nah bruh,' say it ain't so."

"Kill, matter fact the nigga hit me earlier on the text saying he got pulled over or some shit like that. Let's just see if he tell us later," Izzo said.

"No wonder he ain't been answering my calls."

"Let's bounce, Slim."

"Hold fast, look," Dro pointed.

Jroc walked down the steps to an undercover squad car. The driver got out and leaned on the car. "Is that Heather?" She had a pair of keys dangling.

"Yeah, bruh that's what I was talking about, and she got a police belt and a pistol. She the police homes."

"Damn, they set his dumb ass up," Izzo concluded. "Break out before they see us."

❖   ❖   ❖

On Sight Plain 'n Simple
"Draws too, nigga!"
— Black

Black just dropped his sisters off at his house with Keisha. Cruising through the city, smoking some pack, he decided to ride past Victoria's house for no particular reason. Well, maybe to see if he could luck up. He called Izzo earlier, but he was in the studio doing his thing or he would've had him with him.

Riding down his girl's old neighborhood he spoke to himself. "Looky here." Black seen Victoria coming out of the house, walking to a parked car that wasn't there last time he came. He peeked in the car to see it empty. 'GOT YOUR HOT ASS, BITCH!' Black thought as he jumped out of the car.

Noticing Black, Victoria had a bad feeling and tried to close her door to hurry back to the house. Black was on her ass. "In a rush?" Black asked, joggin' in front of her, cutting her off as he drew his gun at her face, forcing her to stop dead in her tracks.

Her hands were to the sky, and she knew what he was here for. "Please, I won't testify."

BOOM!

Black walked over her limp body. "You already did when you drew that picture."

BOOM! BOOM! BOOM!

"Oh my God!!" Black turned to the sound of the scream.

"Victoria! No, no. Somebody help!" The older lady ran up on Black.

"What did you do Shawn. Whyyy!" She hugged the corpse of her grandchild. Black looked to his left, then to his right. "Sorry granny, but I ain't goin' to jail.

BOOM! BOOM! BOOM!

The lady laid on top of Victoria—dead.

Black jogged back to his car and pulled off. He was headed back home. He never went outside without a full clip and he just damn near emptied his gun. Parking his car his phone rang. "Wut it do, boss?" he answered.

"Bruh, I gotta see you asap," Dro stated.

"A'ight, give me a minute. I just came in the house to grab sumthin'."

"Stay home. Me and Izzo on da way there."

"Yup, I'm here."

❖   ❖   ❖

Inside the house Black smelled the food and instantly got hungry. Shaniyah and Shanae was stuffing their faces as Keisha was still cooking in a white short t-shirt and boy shorts. "Aye Boo, Izzo and Dro on the way."

"Okay, I'll make enough for them," she said, not even turning around.

"Fuck day' stomach. I was telling you that so your ass could put some damn clothes on woman." The girls giggled.

Black headed to the basement and started playing his game system. He was tuned in for about an hour with his sisters watching him pay as well. He be in another world when that Call of Duty be on the screen. "Niggah, I know you hear me calling you!" Keisha said with her hands on her hips. Black didn't even turn around. Just responded, "I know you better watch ur' mouth around my babies."

"Tsst." She smacked her teeth. "Sorry bae, but I was callin' you to tell you your brothers here."

"A'ight, send 'em down. What they need to make a grand entrance or some shit."

Coming down the stairs Izzo was the first to speak. "Bruh, you ain't gonna believe this shit—"

"Did you talk to Jroc?" Dro interrupted Izzo.

"Hold up, one at a time. Raise your hands." Black was on joke time. "But nah, I ain't talk to that fool. Sup' wit em'?"

"Moe, we just came from uptown—"

Black put his hand up, cutting Dro off and told his sisters to go upstairs. He knew this conversation wasn't for them. "A'ight go ahead."

"We was picking up some money and seen Jroc come out the police station," Dro finished.

"Nigga, that ain't it. The white bitch he fucking, uhhh what's that bitch name . . . Heather, she them peoples, fuckin' D.E.A., nigga," Izzo said stating the facts.

Black sat there shaking his head. Mad would be an understatement. "Is he tellin' or what?"

"We don't know yet. We was gonna see how he act, but make sure y'all don't do nothing to incriminate yourselves around him until we get to the bottom of this," Dro said.

"What about the witness?" Izzo asked.

Black smiled. "Done."

"We gotta handle that police bitch too," Izzo said. "She done been in my trap and all. Slim, she know too fuckin' much." Everyone agreed on that, but Black was still elsewhere. "What about Jroc?" he asked again.

"I know, I know, but wait. We don't have the facts yet," Dro stated.

"Facts? Yeah, okay. I know what it look like and you was there too," Izzo said while making the talking sign with his hands.

Everybody had mixed thoughts, but Black was more on that get that nigga before he get me type shit. He always told himself he would hold court in the street before he go to jail forever. Smoke filled the air in Black's den. Endless blunts were getting passed back-to-back. In the middle of the bullshit Keisha brung the fellas some munchies. She even had a bottle of Patron' to calm the nerves. She knew something had happened. She could feel the vibes but decided to stay in her place and don't question Black, especially when company was around. As Black opened the bottle, Dro's phone rang. It was a text: 'WHATS GOOD.'

Dro lifted the phone in the air so everyone could see it. They shook their head in disgust.

'SHT, WAT UP.'

'OH, I WAS RETURNING YOUR CALL FROM EARLI-ER.'

'I HAD SOMETHING 4 U BUT THATS DEAD NOW.'

'THATS A BET, WY@'

Dro showed his phone to Black who grabbed it and typed:

'@ BLACK CRIB COME THRU.'

Izzo was geeked in his questioning. "What you gonna do when he get here?"

"Get to the bottom of this shit," Black said smiling.

Black walked to get some air on the porch. He sat on the stoop and watched his sisters play in the yard as he smoked a jack'. Halfway into his cigarette Dro came out and fired one up as well. "It's funny that dudes smoke tree in the crib, but won't smoke no jacks in there," Black said, not even looking at him.

Izzo came out as well. "Let me hit one of them jacks."

Dro ignored him and spoke to Black. "Y'all got a nice spot out here, Slim."

"Yeah, preciate it, and I'm tryna keep it too. I hope I don't have to punish this nigga."

"I feel you bruh, me too," Dro stated, pulling the jack for the final drag, then puttin' it in the ashtray.

"Oh, it's like that?" Izzo said when he realized both jacks was gone. They got up to go back to the den and chill.

After about an hour there was a knock at the door. Keisha opened her front door. "Hey boy!" she said, hugging Jroc.

"Sup girl," Jroc said, half hugging her back. "Where my niggas at?"

"Downstairs . . . BLACK!" she screamed. "Go ahead down there." She pointed to the steps.

Jroc walked down the stairs with a heavy hart and a lot on his mind. "Damn, I smell it. Can I inhale it?" Jroc said making his presence known as he reached the bottom step.

"Sup bruh, wat up wit it?" Dro dapped him up. "You a'ight, fuck you do today?"

"Here, buddy ol' pal, take a pull of the high power and tell us about your day," Izzo said sarcastically.

"My nigga!" Jroc gladly accepted the jay'. "But shit, may day was a'ight up until after I left school, then it got wild."

"Is that right, elaborate," Black said, standing up now in front of Jroc. Jroc didn't even catch the approach. He just inhaled the jay but continued. "Shit was crazy, Slim, on my movah. I got pulled over and booked," Jroc confessed.

"And?" Dro pushed.

"You ain't gonna believe this shit either. My bitch . . . you know, Heather." Jroc shook his own head for what was about to come next.

"What the fuck, nigga, talk!" Black grew impatient.

"She the police homes," Jroc said in defeat. "They gave me to the end of the week to come back and tell them something or girl that lived by Keisha's old house that didn't die from that robbery we did—"

WOP!

Black stole off on him. "Damn bruh. What you hit me for?" Jroc asked from the floor as Dro grabbed Black.

"Shut up nigga! We ain't do shit together. Now strip before I blow your face off," Black said about to whip out his gun.

"Chill Black. Fuck you doing?" Dro asked, trying to intervene, but to no avail.

"You ain't just hear this nigga. Talking 'bout some robbery we did. Nigga, I ain't do shit. Now take that shit off."

Jroc was scared to death. He was thinking he should have chosen his words better. Now his homies think he hot when he didn't give them no information. So, him knowing Black he didn't chance a threat made by him and began to take his shit off down to his briefs. "Drawers too, nigga!" Black said.

"Whoa, whoa, whoa," was Izzo's first words. "Why the fuck the nigga gotta get naked? I don't want no cheeks!"

"Shut your dumb ass up. He might got a wire on him or in his ass," Black said dead ass serious.

"Well, good luck looking for it," Izzo said, turning around flicking the game back on.

Jroc told himself he wasn't goin' out like that. "Fuck you nigga. I ain't taking shit else off. I ain't hot so do you!"

Dro was goin' through Jroc's phone, and everything looked normal. "Put your shit back on, scary ass nigga," Black said.

"That's crazy, moe," Jroc said, pulling up his shorts.

"Ain't shit crazy about it. We seen you coming out the police station," Izzo stated not even looking back as he spoke.

"Fuck all that!" Dro said, shutting them up. "So, what they got! What they know?" Dro quizzed.

"Nothing really. All they got is me hustling in school. Now they investigating the homicides so I gotta get to that witness. Peep this, they even gave me my shit back and told me they had bigger fish to fry, and I got til' the end of the week to tell them something."

"What's up wit' your bitch?" Black spat.

"Already told you," Jroc said, but turned his attention back to everyone. "She smokin' hot, she da' police."

"We gonna have to smoke her ass too," Izzo chimed in.

"First I gotta get the witness," Jroc thought out loud.

Izzo and Dro looked at Black as Jroc said that last comment, but Black responded. "Yeah, that sound 'bout right. Handle your business. Let us know when it's done." Jroc left, headed up the stairs to put his plans of engagement into effect. "Later," he said and was gone.

Izzo looked at Black. "Why you ain't tell him the witness already dead?"

"Cause, I'm still leery. Not sure if I could trust him all the way," Black said.

"So, what y'all think?" Dro asked. Both of them shook their heads, but Izzo asked, "What's the plan?"

"Heather's the plan," Black said with venom.

CHAPTER 39

"Prophet!!"
— Groupie

After leaving Black's house Dro decided to stop by his house to change cars. They were cramped in the coupe, so he wanted to get his '96 Impala. Dro had it repainted and the whole interior looked like this year's model, only the old frame.

In the car many topics came about, one being the situation with Jroc. Black was still on the edge and was trying to knock out any and all loose links out the chain that had the power to cause damage. Last result was to punish Jroc, but only if he had to. The car was smoked out. If Dro would have opened a window, big clouds of OG kush would've came out. They pulled up to the hood and Dro parked in front of his grandmother's house, and they walked down bottom.

Everybody was out. It was a couple crap games, ceelo games, niggas smoking, drinking and hustling.' Just another day in the hood.

"Aye fool, I'll be back. I'm bouta go check my trap," Izzo said, stepping off.

"Me too, Slim. Bouta go check on my lil rugrats," Black said, talking about his sisters.

Dro looked at both of them without words he chucked the deuces. Dro was chilling on the gate by the main intersection of his hood, Rst. His head was heavy. 'SHIT WAS ALL GOOD JUST A WEEK AGO' he thought as he fired up a jack. He walked to the store to get a pint of something to drink on. Entering the store a few of the neighborhood regulars was chilling in the store doing they own thing. "James, what's up?" Dro spoke to the store clerk.

"Hiiiii," the Korean clerk spoke.

"You good, Slim?"

In broken English he responded, "Yah, fine."

"That's what's up, any discounts today?" The clerk smiled. "Just had to check and make sure," Dro giggled. "But uh let me get a pint of Patron and a Lime Tropicana."

"Ice cup?"

"No question."

"24.95."

Dro exited the store stopping in front of it. He poured the ice out. He placed everything on top of a parked car that was in front of the store, and he mixed his drink. His phone buzzed and he answered. "Hey young lady." It was his grandmother.

"Hello sweetie. Are you around here?" she asked before Dro could answer. She continued, "I see your car out front. Can you go and get me a coffee from 7-eleven with a few hazel nut creamers?"

Dro smiled. "Anything for you. I'll get it for you and be there in a few."

❖   ❖   ❖

Izzo walked in the trap and didn't know if he should be mad or what. It was 6 lil' broads dancing to the go-go beat in thongs and nothing else. One getting fucked and another sucking dick. The look on the young boy's face told it all. 'AWWWW SHIT' was the expression. Izzo understood that they wanted to get their dicks wet so he ain't trip. He called his LT. "First things first. I hope you got that if y'all in here like this," Izzo said to the young goon, and he got up and went to the back and came back with the duffle.

Izzo was eyeing all the potential in the room. They watched him as he spoke. "If y'all wanna stay up in my spot, somebody gotta pay the cover fee."

One girl jumped off the young boy's lap. "Prophet!!" she screamed excited. "And what might that cover fee consist of?" She licked her lips.

Looking to the sky, scratching his chin, "Um, nothing much, just get down on your knees and show me you love me."

She didn't waste no time. She sucked the dick with emotion. The crazy part was she would look at it eye to eye, then kiss it and then suck it all over again.

After the deed was done, she got up and smile. "Can I get a picture?"

Izzo ain't have no slow neck like that in a minute, so he definitely enjoyed it. "For that performance, I'll take two." He posed, Izzo tossed her $100 and his phone.

"Put your number in there under slow neck," she complied anxiously.

He headed for the door. "A'ight lil niggas, put them hats on, and make me look good."

Black was walking. To the left at the corner, he noticed the car that had been on his line lately, sitting idle with smoke coming out the slits of the windows. He was watching the window cause if it came down any further, he was gonna let the gun talk and forget anybody was outside. The back passenger window had a paper in his hand and 2 fingertips dangling out the window as it came down slowly. Black drew his weapon but placed it on his side. The inside of the car was dark, but the tattoo on the dude's hand looked familiar, but he couldn't place it.

Dude dropped the paper on the ground and raised the window back up cruising off. Black looked around. 'WHAT DA FUCK.' He walked toward the paper and put it in his pocket and walked to the courtyard off the main street then read it:

THE TIME IS NEAR FOR YOU TO PAY YOUR DEBT.

Black was lost but the tattoo was real familiar, but he couldn't place it for nothing. Black was coolin' in the crib and his sisters was good. They got dropped off by Keisha an hour ago. Really he was there to check on his money and guns. His fingers was itching and it wasn't a money feeling. It was the feeling of death by his hands.

While in his room, he checked his inventory of bullets and pistols to see if he needed to re-up or not. "DONTE!" his mom yelled from the other room.

"Yeah, what up?"

"You got any money?"

"Usually, I try to keep a few dollars. Thanking for asking." Black smiled at his own joke.

"For me boy. I need a couple of dollars."

"Here," he said, tossing her $50.

Black left the crib and made his way outside. He was nervous to see what was up with this situation. He knew if shit went sour, out of the whole crew he would be doin' the most time. If he just go with pistol all would be solved in his mind. There was the devil on one shoulder and an angel on the other having a tug of war in his ear. Then this dude keep poppin' up. He was stuck.

"Fuck!" he screamed to the sky. Then a fat jay of haze was the antidote to ease his mind.

❖   ❖   ❖

Jroc
"Let's run away."
— Heather

'Damn this shit fucked up.'

It's just me and this black and white ivy I'm blowing as I cruise down the street. I gotta see what's up with this chick Victoria, but then my chick acting crazy as well. She hit me with a text, talking 'bout she miss me and come see her. That shit had me trippin' out, but I put that in the back of my mind as I decided to drive to the other shawty's house. I didn't know what I was gonna do, but I had my gun with me.

Heather been blowing my phone up, but I didn't answer it. 'SNAKE BITCH.' She had all the sense, so she thought, but I got her ass. I was on another mission right now. In the car I got closer to her crib, Victoria's that is, unannounced. 'HERE I GO' I thought as I pulled up on her block.

Goin' down her street I was checking the scenery to see what was up. "Oh shit!" I said out loud as I rode past her residence that was taped off with crime scene tape. I parked on the side street. 'I GOTTA SEE WHAT HAPPENED.' I was walking then it hit me. 'WHAT THE FUCK YOU THINKING.' I turned around swiftly, got in my shit and pulled off.

I wanted to call my men, but really right now they ain't fuckin' with me til I fix this shit or Black gonna try and see me. I know that look I seen in his eyes. I'm no fool.

Since Victoria was gone, I decided to pop up on Heather and see what this bitch up to. I went to her door and was about to knock but said fuck it. I grabbed the knob. It was open. I went to the fridge and opened it as well and drank a soda from the bottle and bit into an open sandwich that was in the microwave.

I even fired up a jay and I never smoke in here. Now I know why she didn't want me to smoke weed in her. Fuckin' cop, but now I don't give a fuck. Walking up the steps I heard music in the backroom where I guess her hot ass was at. I followed the music, then opened the door. There she was in the mirror dancing, practicing twerking lookin' silly as shit, but sexy in her panties and pumps. She didn't even hear me come in. I smirked, but quickly wiped the smile off when she turned around. She smelled the weed. "Uh James, put that mess out!" she said, fanning the smoke. I grabbed her hand forcefully and pulled her toward me. She moaned.

I looked at her with evil eyes, trying to hold my composure. But she licked her lips seductively and bit her bottom lip. My hate turned to lust as I grabbed her neck. She breathed in heavy. I forced her to the wall. Her back hit hard. I put my tongue down her throat. She accepted it. "Oh my God James, what are you doing?" she asked in between breaths.

"I love you baby. I can't help it," I said, just to see where her head was at.

"Oh my God baby, I love you too!" she exhaled. "With all my heart."

I smiled, kissing her neck and made my way down to her nipples. 'I GOT HER.'

She loved when I showed each nipple the same amount of attention, then it was her stomach. Sliding her panties off, I lifted her up and put her legs around my shoulders. I followed the trail of hair that led to her clit. She had a landing strp of pubic hairs.

"Daaaadddyyyy!!" she moaned once I got to the end of the path. I ate that the pussy with no regard to the fact that fed was tryna put me and my men away for life. What she didn't know was the power of words and sex would have her doing anything for me. My plan was to get this bitch on the team before I let her bring me down.

I might not be the best hustler, but I'm the world's greatest when it comes to getting into these bitch's heads. Just another one on the list. By the time I finished eating the box, she was shaking, begging for the dick. That's what she wanted; dick, so dick is what I gave her in every hole big enough. We fucked for 'bout 45 minutes and was exhausted.

Getting in the shower together, she washed me, and I returned the favor. Now my game began as she spoke. "You know I love you for real, right?" Heather asked softly.

"I love you too baby, with every breath in my body." I poured it on thick.

"Let's run away," she said, looking me in the eyes.

I had to choose my words carefully. She was really looking for an answer. "Nah boo, we can't. We gonna get through this," I started, took a breath. "If you really love me," I licked my lips. "You'll make sure we be together, free and forever. I wanna make you my wife." I rubbed her cheek. She stopped washing me and put both her hands to her face like I just proposed or some shit and started crying. I pulled her close. "I'll never leave you, okay," I said as she squeezed me tightly.

Heather

"Shid, we getting married."

'OH MY GOD, WHAT AM I DOING?' I fell for the bad guy and I'm in love, I think. He really not bad for real. I wish he could just give his friends up so we could live happily ever after. Never has anybody ever treated me like he does. I don't want to lose this feeling. I'll do anything for my man. He got me and don't even know it. I'll quit all this if he say the word. I don't know if my real daddy would accept him, but I don't care.

We just had an awesome sex session. He said he had something to do and left after his shower. I don't know how he did it to me, but I'm not even disappointed. I sat on my bed flipping channels with thoughts of James in my head and my phone buzzed. 'I HOPE IT AIN'T WORK' I thought, reaching for my purse to grab my phone.

Nope, it was my friend Tiara, my homegirl. That's what she calls me, her homegirl. A newfound friend. I love hanging with the girls. It's a different experience than I'm used to. I never had that either, real girlfriends. They have so much flavah, another word I learned. Sliding my phone, the message read:

> "Hey gurly wats da move 2nite"
>
> "Hey I'm not doin' anything my boo
>
> just sexed me senseless :) so I know he
>
> good 4 2nite, I'm avail"
>
> "sexed you . . . lol . . . girl he fucked
>
> you . . . that's wat us say, we goin
>
> out girls only."
>
> "lol . . . ok . . . time and place"
>
> "be ready @11:00"

I closed my phone excited. I knew I couldn't give up my new life. It was way better than my old life. My baby could take care of me, and I had the inside scoop, so how could we lose? 'FORGET THIS CASE' I thought as I finished getting myself together.

Now I had plans for tonight, but I had to head back to the office to report. After my boo's fragrance lingered from the bathroom it reminded me I needed to get back in the shower too. Thoughts of him had me cumming all over again. The shower felt so good as I washed all the sex away. I was nervous cause when he took his pussy, he didn't even wear a protective hat and I didn't even care.

I got in the car after I locked my house. I was headed back to work. When I walked in my office, my captain was on my heels. "How's the case going?" he asked.

"It's coming along. I am trying to get the subject to turn for us," I told him. He was persistent and stayed on my line, but I was never goin' to turn my baby in. 'SHID, WE GETTING MARRIED.' I wasn't going to mess that up. That's how I felt as I sat at my desk, then I received a text: "I LOVE YOU BABY." That put a smile on my face.

I had a big plate and it seemed to only be getting bigger. But for some reason I didn't even care. Work was goin' by for the most part. I did my recon in my area as I drove through high-risk drug areas uptown. It was incident free, maybe cause I wasn't looking for anything. Now it was time to clock out and head home. Tonight is ladies night and my boo said he just brought me some shit so my girls aren't gonna show out on me . . . again.

CHAPTER 40

Timing Is Everything

"I'm innocent."
— Black

Charmine and Tiara was on the way to Heather's house to pick her up. Tonight, was ladies' night. They had it all planned out. The guys didn't know anything. Each of them told the guys they were goin' out, but not with who and where. Arriving at Heather's, Charmine and Tiara were shocked to see her house.

"Is this the right address?" Charmine scrolled through her google maps.

"Damn girl, what this bitch do to live in this uppity ass neighborhood?" Tiara joked, looking at the nice houses sectioned off by a nice lawn and fences.

"Girl, I don't know, but she better bring her high yellow ass on."

BEEP! BEEP!

Jroc never came back in so she just sent him a text tellin' him she was goin' out and would see him later. Heather came out, locked her door and walked down her stairs. She was all smiles when she seen Tiara and Charmine. "Hey girls."

"Look at this bitch here." Tiara smiled. "Snowflake got ass too!"

"Stop playing." She blushed. "Where's Keisha?" Heather asked, closing the car door.

"She the next stop," Charmine answered.

They rode listening to Ty Dolla $ign ft. Lil' wayne 'LOVE YOU BETTER,' singing to the beat like it was their own song. They were getting in party mood. Arriving at Keisha's house the same routine took place. There was honk but no response. Charmine called, but now answer. Livid, she got out of the car and walked to the door.

KNOCK! KNOCK!

"Sup lil Dro. Why da long face?" Black asked lookin' her up and down. "Where y'all goin' at lookin' how y'all lookin?" He finished, trying to see who was in the car, but to no avail. It was smacked out (tinted).

"We goin' out, now move." She pushed past Black. "Where dat hefa at?"

"Here she is boo!" Keisha was excited. Black stood in front of her with questioning eyes. "Move niccah, it's ladies' night, no dicks allowed."

"BETTER NOT BE NO DICKS!!" Black yelled to her back.

Charmine looked back. "I'll take good care of her for you," and winked.

Black walked back in the crib and decided to call Izzo. "What's up Blacker than me?" Izzo answered.

"Fuck you at?"

"Just left the studio about 5 minutes away from the hood now."

"We goin' through tonight, you down?"

"Sayless."

"I'm on my way."

CLICK!

Black hopped in the shower and made it quick. After getting wet, he threw on some jeans and a light hoodie. It was still hot outside as he left, headed to his car to go up top. His car was in the shop. He was getting it armored proof. Dro had requested it and even paid for it so Black didn't mind. That left him with one of the labels cars to play around in. The record company just dropped it off earlier, but he didn't even come outside to see what type of car it was. The car was sexy, a blacked-out hand-built AMG Coupe by Mercedes. It had the S&G logo on the back window. The only thing Black didn't like, other than that she was exotic. Driving down East Capital, the northeast side of D.C., Black decided to make a pit stop. He pulled around Clay Terrace for a minute to get him a Dipah' (PCP) that usually put him in kill mode. Smoking and driving he hit the wet cigarette to the face, and it had him on his level.

He pulled up around the way with Will Tha Rapper on the repeat and parked in front of Izzo's trap rappin the chorus:

"I pull up hop out you girl she on my dick, whoa I work out and purp out her nigga better shoot, so I told 'em hop out or pull up he say he wanna kill me oh so why he actin' scary, he got a 30 I know he wouldn't blow, no."

It was 11:45 p.m. and still was live outside. He left his car running with the music loud goin' up the steps. One of the young boys must have been new and didn't know better.

"Aye unc. I ain't tell you come up these steps." Black looked behind himself, then the other young boys who looked away, then back to the voice that was talking. Black thought the goop was fucking with him, but lil' man held his stance.

The other young boys were bubble-eyed. Nobody moved or flinched. They knew Black was crazy and any sudden movements could cost you your life, especially in this state of mind.

Black smirked. His face didn't match his actions. "Nigga!" Black whipped out his gun, pointing the cannon dead to the kid's face. "Empty your pockets, fool!" Young boy froze for a second, looked around and seen that nobody was coming to his aid. He emptied his pockets giving Black about $1,500 of Izzo's money.

The kid spoke. "You don't know who money you fuckin' with."

WOP!

Black slapped shawty with the gun. "Nah nigga, you don't know who you fuckin' with. I'm the fuckin' law around here. Tell Izzo Big Black came looking for him and to take this money out your cut for the month, pussy nigga." Black kicked him in his stomach, then looked over to the kid on the step smoking. "Y'all ain't let this new nigga know what's up, um peeettty."

Izzo came from the cut and seen Black leaving his trap. They met in the middle of the block. "Ready!" Black asked.

"No doubt, I guess we ain't doing nothing too crazy. I see that pretty ass exotic bitch parked out front."

"My shit in the shop, we ain't driving that."

They walked through the parking lot and got into one of the many SUVs that were always in the hood. That's all the young boys did; steal cars and joyride, trying to get some pussy. Some sell the parts, the smart ones. It's safe to say if you don't mind the heat you're never stranded. It's always a bucket on standby.

Riding down the street, Izzo fire dup a jay, hit it a few times and passed it to Black. They rode in silence to their own thoughts until Izzo started to notice the area he was in.

"Slim, what the fuck we doing around here?"

"To handle unfinished business once and for all," Black said, as he glared at the house. Shaking his head, Izzo blew smoke. "Cold blooded . . . Did you tell Jroc?" Izzo plucked the jack and rolled the window back up.

"Fuck Jroc!" Black gritted. "I'm not waiting on him to dictate my future."

"Cool wit' me," Izzo agreed.

"You scraped right?"

Izzo reached for his hip, grabbing his gun and chambered a round. "Glock full, like the moon in the sky, nigga."

Pulling up across the street from Heather's house, a few lights was on. This was going to turn the heat up on things. Killing a cop was usually a no-no, but circumstances changed Black's mind. "Call Jroc," Black stated. "See where he at." Izzo called him and found out he was at home, playing his game system. So that meant it was go time.

Looking around, they jogged to the front door and kicked it in. All they heard was music. Running through the house they couldn't find her, or nobody else. Black found her badge and decided to take it. He left her police issued sidearm on the desk. Black wasn't satisfied. He went to the garage to see if she was hiding but ran into a gasoline pail. Rage and the mixture of the different toxic fumes in his body had him ready to lunch-out. He started pouring the gas everywhere in the house.

Izzo ran into him with a look of shock. "Black, what the f—, come on nigga, time to go," he said, pulling Black's arms. He was in a demonic trance of some sort. Black pulled away when he made it to the door and dropped the empty pail, then grabbed a piece of mail that was on the side table at the door. He lit the mail on fire with a psychotic laugh and tossed it. He watched it ignite. A flame trail shot across the house and that's all she wrote.

They hopped back in the car and Black fishtailed out the parking spot. "Fuck you doin'!" Izzo asked, grabbing his seatbelt. "WATCH OUT!"

SMACK!

Water shot to the sky as Black drove through the fire hydrant that was on the corner. "So, they can't put the burning furniture out," he said, laughing hysterically.

"Nigga, you crazy."

"Nah nigga. I just put work in until it all work out," Black said, slowing down after bending the corner. "So, what you 'bout to do?" he nonchalantly asked as if he didn't just set fire to a federal officer's home.

"Slim, you burnt. Take me back around da way," Izzo said, not believing this shit just happened.

Dro been chillin' on the block for a minute. He kept getting texts from his girl, so he knew she was having a good time. Black made it to Dro's and put his hand out for dap after he parked the car and was overly excited. Accepting his hand, Dro asked, "What you just finished doing? You look suspect."

Black raised his arms. "Damn homie, why I had to have just done something? I'm innocent." He flashed his rare smile.

"Yeah, I know it. I was looking for y'all and they told me y'all pulled off in a bucket, Mr. Innocent."

"Damn, somebody always watchin' a nigga. But Izzo at 7-eleven," Black said, dodging the question.

"You right. I don't even wanna know," Dro surrendered.

Black laughed. "It's for the best."

Izzo came back with a bag full of bullshit—all snacks. "Bruh, hurry up. We waiting on you. We 'bout to go up top to hit the bar," Dro said.

"That's a bet. Fuckin' with Black a nigga need a couple of drinks, crazy ass nigga." Dro just shook his head, knowing that they just got done doing some bullshit.

"Moe, Jroc out here?" Black asked.

"Nah, but he posted on Instagram saying he still playing online," Dro answered, scrolling down his phone.

"Fuck dat. Let's go to this bar," Izzo said, taking the lead.

Ladies' night and that's exactly what it was. The girls were having the time of they life, but the night was getting away from them. They had their share of dances, drinks and girls and guys hitting on them. It was a good fun night, and it was time to roll.

If it wasn't for Charmine being the soberest, no telling what they would have gotten into.

"Okay ladies, time to go." Charmine tried to round everyone up. Heather was dancing with a girl who she thought was a man. Keisha and Tiara were with each other, dancing like they were at a strip club. Charmine just started grabbing them one by one.

Finally, she retrieved them all and headed for the exit. Outside the club they were still hyped. Heather began to talk but was slurring. "Oh . . . my . . . God. I never had . . . so much ffffuunn in myyy liiiiiiifffffe you guys."

"Yeah gurl." Tiara slapped fives with Keisha. "That's cause you ain't got no hood bitches as friends in your clique, witcho' uppity ass." They laughed.

"I need a jay," Keisha said, and Tiara was quick to respond.

"Bitch, I got one fat ass spliff in the car."

Charmine didn't like the sound of that. "Bitch, no you didn't."

"Chill girl. It's only a jay, girl," Tiara said. "And ain't that shit legal anyway now?"

They made it to the car and was on the way. "Fire up, bitch!" Keisha said. The blunt was in rotation. Everybody was high out of their mind, even Heather. She tried not to inhale, but the shotguns Keisha was blowing her went straight to her brain.

"No wonder it's called train wreck. I swear I'm seeing stars," Heather said all giggly and goofy like.

Charmine was driving and the first drop-off was Tiara. She was the closest. After that was Heather. As they drove further uptown everybody was in their own world enjoying the ride. Tiara was gone as Charmine turned down heather's block. It was lit with police cruisers everywhere. "What the hell happened in this Mr. Rogers ass neighborhood?" Kiesha joked.

As they got closer, the answer to the question was answered. At the same time, they noticed it was Heather's home looking like burnt sticks and ash. Heather jumped out of the car and ran to her house to be grabbed off her feet by an officer. "Hold on Miss. You can't go in there. Are you a resident?" the uniformed officer asked.

In between sobs she answered, "Yes, that's my home."

"Was anyone in there?"

"No, I don't thin so," she replied in between sniffs.

At the same moment another officer came over in regular clothes and asked, "Heather are you okay?" The voice was familiar as she turned around to see it was her old partner. She rushed into his arms for comfort as her 'new' friends came up beside her and grabbed her.

"We got her sir." Charmine pulled her away.

"I'll talk to you later, officer," Heather said, walking away with the girls, trying to make sure her fellow officer didn't blow her case. They all went to the car and pulled off as Charmine spoke. "What they say happened, girl?"

"They don't know yet."

"I've been calling Jroc but no answer," Charmine said sympathetically. Heather balled up in the backseat of the car as Keisha offered her comfort.

"You can stay with me tonight."

"Thank you," she replied softly. Charmine pulled in front of Keisha's house and said her goodbyes to both of them as they got out, then she pulled off into the night.

CHAPTER 41

Best Of Both Worlds

"Shhh, you loud boy."
— Heather

Keisha and Heather walked in the house and headed to the living room to talk for a while. Heather was distraught and sad, thinking how the day went from great to a disaster. They drank a lot more and smoked to try to change the mood. She smoked as if she didn't even own a badge. This put them on another level, and they decided to call it a night. "Girl, I'm gone to bed. You can use the spare room. Clean linen and shit in the bathroom," Keisha said going up the stairs. Heather decided to take her up on her invitation and followed her up the stairs. "I'ma get in the shower."

"Okay girl. I'll be in there to wash your back," Keisha said, jokingly.

"Whatever girl. I'll leave it unlocked just for you," Heather said going in the bathroom. She didn't waste any time and went straight to it and got naked to let the hot water ease her mind.

Black pulled up at the house, twisted. The bar did him justice. He was surprised to how he made it home without fucking up his whip—well, the S&G company car. Walking through the house he smelled the tree in the air—his tree and it lingered. Climbing the stairs, Black heard the shower. He started to go in the room but decided some shower sex would be better and a great happy ending.

As he walked to the door, thoughts of Keisha's body made his dick jump. Opening the door real slow, he couldn't see anything. It was foggy to the limit of no sight. You had to put your arm out to guide you if you weren't familiar with the layout. Black had one of the sliding doors entrances to the shower. He shut the door and stripped down. Looking at the outline of Keisha's body, his manhood was fully erect. He got up behind Heather, poking her cheeks with his dick. In his mind, it was Keisha.

Heather was high as a kite but felt the dick on her ass. She smiled. Heather thought it was Keisha playing around with a dildo or some other freaky toy. "Um, stop playing," she moaned. That only turned Black on more. He began rubbing her breasts with one hand as he put his dick in her from the back.

"Dayum, it feels so good," Heather said, throwing it back as Black gave her that intoxicated dick. Black felt himself 'bout to cum and gave her the jackrabbit stroke. He was sweating bullets in the hot and steamy shower. He came so hard, he fell on Heather's back with a barely audible grunt, then hugged her from behind through the sweat and fog.

Heather was hunched over, trying to catch her breath as well when she turned the water off. "Damn Keisha, where that come from?" she asked, turning around as Black dropped his arms looking at Heather with pure shock.

"Oh shit!" Black stepped out of the shower. "What the fuck you doing in here?" he asked in hushed tones.

"Oh, my goodness, this is not what I planned nor was my intentions." Heather hurried, wrapping herself in a towel.

"Where Keisha at?" he whispered.

"In her room laying down. We came from the club about 2 hours ago and my home was burned down." Black smirked but hid it well. "She let me stay here for the night."

"Fuck! You better not say shit or she gonna fuck 'you' up," Black said, turning the water back on to wash Heather off his dick.

"I won't, I promise."

"Damn . . . I literally just fucked da police," Black mumbled to himself.

"Huh?" Heather turned around.

"Nothing, I'm 'bout to hop in this shower. Care to join me?" Black laughed. "But for the record, you got some grade A pussy. I see why that nigga gone off you," he said, sliding the door close.

Heather walked to the shower door and opened it. "Shut the fuck up Black. You nasty and you not ever going to get no more of this grade A either," she told him. She was mad at herself because she enjoyed it and was better than Jroc. It felt fuller and more like a glove inside her. She knew it was wrong, but it felt so right.

The next morning Black walked around the house like nothing had happened. He didn't feel bad about it because she was the enemy and if it was up to him he would kill her ass right now, but to many people he was aware of her whereabouts.

"Good morning sleeping beauty," Keisha said to Heather as she walked into the kitchen.

"Hey girl." She spoke just above a whisper. She was drained from the pound game of last night.

"You look like you had a long night and good fuckin' or some shit," Keisha said, laughing. Heather just looked at her plate, but didn't respond but Black did.

"Yeah, she probably did get fucked real good in her dreams."

"Shut up creep," Heather said as Keisha put some bacon on her plate.

The house phone rang. "Girl, you got a house phone?" Heather asked.

"Yeah, and it came with the cable plan." Keisha left to go answer the ring. Black got up and walked to the fridge and got some orange juice. Going back to the table he passed Heather and smacked her ass, which was hanging off the stool.

"Boy Stop!" she said, looking around the corner.

"She ain't coming out here with your scared ass," Black said, sitting down in front of her.

"I thought you didn't mess with me, Black," Heather said. Black took a bite of his waffle.

"Maybe I do, maybe I don't, but what I do know is I'm tryna fuck again . . . and again and see what that thing on your shoulder like."

"Shhhh." She shushed him bubble-eyed. "You loud, boy."

"Fuck dat, what's up?"

Before she could answer, Keisha came back in the kitchen grabbing her keys and spoke to Black. "Boo, I gotta run to my mom's for a minute. I'll be right back." Black just looked at her as he continued to eat. She turned to Heather, "You good til I get back, girl?"

"Yeah, I'm good."

With that being said she left the house. Black was staring at Heather, thinking of a plan on how to use her like she did Jroc. He went to his room, leaving her in the kitchen. In the room he grabbed his camera and set it up in her room—the guest room. He went back downstairs, and she was washing the dishes. He got right up on her and pressed his dick against her ass as she continued to wash. "You better stop."

Black spun her around and kissed her and she accepted it eagerly. He picked her up and walked her to the bedroom and threw her on the bed. He tore her clothes off and she let him. His pants dropped. "Damn, it's so big," she said.

Black walked over to her and smiled. She couldn't stop staring at his dick. She grabbed it like she was gonna take it away. She couldn't even close her hand around it. Stroking it with both hands, Black ran his hands through her hair and pulled her head toward his manhood. Licking her lips, she looked at it first, kissed it second, then started licking it from the base to the head like a lollipop. She sucked the head and felt his dick jumping.

Black stopped her, positioned her on the couch they had in the room with her ass hanging over the edge. He put his manhood all the way inside her until his balls was slapping her ass to the beat. She started screaming in pleasure. Black couldn't fake. She had some good pussy, but his mind was in it for the cause of blackmailing her. Black squeezed her ass and talked dirty to her. "You like this black dick, don't you?"

"Yessss, Daddy. Don't stop!" He pumped faster and faster, then came all on her back and hair, then collapsed. "Dirty bitch."

"But that's what you want," Heather replied as she rolled over and walked to the shower. Now she was in too deep. In the shower many thoughts went through her head. Black on the other hand went to the camera and stopped his featured film. He took it downstairs to his den and watched it again. 'DAMN SHAWTY COULD TAKE A DICK,' he thought as he watched. After it ended, he saved it on a USB and his phone, but put the USB in his safe.

He began to play the game. A little while later Heather came downstairs and sat on the couch across from him. He was smoking. They sat in silence for a couple minutes as Black played online. "So, what is this?" Heather asked, referring to what had happened twice.

Before Black could answer, Keisha walked down the stairs of the den. "What y'all doing?" she asked.

Blowing smoke, Black answered, "Chillin, killin'."

"Nothing girl, watching this fool curse the TV out. I don't understand it. All he doing is killing people."

"That's what he do girl, but you ready to roll?"

"Yeah." Heather got up walking past Black as Keisha walked up the stairs leading the way. When she cleared him, Black squeezed her ass and winked. She smiled and followed Keisha.

CHAPTER 42

Dro

"Was Black there?"

"Shit!" I just woke up from a nice sleep. "That was a long night." I stretched, trying to get myself together. I didn't even feel my girl come in last night as I rolled over almost smashing her little frame. I got up, hopped in the shower to try to wash this hangover off me. My phone was jumping last night and this morning, so I knew I was gonna have to make a lot of moves to-day. I got out of the shower to my girl shitting. "Damn girl, funky ass, what the fuck you eat?" I said, damn near running out the bathroom soak and wet and ass naked, trying to avoid the smell. I couldn't stay in there and get ready or dry off.

Charmine tried to talk to me, but I kept it pushing. 'DAMN I MISS THE DAYS WHEN SHE USE TO HIDE THAT PART

OF HER AWAY FROM ME.' Drying off in our room, I sprayed a shot of that Gucci shit on me. That fragrance smelled good.

Today was gonna be a chilly day so I decided to put on some laid-back attire which was some jeans and a white T with a pair of 990's, New Balance, grey. I finished getting dressed and Charmine walked up on me. "Good morning boo!" she said excited.

I just looked at her, then spoke back with a frown on my face. "What's up stinky?"

"Where you going?"

"Outside, make a few pick ups, why?

"Because." She put her hand on her hip. "I wanna chill with you today," she whined, then got serious. "Did you hear about Heather's house?" Charmine asked.

"Nah, what happened?"

She grabbed the remote to the TV. "Look, it should be still on. It was on the news all morning."

"Damn, was she in there when it happened?" I asked, hoping she was on the low.

"Goodness no! She stayed with Keisha last night after we came from the club and—"

"COUGH, COUGH." I damn near died when she said that, but she continued.

"You okay boo?"

"Yeah, I'm good. Was Black there?"

"Not when I got there, but I'm pretty sure he came in. "Is he okay?"

"Yeah, yeah, he good. I gotta call him 'bout some other shit doe." I stepped off. She followed right behind me. She wasn't gonna leave it at that. "What's goin' on? Can I still go outside with you?"

"Yeah, go get ready." She left as Black answered the phone.

"Sup' Bossman?"

"Where you at, Slim?" I asked him.

"In da crib."

"Shawty still there?" I asked.

"Nope, both of 'em just rolled out."

'WHEW!' I blew a sigh of relief.

"I was hoping you didn't do anything crazy."

He giggled. "Nah, not yet. But I got something to show you."

"True that's cool. I'm 'bout to head uptown, but my girl with me." I hipped him.

"A'ight, fuck dat mean. Soon she get up here and link with Tiara, we slide."

"I hear you."

I was glad he didn't do anything to that girl cause now was not a good time. Knowing Black, he would've tried to do her right there, but I'm glad he didn't. I'm pretty sure he was the reason her house went up in flames. I sat and played the game until Charmine was ready to leave.

Izzo was outside early. He spent the night over at Tiara's house and they fucked all night. That's the reason why her mother put his ass out this morning. The noise Tiara was making made sure that the mother knew Izzo's first, middle and last name. All he had the chance to do was bird bath and headed straight to his trap. The only good part of the situation was that he's pumping outside, and he was there to catch all the sales. Wasn't no shame in his game. He had weight but wasn't letting no money pass him. His young boys were still asleep and hung over. He didn't mind, it was Sunday, a down day, but still a working day—people smoke 7 days a week.

Izzo decided to walk to Tiki's, the neighborhood carryout that sold breakfast as well. When he walked in the store, he seen Jroc in there waiting on his food. "Pretty boy, what it do?" Jroc spoke.

"Shit, what up Slim?"

"Fuck you doin' up this early?" With his head lowered he

sighed. "Heather's house got burned down last night and Keisha dropped her off at my crib this morning and she was hungry."

"Dayum homie, they say white girls can't cook, unless you Martha Stewart, now that's different," Izzo said, tryna lighten the mood.

"Wasn't she at the club with your girl and them last night?"

"Yeah. I wasn't hipped til they came back though, but speaking on that what's up wit' your lil snowbunny?"

"I'm working on it, so she won't testify against me. Once she fall in love, it's over. Ya dig," Jroc said like he had it all figured out.

"Yeah, a'ight nigga, we'll see." Izzo noticed Black riding a bike across the street. "AYE!" he yelled, running out the store. "Black!"

Black turned around and rode the bike back toward where Izzo was at. Black been on moves since he made it uptown earlier. He didn't even know Izzo was out, or he would have brought him along.

"Fuck you doing up this early, it's Sunday?" Black asked as he approached Izzo.

"Nigga it's 10:30 a.m. That ain't early, moe, but what's goodie?"

"Shit, back on my bullshit, missions and shit." Izzo nodded to the store. "Jroc in there too."

"Oh yeah." Black opened the door after he dropped his bike. "Come here fool," he said to Jroc. He came out and gave Black a head nod. "What's up, bruh?"

"Not a damn thing." Jroc frowned, as Black continued.

"I see you handle your business last night." Black fishing trying to see if he was gonna take the credit for it.

"Nah, she wasn't even there, and I didn't do that shit. They calling that shit a robbery, arson or some shit. She in my house right now, but you knew that since she was at your crib last night," Jroc said, pulling his card.

Black ignored him. "But uh Izzo, hit me when Dro get up here. He supposed to be on his way and we 'ALL' gotta talk,"

Black said, looking at both of them.

Izzo and Jroc got the food and started walking back 'round the way. It was a new day and for the most part it started off just fine. They walked through the hood and noticed it was quiet with only a few people out and about. A few kids were out, the ones whose parents let them do whatever they want. Sometimes the kids beat the hustlers out. They wake up and go, like firemen and get up and be outside all day. "Let me drop this food off. I'll be back," Jroc said, dapping Izzo up.

Izzo stood on the gate, eating his sandwich he just bought. By the time he finished, Dro was pulling up and had his girl with him. "What's goodie, Prophet?" Dro said, smiling from his exotic car he was in today.

"Shit coolin.' Tryna pull up like you did." Izzo admired the car. "I'm tryna get on your level." Dro left the Benz at the house and today he drove a rented Ferrari F12 Berlinetta from Exotic Rentals in Arlington, Virginia.

"I'm 'bout to park and come holla at you."

Dro parked and him and Charmine walked back to the gate when Charmine decided to go see her friend. "I'm 'bout to go see what Tiara doing."

"I'll be out here," Dro said.

"Don't disappear." Her eyes narrowed. Dro smiled. "Foreal, don't leave. I'm chillin' with you today."

"Go ahead, I hear you," Dro said, waving her off.

Dro made it to the gate and Izzo had a jay in the air. "Boss-man, how much that shit cost?"

"That bitch right there." Dro smiled looking back at the car. "That shit was nothing, slight work only $315K."

"Slight work huh?" Izzo laughed.

"But it's rented, so you know I didn't pay nowhere near that shit," Dro confessed.

They smoked weed like hippies and had plenty of it. It was just them two for a while and they ping pong jays back and forth. Black rode up on the bike. "Right on time," he said as he reached for the jay. "I thought I told you hit me when Dro got up here."

"I knew you was gonna just roll up anyway," Izzo said as he passed the smoke.

"What you wanted with me?" Dro asked.

"What y'all think of Jroc's lil white chick?" Black asked.

"Hmp, I think that bitch got that nigga on some type of pussy spell," Dro said, smirking. "And let's not forget she da' police."

"Shid, I'm tryna see what the hype about," Izzo said, half joking.

"Go ahead playa, so Tiara could kill yo ass. You see what she did to that girl at the club you performed at the other night."

"That was different."

"Fuck all that shit doe," Black said. "But don't tell the girls about the bitch yet. We gonna pull up on her."

"Cool wit' me," Dro said.

"But look, this the shit I wanted to show y'all."

After they watched the featured film, they looked at each other with blank expressions. They were lost for words. She a hoe and now that Black had her on film, it gave the team leverage that they would exploit, when needed. Chilling around the way, they had a few dollars in their pocket, nobody hustled on the corner, but Izzo caught a few sales just cause he was addicted to the lifestyle. He acted as if his record not Gold on iTunes and hadn't been #1 for the past two weeks and counting.

Across the street beside the Ferrari, parked Izzo's Audi R-8 sportscar. The hood lifestyle was treating them well. Jroc came up the street looking high as ever. He had the walk when it look like you just floating on air on a bed of pillows. He finally made it to the gate where everyone else was at and spoke. "Wat up! It's looking like a car show out this bitch." Jroc smiled as he extended his hand.

On the street was the S&G Amg Coupe that Black drove, the rented Ferrari that Dro had and Izzo's Audi R-8. They was making a statement and it was well received. Everybody had their signature jews on reppin' the city and putting the label on. "Shit coolin,' " Dro responded as Izzo nodded.

"What's the move for today?" Jroc asked.

"I'm 'bout to head uptown and make a few moves and check on a few spots," Dro said and Black quickly included himself on the move but was gated. "I'm good, my girl coming, no telling what else she might want to do, so I'm riding solo today."

"A'ight Bossman, just tryna earn the money you been paying a nigga, ya dig," Black said with a nod of his head.

"Oh, you will," Dro said matter factly.

"Damn, you must got a sensor on your shit, cause here lil Dro come now, right on cue," Black said, joking, but nodding his head in the direction that Charmine was coming from. Dro looked and walked toward her as they walked toward the car.

"Let's go boo." She grabbed his arm and walked off, but then looked back. "Izzo! Tiara want you."

Black caught the move and didn't want to get stuck with Jroc. "I'll be back," he said as he stepped off, heading to get on a bike.

"Fuck dat nigga get a police mountain bike from?" Izzo asked.

Jroc just shook his head and said, "Same shit I was thinking, but that's Black, it's no telling."

CHAPTER 43

Everybody Mad

"It's a video joint from—"
— Jroc

Back on his bullshit, Black was cruising down the street in a pair of jeans and a white tee. He tucked his chain; he was bored. They say a bored mind is the devil's playground. He was riding through random neighborhoods looking for a quick come up. He rode around a hood on 5th-n-O street. It was a few blocks from his neighborhood. It was a dangerous complex. Dudes wasn't sweet for the bullshit, but Black didn't care, he was the type to shoot his way out a jam.

It was still early, 'bout 12:00 p.m. He spotted a crap game and rolled up on it dropping his bike. "Police! Put your fuckin' hands up," Black said with his hand on his gun, but flashing Heather's badge that he took from her house.

"Oh shit!" They put their hands up and one dude looked like he wanted to run. "Damn, all this for gambling?"

"Shut the fuck up and lay on your stomach before I blow your fuckin' face off and say it was self-defense," Black ordered. They did as they were told and Black went through all their pockets, taking all their money. "Oh! What's this, huh?"

Dangling from Black's hand was a pretty two-tone nine-millimeter he found in the dirt beside them. Nobody said a word. He put it on his waistline. "Whose is it?" Black was in character. A small crowd watched from across the street in the parking lot. Silence was their only reply. "Let's make a deal, tell me—"

"Fuck you, pig!" one dude spat.

Black forgot he was in character. "Fuck you call me?"

BOC! A shot went through the guy's leg.

"Yooooooo! Fuck you doing?" the guy's friend asked. "You da' police, you can't just shoot people."

"He pulled a gun on me; you didn't see it?" Black stated, picking up their money off the ground. "You boys place nice and stay out of trouble. Have a nice day. If you have any problems, call me. You know the number, 911."

Black rode all the way back around the way in like 2 to 3 minutes flat. Headed straight to his mom's house. He brought the bike upstairs to get it off the street. His mother was hipped to him. "Boy, where you get that damn bike from?"

"Chill lady," Black said, ignoring her question and walking to the girls' bedroom.

"Don't be walking away from me when—"

SLAM!!! Was the sound of the door cutting off her statements.

"What up, stinks?" he asked his sisters.

"Nothing, watching SpongeBob."

"Let me get some money," Black said with his hands out. They laughed.

"We ain't got no money!"

"Here." He gave them both a hundred-dollar bill and told

them to hide it. Their little faces lit up at the sight of the blue money. They never seen it before. Running to Black they embraced him with hugs and kisses to thank him.

Leaving their room, Black headed to his. He counted the money from the caper he just pulled, and it rounded off at $8,000. 'THEM BOYS WAS HEAVY.' He smiled. Black put most of the money into the safe and kept a few hundred in his pocket. He also did inventory on his bullets to make sure he was good, since he been using a lot lately.

Walking through the living room he expected his mom to ask him for some money, but he decided to beat her to the punch and gave her $50 that he knew she wanted and headed straight for the door and headed back outside.

Jroc was in the crib with Izzo and Tiara, but Izzo left him in the living room. Jroc was waiting for a minute after Izzo had told him that he was going to 'holla' at Tiara. He knew Izzo spent him (lied to him) and was in there fucking, so he decided to roll out. 'SHID, I GOT PUSSY IN THE CRIB TOO,' he thought as he closed the apartment door.

Walking down the stairs he exited the building and headed through the courtyard where he noticed Black coming out of his mom's house, but Black kept it pushing. He fired up a stogy in efforts to relieve his stressful problems that were his reality.

Jroc made it to his house and seen Heather in his room watching TV. "Sup' boo?" he spoke, breaking her out of her daydream.

"Hey baby!" She was excited. "Guess what? I found an apartment I could afford until my house is repaired," Heather said, jumping up and down, then straight into his arms.

Jroc tried to play the game and be Casanova but lost. He done fell in love with this girl and didn't even realize he was that gone off her. Heather was a good girl until she was exposed to another lifestyle and met Jroc, but when she 'met' Black, he turned her sour. Heather loved Jroc but would give Black the pussy on demand. She didn't understand her logic and heart at this moment in life. Black had her sprung. That one night of pleasure was all it took. She loved to be controlled and talked to dirty. Now she had 2 friends, and 2 murders, but different qualities. She wanted both.

"Where is the apartment at?" Jroc asked.

"It's actually around the corner." She smiled. "Two blocks over to be exact."

"That's what's up boo. How much money you need for a deposit?" He dug into his pocket, pulling out a wad of money. "You know I got you."

"Come on, we can go together!" Excitement evident in her voice.

They got dressed after a quick sex session that took place in the shower. Jroc thought Heather was a little more aggressive than usual but waved it off. 'SHE A WHITE GIRL.' The whole time Black had opened her freakier side up to new heights.

Getting in the car, Jroc drove to the rental office. Entering, they were greeted and taken care of. They completed the objective, leaving with a 1-year signed lease. Jroc didn't know he was going to be on the paperwork, but the power of pussy had him signing on the dotted lines. He dropped her off with a lot of cash so she could furbish her new condo. Inside Jroc's house Heather was getting ready so she could head to work. Jroc kissed her and headed to the door to make his exit.

Jroc went back down the street and chilled in the hood. Izzo was just coming back outside with a smile on his face and some loose legs. "Damn bruh,' you left?" Izzo asked.

"Nah, I was right here, coolin'." Jroc lied.

"My bad, bruh." Izzo grabbed his nuts. "You know how shit just happens, ya dig." He smirked.

"Whatever nigga."

"Dro ain't been through yet?"

"Nope." Jroc started patting his pockets. "Damn, I left my phone Slim. Let me see you horn right quick."

Izzo dug into his pocket and gave it to him, not noticing he had an unread message. He was busy tryna find his lighter for the blunt he had dangling from his lips. 'FUCK MY LIGHTER.' Izzo looked around in circles as if it was in the area.

Meanwhile, Jroc was about to dial a number and seen a video message on the screen.

"Bruh, you got a message on this joint, Slim." Jroc flashed the phone to Izzo who wasn't paying attention and waved him off.

"Open it, read it, so I could hear you."

"It's a video joint from—"

As soon as Izzo heard the word video he came to his senses, but it was too late. Jroc opened the message and seen Black carrying a white girl to the couch, toss her on it as she giggled. The laugh caught his attention and made him zoom in so he could look a little bit closer and harder. He noticed the white girl was his white girl, Heather.

He was beyond made. He was furious. "What the fuck is this, moe?" Izzo put the lost face on and grabbed the phone to get a look at the video.

"Let me see." Izzo looked at the phone. "What?! Looks like fucking." Izzo tried to downplay it. He never knew Black sent him the link after they watched it.

"That's my girl, Heather! Look!" Jroc yelled.

"What! Fuck no, Slim." Izzo looked at the phone again, playing oblivious to the content. "Nah, Slim that ain't her. You know all them white bitches look alike."

"Fuck dat! That nigga got me fucked up," Jroc huffed.

"Bruh chill . . . Bro's ova' hoes remember." Izzo grabbed him, making him face him. "You know she tryna get us all bagged up," he tried to reason.

Jroc wasn't trying to hear none of that. It's like he wasn't even mad at Heather, only Black. "He tricked her, bruh."

"What?! Nigga is you stupid?" Izzo questioned. Jroc was gone and Heather was seeming like she was going to be his downfall. Jroc stormed off down the street and disappeared as he turned the corner.

'DAMN.' Izzo shook his head, then looked around to notice he was on the block by his lonesome, solo. After thinking 'bout what just happened he decided to hit Black:

'AYE CUZ JROC SEEN THE
FLICK
HE MIGHT BE TRYNA C U, HE
HEATED.'

'FUK HIM, SEE EM WHN I C
EM'

"Shit, these niggas 'bout to start trippin," Izzo said to himself after reading Black's response. He flipped through his contacts and decided to call Dro.

CHAPTER 44

Dro

"A lot of bullshit, that's all"

Charmine was happy. I was making my rounds, cruising, riding with the window half down so the jet smoke wouldn't stain my interior. 'CAME ALL LONG WAY FROM RIDING MET-RO' I thought as I pulled up at my last stop. It was an older dude who I be serving. He was about 35 to 40 years old. Usually he buy whole bird' (kilo) from me, but today his shipment was sliced in half. I never tried to keep him waiting.

This day he looked kind of crazy. I think he was high off that dipah'. All in all, he didn't look himself, but me being used to him I looked past it and still got out of the car to greet him.

Usually, he would hop in my car, but I had my lady with me today so that wasn't happening. I don't let niggas get comfortable around her. She was safe behind the limo tints. I noticed all the young boys eyeing me. I was kinda glad he was the last stop; the scenery looked suspect. I walked to the ol' head and gave him the plastic carry out bag with the yellow smiley face full of work inside it. He grabbed it and stepped off.

"Slim, what's up, bob?" I asked with hand gestures referring to my money that he didn't give me. The nigga laughed at me and kept it moving.

He looked back. "I know some lil' niggas that would murk you for the rest of it." His young boys stood up.

I'm from the streets, so I caught the hint and turned on my heels headed back to my whip. As I pulled off, he had a nerve to wave at me. I cruised down the street listening to Lil Wayne and a verse made me smile: 'MY POCKETS FLOODED WITH MONEY, LIKE IT WAS RAINING FOR MONTHS.' It was a shame them niggas was gonna die. They robbed the wrong nigga, thinking I was a sweet lick. 'I'LL BE BACK UP THIS BITCH TONIGHT,' I told myself.

If them niggas would have went in my pockets, they would have come off with about $10,000 dirty money. Driving back 'round the way, I was still tight (mad). I told Charmine I had a change of plans. She looked like she didn't like it but understood. She knew something had happened but wouldn't ask me. That's one of the reasons I always tell her she don't need to be around me when I'm making moves. "Where you tryna go?" I asked her.

"Take me back to Tiara's house, or home if you don't want me uptown." Charmine tried to guilt trip me. That shit don't work no more, but I play the game for her.

"I'll take you to Tiara's apartment." She smiled as I fired up a jay of loud. My phone rang and I seen it was Izzo. "Sup' Prophet?"

"Bruh, Black sent me that video and Jroc saw it. Now they beefin'," Izzo said, talking fast.

"Beefin?"

Desperately tryna explain the shit to me he said, "Yeah beefin'. Jroc stormed off, talking 'bout he got 'em and all this shit. Black was like whatever, so you need to talk to them niggas.

"I'll be there in a minute. I'm on Georgia Avenue, leaving from around Morton Street." I disconnected.

Charmine ain't miss a beat. "What's up boo?" With concern all in her voice.

"A lot of bullshit, that's all."

Jroc walked back to his house and hopped in his car. He was furious. Words couldn't even describe the hurt. Pussy had him so blind he forgot that Black was his homie form the sandbox. He opened his glove compartment. You would have thought he wanted to beat Black up, but that wasn't possible. He was scared. He was sitting there debating the unthinkable. As he sat there reading the card that read: DETECTIVE GUN, HOMICIDE, he felt it was his only option to get Black out of the way and securing his girl.

Black was really trying to save his crew, along with Jroc by making that movie. Jroc's relationship wasn't even in his thoughts. All he was thinking was to gain leverage to taint the police case, if he couldn't smoke her.

When the pressure hit, Jroc got busted, pressed out and set up by the police. When the detective told him all he want is a shooter and he was a free man, it seemed so easy now. Now that Black fucked his woman, he going to give him to the police on a silver platter, not knowing by saying one word would incriminate the whole crew, including himself. The whole time Jroc thinking he had all the sense and walked right into the police station and spilled the beans. Now he done crossed over to the other side.

CHAPTER 45

Black

"Damn, they made you mad."
— Black

My phone rang. "So, you still thinking of me like I knew you would."

"Baby, we have a problem," Heather said.

"What problem?" I was confused.

"Your homeboy just turned state and told 'bout that heist y'all was in," Heather said.

'CLICK'

I hung the phone up so fast like it was burning my ear. I didn't want to talk over the phone in that manner that she seemed to be talking. She still the police. I looked at my phone as it vibrated:

"CAN I SEE U LATER," she texted.

"I'LL CALL U LATER B READY."

I was walking down the street and heard the engine before I seen the car as it rode by me. It was Dro's Ferrari. Then in 'about 3 minutes he pulled up on me in another whip, a bucket. "Get in."

"Sup bossman?"

"Time to earn that money I pay you good for. We gotta handle something uptown before these niggas roll out."

"What happened?" I asked as he pulled off.

"Nigga robbed me, and it's payback time, hit with they lives." I seen the venom in Dro's eyes.

"Damn, I was wondering why you pulled up in this piece of shit." I laughed. We were riding on the backside, heading uptown, but on Sherman Avenue. I realized I only had my 38 special on me. "Bruh, I only got my up close and personal on me." Dro pulled over on Harvard Street, got out and popped the trunk. I looked inside. "Dayum, they made you mad." I smiled. He had an arsenal.

I looked in his trunk and my smile got wider. Dro seen my smirk and gave me the rundown. I swore he loved doin' this part. It hypes him up.

"Bruh, this a LAR-15, semi-automatic with 5.56 NATO rounds. If you don't know what that is, it's similar to .223's. It holds 30 rounds in this clip I got. This navy shit. It has a Delta Quad rail two piece drop in and gas system, no jammin', plus an Ergo grip and a two-stage tripper."

I was lost and amazed at the same time. I just nodded like I understood and pointed to the next option. He continued. "This is a UTS-15, pump action—"

"That's a shotgun?" I cut him off, amazed at the gun.

Dro smiled. "Yup, and it holds 15 rounds, 12 gauge."

"Damn, and those pretty bitches right there are?" I pointed.

"These bitches are twins, Ruger SR 45's that hold 10 and 1 in the head, and they lightweight. So what's it gonna be?" he asked.

I grabbed the LAR-15. I like to make a mess on the scene. He grabbed the two pretty bitches. We got back in the car and rode past a few niggas, then parked in the middle of the block. "Why we park all the way down here? Fuck we waiting for?" I asked.

"I don't do driveby's. This ain't the 90's no more. We walkin' up on them niggas."

I looked at Dro like he was crazy. Niggas think I'm the loose cannon, but this quiet ass nigga here is the worst. If I would've known this part, I would have grabbed the twins. Now here we are creeping behind cars, and I got this big ass choppa closing in on these niggas. I ain't have no type. All them niggas seen was two fly ass niggas come out of nowhere with that shit. Dro had a target I see. He only fired at one nigga. He took aim.

BOC! BOC! BOC! BOC! BOC! BOC! and hit 'em, then kept firing at him. You know my baby got jealous and was never the type not to express herself.

'TAT TAT TAT TAT!'

"I hate this semi shit," I said out loud. I then put it on auto by hitting the switch.

'BRRRRRRRAT BRRRRRRRATT TAT.' It sounded like it was stuttering as it fucked everything up in sight.

Dro was on top of his victim, letting it ring. BOC! BOC! BOC! He didn't tell me who not to shoot, so everybody got some. I was the clean-up man. After the smoke cleared, we jogged back to the car. Dro pulled off and stopped at the red light like shit just ain't go down. I hear sirens and some mo' shit. This shit get me mad every time he do this shit. But the crazy part it works every time. As we cruised, I decided to tell him the news.

"Bruh, now that's over—"

"What?"

"The nigga Jroc—"

"I heard what happened. Izzo told me earlier," Dro said, cutting him off. It was blowing me like shit.

"Nigga! If you just listen for a second . . ." Dro looked at me, then back to the road. "The nigga was so mad about the video, tsst . . ." I paused and sighed. "Your man, yup 'your' man turned state on us, thinking if I'm gone, he could have Heather to himself like I'm really into her or some shit. That's some sucka shit, moe."

SKRRRRRRR.

"What!?" He slammed the brakes as I looked around and continued. "Crazy part, the bitch the one that told right after he left the station. Matter fact go to the gas station so I could call her on the payphone."

The nigga looked at me like I was trippin' or some shit, then said, "Nigga! Ain't no more damn payphone out here. Maybe at the train station."

"A'ight go there then. She tried to tell me the whole scoop, but I banged (hung up) on her ass."

"Smart shit," Dro said.

We dumped the bucket and walked down Shaw Howard train station on the 7th and S Street side to use the payphone. "Listen." I put the phone to Dro's ear.

"Yes?" she answered. "Who's calling?"

"Tell me what happened again today," I said, dodging her question and saying my name. She repeated it, not leaving a word out and added the parts that I didn't hear earlier. "You a bad girl," I whispered through the receiver into her ear.

"I may be bad, but I'm perfectly good at it." I smiled at her wittiness.

CLICK

Looking at Dro I smirked. "See bruh, I got her under the wing. She dick-sick."

"Yeah, okay wit' your trickin' ass."

"If I buy the pussy, she paying for it," I said, laughing.

We were back around the way and Izzo was out there holding up the light pole posted up. Dro walked back to the bucket. I guess to get the guns out and put in a safer place. Niggas were outside coolin' but anybody liable to jump in one of the buckets and pull off. I know I didn't really want to be around here. I didn't know how quick they would react to the information and if shit just got real as of now.

But in my mind, I knew I was gonna kill Jroc and probably that bitch too in due time. For now, I'ma play dumb and get all the information out of my newfound friend, Heather. I'm supposed to see her later. She wanna make me dinner, but on the low she gonna make me rich.

Me and Izzo was ping ponging the doooby (blunt), then out of nowhere I seen a squad car pulled up on the corner. Nigga damn near choked to death as Izzo tossed the blunt. Dro walked back up and asked for a jack.' I gave him a light, but really, I was concentrating on the squad car and didn't even notice the other car parked across the street.

It was the same car that been poppin' up dropping letters off in shit. I got instantly tight after seeing it. Police was posted, and this wild car was keep showing up. Everybody must have noticed my face and wondered.

"Sup' Killer? You got that look in your eye," Dro said. I just nodded to the car and the eyes followed.

Four doors and four guys got out. They were fresh and iced out. I mean these niggas was drippin' and tailored. They walked toward us and stopped. All I had was my 38 on me so I stepped in front of my men. The dude with the tattoo stepped forward. My mind was buggin.' I was still tryna place the tattoo but couldn't recognize it or the owner of it.

Tattoo smiled. "You like my tattoo, huh?" He extended his arm to show me the whole thing. "Yeah, me and my pops had matchin' tats." He paused and stared at me. "But I'm sure you remember my pops, right?" He waited for an answer, but I gave him nothing. "Well, his name was Fred, and he was fuckin' your mother. Ring any bells?"

"And so, what the fuck you want?" I grilled.

"Ha!" He chuckled. "I'ma get what I want now that I know it's you that dawged my pops out like that. I just wanted to give you fair warning of what's to come. When I come, you gonna feel it." He leaned in a little too close for comfort. "here's my card. Offer me a nice amount and I might just say fuck it. I know my pops was a piece of shit and I don't know what he did, but he was my pops and I'm not goin' like dat." He tossed his car and stepped off.

CHAPTER 46

Jroc left the station with a sense of satisfaction but on the inside he was sick. The bottom of the barrel. He done switched jerseys and was now playing for the other team. He let his attitude and jealousy get in the way of his reasoning. All he could do now was recant and take back his statement, but if he do that it's a big possibility he could go to jail for that. 'FUCK IT' was his answer to all his previous actions.

Jroc parked his car in front of the crib and decided to walk down the street and past a fiend who offered to wash his car. He gave the guy $10 and kept it pushing. First person he seen was Izzo posted up in front of the train station. He walked up on him and spoke, "Sup playboy."

"Oh shit, look y'all it's the Hulk," Izzo said to the imaginary crowd as he looked over his shoulder talkin' about Jroc's actions earlier when he stormed off. "You good homeslice?"

"Yeah, actually I am. Just had to ride if off, no worries." Jroc fanned himself. "It's hot as shit out here, but Black gonna get his," Jroc said, rubbing his hands together.

"Fuck you talking 'bout, that's our homie, nigga. I'm not just gonna sit back and let y'all hurt each other."

"Nah, I'm good. I ain't gonna do shit to the guy. Karma is."

"That's some wild shit to say, Slim. That bitch you tryna cuff gonna have you in cuffs, you keep bullshittin'," Izzo said nodding his head, not believing what Jroc was saying.

Jroc was willing to fuck up everything he had going for himself in the name of pride. Can't nobody fuck one of his bitches in his mind. He realized that they all come from the sandbox, but he was out for self.

Izzo, on the other hand, was taking mental notes. He noticed Jroc wasn't the same guy he grew up with. This nigga in front of him was a mirror image. The little hood he had in him was long gone.

"Fuck all that Black shit doe, fire this up," Jroc said, giving Izzo a jay'.

Izzo grabbed it and sparked it up. he took a couple pulls. "Nigga, I hope you know I ain't giving you shit on this jay' either, wit your wild ass."

"Damn bruh, you ain't got 5 dollars wit your broke ass." Jroc was on joke time.

"Broke? Yeah, right! Being broke is behind me. You must not have seen that record of mines on the billboard. Number 1 nigga and my trap jumpin'," Izzo boasted. "Plus, I ain't giving you shit for this boney ass rollup." He held the jay to the sky.

"Nigga that joint pearled. I rolled that joint like a cigarette," Jroc said as he noticed Black coming up the street.

Izzo followed his gaze and saw Black as well. That nigga came out of nowhere. He stay on that pop up shit. Niggas be wondering how he get his victim's. Je just a smooth criminal with light feet.

"Sup' boy?" Izzo spoke. Black walked straight past Izzo's hand, leaving it dangling in the air. He was still mad at Fred's son for the threats he made. He seen Jroc and decided to see what's up with him.

"What's up wit all that fly shit you talkin' 'bout?" Black asked, damn near nose to nose.

Jroc backed up to create space between them. "You got it, Slim. I don't want no smoke," he copped out.

"Yeah a'ight, fuck you been at? My man said he seen you driving uptown." Black was pressing him out, tryna get a reaction out of him.

"Minding my fucking business nigga! Now get the fuck off my line, damn." Jroc pushed Black. Black drew a punch back that was intercepted by Dro.

"Chill big boy. You don't see them peoples on the corner?" Black laughed and continued to talk to Jroc. "Your scary ass, I should smack fire out your ass, all that purpin' (portraying an image) you doing."

"Do you, bruh," Jroc bluffed, knowing he didn't wan it.

Dro got in front of both of them and forced them to walk. Standing in front of the train station, another jay' was fired up as they watched the day go by. Everybody was in their own thoughts. Dro had mixed feelings about his man. Him and Jroc was the closest. He knew if it came down to it, he wasn't going to jail for no snitch ass nigga. he'll be the one to pull the trigger and mourn him later.

Izzo wasn't even thinking about Jroc. All his thoughts was wrapped around his new single he wrote and his trap. He was trying to blow up. All Black did was think of work. He had murder money and mayhem on his mind, all at the same time and not always in that order. But whichever way it came, it didn't matter, they all compliment each other in his mind.

As the day turned into night, it felt like old times before the money and all the bullshit that came with it. They were coolin', sippin' and enjoying each others company for the most part. The neighborhood thots' (them hoes over there) was out and about and thought they were the shit. Some of them were looking good with their 4 bundles of 30-inch Brazilian virgin lace hair, and the Instagram freak 'em dresses on. The busted-up ones tried even harder and had them new butt lift panties and extra thin waist trainers, tryna hide that ran through body, but some niggas was thirty and just didn't care.

There was a cool breeze in the air. It felt good and mellowed everybody out. The police was riding but wasn't messing with nobody, which was odd, but nobody dared to complain. After chillin' on the frontline, the next destination was the courtyard. It was like the chill area for all ages.

Kids, couples, young and old all graced the courtyard. It was a neutral zone with a playground in the middle and benches surrounding it. In front of the buildings were different groups, doing different shit.

Following the smoke cloud, they ended up in front of Izzo's mom's building where they stopped and sat on the steps. Sitting for a moment Izzo hopped right back up. "I'll be back."

"Nigga, that's why you wanted to come in here anyway. You think you got all the sense," Black said laughing. Izzo jogged to the next building heading to Tiara's spot and disappeared behind the door. Jroc just stepped off, flashing the deuces letting them know he was gone.

"Fuck yuh!" Black said, flickin' him off. Jroc looked back and smile. The comment pissed him off and he was guh' (irritated or embarrassed), but he brushed it off and mumbled, "Fuck me, nah fuck you coming soon, bitch ass."

Dro and Black chilled on the stairs, talking about the label and plans to handle this ongoing problem. A lot of ideas was being tossed around, but they needed to put it into effect before they start handing down indictments.

Dro felt some arms wrapped around his neck and the scent of who it was was a dead giveaway. He purchased it, Chanel no. 5. "Hey baby."

"That's crazy. What, you forgot I was out here?" Charmine

asked.

"Nah boo, I had to handle some business. You know that."

"Nigga, you been handled your 'business.' It's all over the news," she said, standing in front of him with her hand on her hip. Dro had bubbled eyes after hearing that.

"For real?" he asked.

"Yup, but you good boo. They ain't got nothing on you baby, nothing but a bunch of shell casings." Black was excited with the news. "Yeah boy! Nigga they can't touch us, moe."

Dro laughed. Tiara came outside with Izzo behind her. "Damn bitch, just roll out on a bitch when yo man pop up, huh?"

"So, and . . ." Charmine rolled her eyes. "I missed by boo, stop hatin', " she said, kissing Dro on the cheek.

"I'm gone." Black stood up. "I was cool wit being the third wheel, but y'all doin' too much now. Time to go frisk some niggas," he said, pulling out Heather's badge that he had put on a chain lookin' like a detective.

"Nigga you crazy," Dro said as Black went to the next building to get his police bike out the cut. "So, what y'all 'bout to get into?" he asked the girls.

"Heather about to come through. We probably chill or go to the bar down the street," Tiara answered. Charmine looked at Dro and put on her puppy face. "If you staying out, could I chill with Tiara?"

"Do you bay, Izzo walk with me. We'll be right back."

Walking around the corner they headed to the liquor store trying to catch it before it closed. It was packed because of the hour. They decided to get them a bottle before they had to start paying bar prices. There was about seven sexy women in line talkin' together. They looked like they were about to show off tonight. The girls noticed them and Izzo could hear his name 'Prophet' being whispered amongst the group. Izzo did some thirsty shit and pulled out a wad of money. Dro looked at him and smirked.

Little did Izzo know, but 3 of them were friends of Tiara from the club. She made sure all the girls that worked in there knew he was taken, so she wouldn't have to fuck nobody's child up.

"Damn gorgeous . . ." Izzo stepped up. "What y'all drinking?"

"Ain't you that rapper?" a chick asked.

Licking his lips and shrugging his shoulders he purped out, "I do a lil rappin', but that shit ain't 'bout nothing."

"Can I get a picture and your numba?" Three girls pulled out their phones.

Dro laughed, but Izzo replied, "Whoa, whoa, whoa, slow down. It's enough of me to go around," Izzo said, looking back at Dro giving the expression asking for help. he posed, grabbing asses and breast and they didn't mind. He got the number and started talkin' to the remaining friends.

"What about y'all?"

"No than you, Izzo. I mean Prophet. We don't want no smoke with your crazy ass girlfriend, Red Bottom." Then it hit him; they work at the club.

"Shit!"

"Damn brush,' " Dro shook his head, smiling.

After buying about 3 bottles, they left the store and seen Jroc riding past. 'FUCK HE GOIN,' Dro thought as Izzo popped a bottle of Rose screaming, "Happy New Year!" as the sudds came out. Dro looked at him like he was wild. "Fuck is wrong wit you."

"We good bruh,' chill." Izzo leaned on a parked car and began drinking from the bottle. Dro opened his bottle and sipped as they enjoyed the night, undecided on the next move.

CHAPTER 47

Heather

". . . Don't wait up."

It was nearing the time for me to punch out and I couldn't wait. It had been a long day, my boo been blowing my phone up, James. I haven't been answering and he just going to have to be mad at me tonight because I've been invited to hang out with the ladies. Tiara texted me earlier asking me to come over. I told her yup, but I had to go and pick up Keisha because she wanted to come as well.

First stop will be my apartment. I have to get out of these wranglers I had on. I'm pretty sure Jroc wouldn't tell the girls who I really am, or they wouldn't be asking me to hang out, right? Walking down the parking garage I ran into my boss, and he asked me so many questions. He also informed me that the warrants for questioning will be issued tomorrow so for me to keep the accused in the city. 'DARN IT' was all I thought. Didn't think it would be this quick.

I left and drove down the avenue like a bat out of hell. I was trying to hurry and get changed. I got pulled over and sat—I waited. The officer must have run my tags because he didn't even get out of the car. He pulled beside me, looked at me and winked. I smiled and he bucked a U-turn and rode asway. The officer must have wanted to make sure it was me—one of the team.

Making it to my residence I noticed James wasn't there, but he brought me a few outfits—designer outfits. I texted Keisha to let her know I was on my way.

Getting in the shower, inside of the water, thoughts of Black flooded my mind and I started to touch myself. I realized I would need some of that good loving from him asap. I exited the shower and decided to give him a call. "Hello big daddy."

"Sup slut," he answered.

I bit my bottom lip once I heard his voice.

"Um, you."

"You ready for me, again?"

"I'm waiting on you."

I think Black was happy that I lived so close around his way now. He had to be because he must have stopped whatever he was doing and came straight over. He was there in about 5 minutes. The door was open, and he came straight in. He walked into my room and the brother didn't waste any time as he whipped out that elephant trunk and put it in my face.

After our session, my va jay' was sore. Aggressive. That's how I seemed to love it and he delivered each time. I was about to tell him about the warrants, but the unexpected happened when I heard a voice. "Baby, you home?" James screamed from the front door of the apartment. Black heard him and headed straight for the window. Gladly I was on the ground floor.

"In here, boo!" I screamed as I sprayed some fragrance in the air to change the aroma.

"Where you going?" James asked as he entered the room.

I looked at him and answered, "I'm headed out to hang with the ladies tonight. I had a long day. Why you aren't with your friends?"

"I just left from round there wit them."

I noticed him trying to scan my apartment, so I grabbed his attention. "My captain told me you came up there today." I could tell James was guh' (Tiara taught me that word.)

"Yeah, so?" he said, and I giggled, then walked off to continue getting ready. That was a turn off. The more I hung with the girls, the more they started to affect me, and I was starting to hate my job and soft ass men. They all suppose to be childhood friends, now he acting shady. 'YEAH, I HAVE TO TELL BLACK WHATS UP' I thought, heading to the door.

"I'll see you later. Don't wait up!"

Keisha was waiting on Heather to come pick her up. She been looking forward to a ladies night. Over the last few months, she became close with this group of ladies, mainly because they all had men in their lives that were connected. Black been treating her so well and she thought life couldn't get any better. Keisha sipped her Merlot until she heard the horn beep. Hearing that, she was up and out the door.

Walking to the car she seen Heather singing all ghetto-like in the car. 'WE DONE TURNED HER OUT' she thought, opening the door. They drove and the next stop was Tiara's house. As they drove, they had general conversation about their day and girl talk.

Finally pulling uptown, they were surprised to see it was still a lot of people outside. Heather called Tiara to find out the move for tonight.

"Hey girl, what's up!" Tiara answered.

"We in the parking area," Heather spoke.

Tiara made fun of Heather's choice of words and mimicked her in her own white voice. "We in the parking area. Girl, bring your intelligent ass in the courtyard. We in here."

Heather parked and they got out of the car and walked toward the courtyard. Everybody was out, some smoking, coolin' and drinking.

"Nigga's stay getting it in round here," Keisha said, holding Heather's hand as they walked. They soon noticed Tiara and Charmine who was already saucy'. It was them and a couple other neighborhood girls.

They had a folding table out and speakers in the window pumpin' out the music. Tiara decided to start a game of spades. "I thought we was goin' out?" Keisha asked.

"We are out. Ain't you out the house?" Charmine said, shuffling the cards. "We got drinks and some good week, so find a spot and chill."

"Girl, if I would have known we was gonna be in the hood, I wouldn't have worn this lil ass skirt. I hope Black ain't out here." Keisha looked around nervously.

"Nobody told your ass we was goin' out. All I said was we chilling," Tiara confirmed. Keisha looked at Heather rolling her eyes.

"That's not what this hefa said. If Black come around here and see me, he might black my fuckin' eye, girl," Keisha said knowingly.

"If you scared, just go in my house and change your shit. Damn, we ain't keep tryna hear about it," Tiara said, nodding at her door as she shuffled the cards.

With that last statement it silenced her as the cards were dealt. They were having a good time when Dro and Izzo came through the courtyard blowing smoke. You could smell the potency before they even turned the corner. Dro was walking but could feel his girl's eyes on him and tried not to look. That didn't stop Charmine from calling out to him, "Boo!" she yelled across the courtyard.

Dro looked and gave her the deuces and tried to keep it pushing. Without looking back, Izzo said, "She coming, fool," in a low tone, trying to be discreet.

"Nigga I know you heard me!" Charmine grabbed Dro's arm, spinning him around, forcing a kiss. She was tipsy and he could see it all in her eyes.

"I said what's up boo. I thought y'all was goin' out somewhere."

"We are out, can't you see?" she said with her arms widespread.

"Yeah, okay. I'll be back. We walking to the store. You need something?" Dro asked.

"Hold on, let me see if—"

"Nah, I said 'you.' If not, I'll be back."

"Mean ass!" she said, turning on her heels headed back to the group of girls.

Meanwhile not too far off around a few corners, Black was lurking. He was riding around on the police bike heckling everybody who he thought was worth his time. Dro just dropped $10 bands on him, and he had money, but the rush was too explosive for him to stop. Black decided to ride through Adams Morgan, a somewhat wealthy part of the city. You could always find a sweet lick in that area. White, black and/or whatever else could be a potential come up.

It was the bar scene and Black knew people would be out and about. He rode past a group of white boys. The scent in the air made him stop. His presence was so hood, the white boys didn't even notice the type of bike he was on. "You got a problem?" one of the white boys asked, trying to intimidate. Black laughed.

"You think it's funny?" another asked.

In two sift moves, Black stole off on one of the white boys as he whipped his gun out in the same action. "Police!" He let his badge hang. "Put your fucking hands in the air!

Their demeanor changed instantly. "Sorry sir, we didn't know you were an officer," one pleaded.

"Is that pot I smell?" Black pointed his gun. "Empty y'all pockets." They complied and Black found an ounce of OG Kush. "Ummmm um, smells good." Black put it in his pocket along with all their money which added up to about $900. "Get the fuck outta here before I change my mind."

They ran and Black got back on his bike, rode down U Street headed back to the hood. 'LOVE THIS BADGE. MAKES SHIT SO EASY' he thought as he cruised. making it back around the way he seen it was still lit and it was 12:20 a.m. He rode through 9th Street to see if Dro or Izzo was still out there but didn't see them, so he kept pedaling down bottom.

He went into the courtyard and seen his girl playing cards. Black's face frowned when he noticed her outfit. He rode right up on the table and dropped the bike. Charmine seen his face and tried to intercept. "Hey brova, what's up!" He ignored her.

"What the hell you doing out there?" he asked Keisha.

"Why you yellin' baby. I'm just chillin' with the ladies," Keisha said as she tried to pull her skirt down some, but it didn't work cause her thighs was too juicy and thick.

"Stand the fuck up." She hesitated, but complied, slowly. "What you got on? You know what, come on." Black grabbed her arm. "We outta here."

Tiara stood up. "Chill Black, damn. She could change in my house. She only out here with us."

Black released her and gave her a slight push. "What you waiting for? I should fuck you up for playing wit me." They all stood and headed to Tiara's house, but he stopped Heather. "Aye, Heather, come here right quick."

"Sup Black." She tried to contain her smile.

"Walk wit me to the store," he told her, and she agreed.

While they walked to the store, Heather told Black everything the captain told her. He knew it was time for action. Coming back from the store he sent Heather back around the corner to the girls. Black seen Dro and Izzo walking and flagged them down.

They dapped each other up and bean to speak.

"Moe, you ain't gonna believe this shit. It's gonna fuck y'all up."

"What's up bruh?" Izzo asked.

Black told them all the information Heather had just laid on him. They were heated. Now at any moment they could get picked up for questioning on whatever they had cooking. All sorts of ideas was floating in the air. Jroc's name was getting tossed around and not in a good light. They was walking down the street and Black stopped at his car.

Izzo smiled at the car. "That joint look sweet now Slim, like a fuckin' tank," he said, admiring the armor. "I need to do my shit like yours."

Black smiled, but his mind was elsewhere. "When she told me that shit it made me mad all over again, but I'm 'bout to get me something to smoke," Black said.

"I'm 'bout to ride with you," Dro said.

"You could ride, but I'm 'bout to get me a dipah' (PCP)," Black told him. Izzo was already in the car. he smoke it occasionally so it was nothing to him. Dro contemplated then gave in. "I don't care. Matter fact I need a different high, But Izzo get in the back, nigga."

Climbing over the seat, Izzo chimed in, "They say it effect people differently, but we got you bossman."

Driving, Black didn't feel like goin' too far so he rode to Benning Courts in Northeast. It would be a first for Dro, but Black and Izzo was ready. They were riding dirty with pistols on deck, just in case. This was normal, it always better to be with them than without. It was proven true on several occasions.

Pulling up in the alley, they parked in the lot. Niggas was looking all crazy cause they couldn't see inside the car. Black got out first and his men followed suit walking beside him. Coming up on the crowd Black spoke.

"Sup' Slim, anybody good?"

"Who you?" one dude asked.

"Not the fuckin' police if that's what you thinking?" Black said with attitude all in his voice. The tension was rising quickly until another guy in the crowd got star struck when he noticed Izzo.

"Oh shit! It's dat nigga Prophet from Uptown. What it do boy! Your shit cranking on the radio."

"Respect homie, 'preciate dat."

"What y'all tryna get?" the fan asked.

Black stepped up. "We tryna get two sticks."

One of the young boys ran in the cut while dude chopped it up with Izzo. Izzo wasn't used to the fame yet, but he enjoyed it when it came. The kid came back with two capsules of the liquid. The exchange went smoothly, and everyone went their separate ways. Izzo even got booked for a block party by one of the ol' heads in the neighborhood.

In the car Dro spoke to Black. "Bruh, you need to chill sometimes. You always ready to go off."

"Nah, the city gonna know me."

"He must not know I'll blow his face off," Black countered as he pulled off.

They were driving, smoking with the window down. It wasn't like smoking weed with a great scent. The dipah' stink for real, but they was where they wanted to be, high. They didn't even know how they got on Interstate 295 from Benning Road. Cruising in his mind, Black noticed some police lights behind him. He must have been speeding they thought. He didn't trip, so he pulled over, forgetting how dirty they were.

Sitting in idle, the officer came to the window. Izzo was paranoid. He seen the officer walk past and instantly played asleep. Black looked at the officer, Dro was bubble eyed, but he kept his gaze straight forward, not blinking. 'I'M INVISIBLE,' he thought.

The officer looked at Black, who had his license and registration already in his hand. "Sir, do you know how fast you were going?"

Black looked around, trying to spot a speed limit sign, and it read 45 mph, so that was his answer.

"No sir." The officer chuckled. "Actually, you were going 15 mph in the fast lane. I'ma need you to speed it up or stay off the city streets," the officer said and grabbed his information and walked back to his squad car.

Black looked at Dro. "Bruh, let me get your lighter."

Dro turned slowly to Black.

"Shhhh, nigga! He can't see me," then looked back forward.

Izzo heard what Dro said and lifted up to look at him. He was about to say something but noticed the officer walking back through the tints and fell back on the seat, playing asleep again. The officer gave Black his information and told him to move along. Black pulled off and Izzo laughed. "Moe, we got pulled over for going too slow, tragic."

"Oh, you awake now, huh?"

"But bruh, I thought I was floating this joint." Black chuckled.

Dro didn't say anything the whole ride. He was in his own world. Making it back around the way Black parked on 8th Street by Dro's grandmother's house. They all got out of the car and began walking back to where the girls was chillin' at. Dro stopped walking and paused.

"What's up bossman?" Black asked.

Dro turned around and walked the other way. Izzo and Black looked at each other with the 'what the fuck' look but decided to follow him. This was his first 'wet' high, so they wouldn't leave him alone by himself. They followed him and they noticed Dro was walking toward Jroc's house. Dro screamed out of nowhere to nobody, "Nigga, I'm straight from these streets. I'm carved from the pavement!" He banged on Jroc's door. Black walked up on him. "What you doing bruh?"

Dro was looking high and crazy. Jroc opened the door and seen Dro, then smiled. In a split second Dro whipped out and had a pretty .40 cal, two-tone Glock pointed in Jroc's face.

"Night, night hot ass nigga!"

CHAPTER 48

"Oh yeah, let me refresh you."
— Black

Dro woke up with the meanest hangover he felt in a long while. He had memories of last night, but it was blurry and inconclusive. Nightmares and different pictures flashed through his head. He was trying to figure out what was real and what was a dream. 'NOT SMOKING THAT SHIT NO MORE,' Dro thought as he made his way to the bathroom. Last night was his first date with the dipah' and in his head the last.

Dro threw some water on his face as the shower heated up. Charmine, his girlfriend, woke up a few minutes later and went to the bathroom, noticing Dro in the shower. That didn't stop her from sitting right on the toilet and let it go. Dro snatched the curtain open. "Ugh, what the fuck, moe!" He seen her on the toilet, shitting, and scrolling through her phone. "I can't believe a little girl like you could smell like that," he said, sliding the curtain back close.

"Whatever, nigga!" Charmine said, then flushed the toilet. "Didn't you say it was called a courtesy flush." She giggled as the shower heated up.

"Ahhhhh!" Dro screamed as the water temperature started to burn his skin and he slipped and fell.

Charmine giggled, wiped herself and got up to wash her hands. "Hurry up, I gotta get ready for work." She left out, shaking her hands dry.

Dro finished and left the bathroom, smoking a jack' (cigarette) while he put his clothes on. He didn't have plans for today. He had to go to the studio and check on some of the projects he had goin' on. Really, he didn't want to around the neighborhood because he did remember what Black told him about the police and didn't know if the warrants were active as of yet. "HOW THE FUCK I'MA DEAL WITH THIS SHIT,' Dro thought as he sat in the kitchen eating a big bowl of Cookie Crisp.

"What a night," Izzo said to Tiara as she finished topping him off with some morning head. All they did for the whole night was fuck. That dipah had Izzo shit brick all night. Tiara loved it and definitely took advantage of the effects. Now it was a new day and Izzo had money on his mind. He kissed Tiara and headed outside to check his trap.

Everything was business as usual for Izzo. He was a show-me type nigga, so until he seen a warrant or heard niggas tell him them peoples came looking for him, he was gonna grind like always.

Entering his trap his lil' men was coolin.' It was still early. Some of them didn't even make it home the night before. Izzo smelt the smoke in the air and followed the scent to the backroom where a few more youngin's was blowing heavy. The backroom was full of smoke clouds so thick he couldn't even tell who was in there. All he saw was about 5 different cherries lit in different areas of the room, letting him know it was at least that many blunts in circulation. Izzo went to the closest one, grabbed it and stepped off. "Thanks," was his only words as he left the back. He felt his hip vibrate to see he had a call from Black.

"Where you at, Slim?"

"Outside," Izzo answered.

"Damn, already?"

"All day, nigga!"

"Come up top. I got a sale for you, and I need to put a bug in your ear."

"Bet, I'm walking up outta the trap now." Izzo ended the call.

Heading up top, Izzo walked the 8th Street way up the middle of the hood. Passing Jroc's house, he just shook his head. 'DAMN HOMIE.' Bending the corner, he was now on T Street looking for Black. He spotted him chillin' in the middle of the block sitting in one of them folding beach chairs that had the cup holder attached.

Izzo walked up on him. "What's up bruh? I see you really chillin' like shit."

"Yeah, I'm coolin'. Wanna hit this OG Kush I got off these frat boys last night?" Black asked, passing it. "But uh, the dude I was talkin' 'bout that I had for you is on his way. He want a whole thing, he geekin' too."

"Yeah, I kinda figured that's what you was talking 'bout. I got what he need."

"That's a bet. I told him $16,500 for it," Black said so sure of himself.

"WHAT!?" Izzo's eyes got big. "No wonder he geekin.' Call him back. I need $37,000 for one of these nigga. You trippin' good, ain't you."

"My bad, shit all the rap songs say they got it for that, so I thought it was the right price," Black said.

"Nigga, do I look like Jeezy, Mr. 17.5 USDA, HELL NAH!"

Waiting for the sale to come, they just kicked it on the block as the day started to unfold. Dro pulled and seen his men cooling on the block without a care in the world. He parked but wondered why they were acting like shit wasn't about to get real and could be possible felons. Dro even drove his girl's Infiniti instead of one of his cars, just to be safe.

Walking toward them, Izzo and Black started laughing. They were high, but when Dro pulled up, it reminded them of last night's events, that shit was unexpected and crazy to say the least.

"Bruh, you was high as Pookie last night," Izzo revealed.

"I'm hip. I'm not fuckin' with shit no more," Dro said, shaking his head, tryna remember.

"Yeah bruh, you was lunchin' good," Black added.

"I don't even remember what happened."

"Oh yeah! Let me refresh your memory."

❖   ❖   ❖

"Bruh, the shit was crazy. You whipped out the cannon on Jroc after you walked to his house bangin' on his door. I swear you was about to squeeze." Black replayed the night:

"What you doing bruh?" Black asked Dro. He was looking too high and crazy. Jroc opened the door and seen Jroc and smiled, then in a split second Dro whipped out and had the gun pointed dead in Jroc's face, point blank range. "Night night, hot ass nigga!" Dro was livid as his finger was about to squeeze.

He was saved by the bell. "Who is that at the door?" Jroc's mother asked. Jroc was still froze from the gun pointed at his head and was unable to respond. She got suspicious and began walking toward the door.

Izzo grabbed Dro as he was about to let the cannon blow. The only reason Dro hesitated was because of the sound of madukes. He knew if he shot Jroc, madukes would have to go too and he loved moms.

Jroc's mother only wanted what's good for her son and was supportive of his company of friends even when she saw them doing things they weren't supposed to; she'll turn the other cheek. For that reason, Dro let Izzo take his gun away as angry tears came down his face. He looked at Jroc with hurt, hatred, and betrayal in his eyes. 'You foul, Slim.'

Jroc just looked down as Black grabbed Dro by his shoulders and walked off. Jroc's mom made it to the door as he was closing it. 'What's wrong baby? Who was at the door?'

Jroc looked at his mother with his shoulders low. 'Ma, I might gotta go away for awhile, just until things get right.'

❖   ❖   ❖

Exposed (The night continued.)
"Chill . . . chill . . ."

Dro

The night has just turned for the worst. Now Dro has just exposed his hand. Jroc now knew that his days were limited. Dro and the crew walked down the street still high. Some higher than others, Dro was ahead of Izzo and Black who were tailing behind, talking to each other.

"That nigga lunched out. He was about to smoke Slim right on his momma's porch, off some Soulja Slim type shit and y'all call me crazy," Black said.

"Yeah fool, that goop bring out your real emotions and shit must have hit 'em like a ton of bricks," Izzo reasoned.

"Fuck dat. I probably still would have smoked 'em and his moms. I never like the bitch anyway with her uppity ass."

Making it back down the street, Dro just leaned up against the fence. He was trying to mellow out, so he could get his thoughts together. The seriousness of their problem was starting to set in.

Dro was wondering how much mess they were really in. His sandbox brother, Jroc, the star witness to send him away. Lawyer fees and all that other bullshit rushed his head. "Fuck!" Dro screamed, but luckily, he always had a lawyer on retainer.

"You a'ight, bruh?" Izzo asked, concerned. Black looked at Izzo with a wild and crazy look. "What the fuck you think, dumbass," he answered for him.

"Nigga, I ain't talking to you."

"Both y'all . . .," Dro rubbed his yead. "Shut up for a minute. This nigga turned state . . . fuck! . . . this nigga got a lot of shit on us."

"I'm hip. Y'all should have let me smoke that hot ass nigga," Black said, rubbing his waistline.

Tiara came around the corner and stopped in front of them. Where you been, boo?" She grabbed Izzo in an embrace. "You stink. Let me smell your dick," she told him as the rest of the girls bent the corner. "Are you high?"

"Are YOU high?" Izzo flipped the question on her. "Talking 'bout sniffin' my dick. Girl you trippin.' But on the low you'll be mad as shit if I whip this muthafucka out for the world to see."

Dro was tippin' (making aware), just looking at the sky trying not to make eye contact with Charmine. She could see right through all his bullshit and walked straight up on him, looking him directly in his face. "OH my God Black! Why you give him that bullshit?"

"Damn, why I had to give it to him?" Black countered.

Screaming, she responded, "YOU THE ONLY ONE THAT SMOKE THAT SHIT!!"

"Chill, chill . . .," Dro said in a slow tone, trying to intervene. Charmine grabbed Dro like a child in trouble by his sleeves. "WE GONE!"

Everybody looked at them storm off and knew Charmine was

mad as shit. It was late, but everybody felt good and was on their own wave and decided to call it a night. The girls were oblivious to what was really goin' on in their circle but would soon get hip. Keisha grabbed Black and informed him that she was ready to go. They said their goodbyes for the night then bounced.

Heather was undecided as Tiara and Izzo stepped off as well. "Damn Keish. You forgot we came together," she said to herself out loud. She walked down the street. Her new apartment wasn't too far from the hood, but Jroc's house was closer. "Let me see if this boy up." Heather dialed the digits.

"Yeah boo. I was waiting on your call. You a'ight?" Jroc asked.

She put on her sexy voice as she responded, "I'm fine, but looking for some company tonight. Are you available?"

"Where you at?"

"Walking down your block."

Nervously he asked, "You by yourself?"

"Yes, why wouldn't I be?"

"Come on. I'll unlock the door. Come straight to my room."

Heather made her way up the street and entered Jroc's house. It was dark and quiet with no lights on throughout the block. Opening the door, she walked with her hands out trying to find the light switch. She never had to use it before. She finally made it to his room and asked, "Damn boo, why you ain't leave no lights on for me to see?"

"My bad, my mind not even here," Jroc admitted, then quickly jumped off his bed. "Did you lock the door?"

"Why you so jumpy? And yes, it's locked."

Jroc was paranoid and it didn't make any sense to Heather, even though she was the reason his homies knew stuff that was supposed to be undisclosed and heard only by his team, his new team of detectives. Them closed doors that were supposed to be heard only by his team, his new team. Jroc sat on the bed and decided to confide to Heather his feelings. She listened and now understood why he was so scared and jumpy. She also knew why Dro and the rest of them looked so zombie-like and were acting different.

"Um, so what you going to do?" she asked, fishing.

"I don't know. You tryna run away with me until this shit blow over?"

"I have to think about it. You know I got a job. I just can't run with," Heather reasoned, but really not trying to go anywhere with him now that Black was in the picture.

She inched closer to him, trying to get his mind off the bull-shit he put himself into. Sex is always a good distraction. She was feeling nice and mellow. She couldn't get fucked by Black, so she settled for some lovemaking from Jroc.

Charmine drove home with Dro in the passenger seat lookin' like a zombie. She never seen him in such a state of mind. It was foreign. He looked normal but lost on the inside as he stared at the sky staring at nothing in particular. She could tell he had a lot on his mind but decided against asking any questions.

Dro was still high, but not as high as he was about 30 minutes ago. He started to mellow out as scenes from today started to flicker back into his head. He reached in the backseat where he found a pint of Patron. He took a swig. "I was about to smoke dat nigga," Dro said in a soft whisper.

Charmine looked over, but wasn't sure of what she just heard and asked, "What you say boo?"

Dro just looked over at her and shook his head. "Nothing boo."

Pulling up to the apartment, the Patron was empty. Charmine helped Dro to their room. As soon as she let him go, he fell face first. It was like his legs couldn't hold the pressure of standing up. Charmine stood over top of him, taking his clothes off and then tucked him in. She got in the bed to cuddle, putting herself to sleep.

CHAPTER 49

Honeycomb Hideout
(90 Days Later)

Jroc been dipping in and out the city for a few months now. After that chilling night when Dro was about to take his life, he has been sneaking around his neighborhood to see his mother. He even traded his Beamer so he wouldn't be a target. He now drove a nice Audi A-8.

It was a long sensual night for Jroc after he woke up in his mother's crib with a smile on his face. He touched the side of his bed, and it was cold. It had to be early if Heather was already gone. She leaves around 6:00 a.m. to head to work. They were still going strong, in his eyes. 'I GOTTA GET UP OUTTA HERE,' Jroc thought, thinking of how his men, especially Black and Izzo would come outside early to catch the morning rush, or next victim in Black's case.

Jroc exited the neighborhood, riding behind limo tints. He was headed to his other girl's house out in Maryland where he been laying low at. He been lampin' (chillin) out there for about 3 months now. The sweet part about the location was that he could hustle around there and make money. He basically relocated.

Tiffany is a lesbian, but Jroc was her first and only since their high school days and she still had a place in her heart for him. So, usually she continued to let him dick her down when her girlfriend don't act right.

Jroc loved that he was the only one fucking her and she let him stay in the guest room 'cause he was droppin' bands on her on the regular as he waited on the outcome of the case. He been gave his statements, so all he had to do was wait on the day he gets to testify, and he could come back to the hood.

Jroc's thoughts were crazy. It's never that easy. The life of a snitch is never that easy, especially when the guy or group of guys you telling has men ready to kill on demand. Your life becomes a lottery ticket. Whoever hit you first, get the big payout.

Pulling up at Tiffany's house, a smile crept across Jroc's face as Tiffany stood at the complex door wearing boy shorts and a tank top. Her nipples was hard looking like baby inky fingertips. 'UM SHE READY.' Jroc was excited that he got the text, letting him know Tiffany and her girl was beefin.' That was one of his favorite texts to receive.

Walking up on her they hugged and kissed. The way she was kissing Jroc you would have thought they were still together. Tiffany pulled him inside and Jroc acted like he didn't have a care in the world. He was safe. He loved her down just like she loves it to be done and rolled over when he was finished.

"Nah nigga, that ain't it. You not done yet." She spread her legs wide.

He licked his lips. "Damn, I miss you." He leaned over and at her box like it was his favorite dish.

Meanwhile Dro was in the studio working with Izzo on his new track. The Feds never came to swarm as of yet, so the grind didn't stop. Black got word from Heather that her boss was on leave for medical purposes and the files were still in the boss's office. He had forgot to give them to Heather before he took off. Jroc's statements just sat in the file box and hasn't even been seen by the Grand Jury as of yet. Heather never reminded him either, per Black.

Izzo was in the booth killing the track with a fat jay' of lemon Haze in his hand putting him in the mood. Dro produced most of his tracks and the music was good. Over the course of the summer and the beginning of Fall, Prophet (Izzo's Rap name) started to get a buzz in the streets. He had a few features from some tycoons in the game and things were looking up.

"Aye Izzo, that was good, but hit the course again so I could place the ad lips on it," Dro said from behind the booth.

'THESE NIGGAS BE FAKIN,
I SWEAR DEY BE HATIN
YOU COME THRU UP TOP,
YOUR BODY GON DROP
BOW BOW 2 TOO DA HEAD,
BOW BOW NIGGA YOU DEAD
NIGGAS BE PURPIN THEY
DON'T WAN NO WORK
PULL UP AND HOP OUT
PUT YOUR NIGGAS IN DIRT
BOW BOW 2 TOO DA HEAD,
BOW BOW NIGGA YOU DEAD.

"That's a wrap baby, you like dat, Slim," Dro spoke into the receiver. As Dro was wrapping things up, Black came in. He was talking to Dro about Heather and how the shit was about to stir back up into motion about their case.

Dro was the logical thinker of the crew. Really he wanted Black to squeeze Heather for the information he could get, but decided against it. It was better for him to take matters into his own hands.

"So, what's da plan?" Black asked, rubbing his hands together.

Izzo looked back from Dro and Black catching the end of the conversation as he came out of the booth. He noticed Dro had a smirk on his face as he looked to the sky.

"Don't even trip, Slim. I'ma holla at her. I'ma see if you really do fuck her better than Jroc and see who team she really on."

"Nigga, I laid it down, and still is might I add. She keeps me hip about everything and willing to do whatever I say when the fuck I say I say it," Black boasted.

"Yeah, right. Only time will tell, but what time she get off?" Dro asked.

"About 3, if she don't work OT."

"Bet, I'ma pull up on her."

❖   ❖   ❖

Heather

Today, actually is the beginning of a good day. I may have a little drama in my life that is spilling over into my professional life, but I'll manage. I've been chilling with the girls a lot and been juggling my situation with Jroc and Black. Well Black is cool. He just come through when I ask or whenever he want, no strings attached, but Jroc is another story.

But back to reality. I'm at work sitting at my desk when my captain came back to work from his health scare and dropped this big caseload on my desk. He was smiling for some reason. I decided against asking because really, I didn't care. But luck is hardly ever on my side 'cause here he comes anyway telling me all about it.

"I'm proud of you Heather. I'm sorry I never told you that before I left. I can't believe I left all this in my office putting this case on a standstill. Them guys probably think they are home free." He giggled. "But whatever you did to get that hoodlum to confess, it worked. On your desk in the original signed statements. It's your case so you can file everything and take it to the Grand Jury, no later than tomorrow. I need them behind bars," the captain stated.

"I have all this other stuff I have to get done, sir," I countered.

"Yeah, I know. That's why I said no later than tomorrow, thank you."

"Okay Cap', I'm on it," I relented.

The case was about to get real once it hit the Grand Jury. Sitting here actually reading the statements for the first time, Jroc basically said he was a lookout and Black did the whole thing while Dro and Izzo watched the truck. 'BLACK IS CRAZY,' I thought as I read the details of how Jroc said Black did the people in the house and also the officers that gave chase.

I had to let Black know what he was up against. Leaving the office, my day was finally over. I been calling Jroc but to no avail. Black been answering all day and wanted to see me later. I made a mental note to call him after I get out of this uniform.

Tiara hit me up too and I told her I'll come around her neighborhood to see her. I was undecided if I really wanted to go around her way. Since that night all that shit happened, I've been a little leery. I know that all the guys knew my occupation, but the girls didn't. Dro scared me the most. He was unreadable and I really couldn't tell his feelings toward me.

Pulling up at my complex it was quiet as usual. My new apartment, well 3 months old, was brand new and the surrounding areas was going through gentrification. It was all type of people in and out of my building. I rode past Jroc's house but didn't see his car, so home is where I'm at.

Going up the steps I went to unlock my door and felt a presence behind me in the hallway. The light behind me turned into a shadow as I turned around to see Dro standing directly behind me. Damn near on my ass. "OH!" I jumped. "Hey Dro, you scared the mess out me," I said, facing him, trying to act normal even though I was scared to death.

Dro had the appearance that screamed authority, defy me and you'll pay. He was dressed in an Armani suit and Cartier frames. "Open the door," he demanded. I fumbled for my keys and found them. I opened the door with my face facing the door and Dro came all the way up on me. His manhood pressed against my behind and I felt him. He wrapped his arms around my waist, pulling his body closer.

I didn't know what to expect. All I knew was his body felt fit and toned pressed up behind me. That was short-lived as I realized what he was doing as my police belt was unhooked, disarming me of my weapons. The lust left, and nerves came back.

Closing the door, he tossed my belt on the couch and turned me around to face him. Face to face I could smell the Big Red gum he crew. I inhaled as he said, "We need to talk."

I looked at him and nodded because I didn't want to make any wrong moves. His appearance is deceitful. Him talking is always better than him quiet. "I need that confession," he stated.

As he spoke, my head was on the ground looking at his shoes. I couldn't give him eye contact, or he could see my fear. He lifted my head as I said, "I have it at the office. I didn't turn it into the Grand Jury or Judge yet," I said softly.

"That's good. I need to know what I'm up against," Dro said.

"He signed it and—"

"Shhhh . . . don't worry about nothing. Just get it to me tomorrow," he said, cutting me off.

"Okay I will, but he didn't say you did anything, only Black."

He nodded his head and said, "Tomar.' we got a date, okay."

"Okay," I replied softly, barely above a whisper.

He left.

I was happy. I thought he was there to kill me or something like that. Especially how he was about to shoot his best friend in front of his mother, so I know my life didn't mean anything to him. Sorry Jroc but I hope it was worth it 'cause I'm playing for the winning team.

❖   ❖   ❖

Black

"Come on boy! I'm ready," Keisha screamed from somewhere in the house. I heard her but really wasn't paying any attention because my mind was elsewhere. I received another note with all types of threats. The shit was starting to blow me and make me want to punish dude on sight. But thoughts of Fred faded when I talked to Dro and he told me he talked to Heather and things should be good by tomorrow, but me, I was tryna see Jroc before then. He been hiding out good and niggas ain't be seeing him. When I see him, he another one that's gonna be on sight.

"Boo, I know you hear me calling you!" Keisha yelled again.

"I'm comin' now."

Walking down the hallway I seen her. "You ready, I been calling you," I asked her, being sarcastic. She just looked at me and walked out the door. I laughed to myself as I followed her.

Getting in the car, Keisha got on her phone and really, I paid her no mind as I listened to Prophet's mixtape. His glow up was real, and he been putting the city on. I heard my girl say she was on her way somewhere and it caught my attention as I turned down the music. "Where the fuck you think you going at?" I asked. "Don't you got work?"

Covering her phone, she spoke. "Nah boo, I'm goin' around your way to meet Heather and Tiara."

When I heard Heather's name, I got tight. She ain't been around the way in a minute and that's the way I preferred it. I really didn't want them getting any closer than they already was because I was fuckin' both of them but fuck it. "Oh," was all that I could muster up as a response.

Pulling around the way, Keisha hopped out and waited for me

to park. Getting out of the car she looked at me. "What? You need an escort?" I asked joking, but serious.

"Tsst." She sucked her teeth and walked off.

"Love you too, boo," I said, more to her back because she was gone.

I was headed to my mom's house. It was my lil sisters birthday and they were turning 13. I had big plans for them. I called a few times, but their cell went straight to voicemail. My mom's phone just rang. I'm used to that. She only answers when she's in need.

Walking toward the crib, it was endless people outside but that's to be expected. It was the weekend and kids was at school all week and parents worked, so this was a chill day for all. Summertime was over, so everybody looked forward to these 2 days off.

Making it to the apartment, I pushed the door open. It was unlocked. Some random nigga was on my couch. That was the first thing I noticed. The nigga had a nerve to be smokin' with his feet up.

"Who the fuck are you? And the fuck my lil sisters at?" I grilled him, walking through the house. "Shanae, Shaniyah!!" I screamed through the apartment as I whipped my pistol out.

The dude laughed at me and then blew smoke out his mouth as he stood up. "I'm the messenger big boy." He had his hands up with a note. "Have a good day." He pulled an envelope out, plucking it to the floor in front of me. "I'm leaving now. Don't you follow or them pretty twins we got won't make it." He smirked. "Your mom's tied up in the room. We ain't take her. Fred know you love them girls more than your momma." He walked toward the door. "Our way or no way, be good." He left.

I fell to my knees, pistol in hand, gripping the hand real tight. "Fuuuuuuuuuukkk!!!" I screamed.

CHAPTER 50

Dro

"Put cho hands down nigga . . ."
— Dro

Walking to my whip I had a plan. I took a ride. Jroc so smart that he dumb. I had a good hunch to where he was at. he so transparent, it's crazy. He still posting pictures and not turning off the location bar. The buildings behind him told me he was in some type of complex.

When he would get mad at his mother back when we was younger, he would run to this same spot. I seen his mother earlier at the deli where she was having her lunch break. Actually, she seen me and called me over. Her being oblivious to the situation she spilled the beans. All I had to do was ask and it rolled right off her tongue.

"Um, he probably still at that confused girl's house. You know, the one he took to the junior and senior prom," she said as I smiled. The guy is so predicable.

I could have told Black and he would have been geeking to do the deed. I still had a soft spot for the guy though and couldn't let Black do him dirty per me putting him on. Now what happens in the streets is whatever. I'm not gonna gate them dice. That's not gonna stop me from pulling up on him to look in his eyes to let him know that he could run but he can't hide.

On the highway I was on the way to Jroc's 'alias' Honeycomb hide out or so he thought. Tiffany's house was only like 20 minutes outside the city. I had the window up as I cruised to the sounds of some classic raps by 'Ghetto Boyz' blowing kush just me and the highway.

I pulled up in Tiffany's complex. The neighborhood was live and jumpin'. It looked like a goldmine, as far as the hustle go. I made a mental note to drop some work off on a few niggas and try to secure this complex. I decided to park and walk the rest of the way through the apartments. I didn't want Jroc to notice my car or see me before I saw him. The best pat about this complex was that it had so many cuts you could pop up out of on this nigga. This would be a perfect complex to snake a nigga out.

Coming through the cut I seen Jroc chilling at another building. I really didn't want to confront him in front of everybody, so I backed up and went around the building as few niggas was watching me. I didn't care. I had 30 rounds for them if they wanted 'em.

In front of Tiffany's building, I seen she had the same car from high school. I came around the other side and slid into the building undetected. Climbing the stairs, I reached her door.

KNOCK KNOCK.

The door opened with Tiffany in some leggings with a tank top on, no bra. She still looked flawless. I know Jroc been in her crushing this pussy. She loved some Jroc.

"Oh . . . my . . . God!" She put her hands over her mouth as she screamed in excitement, jumping for joy. She jumped in my arms and wrapped her legs around my waist. I held her up by her ass. Her body was so soft. My dick jumped. "How you been, brova? I always ask about you. I heard you and Prophet on the radio," she said as I smiled naturally.

"I've been good. I see you still looking how you lookin'." I licked my lips as she blushed.

"Boy, stop. You terrible. What brings you here?" She closed the door. "I know it wasn't you wondering how I'm doing." She looked in my eyes. "All I get from you is a 'like' on Instagram, not even a comment. So I know you must be here for Jroc's tired ass." She answered her own questions, grabbing her phone to call him.

I grabbed her arm slightly. "Don't tell him I'm here. It's a surprise," I whispered in her ear like it was a secret. "Just tell him to come here and when he do just give us a minute."

She narrowed her eyes and walked in my personal face. She kissed slowly and seductively while grabbing my manhood, then let it go. "I got you boo," and got on her phone.

The kiss wasn't nothing. She always was like that toward me in school, always flirting, but we had a friendship and that was the type of shit she would do.

I heard her on the phone. "Hey boo! I need you to come here asap. I gotta talk to you." Tiffany winked at me. After a pause, she was listening, then hung up and tossed her phone on the couch.

I must have been looking crazy or had a wild expression on my face because she asked, "What's wrong?"

"Nothing, what he day doe?"

"Oh, he went to the store. He'll be back in a half hour or so," she said, walking to the back of her apartment. "Make yourself at home."

I sat down and started flipping through the channels. From the back I heard Tiffany calling for me. "BROVA!" I got up and followed the sound and it came from the bathroom.

"Yeah," I answered from outside the door.

"Go in my room and get me that wash rag on my bed."

I walked to her bedroom and saw her towel and panty set laid out with lotion and other shit surrounding it. I grabbed the rag and left out. Opening the bathroom door, I reached around it to pass her the cloth. She slid the shower curtain open and exposed her flawless body. "Damn, you bad and sexy all in one breath," I told her, giving her the cloth. She looked at the cloth and told me to bathe her. "Shid, a'ight." I didn't think twice.

I always used to like feeling her up and she liked when I did it as well. Back in the day she wanted me to be her first, and I've been in this same situation plenty of times. But Jroc was my man, and I knew he had the biggest crush on her, so I always declined her, plus I had a girl. But now it ain't his girl and if it was, I wouldn't give a fuck. Times has changed.

I got to rubbing her body down, touching every part of her body, even slid my finger over her clit a few times as she moaned. After getting all the soap off her, I looked for the towel, but she got out dripping wet and walked to her room with a slow switch of her hips. 'DAMN.' I watched her walk.

She gave me the come here fingers, not even looking my way. It's like she knew I was watching her. Like a puppy I was on her heels. She made it to her bedroom, grabbed the towel and tossed it to me. "Dry me off." I walked up on her, wrapped the towel around her and her arms wrapped around me as she started kissing me. I accepted her kisses as she went to undo my pants, taking them off. She moaned in between kisses and said, "Um, finally you gonna let me get some." She grinned.

"Hell yeah, get you some," I told her as she dropped to her knees and started sucking the skin off my shit. She had the prettiest lips, and she kept her eyes on me as she worked.

Grabbing her up, I pushed her on the bed. She was ready. I was gonna ask her for a rubber, but said, fuck it, only me and Jroc probably the only ones that sample this box, because it was super tight. She wasn't the roller type. If I didn't already have me a ride or die, I would have made her mines. Her and her girlfriend.

She was dripping wet, which made her even sexier with the

shower scent still strong. Her walls felt like a glove, maybe even virgin pussy and I was in love . . . with the box of course. The pussy was good. She must have felt the same way about the dick because she was loud as shit. She was a screamer. I swear I was in that joint for like 15 minutes and came all in her. I could have went another round, but I wasn't tryna be that nigga that got caught with his pants down and his ass out.

She cleaned my dick and told me I could have her however and whenever I wanted. The offer sounded good, and I might just take her up on that offer. I left the room to let her get herself straight.

In the living room I fired up a jay' and almost got to relax as I remembered why I was here. Tiffany's phone was ringing, and it sat on the table. I looked to see it was a message from Jroc: 'PARKING NOW:)'

I told Tiffany, but she was still in her room. Then seconds later I heard the shower water come on. I stood behind the door as I heard it opening. Jroc walked in, not even noticing me behind him. "Ol' pretty Ricky," I said to his back. He froze in place, then put his head down.

"Damn," he said.

"Yeah nigga. You need to change it up if your sucka ass was gonna try and run and hide."

Turning around slowly, he spoke, "Only nigga knew about this spot is you."

"Put your hands down nigga. What? You expected to see a gun pointed at you. I'm not here to kill you. I loved you man, like a brother. I just wanna know why?"

"It wasn't even supposed to be like this, Slim. I only told on Black," he said.

"But you told bruh', where they do that at?"

Jroc just shook his head. I looked at him in his eyes. "I'm not gonna tell nobody where you at. I just wanted to look you in the eyes to let you know I'm not gonna touch you, but you dead to me. Be afraid, be very afraid."

"I'm sorry bruh', for real. It wasn't supposed to be like this."

"Nah, you ain't sorry, but you will be," I told him, closing the gap between us, giving him a bro hug, ending our friendship. "Tell baby girl bye for me and for the record she don't know you a firecracker unless you told her."

Jroc was at a loss for words. I walked out of the apartment. I know I just word fucked him and rolled the dice by letting him live. Walking through the parking lot I reached my car. I had plans for tonight. It was a listening party for Prophets' new mixtape, that was the move.

CHAPTER 51

"He's gonna kill you."
— Shanae

Shanae and Shaniyah sat in a big room. It was surrounded by toys, a big 75-inch plasma and a shitload of DVDs. They were taken in the early morning hours of the night. Shaniyah was nervous. She was more timid of the two. Shanae was anxious, but she didn't scare easy.

Shanae was mean mugging the man watching them from across the room at the door. A face that Black had taught her. The goon felt uncomfortable as he asked, "What you looking at little girl?"

Shanae looked at him and narrowed her eyes before she responded. Shaniyah gave her a pleading look to be quiet and Shanae hugged her sister. "It's gonna be okay. Donte gonna come get us, promise."

The goon laughed.

KNOCK.

The girls looked at the door. It opened. There stood Fred, Jr. He held the door open for a servant, a young Brazilian woman. She was gorgeous as she walked in with a silver platter full of food. The young lady approached the twins with a smile and set the small table up and placed the food on it so the girls could eat.

Fred sat on the couch and looked at the girls. He shook his head. He recently found out what his father had done to one of the girls and now understood Black's fury. If he would have known this from the beginning, he probably wouldn't even have approached Black about it, but during the last few months him and Black had grown to hate each other.

He put a ransom on the kids' head for the fun of it, off 'GP.' He didn't need the money, just a reason to make Black hurt and sweat.

Fred moved closer to Shaniyah. She cringed up and leaned into Shanae's arms. She held her and stared at Fred as he began to speak.

"You don't have to be scared. I'm not gonna hurt you." He had a daughter and was disgusted at what his father did to such an innocent child.

"We ain't scared?" Shanae jumped to Shaniyah's defense. "He's gonna kill you."

Fred smiled at the comment and got up. "Enjoy your dinner. I know y'all not used to good food like this. I've seen your house." He left.

He walked around his house. it was massive, just for him and a little girl. It was in Chevy Chase, Maryland. Six bedrooms, 5 and a half bathrooms, 4-car garage, private pool and an outdoor kitchen. Can't forget the lower level had an entertainment room and an exercise room. The place was laid out and Fred was heavy' (a lot of money). He pushed heroin through the city and owned a few car lots. He was getting money, quietly.

His righthand man, Cigar, was the front man. He was of Italian descent, but American born, straight out of the hood. He ran the empire with an iron fist, no shorts, no loses.

Fred and Cigar sat in front of the pool and chopped it up. "So, what's the move for the little girls?" Cigar asked.

"I'm just tryna ruffle a few feathers, beat his, maybe even shoot 'em, but I'm not gonna hurt them little girls." He took a pull of the blunt. "Unless he makes me, but that one sister got a smart mouth. She remind me of him so much." Fred released the smoke from his nostrils.

"Okay boss, well I'm 'bout to go pick your money up from the traps and make a few runs."

"Be safe."

A smile was on his face, even though it was all bad. Black was at the police station sitting in the car. His mother forced him to take her there to file a missing person's report. She wanted to say a kidnapping, but she didn't have any details that would help her in that situation.

Black was thinking of the good times he shared with his sisters and was determined to get them back. He had to do something. He damn sure wasn't going to wait on the police. He exited the car and leaned on the hood and decided to re-read the letter the goon left for him:

> 'It's time to pay the piper Donte.
> How could you leave your Queens un-
> protected in this game of chess. Did
> you think I wouldn't follow up on my
> promises I made to you at our last meet-
> ing? Did you think I was all talk? I'm
> in the big league's boy! You small time,
> stay in your lane and things like this

wouldn't happen. Remember, you have to always use your brain in this game. And you always have to use your gun. On the card is an address to one of my car lots. Drop off $250,000 big face blues. I hope you got it, Big Bank, matter fact you better have it if you want to see these lil bitches for another birthday. They getting old too, you think they old enough to make me some money? You got one week.'

The pint of syrup that Black drank had him sitting on the curb as he placed the letter back in his pocket. His mother came out of the station livid. "It's all your damn fault, it has to be!" she spat. She was hysterical. The sad part was that she was knocked out when Black came in the house. She didn't get to hear the conversation he had with the goon in the living room.

"MY FAULT?!" Black matched her tone. "I ain't do shit! You let whoever take them." He tried to push the blame and guilt off him.

Black dropped his mom's off at the crib and headed straight to the Same Guy Entertainment Studio. He walked straight through the metal detector as it sounded. The officer tried to grab Black but was punched in the face. Black looked at the other officer who apologized. "Sorry Black, he didn't know," he pleased with his hands raised. Black continued to walk as he headed to Studio A, the biggest one where Dro sat in a chair behind the soundboard. Izzo was in the booth, vibing to the beat with Kush in the air as he rapped.

Dro seen the look in Black's eyes and stopped the track. Izzo opened his eyes to see what was goin' on because the music had stopped in his ears. He seen Black and Dro talking with a bunch of hand gestures and Black pacing as Dro read the ransom letter. "Damn, it's always something," Izzo said out loud entering the room with them.

"Don't trip off the money. I got whatever you need," Dro said as he handed Izzo the note to read.

"Fuck is this?" he asked.

Talking to himself, Black paced some more. "This nigga got my babies, Slim. I'm 'bout to paint da city. It's 'bout to rain blood 'round dis bitch." Black was furious. Izzo read it and was ready. "What's the move cuz?"

Black had an idea to go to the car lot but decided against it. It would draw too much attention. Instead, he got the name of the manager off the card and gave Heather a call. "I got an ideal, hol' fast," he said as the phone rang.

The call ended and Black was scheming with his men as a plan came to light. After about 5 minutes Heather called back with a home address on the guy. "Let's go," black said, smirking.

Dro made a call to his connect and he agreed for them to all come see him at a warehouse off the outskirts of the city. They pulled up in Black's armor proofed, smoked out Charger. "Lead the way, playa," black said to Dro as they got out of the car.

Entering the warehouse Dro was greeted by Purple. This was the guy's name, 'Purp' for short. He was a huge, massive man. It looked like he could have played for the NFL in his younger days. His shoulders and back were wide, his chest huge. A true definition of African descent, when his skin was so black it looked purple. His appearance always worked in his favor, especially in the business he was in, but not so much with the ladies. He was ugly.

Shockingly in a tiny voice that of a child or young teenager, Purp spoke smiling naturally. "Dro, my man . . ." Izzo chuckled after hearing his voice. Purp narrowed his eyes, still in the embrace of Dro. Izzo felt the stare and turned his laugh into a cough.

Dro was released and he introduced Izzo and Black. The frown that was once on his face left and a smile reappeared.

"Oh shit! You Prophet, huh?" Purp said as he rapped a verse like it was his own song as his hands waved up and down to the flow. Izzo smiled and was pulled into a half hug along with Black in a quick second. The scene looked like when 'Damon' came home from prison off the movie, Friday After Next, when he had Craig and Day heads pressed against his chest. "And you must be the muscle, huh, big guy," Purp said to Black. "Follow me."

Men were everywhere on the floor and top tiers. 'THIS NIGGA GOT TO BE DONING MORE THAN SELLING GUNS,' Black thought as he looked around. Making it to the office he had a sign hanging that read: BLACK IS BEAUTIFUL, BUT MY GUNS ARE SEXY AND EMOTIONAL. Izzo smiled after reading that. It looked like a library how books were on every wall and in the back sat one desk. It was a cherry wood table and three matching chairs that all looked comfortable.

He sat behind his desk, smiled, then hit some type of button or switch. The walls rotated as it showed an arsenal of weapons, guns galore. Black giggled. The sight of so many weapons tickled him. He went straight to the assault rifles and his first choice that he grabbed was FNH FNAR STANDARD. It was a gas operated autoloader with .308 win caliber bullets with a 20 round magazine. Then he grabbed a FNH SCAR 17s CARBINE. It weighed 8 lbs. with an adjustable folding or removable sight set. it also held 20 rounds, standard. "Pack these up!" Black said as he continued.

Dro and Izzo stared at him as he grabbed another big gun. It was a Barrett 82 A1. This weapon was massive. You couldn't even run fast with it. It had a detachable 100 round box, adjustable and detachable bipod legs and flip up sights. "Hey, sweet things, where you been? I'ma look like Scarface when I bust this joint," Black said as he posed. "Say hello to my little friend." He cheesed a big smile.

Dro and Izzo grabbed a shitload of handguns and even a case of Semtex grenades. Purp looked at them with wild eyes and excitement. "Damn, y'all 'bout to do damage."

"Send me an invoice," Dro said, not even looking at him.

"Nuff' said."
They left.

CHAPTER 52

Squeeze 'em

"No, No, I told you everything."
— Tony

Black and Izzo pulled up at the manager's house. Tony 'swindle' Harris. He earned his name from the type of business he conducted at the lot. He owned a nice home and had this years Benz in the driveway.

Tony's light was on, only on the lower level of the house. Only one light shined upstairs. They didn't own any curtains and Izzo noticed it was a child's room. "That nigga gotta be downstairs," Black said.

This was one of the nicer neighborhoods. Even though it was almost dark you could notice that everyone's grass was green, and you had to have a few dollars to stay in the area.

It was about 7:00 p.m. and the sun was down. Izzo slid his

mask down. The bare face days were now over with now because of his recent status. He was a mogul and people recognize him all the time now. Black didn't give a fuck that he was bare faced.

Black went out the front door and turned the knob. It was locked. "Shit!" Black sighed. "I see this nigga ain't get comfortable out here in the boonies."

KNOCK KNOCK.

Black stepped back off the porch as Izzo leaned with his back against the house. A beautiful Asian woman opened the door in a silk nightgown. To be foreign she was cut up like a bag of dope as if she was mixed. Her nipples were busting through the silk blouse as the autumn wind stiffened them. "Can I help you?" she asked.

"Hello Mr. Harris. Is Tony home?" Black smiled.

She looked back. "Uh, hold—"

Izzo placed the gun to the back of her head. "Scream and you dead, and the kid upstairs." Black casually walked past Izzo and Tony's wife, then asked, "Which way?"

The wife pointed to the sound of the T.V. Black led the way with the wife behind him and Izzo behind her with the pistol trained at her head. Turning the corner of the living room entrance there he was. Tony. He was sitting in his Lazy Boy recliner watching football with a beer in his hand.

Not even looking back, Tony heard the footsteps. "Baby, who was at the door? I hope it wasn't them fuckin' neighbors complaining about Murder barking in the backyard."

Black answered, "Who winning the game?"

Tony turned around and faced Black to see him pointing his custom-made Mark XIX Desert Eagle, with 24K gold finish. "Hey man, whatever you want , you got it!"

"Information."

"What information man?"

"Tell me about your boss, Fred."

Tony put his head down and blew air out as if he was not going to answer.

"Izzo!" Black called out. Izzo grabbed the wife and snatched her gown off. She was now naked, tryna cover up. "Put your hands to the fuckin' sky, bitch!" Black demanded. Izzo never looked away. He was happy to see her exposed boy. She was flawless.

"Wait! You didn't even give me a chance to speak." He tried to reach out for his wife who was scared and shaking. Izzo was creeped out as he watched her ass shake as she shivered.

'WOP!' Black smacked Tony with the gun. "Nobody told you to move."

"Okay, listen." Tony sang like a canary, telling all he knew. He didn't like Fred, so it came naturally.

Fred treated his staff like trash and paid them crumbs compared to the money that was being brought in. Black looked on the counter and grabbed Tony's and his wife's IDs. "I won't be back unless anything you told me was a lie. If I come back, I'm not gonna kill you. I'ma kill her and that pretty little girl in this picture that I know is upstairs, understood?"

Tony nodded.

"You wanna add anything?" Izzo asked as he chambered a round.

"No, no I told you everything," Tony spoke rapidly.

"Well, goodnight. Hopefully, I don't see you again." Black walked off. Izzo smacked the wife on her bare ass and winked.

"Buh Bye!"

Black checked his watch. All that happened in 10 minutes flat but felt like an hour. Black called Heather and she told him that she left a package at her apartment for him. He told Izzo he needed a few soldiers, but loyal for the next move, like ASAP. Izzo made the call as they cruise din the car, headed uptown to put things into motion. Black had a list of things to do. One by one he planned on completing each and every task until his sisters were returned and Fred was dead for the disrespect.

❖   ❖   ❖

The nigh was still young. Black just left Heather's house, picking up all the gifts she left behind for him, along with more information that he requested. It was always a plus to have somebody on the inside. It makes things so much easier.

Fred gave Black 7 days to get the money. This was going to be 7 days of murder and corruption in search for him. Black, Izzo and 3 other young boys, no older than 16, was in a stolen Excursion truck. Tony had given Black an address to a trap house where he was to drop money off to Fred at a later date.

It was crazy. The trap house wasn't far from his own neighborhood, maybe about 10 blocks away. Pulling up, they were strapped like Taliban. Black and Izzo was scrapped with two of the three assault rifles they had just gotten. They decided to leave the showstopper for another day.

The young goons were strapped with .40 caliber Glocks with 30 round extensions hanging from the butt of the pistol. Black and Izzo leaned on opposite sides of the door and knocked loud with two kicks of the door. "POLICE!" as two of the young boys ran full speed with a police door ram in tow, courtesy of Heather.

BOOM!!

The door flew open as Izzo and Black threw two canisters of tear gas through the door, another courtesy. "Police! Hands up! Let me see your fuckin' hands!" Black ordered. He got pretty good at playing the role. Black stood in front with Heather's badge hanging from his neck. He looked at the young boys. "Search this shithole." The complied as they spread out. Black turned his attention to the guys in the house. "Where's Fred?" He paced. It was silent.

Two of the young boys came back with guns and drugs. They placed it on the table. Izzo had them lined up against the wall. It was 7 of them. Everybody had a mask on except Black. Izzo and the young boys were masked up in all Black with D.E.A> vest on.

"You all wanna go down for all of this? You know it's a life sentence." He put on the act.

Silence.

"Sir, he has them trained. They are tight-lipped. If we hang them by their thumbs for two weeks, they might tell us their names." Izzo joined the show. The last young goon came down the stairs, dragging a big bag of money. He had his gun in one hand, the bag in the other. "Whoa!" The carpet tripped him, forcing him to fall.

BOC!!

Everybody ducked for cover as a round went off. "Oh shit! My bad." One of the seven hustlers slid down the wall slowly with a circle in the middle of his head, headshot. Brains splatter was on the wall behind him.

"Damn," Black said. "You can't do nothing right."

Izzo laughed. "That's why they call 'em Lefty." The rest of Fred's men were visibly shook, but still didn't relent. "Last time asking." Izzo and the young boys stood beside Black.

Silence.

"Okay, have it your way. For the record we ain't the police."

'TAT TAT TAT BRRRRRRATT TAT TAT BOC! BOC! BOC! . . . BRRRRRAT TAT TAT! Endless shots pierced their bodies, and the bodies didn't fall until the shots stopped.

The wall looked like artwork, maybe a Picasso of some sorts, no survivors. They picked up all the work off the table and bounced.

Entering Izzo's trap, Black took all the money and Izzo, the drugs. They split the guns as Izzo broke off his lil men with some work of their own and gave his as a front.

Black came off with $100,000 big blue faces. "This would go toward the ransom. If dude other spots like this, I might need Dro's help." He smirked. Izzo came off with 7 bricks of soft, pure uncut. He was excited from the possible revenue, then his phone vibrated.

"Aye, we still goin' that listening party. Tiara blowing my horn up about that shit," Izzo asked, looking at his missed call.

"Keisha blowing mines up too. I ain't gonna stop your shine supastar. I'm 'bout to go get her and get ready. I need to get my mind off the things for a minute. I'll see you later." They separated.

CHAPTER 53

Prophets Listening Party

"So, what will it be supastar?"
— *Bartender*

Dro put everything in motion for tonight's events. The girls thought it was a date night, but in all actuality, it was a surprise listening party for Izzo that wasn't a surprise because everybody knew about it. He had the girls ride together and the men did the same. The females rode in a stretched pearl white Rolls-Royce Phantom, valued at $298,000 standard. The good men rode in three Bugatti Veyron, 16.4 Grand sport Vitesse. It valued at $2.5 million a piece. They smelled like money, but whips were rented.

You know you winning when you pull up to a Dave and Busters and it don't open until you walk the red carpet to the entrance. Heavy'. It's a word to describe the weight they carried.

It's nothing like the feeling of being a kid again while playing games, but yet feeling grown being able to get twisted as you do it. This was the feel in the location as Prophet introduced each song as it played. That was the game plan in Dro's mind.

Getting out of the cars, cameras flashed, and the girls were shocked and didn't know it was goin' to be this big of an event. Dro invited paparazzi to shed light on his homie/artist. They had their chains out representing the label which were big S*G interlock links meaning Same Guy, a gift that Dro gave each of his homies when he first got on. Pictures were taken and everyone looked good in their casual but expensive fits.

Walking in, a massive crowd followed close behind. Photos of Prophet graced the walls of the establishment along with a full life size wax figure of him as well. The girls looked around as about 10 women with sparkling bottles came to congratulate Izzo on his Platinum single. Izzo was shocked. Dro went all out for him and never did he expect this much.

"First spot, the liquor spot," Black sang and Izzo along with Dro agreed as the girls still stood in awe of the place, not noticing the guys step off.

"So, what will it be supastar?" the bartender asked.

Everybody ordered their drinks and sat at the bar. The hostess of the party came with a headset and gave it to Izzo. "As the songs come on, hit the switch on the side to turn the mic on so you can introduce the songs. You could rap along with it too if you would like. I'm sure they would enjoy that." She winked.

"A'ight bet," he said, putting it on. Dro hopped up and looked around. He liked the scene around him. "Moe, I ain't set this shit up so we could just sit at the bar and get twisted."

"You ain't said nothing slick, Slim. You want work, point any game out in this joint and I'll beat that ass," Izzo boasted.

"Don't rap me up." Dro and Izzo headed to play whatever game that was multiple players. A crowd followed them as Izzo turned his mic on. "Yo, this track right here is called 'Niggas Be Purpin'. I hope you enjoying it like I'm enjoying whooping my man's ass in this motor cross race." He turned the mic off.

"Damn, why we just can't chill," Black said to the bartenders. He got up and followed behind the crowd. He was literally the only security.

Black wanted to stay at the bar, but out the corner of his eye he seen Keisha and Heather walking toward the bar. He didn't want to be stuck with both of them by himself.

Coming up behind Dro was Charmine and Tiara with a bunch of tickets from whatever game they were playing. The first game was over and Izzo was the winner. Now all 4 of them was in straight gunning for a victory as they raced side by side. Cameras flashed, taking in different moments of the night. The race was intense. It was for bragging rights and sexual favors later in the night.

The next track came on. "I hope y'all enjoyed that." The fans clapped. "Well, this right here is a track I wrote for my baby, Ti-ara. She right here wit me y'all, from day one." Tiara blushed and covered her face. "It's called 'Dreams Come True'."

Black was really in another world. He was tossing back shots left and right while Keisha and Heather waited to get in the next race. About 2 hours passed. It was a good turnout, and everyone continually thanked Dro as it neared closing hours.

"I gotta go drain the anaconda," Black said to nobody in particular as he wobbled to the bathroom.

Izzo looked at Dro and Dro just followed behind Black as he walked. He leaned on the wall outside the bathroom as he listened to the echo of the music. Black went into the bathroom. Walking to the urinal, Black went to handle his business. He heard a toilet flush and it made him look at the mirror to see who walked behind him as he pissed. Black rubbed his eye a few times to make sure his eyes wasn't playing tricks on him.

Dude walked past and went to wash his hands. Black shook his man a couple times, then flushed the pisser. Walking up behind the guy, he hit him in the back of his neck with a straight jab, pushing the guy's face toward the mirror and shattering it.

"Ahhhhh shit! You bitch ass—" Jroc's mouth was shut with another jab, forcing him to the ground.

2 hours before . . .

Jroc didn't have a clue as to what he was getting himself into. He was with his female fuck buddy and she invited him to a listening party. She didn't remember the name of the artist. All she kept telling him was that he should know him because the guy was from the city. Jroc didn't put the pieces to the puzzle together. Once he arrived he was shocked to see the turnout.

She even had tickets for them to get in V.I.P. Once Jroc entered and seen the pictures and posters, he got instantly nervous. He couldn't turn around and leave. He was already in the building. He thought he would be good if he just avoided Dro and Izzo. He didn't see Black all night. It was pretty crowded. He didn't even see none of the girls. He made sure he stayed out of the light of the flashing cameras. All was good until he had to shit . . .

❖   ❖   ❖

. . . Jroc looked like he seen a ghost. He tried to get back up and try to fight. Black wasn't have it. Black hasn't seen him in about 3 to 4 months. He was furious and twisted. "Nigga you gonna snitch doe . . ."

PUNCH, KICK!

"Over a bitch, doe!"

STOMP! STOMP! Black screamed on him as he continued to beat shit down Jroc's legs. Each punch Black threw, a word was said before it landed.

Curling up, Jroc pleased, "Come on, bruh . . . stop," he cried out.

Black stopped to look at him. He shook his head as he started to walk off, heading to the door. He paused. 'FUCK THAT!!' Black ran back and jumped in the air to do an elbow drop like he was in a wrestling ring. Landing it, he got up and started the beating all over again.

Meanwhile, outside the bathroom, Dro was leaning against the wall, playing with his phone oblivious to what was goin' on on the other side of the door. He reached into his pocket to retrieve a jack' (cigarettes), never taking his eyes off his phone. The listening party was trending on Instagram. Out of nowhere some little fingers sparked a flame for his jack.

Dro looked up to see Tiffany, a friend from school. The young lady that Jroc was lamped with when he paid him a visit a while back. A big smile came across her face as she rushed to kiss Dro all in his mouth. Dro accepted the kiss, then pulled back, thinking of Charmine. "Hey boo!!" Tiffany spoke, excited as always.

"Sup' shawty. What you doing here?" Dro asked, looking around.

"Don't get nervous. I know your boo here. I just spoke to her. She still looking good too. Maybe us 3 could have some fun." She reached and grabbed his dick, slightly squeezing it.

"Girl, you better stop."

She smiled and licked her lips. "Make me." Dro shook his head as she continued.

"But I'm chillaxing. Jroc came with me so we could get out the city, yak no."

"Same here, but mostly to promote my artist and homie Prophet."

"Did he go to school with us?"

"Elementary but not high school. He stop going by then." Dro hipped her as another thought came to mind. "You said you was with Jroc?"

"Yeah, he in the bathroom. He gonna be happy to see you. He always talking about ol' times like y'all don't see each other no more."

"That's what's up . . ." Dro paused. "Hold up, he in the bathroom?" She nodded yes. "Oh shit!!" He rushed to the bathroom.

Busting through the door he seen Black with Jroc's head in the toilet trying to drown him as he flushed the toilet with his foot continuously. "Black! Let 'em go!" Dro ran over to pull him off Jroc.

Black kicked Jroc one more time before Dro was able to separate the two. Leaving the bathroom Dro told Tiffany to go and help Jroc while he and Black left the area. Black looked back at Tiffany, "Ayo, ain't that Tiff from junior high, Slim?"

"Yeah fool, but fuck dat, we gotta go. I was talking to her when she told me she came with Jroc. I knew it was gonna be a crazy scene in the there," Dro said, looking around, scanning the room tryna find everybody else.

Dro spotted the rest of the crew. They were at the door, smiling for pictures as Prophet signed autographs. Black grabbed a few napkins off a table to wipe his hands and face. He then grabbed a drink out of a dude's hand, drank it and tossed the glass. "What nigga, bill me," he said walking at the guy who had the stuck face. They all make it to the front and Izzo glance to notice everyone where he was. "Y'all ready?"

"Yup," Black belched.

Exiting the spot, their rides was already waiting. Charmine smiled and looked into Dro's eyes with a glossy smirk. "That was fun baby and unexpected. I really enjoyed it."

Getting into the whips, the next location was this nice restaurant that was 5-stars for service and food. Dro really pulled all the tricks out for his man to do it big and get a taste of the life to come.

Tomorrow was back to business to secure their future, but tonight was all about the glow up. In the restaurant they were seated. Heather began talking code to Black and a message was exchanged. Black stood up and headed to the bathroom. It had to be important if she had to tell him now. Heather crept off behind him, but went the long way, giving the illusion she was being sneaky, telling everyone she was going to make a call.

Entering the male bathroom she spotted Black's shoes and opened the stall. He was surprised. "What the fuck!" Black reached for his weapon, but looking over his shoulder to see Heather standing there. "Girl, you almost got smoked," he said, putting his shirt back over his waist.

"Quickie or nah', ain't that how you say it." She giggled.

"You crazy girl," he said, looking around her.

"Yeah, in love with that." She pointed to his rising print. She went to grab it and began stroking git.

"Fuck it!"

Black bent her over the stall and punished her from the back. Meanwhile, everybody else was at the table eating, oblivious to what the other two was up to. Good conversation and re-membrance of good times became the topic of conversation. Black returned and minutes later Heather came back as well. Dro looked at both of them and read between the lines. Black smiled at Dro, which confirmed his thoughts.

After the meal and a few drinks, and even a little dancing, they were ready to leave. Leaving was different from coming. Dro, Charmine and Heather rode in the Rolls Royce and the rest of the crew rode in the other cars.

Dro decided to give Heather a ride in the morning. She was too drunk. Actually, he slipped something in her wine so he could ensure he get them papers in the morning.

Pulling up to Dro's crib, Charmine headed to open the door as Dro carried Heather. She was busted. Her skirt was blowing and Dro noticed she ain't have any panties on and her pussy was bald as the day she was born with pretty pink lips. Charmine seen her as he walked by her. "Cover her ass up, boo. Got her twat all out."

"Shit, my bad."

Charmine went straight to the bathroom. Dro carried Heather to one of the guest rooms and tossed her on the bed. Heather landed on the bed then fell over to the other side. Dro ran to the other side. "Damn, my bad snowflake, you a'ight?"

He went to pick her up and she was eagle spread on the floor. Her pussy was exposed for Dro to see as Heather licked her fin-ger and put it between her walls. Dro looked around the corner. He was tempted. He picked her up and laid her on the bed.

She rolled over and grabbed his belt buckle so she could pull him closer. She moaned. "I just want a taste. I won't tell if you don't." She tried to unbuckle his belt. He grabbed her hand, stop-ping her dead in her tracks before anything could get started. "Sorry baby girl, I'm not tryna die tonight," he told her, thinking of Charmine in the next room.

She stood up wobbling and dropped her straps from her dress. It fell to the floor and her breast set upright. 'DAMN.' Dro looked at her playboy naked body in awe. Shaking his head he walked toward her. "Do what you suppose to do for me to-morrow and I'll beat this pussy like I know you want me to." He had three fingers in her wet tunnel as he spoke. She moaned and backpedaled to the bed, falling out, instantly snoring.

Dro came out of the room as Charmine was walking past. "Is she alright?" she asked.

Closing the door quickly he responded, "Yup, sleeping like a baby."

"Okay, come to bed. I wanna show you something . . ."

CHAPTER 54

Dro

"Congrats pops!"

I woke up early as shit. I slept about 3 hours, and it was over. It was now 6:30 a.m. I was on my way down the hall to the guest room. Opening the door, I see Heather asleep in the middle of the bed still ass naked, curled up with a thumb in her mouth.

I walked over to her. As I got closer, I picked her dress off the floor. I smacked her ass. She moaned. "Ooh." She rolled over, looked at me and smiled. "Hey Dro," she said with sleepy eyes as I tossed her the dress.

"Rise and shine, time to head to your crib," I said, turning around to leave the room.

I was already dressed and ready. Charmine was still asleep. She was twisted from the night before, plus you know I laid it down last night. She was sound asleep.

Today was the day to get the ball rolling on this situation. Looking at my phone I had 3 texts. One from Black and 2 from Izzo. I opened the first two from Izzo. He ain't want shit. He was laughing and cursing me out for not telling him that Black was beating Jroc's ass in the bathroom. The second text informed that he was home and safe. 'BLACK HAD TO TELL THAT NIG-GA, HE CAN'T HOLD NOTHING,' I thought as I scrolled to the next text to see what Black wanted.

Black on the other hand texted me that him and Keisha was at the hospital. I called him ASAP.

"Yeah bruh'," he answered.

"What's up? Everything good?"

"Yeah . . . Keisha had alcohol poison and she prego, moe." He sounded defeated.

"Con grats, pops!" I said to lift his spirits.

"Yeah, I hear you, but I got shit to do. I'll hit you later."
CLICK.

After he hung up, I just looked at the phone shaking my head. I know Black was going through it, especially the shit with his lil sisters. Heather came down the stairs looking like a new person and wide awake.

"Good morning'!" She spoke, sounding all country in shit.

"Ready?" I asked as I made my way to the door. She was on my heels as I walked to my garage. I decided to pull my '96 Impala from under the sheets. Getting in the car, we pulled off on our way to her apartment. We made it there in about 20 minutes. The traffic wasn't heavy yet. We beat rush hour by like 15 minutes.

I stayed outside as she got herself together. She came back outside with her gun and badge hanging around her neck. That shit threw me off to actually see her in work mode. She came to my car and opened the door.

"Girl, close my damn door. I ain't driving your ass to work."

"Why not?" she asked with her hand on her hip.

"You got a damn car. I'll be right behind you."
'BITCH CRAZY, SHE AIN'T RIDING WIT ME AND

THINK I'MA PICK HER UP LATER. SHE LUNCHIN', I said to myself.

Following behind Heather I parked in the McDonald's parking lot uptown on Georgia Avenue. The police station was across the street. About 5 minutes later she came out the station looking for me. I hit her phone with a text: "ACROSS STREET@ MICKY D's."

She received the message and looked toward my direction. I flagged her down and she came with a big magnolia folder in her arm. I was a lil noid' (paranoid) to see what was inside. Heather came and asked where we were goin'. I had to think about it for a second. Really, I didn't want her in my car, but I couldn't think of a place off the top of my head.

"Let's head to the label," I suggested. She got in her whip and followed me to my building, The Same Guy Entertainment facility to conduct my business. He arrived and headed to my office. "So, let's see what you got."

❖   ❖   ❖

"Talk to me."
— Lefty

Black left the hospital and dropped Keisha off. He was on moves and didn't include her. Pulling up around his neighborhood it was early, 7:30 a.m. was the time. Black was headed to his mom's house to pick up a few things.

Going in the house he seen his mother staring at the T.V. with tears in her eyes. He knew she was in an emotional state, so he decided to ask, "What's wrong wit you?" She looked at him and debated on telling him. His patience was wearing thin. "What!?

Say something."

She took a breath and wiped a tear. "I called the station to check on the case and they said it wasn't even on file."

"What!" Black raised his voice. "Give me that card that 'pig' (officer) gave you yesterday."

Black left out and called Heather. She answered and told Black that she was in a meeting with Dro, but still sent him a picture of the officer that was in question.

It was slightly chilly today. Black had on some fitted jeans and a Columbia lightweight jacket and his backpack. He got in the car and drove to the 3rd District police station. Officers were still arriving. The shift had just started at 8:00 a.m. and it was 15 minutes til the hour. He sat and waited.

Black watched the parking lot from across the street of the entrance. His phone buzzed and it was a text: "5 DAYZ IN COUNTING."

Black called the number back. "Sup playboy, how that money coming along?" Fred answered.

"Let me talk to them."

"Listen, I'm in charge here. Now answer my damn question." Black inhaled and clenched his teeth. "Halfway there, Slim."

"That's more like it. Now hold on, I'ma put the lil gangsta one on the phone." He chuckled.

"Dontel!!" Shanae spoke into the phone.

"Hey princess. He didn't hurt you, did he?"

"No, but Shaniyah scared, but I got her."

"Put her on," Black told her.

"He won't let me. I told him to let us go and you might not ki—"

Black clucked the phone. "Hello!!" Black screamed as the line got quiet. Then Fred came back to the phone. "She got a mouth on her, don't she . . . but uh, 5 days, Slim."

CLICK.

Black was livid. "I'ma kill this nigga!" he yelled to the air.

Officer Johnson pulled into the parking lot, looked himself

over in the mirror and exited the car. Black walked around the corner and started jogging once he reached U Street Northwest in between 15th and 16th Streets. He stood in front of the fire station. They were literally back-to-back of the building. It was a narrow alley that led to a garage that both departments shared. When Black and his friends were younger, they would use this same alley way to come steal the dirt bikes that the officers would take from other people and impound.

Black entered the parking lot through the rear and found the officers police car number, his spot. He was masked up as he crept and ducked beside it. Cars came in and parked, not even paying attention to their surroundings. They were safe at the station, right?

Black pulled out his burner phone and called the department. "Hello, 3rd district. How can I be of service?"

"Yes, good morning. May you transfer me to Officer Johnson's desk."

"Hold please . . . Johnson here," the officer answered.

"Hey buddy, it's Pete. Your car has me boxed in. Can you come move it please? I have an emergency. My wife is in labor," Black lied.

"Pete?"

"Yeah, I'm a rookie. You probably didn't even notice me, but can you please hurry!" He was trying to find a face for his name.

"Oh yeah, yeah, I'm coming."

CLICK!

Black smiled.

Officer Johnson came running around the corner, looking around. He made it to his car. It was pretty tight. A few cars came since he made it to work. He didn't see 'Pete' as he put his key in the door.

Black came from around the back of the car, quickly pulling out his gun. He was about to squeeze but decided against it. He would never make it outta there if he did. he made the decision to hit him instead.

WHOP!

The officer fell in the car with his head leaning on the horn. It blared loud. Black hurried and pushed his body all the way into the car. Grabbing his keys out of the door he placed them in the ignition. Officer Johnson was asleep.

Black opened his backpack and grinned. He grabbed two hand grenades and pulled the pins. Now he had 30 seconds. He dropped them in the car and hauled ass through the gate and through the alley way, pulling his skully off as he made it back to the main street.

BOOOOOOOOM!!!!!

A fireball shot to the sky. "DAAAAMMMM." Black looked up to the sky as he casually walked to his car. 'DIDN'T WANT TO DO YOUR JOB, HUH, CRACKA.' Fire trucks started up and was headed to the front of the police station as Black pulled off.

That incident wasn't a part of his day, but the way Black was feeling, anybody that was in the way of him getting his sisters back was a target. Black was now about to go follow up on some information Tony gave him. It was a couple of guys Fred had to do the kidnapping for him for a nice fee. Black called Izzo to see if he wanted to make a trip, but no answer. He figured he was still passed out from the party last night. Black called one of the young goons that helped him out yesterday. "Talk to me," Young boy answered.

"What's up, Lefty, tryna work?" Black asked.

"Who dis, bob?"

"Black, fool."

"Oh shit, my bad big homie. Yeah, I want smoke, what you need?"

"I need you to ride out wit me, you know I got you."

"Shid, a'ight, I'm in da trap . . . my other two homies right here too." He tried to put his homies on.

"Next time, only need one extra. I'm 'bout to pull up."

CLICK.

It was still early, 9:00 a.m. and Black already had a body under his belt for the day. He pulled up and honked his horn.

BEEP BEEEEEP!!!

Lefty came running down the steps jumping every two steps with some skinny jeans on. Black shook his head. Lefty resembled the light skin guy from the rap due Rae Sremmurd, dreads and all.

"You scraped?" Black asked looking at Lefty's jeans.

"Pants too tight. I 'on hold no gun. But believe me this North Face backpack sure do hold sumthing'." He smirked.

"Well, make sure that bitch on safety in my fuckin' car."

"Dayum big homie. You know that was an accident when I slipped and fell," Lefty defended.

"Yeah, I know it, especially that headshot—"

Lefty put his bookbag down in front of him inside the car. "Hol' up big homie, that's crazy. You know when I fell everything else after was planned on my way to the ground, right. I seen the nigga reaching for his joint, so I squeezed. I saved lives that day. I'm something like a big deal . . .," he stated, like it was fact. ". . . I'm something like the transporter, nigga."

Black but out laughing. "I like you lil nigga."

"I like me too." He nodded his head passing the jay he was smoking.

The both of them pulled into traffic headed to 3rd Street tunnel. The next destination was Maryland. Black pulled up to a rinky dink shack in College Park. It was a decent neighborhood, but this house was the only house on the block where the grass wasn't cut. Cars and half-fixed vehicles were on the lawn, some rusted, others in good condition.

Black looked at his phone. He was reading the information he had on his vic's. They were both brothers that was sick, mentally, not unhealthy sick, but only in the mind. The brothers were arrested a total of 46 times combined from charges of robbery, rape, sexual assault, and kidnapping for hire.

"What you holding?" black asked. Lefty pulled out the same

.40 caliber Glock he used the day before. Black frowned his face up. "Give me dat! Once you body a nigga wit it, get rid of it," he schooled him. "You don't wanna get caught on the humbug (Humble) and to the job for them. Here, take this one." Lefty smiled.

It was the same gun but a .45 caliber Glock, standard, no extension. They exited the car after parking it across the street from the house. Black noticed the garage was open. Coming up the driveway they seen a guy with the hood up in a car, working on the vehicle. Black was on one side, Lefty on the other as they crept. Making it to the front window Black mouthed, "Get his attention."

Lefty nodded. "Hey buddy." The man looked at Lefty as Black came around the corner. He looked lost as he asked. "Who are you, boy, lost?"

Lefty shook his head. "Oh, you one of them type huh, racist bitch."

WHOP!

Black hit 'em over the top of his head. He fell over unconscious. Black rolled him over and looked at the guys' face. "Yup, it's him. Let's go find his brother."

They tied his legs and arms also putting tape over his mouth and leaving him on the ground. Closing the garage door, they entered the house through the side door. The house was laid out. From the outside it would trick you. Home invaders would have missed a good lick if judging from the exterior.

A massive 70-inch T.V. was mounted on the wall, a 50 inch in the kitchen, and it had marble floors. They continued to search and seen the next room had white carpets, the expensive fluffy type. They climbed the stairs, guns pointed at the master bedroom. Lefty stayed at the door as Black did a body search looking for the brother and came up empty.

There were four rooms on this level of the house. Room 2 was creepy as they looked around. Weird for two grown men to be living in. It had dolls and oversized teddy bears everywhere.

The creepy part was the door and how many locks it had on the outside of it. Ten with no knob on the inside. Black was livid, evil thought in his mind.

Third room.

Bingo!

"You sick bastard, stand up!" Black yelled, pointing his gun. Lefty came in behind him. He was shocked to see the sight before him.

"Oh, shit man, what the fuck goin' on in here?!"

There was a girl strapped to some type of sex machine. She was naked and curvaceous. The machine had switches that opened and closed her legs, bend her open and basically forced her into any position that is wanted.

The man had his face buried in her juice box as she cried out. She was older than 16. "Who the fuck are you!" He stood up.

"You sick bitch! Don't fuckin' question me."

BOC!

"Ahhhh!!" Black shot him in the knee. He tried to pull himself up.

BOC! BOC! Left shot him in his other knee and thigh. He fell.

"Go get his brother," Black said as Lefty complied.

The creep was in pain with 3 bullets in his legs. Black walked to the teenage girl. "It's okay sweetie, it's over. I'm not gonna hurt you." Black pulled the gag and ball out of her mouth.

"Thank you . . . so . . . much," she said in between sobs. "They had me for a week," she said looking ashamed.

Black looked around the machine trying to learn its functions. "How do I get you out of this freak ass joint?" He found the controls and unlocked the clamps and she fell to the floor. Black ran to her aid. "Are you cold snowflake?"

She jumped in his arms, naked and all. Holding her close he looked around for something to cover her up. Coming up empty he took his jacket off, giving it to her. "Sit right here. We'll be gone in a few." She complied. "LEFTY!!" Black screamed.

"Yeah! I'm . . . coming," he said breathing heavy.

Black walked to the door to see him dragging the brother up the steps. Lefty dropped him and looked at Black. "You gonna help or watch big homie?"

"Make dat nigga walk!"

"His legs tied up with the ropes."

"Take it off him then, dumbass." Black shook his head.

"Oh . . . yeah, I knew that. I was just tryna see if you knew."

Lefty sat both brothers up and leaned them against the wall. Black found out that the girl was 16 years old, and her name was Susan. Her body suggested otherwise. She had at least a C-cup breast and a heavy bush and hips ready to bare kids. The only thing that told her age was her baby face and innocent eyes that was slowly turning cold.

Susan told Black that his sisters was there the other night, and they shared a night with her. She gave Black Shanae's bracelet and told her that he was gonna find them. That made him smile. They didn't give up on him. She didn't know if they were touched or not and dreaded the thought.

Black was mad.

WHOP!

He smacked blood out one of the brothers back-to-back. "Where are they?" Susan covered her eyes as blood landed on her, along with a tooth landing in front of her.

"Who?" a brother asked.

WHOP! WHOP!

"The two little black twins that was here!" he screamed, looking demonic.

WHOP! WHOP! He pistol whipped him with each word.

Lefty seen Susan squinting her eyes after each blow. They were the same age, but she hadn't seen nearing as much as he did in his 16 years of life. "Come on Susan, let's go find you some clothes." They left to go to the 'kids' room.

Black noticed a silver pan with knives. "You guys were gonna torture that lil girl." He grabbed the wounded brother. He tried to fight back. Black dropped him with a slight squeeze.

BOC! BOC!

"Ahhhhh shit! You fuckin' nigger!" he screamed.

Black picked him back up and placed him on the machine the girl was attached to. "Where are they?"

"I don't know."

Black hit a button on the machine, and it arched his back, bending him over. Black grabbed the knife and cut his sweatpants off. He wore no underwear. "I have an idea, since you don't know maybe this will refresh your memory." Black put the red ball in his mouth and strapped it tight. Black looked at the brother that was still on the floor. "I'll as you a question. If I don't get the right answer, your brother gets it."

"Okay, okay, what do you want to know?"

"Where the fuck are they?"

"All I have is a number."

"Wrong answer." Black dismembered his balls and threw them at the brother. The strapped in brother let out an agonizing yelp. "I'ma ask you again, where—"

"I dropped them off at Cigar's house."

"Address?"

"I don't know the—"

CHOP! Off came the brother's dick. It fell to the floor as it leaked blood. Black grabbed a crowbar as the brother passed out.

"Wait! You didn't let me finish. I don't know it by heart, please stop."

"What is it?"

The brother gave the necessary information. "Lefty! Bring Susan in here." They both walked in the room. Susan walked to Black like he was her savior. "Yes," she answered softly.

"Come here sweetie." Black wrapped his arms around her, her back to his chest. "Just aim and squeeze, don't pull."

She looked at the brother on the floor. He did some crazy things to her this past week. All them memories rushed into her head. She took a breath and screamed.

BOC! BOC! BOC! BOC! BOC! BOC! CLICK CLICK.

Black grabbed the gun as she wrapped her arms around Black's shoulders in an embrace as she cried. Black was her hero. Black walked past Lefty and Susan in tow and noticed a bag. "What's in that bag?"

"Our earnings. Shid they can't use it, right. Let me ask them. Uh, mister creep, can we get this bag of yours?" He laughed. "Nah, but uh, me and Susan searched the spot. These creeps had some bread, they was heavy'."

"Whatever nigga, finish that other nigga off. I'm out," Black said as he held his empty gun.

"Don't mind if I do . . ."

BOC! BOC! BOC!

". . . See you on the other side.

CHAPTER 55

WAR READY

"What's the move, bossman?"
— Izzo

It was noon, Tiara and Charmine were together. Keisha was supposed to be with them but decided to stay home and rest after the news she received about her pregnancy. She was happy to bring a so in this world for Black.

Dro insisted that the girls meet him at this location that they were posted in front of. Confused, the ladies stood outside a gun range looking at the Goggle Maps App as if they were in the wrong location. They looked at each other and shrugged as they walked in.

Entering the range Izzo and Dro laughed. "Fuck so funny?" Charmine asked as Tiara co-signed with body movements.

"Nah, question is fuck y'all go on?" Izzo said, pulling down his shades. They had on camouflage pants and tight tees with bandannas wrapped around their heads, looking like some ghetto G.I. Joes.

The white lady laughed as well as she stood behind the counter waiting to service them. Both Charmine and Tiara looked around the fellas giving the lady the attention she was seeking.

"Something funny?" Charmine asked in a snappy tone. "Bitch looking like Germs from the Mucinex commercial."

Tiara laughed. "Uh uh girl, not that fat little green monster." The slapped five's laughing as they sat on the benches.

Dro decided it was time to teach them how to shoot. They were getting deep in the game, and he didn't want their women not able to shoot that pistol if they had to defend the throne. Dro and Izzo taught them how to shoot. After the lesson Dro signed them up for shooting lessons every other day for the next 2 weeks. It was mandatory.

After they left, the hood was the next location. Dro been calling Black all morning but to no avail. He finally called him back when they was at the range and told him that he was around the way. They pulled up, the girls stepped off and went on about their day.

Dro and Izzo posted in front of Izzo's trap. A car full of females rode by hanging out the window. "Hey Prophet!" they screamed flashing their breast. Izzo smiled. That was a regular thing as of lately. Izzo would put on Instagram for the girls that had the best set of tits and would get tickets to his show.

He would say all type of stuff on his IG just for the fun of it not knowing that people would really do it. he was city famous and steadily blowing up larger. His new single stayed on the radio, courtesy of the listening party put together for him and the radio connects. YouTube had over a million hits in a day. Izzo was on his way.

"What's the move, bossman?" Izzo asked.

"Waiting on Black to come around the corner."

"Is that nigga a'ight? I know he still counting the day to get his lil sisters back."

"Yeah, he good. Matter fact there he go right there." Dro nodded to Black's direction.

Black came around the corner with Susan with him. Lefty had rolled out. Black tried to drop her off, but she told him that the brothers killed her parents in front of her and she had nowhere to go. Black was now her guardian, for now.

Susan actually liked Black. She was grateful for him rescuing her and giving her a second chance at life. She vowed her loyalty.

"What's up bruh'?" Black spoke. Dro and Izzo looked at Black with questioning eyes. "Who dat, Slim?"

"Her name is Susan," Black introduced.

"She look a little on the young side, bob," Izzo said, sizing her up.

"It's not like that fool. She only 16 years old. She was in that same house that my lil sisters were being held at."

Izzo was vexed. "Damn homie, you don't fuck with me huh . . ." Izzo wanted to go when Black put in work. "I couldn't roll?"

"Nigga, you know I called you. I took Lefty with me, shawty cool as shit. He a lunchbox but I could help lil shawty out. I'ma use him again," Black stated, then continued but was talking to Susan. "Go sit in the car." She jogged off. "Yeah, about that. I need you to find out where that dude that you just signed on your label is from. I heard he with Fed lil clique of nigga on the southside."

"I got you bruh', I'm 'bout to be on my way to the studio now, anything else?"

"Nah, I'm 'bout to head to the crib and get Susan set up with some clothes and shit. I gotta count this money too. I should be good, might not even need you but I'll let you know."

"A'ight, Slim."

"Hold on bruh'!" Izzo called out. "Next move you make, don't leave me out, I'm hip to you and what's goin' on, so yeah . . ."

Black smiled. "Don't you got a video shoot or sum shit, supastar," he said, walking off.

❖   ❖   ❖

4 DAYS
"It's yours, on me."
— Big Purple

Heather was in her condo. She hadn't seen Black in a couple of days, and she yearned for his touch. She spoke to him every-day, doing things for him but she knew he was goin' through something involving his sisters.

She walked back in her room to see Jroc laid out in the bed stretched out watching T.V. She called him last night 'cause she had an itch that needed to be scratched. Jroc did what he was supposed to do, but she wanted to be fucked, not loved and only someone else could do that for her.

"Hey sunshine," Jroc spoke.

She smiled. "Hey boo, what you doing today?"

"Shit . . . not staying in this neck of the woods doe. You know I can' be around this spot for too long."

Dro held his word. Nobody seen Jroc since a few months ago except when they ran into him at the party. Dro knew where he been hiding out at, but he wasn't going to be the one to tell.

Jroc been winning in the projects where he hustled in Tiffany's complex was a goldmine and he had it jumping selling molly, PCP and deuce (K2). He was in Forest Hills Apartments, a neighborhood called 'The Creek'. He was heavy as his pockets were swollen.

Heather knew he had money and made sure he gave her a piece of the pie. "Well, I need a couple dollars. I have a few errands that I need to run. You got me hubby?" she purred, stroking his ego.

Jroc pulled a few hundreds off his stack and gave it to her. "You know I got you, boo." He got up. "I'm 'bout go get up outta here. I'ma hit you later." Heather gave him a long kiss, grabbing his manhood and giving it a slight squeeze.

"Can't wait."

He left.

Heather had a list of things to do for Black. She had to please her boo, so she was up and out the door, headed for work.

❖   ❖   ❖

Meanwhile Dro was cruising the street. He had received information for Black last night, but it was too late to call when he got it. He spent the night at the studio working with a few of his artists, mainly the one Black as interested in. Dro told Rodney 'Slim Dunkin' Green, he would drop him off after the session. They rode and talked shit during the ride.

Dro got him to open up about his life and background. Then what do you know, Fred's name popped in the conversation and Dro was all ears. Slim Dunkin and Fred was childhood friends. He was Fred's daughter's godfather and she always stayed at his house from time to time.

Dro smiled as he thought how crazy it was the way people just give up so information for the sake of convo'. "Let me see the picture of the little princess," Dro asked.

"Yeah, yeah, she beautiful. Just swipe left." Slim passed the phone. "I suppose to get her tomorrow after she leaves her mom's. Fred told me he had something goin' on at his house and didn't want her home, but whatever. That's why I worked so late tonight. Ya dig. I'm tryna blow."

Dro pulled up in an average neighborhood and parked. "This where y'all gonna be. This a nice neighborhood compared to the one I grew up in," Dro said as he tried to fish confirming the location.

"Yup, my palace, don't let the looks fool you. Everything I rap about come from these streets you parked on."

"True shit, you know I respect the grind. Well, take it easy big guy. I'll see you in the studio in a couple."

"Love," he said, pounding his own chest.

Dro pulled off.

❖   ❖   ❖

Black laid in a pile of money, stressin'. The last lick grossed him $80,000 cash and a total of $180,000, $70,000 short of the ransom. He was in his den, smoking a jay' of purple haze, a pound of weed was also a part of the come up and it had the whole basement funky smelling good.

Black walked up the stairs to see Keisha and Susan eating lunch. Leisha didn't know how she felt about the little white girl, but she knew Black was goin' through something, so she never expressed it.

"Damn, what time is it?" Black asked.

"Good morning to you too. It's 12:30 p.m.," Keisha said, and Susan giggled. "And your phone been ringing off the hook all morning. It was Dro and a dude named Fred."

As soon as Black heard the name, Susan's eyes lit up. She was hip and she saw Black run up the stairs to the bedroom to retrieve his phone, skippin' two steps at a time as he ran. He grabbed his phone. It was 2 texts and a missed call from Fred and 3 missed calls from Dro and Izzo.

Black opened the text from Fred first: '4 DAYZ' was the first. 'WE MISS YU PLZ. HURRY!!' was the second.

Black was heated.

He called Fred back.

"Heeeeeeyyyy, Mr. Donte," Fred answered.

"Where my sisters?"

"Hold please, your call is important. The operator will connect you."

Black clutched the phone tightly. He was growing really impatient with Fred's sarcasm. A small voice came to life. "He-hello?" Black let go a sigh of relief. Fred purposely put Shaniyah on the phone. She was the most vulnerable.

"Hey baby, are you okay?" Black asked.

SNIFF. SNIFF.

"I thought you was coming to get us. I wanna go home," she whined.

"I promise I'll—"

"Uh uuuuuuuuuhh." Fred cut him off. "Now don't you go making promises that you can't keep."

"Listen, Slim. I'm 'bout there. Can we exchange more sooner than later."

CLICK! Fred hung up.

"Fuuuuuucckkkk!!!!" Black screamed. He tossed the phone on the bed. No sooner as it landed, it rang. Black ran to the phone to answer it, but it was a text from Fred:

'LOL :)' He was taunting him.

Black scrolled to the message from Dro. After reading it a smile reappeared on his face.

Dro had just dropped Charmine and Tiara off at the gun range. He was serious about getting them gun ready. He made a pit stop to go holla at Big Purple. He owed him a few bands and was headed there to pay his debt. Pulling up at the warehouse, it was routine. "Spread 'em," the big doorman ordered Dro.

"Really, those the choice of words you use," Dro said as the goon patted him down, taking his gun. "Damn, where that come from?" Dro smiled. The doorman gave him a stupid look. "I don't know why you lookin' like that. You gonna have to take it every time."

Purp walked up massive and spoke in his signature high pitch childlike voice. "Hey, my man!! I see you come bringing gifts."

Dro smiled and handed him the duffle as he looked around the warehouse. His eyes got big. "Aye, fuck is that?" He pointed.

Purp looked in the direction of Dro's glare. "Oh, that's Bubblez Hot. I have her for another 2 hours." Purp extended his hand for some dap.

"Nah, big boy, I'm talking 'bout that shit she holding."

"Ooooooohhh that . . . you want it?" Purp asked. "I just got a shit load of them."

"Fuck yeah, but what is it?"

"It's the new model 700 SPS Tactical AAC-SD."

"What!?"

"It's a sniper, but it's a hitman's dream gun. It's 7 pounds bolt action with .308 win. caliber bullets. It's only weight for real is the heavy barrel with a threaded muzzle. You could take it off, but it disables the flash hider and suppressor. It's loud as shit without it. Oh yeah, it also had a Leopold Mark IV scope, so you could really zoom in."

"I'll take it. How much?"

"It's yours. On me."

Dro told Purp he would see him later. He didn't mind Dro leaving. He had a pretty lil vixen in his office waiting for him.

Dro was satisfied with his transaction. He had no plans for the sniper, but it would definitely come in handy one day. He pulled off and was cruising down the highway when his phone rang. It was Izzo. "What's goodie?" Dro answered.

"Sup Playboy. My lil man Lefty been doin' his homework and told me he spotted that nigga Cigar."

"Who the fuck is that?"

Izzo looked at his phone. "Oh shit! My bad bossman, I thought you was Black. I been hittin' his phone and he ain't answer."

"I'm hip. Earlier he told me he had moves to make today, if you know what I mean. But that wasn't supposed to be til tomar."

"Damn . . ." Izzo was thinking. "What you 'bouta do?"

"Shit, probably head to the studio and check on things."

"You tryna ride out with me and holla at this nigga on Black's behalf?" Izzo asked. "Or did you hang up your Nike boots for a pair of Gucci loafers?"

"Oh, you got jokes, huh? Don't even trip. I did just get a new toy and I'm tryna see what the hype about."

❖   ❖   ❖

Black drove through the southside of the city. He was out of his element. This wasn't his side of town. Dro gave him instructions to a hood where Slim Dunkin be hustlin' at. He was riding down Southern Avenue, right behind the 32 Metro bus. It was a gang of niggas out there as he coasted by, staying behind the bus to get a feel of the area.

He didn't want to jump out of the car in front of all these niggas. It was chilly and all their hands were in unexposed, hiding in their pockets or jeans. He was crazy, but not stupid. Black pulled in one of the parking lots close to an exit, just in case a quick departure was needed.

Driving his bulletproof Charger, he was safe in the vehicle. Parking his car, he approached a dude that was posted up by himself on a light pole. "Aye homie, what's up?" Black spoke and the guy nodded, not really tryna be bothered. "Fred been through here?"

"Fuck is you, da police?"

Black clenched his teeth. He hated being called the police, but he held his composure. "Nah big guy. I'm supposed to drop some bead off at his trap. He told me the whole hood knew 'em, but you right, never mind. I'll let him know you wasn't fuckin' with me."

"Hold on, it's the top building, Apt. 101."

"Preciate it."

Black walked to the building. The lost was empty but the frontline had endless niggas. He knew he had to be cautious, or he wouldn't make it outta there. After smoking a jay' of OG Kush out front of the building, he was acting like he was from around there or just visiting someone. Finally, somebody came out so Black could gain entry.

Catching the door, he slid in. He adjusted his vest he still had from Heather. It was a tactical vest, a lightweight, but effective.

Under his shirt it was not visible. He still had on his Northface Steep Tech coat.

KNOCK.

"Who is it?" a voice answered.

Black took a breath. "Fred sent me." There was a slight pause, then the door opened slowly. "What's up homie?"

Black ignored the guy, walked in like he belonged there and started talking. Izzo been calling his phone, but he ignored the call. Heather has been shooting him information as soon as it became available. She gave him a couple names, so he decided to use the info and name drop.

"Cigar in the car. He on his way up. You can direct all your questions to him when he get up here."

"Oh nah, it's cool homie. We don't want no problems from that crazy mother fucker, mi casa su casa hombre."

Black looked around and did a head count. It was three dudes and a chick in his eyesight. "Who else in here?"

"Nobody. Well, shawty friend in the bathroom."

"Good," Black whipped out. "Everybody on the wall."

"FUCK!" It seemed like they all said it at one time in unison. "I knew this was some bullshit. Cigar always come by himself." A guy cursed to himself.

"Always go wit' you instincts young boy." Black lined them up and told the girl to go get her friend out of the bathroom and don't take too long. "Okay, listen, this how it's gonna go . . ." Black put the gun on his hip and pulled out a grenade from his pouch on his coat. he fell in love with grenades and made a mental note to get some more.

"Y'all gonna tell me everything you know about our friend Fred." The girls cried, the young boys was silent. "Oh, y'all got heart huh?" Black mimicked the movie 'Babyboy,' then laughed at his own joke. "Y'all know how many times I've been in this same situation, and it always seems to end the same way." He put the grenade up and pulled the pistol out, twisting the silencer on it. "First to talk, lives."

What looked like the youngest of the three, stepped forward and began talking, telling all that he knew. Black looked at the kid as he spoke, letting him tell it all, but when he finished, he asked him, "Aye kid, how old are you?"

He stuttered. "I-I-I'm thirteen." The other two had to be around 17 or 18 years of age.

"Come here lil man." Black handed the kid a bookbag and told him to go fill it up with everything in here.

The kid ran in the back and complied. Black looked at the girls. "Put y'all fuckin' clothes on." The girls scattered. The other two boys cursed the youngest one out when he retrieved all the funds and gave the backpack to Black.

"Look kid, you ain't built for this life. On my mova' if I wasn't goin' through some personal shit, I would've blown your melon off . . ."

PST! PST!

"Just like that."

Black shot the two other guys in their head. A small hole dripped blood down the side of their faces. "Look kid, I'ma have to shoot you too, but it's gonna save your life, so you could tell the story and why you still living. I'ma count to 3, okay. 1 . . ."

PST! PST!

"Ahhhhh, shit!"

"2, 3." Black shot him in his arm and high in his thigh. "If I come back around here and I see you, I won't be so nice next time."

Izzo was in front of the trap just chillin' around the way. He recently rented the apartment next door to the one he was already renting. The money was flowing. Dro just got in good with a connect in Miami but couldn't make any moves as of yet because of the shit going on.

That was placed on the back burner for now. Dro pulled up in a Tahoe XL. It was used new straight off the lot. It was an older model, like 2006. He got it dirt cheap at the auction. The back story was that 3 guys were killed in it, so no one wanted to bid on it.

Izzo hopped right in the passenger seat, and they pulled off. "Nice ship."

"Oh, you got jokes, huh?" Dro asked. Izzo laughed. "So, what's da move?" Dro asked.

"Young boy Lefty told me the nigga Cigar owns a little Italian Pizzeria downtown. He just recently got into a dispute with a rival neighborhood about some profits he refused to split. I was thinking we—"

"Hold fast," Dro cut him off. "I got a better plan."

Dro pulled up downtown. He was on Pennsylvania Avenue southwest. Across the street was a hotel and directly on the other side of the street was the Pizzeria. Izzo seen Cigar sitting on the patio with a cuban in his mouth, puffing away with a beer in front of him.

Cigar didn't have it all. He was clinically diagnosed a psychopath and it showed in his everyday dealings. he escaped from a crazy house a year ago and the institution came up on the search.

Izzo crossed the street and headed to where Cigar was seated. They eyed each other as they neared. Izzo made sure to keep his hands visible as he approached. He sat right down as if he was expected to be there.

"What the fuck you doin', boy?" Cigar spat.

Izzo wiped his face of the slight spit that hit his face, then got into character. "Listen, I thought we had a deal. How you wanna try and muscle me out."

"Fuck you nigger and that chump that sent you. I lay the rules 'round here. either get wit it or get lost."

Izzo lifted his hand as if to say stop or hold on. But really it was a signal. Dro was on the roof of the hotel with his new gifted friend. Inside his sights was the signal. He turned his red beam on. Izzo pointed to Cigar's chest. Cigar acted like it was nothing and brushed it off like it was lint. Izzo smiled as he spoke. "Actually, I'm not here for that dumbass turf shit. I'm here courtesy of my brother. Fuck you and dat nigga Fred. He next."

Cigar looked at his chest. The dot began to rise as he asked, "Who the fuck is your brother?"

"Black. Do you know the name? You had his sisters, the twins. I'm guessin' now your boss has 'em, right?" Izzo said. Cigar blew smoke in Izzo's face and smirked at him.

PST!

Izzo smiled as the power from the high caliber bullet knocked Cigar right out of the chair, sending his body to the glass, shattering it upon impact. The glass didn't break as Cigar slid slowly down the glass, leaving a trail of brain splatter.

Izzo grabbed the napkin and threw it on him. "Fake ass Italian." He died with his signature trademark; a cigar still clutched between his teeth.

CHAPTER 56

3 Days Left

"He left me no options."
— Black

Today was a big day. It was time to level the playing field. Black, Izzo, Dro and Lefty were all in the studio. A plan was discussed to even the odds. Black wasn't sure why he felt a strange feeling in his stomach. It was the kind of feeling that comes right before something bad is about to happen. Black pushed it in the back of his head. 'IT IS WHAT IT IS.'

Dro pulled up, the truck slowed to a standstill. It was smacked out (tinted), which made it impossible to see inside of it. The doors opened. Four pair of Nike boots hit the pavement.

Everybody looked around briefly and spoke amongst themselves. One man rang the doorbell, Lefty. Everybody else had the mask down, covering their face. A kid about 12 years of age opened the door without even asking or seeing who was behind the door.

WHOP!

Black hit the kid with the butt of the gun as Lefty pulled his skully over his face. Everyone entered. In the living room were 2 men playing Madden. In the kitchen was a lady cooking over the stove. Lefty ran p the stairs and found Slim Dunkin. He was in the shower, Dro had the two dudes that were in the living room helmed up. Izzo had the lady face down on the floor.

Black had little Fredricka around his arms. She was the same age as his lil sisters were. He felt terrible that he had to stoop to this level, but it was an eye for an eye with him.

Lefty kicked Slim Dunkin down the stairs, and he landed in front of Black. Fredricka was hysterical as she tried to reach for him. Slim looked to Black. "What's this shit about homie?"

"Nothing to do with you, but I'm taking the girl," Black said through clenched teeth. "Your man has something of mines. Now I have something of his."

"I can't let you take her," he said, like he had a choice.

"I hoped you wouldn't so you could give me a reason."

BOC! BOC! BOC!

Black shot him dead, ass naked on the floor.

BOC! BOC! BOC! BOC! BOC! BOC!

Dro punished the other two dudes that sat on the couch. Izzo felt left out and pointed his gun at the woman on the floor who was crying. "I can't man, she might be a fan."

Black shook his head. "You wild for dat, leave her, let's go."

"What about this lil nigga here that's knocked out?" Lefty stood over him geeking for the green light. The lady that was on the floor screamed, "Noooooo! That's my son, he's innocent."

"Leave 'em," Black ordered.

They left out the house. Black had the girl over his shoulder and jumped in the 3rd row seat of the truck. Dro dropped Black off at the house. Him and the little girl was in the room. He took the mask off her face. She was crying. You could tell she was a sheltered little girl. She wasn't seasoned like his sisters, well at least like Shanae.

Susan came in the room. "Who is that?"

"This is Fredricka. She will be our guest, treat her well." Susan gave him a look and he already knew what was to come next and he wasn't gonna lie. "Did you take her?" Susan asked with a hand on her hip.

"I did, but only so I could get my sisters back from her father." Fredricka looked back and forth, listening to the whole conversation. "Now he have to trade," Black said, getting up.

In the short time Susan been with Black, she began getting hip to a lot of the things goin' on around her. She wanted in. Black already been molding her for the future. He seen the fire in her eyes.

Black left the room and called Fred. He answered, "Well, well, well, thought you didn't care anymore. I was beginning to—"

"Shut the fuck up!" Black cut him off. "Listen you fuckin' bitch ass nigga. The playing field is even now so cut the bullshit."

"How do you figure?" Fred questioned and laughed. "This should be interesting."

"Oh, it is. How is Fredricka doing? Won't I go ask her?" Silence. "Cat got your tongue, you slick talkin' lil bitch."

CLICK.

Black walked in the room to see Keisha watching T.V. She frowned her face when she seen him. "I don't even know you anymore."

Before Black could respond, his phone rang. "Talk."

"Time and place."

"Tonight at 8:00 p.m. Meet me at Stadium Armory parking lot on the Benning Roadside."

"Don't hurt my baby."

"Shut your suck ass up."

CLICK.

Keisha rolled over after listening to the conversation. "Go ahead." Black looked at her and told her. "He let me no options."

❖ ❖ ❖

It was a clear black night, a clear white moon. Black sat in Dro's Tahoe with Lefty in the backseat with Fredricka. Dro was yards away laying on the turf of the golf course that was across the street from the parking lot with his trusted sniper ready.

Fred pulled up in the Porsche 918 Spyder. The sight of the car made Black mad. It reminded him of Jroc. Both cars faced each other, and Fred got out of the car. Black opened his door as well. "Fuck my sisters at?" Black yelled.

"Fuck my daughter at chump."

Both men had pistols in hand. They were the only two on the lot. Black nodded to Lefty, and he opened the door, out came Fredricka and stood at Black's side. The twins did the same as they walked slowly, passing each other with their heads down.

An officer was riding down Benning Road and noticed the two cars. He thought it was a drug deal of some sorts and dispatched backup as he entered the vacant lot. Fred and Black didn't even notice.

They turned too late as he flashed his lights and got out of the car. "Hands!" Fred jumped in his car and peeled off. They had no chance catching the Porsche. Black was boxed in that quick. He debated ramming the cop cars, but more cars swarmed.

Black got on his knees with his hands up. His sisters just hugged him like a shield as he surrendered. Dro peeped the move and ran to his car. They were arresting Black and Lefty on weapon charges. Dro pulled up just in time to claim custody of the girls.

"I'ma send you a lawyer fool," Dro yelled as the transport wagon pulled off.

❖ ❖ ❖

A year later.

For the past year Dro been stacking money and putting all his affairs in place. Black was sentenced to 6 months for the gun charge and Lefty received probation. They never released Black because of the pending charges and was considered a flight risk. Today was sentencing day for the charges against all of them.

Dro, Izzo and Black stood side by side. Black was in an orange jail jumper, courtesy of the jail. Dro and Izzo was on bond and came to court from the street. Jroc been hiding out but would pop up every few months, trying to sneak in and out of the city.

Jroc thought he had all the sense as he walked in the court-room to sit with everybody else. He basically hid out since the day he confessed. Once the warrants were issued, Dro and Izzo turned themselves in with lawyers in tow. Being that Jroc already turned in his statement, all Dro had to do was get Izzo to agree to what was written and documented, and the sentencing date was set to enter guilty pleas.

Jroc tried to speak to Dro, but all he got for a response was a shake of the head. Four of them stood side-by-side with 3 law-yers separating each of them. Jroc didn't have a lawyer. He was the key witness. The state had his back, so he thought.

The moment the truth was about to be heard for all ears to hear. As the proceedings went along and the charges were read, Jroc had a puzzled face when he heard his charges labeled him as the mastermind of the whole conspiracy.

"Hold on, that's not right!" Jroc yelled.

BANG! BANG!

"Order in this courtroom." Dro and Izzo smiled.

A year ago, Dro had changed the statements, courtesy of Heather. Basically, it said everybody was in the car when Jroc de-cided to see his girlfriend to find her cheating with the armored truck driver. His emotions go tin the way and he killed EV-ERYBODY! He fled the scene and got pulled over. His friends thought he was gonna confess and turn himself in, but instead he shot and killed both officers and if they told on him, he would kill their family. But when the girl he shot survived and drew the picture of him, he had to go finish the job.

The statement was signed and sealed by the captain and Jroc. Heather did her part and played by the rules.

As the sentences were handed down, Dro received 36 months for his role in being in a car driving away from the scene of a crime along with Izzo and Black. Black already had a year in, so he would be home first.

Jroc on the other hand received 720 months plus life for a shitload of charges. He was labeled the head and the Judge threw the book at him. Tears ran don his face as he tried to plead his case while his co-defendants looked on silently laughing.

"Court adjourned!" the Judge announced. "Next case."

Dro blew his now wife, Charmine a kiss and Izzo gave Tiara a wink. The media was loving this case as it got bigger. The headline was 'LOCAL RAPPER, MURDERER?' Izzo's statics just went to the sky, and he had big plans upon his release.

Black gave Keisha a head nod. Their relationship has been strained since she lost the child she was carrying. Shanae and Shaniyah waved at their big brother, along with Susan who still lived with Keisha.

Heather was in the back of the courtroom where no one could see her. When Black got locked up, she disappeared for the sake of her job. Black spotted her in the back, and they locked eyes. Heather had a baby in her arms and mouthed the words, "Black, Jr." and Kisha read her lips after following his gaze.

Everybody left the courtroom and headed to their cars. Keisha went her own way with empty promises to kick it later. She had plans for Black.

Charmine and Tiara rode together in Dro's newly purchased Audi TT RS Sport. In the car they just looked at each other as the engine roared. Dro left them the blueprint to keep things afloat until he was released, so it was up to them to make it work.

"So, you ready to get this money?" Charmine asked.

"No doubt, bitch. We gonna hold our niggas down."

"Damn right. It's gonna be a paradise." Charmine looked to the sky.

"And a warzone," Tiara said, as she grabbed her gun from the glove compartment, cocking it and placing a bullet in the head.

CHAPTER 57

(1901 D Street)

Receiving and discharge, R&D. The casualties of war. A good and a bad section to be in, all depending on which side of the door you're headed.

1901 D Street, a cold place to be. Home for numerous fallen soldiers and good men. Temporary housing until the Feds come and drop you off anywhere in their system. New York to California, it doesn't matter. You're no longer a person, only a number, cargo. The Department of Corrections, in other words, Gladiator school in the Nations Capital.

Getting off the bus, Dro, Izzo and Black were headed to the jail. Jroc was held on a separate bus, voluntarily admitted to segregation. He didn't want to walk population in fear of running into one of his co-defendants.

Black was already in population. After he was searched and received, he was told to head to his unit, Northwest I, Max custody. Dro and Izzo was left behind. They had to go through the motions of intake. This was a process that drags and could take up to 4 to 5 hours.

The first stop, the infirmary. This was a part of the classification process. Oddly the Warden did a walk through. Izzo and Dro sat in the holding tank with a few others awaiting convicts trying to see the doctor.

"Grab that inmate for me," the Warden told one of his officers as he looked through the face cards of inmates.

Everyone in the holding area looked around, following the finger that landed on Izzo. Dro and Izzo looked at each other with a look of confusion. "Fuck is dat?" Izzo asked.

The Warden had on a tailored suit with some nice loafers, a respectable appearance. His towering dominance froze Izzo in place. He just looked important. The Warden didn't have any type of identification visible to inform Izzo of who he might be.

Izzo ignored the finger being pointed at him and continued to talk to Dro, but quickly was interrupted. "Aye! Dreadhead, the Warden wants you, so come on, now!" the C.O. barked commands.

Izzo looked at the C.O. and back to Dro as he stood up, "Bruh', I'ma see you later, Slim. Stay safe," and dapped him up.

Izzo was pulled down a long hallway. "Damn homie, slow down. You draggin' the shit out me, moe." His arms were cuffed to the front with chains around his waist attached to some leg shackles. His mobility was real slow and calculated.

"You ain't shit in here, punk!" the C.O. cursed. Izzo just kept quiet, shaking his head. He watched too many episodes of COPS and many other jailhouse TV shows on A&E to talk smack while in restraints.

Making it to the Warden's office he was placed in a seat, still shackled. "Well, well, well . . ." the Warden began. ". . . look what we have here." He smiled, then looked at the officer. "You can leave officer, me and my friend are gonna get a little more acquainted." The warden stood up and with hand gestures said, "Before you leave, take his arms out them restraints, please."

Izzo looked around the office and noticed the warden was real familiar with what was hip and trending. On his walls were pictures of video vixens and a couple Straight Stuntin' Models. On the other side were trophies, pictures of his own children and their accomplishments. In the corner, Izzo spotted a picture of himself—well, of his mixtape album cover.

After removing Izzo's handcuffs the officer left, closing the door behind himself. The warden and Izzo made eye contact.

"So, what's up?" the warden asked.

Silence.

Izzo had his mean mug on. They weren't friends and he was making this fact known. The warden chuckled. "Look the reason you're here is because I'm a fan of your work, and when I say that I mean the stuff you do for the lower-class neighborhoods. I'm from the streets too, but that's neither her nor there. My son and daughter are fans of your music. I'm Warden Marshall by the way. Don't really care for the hippy hop thing your generation done messed up, but I'm here to offer you a deal."

Izzo frowned. "What kind of deal?"

"You're already sentenced. You'll be here for at least a month before the Feds come get you. My proposition to you is that if you sign me an autograph and a contract stating you would do a mini appearance at my daughter's 18th birthday, I'll let you go to population and not put you in the hold, South I, nor the north side either."

South I was the real hole, more like hell. It was a segregated part of the jail for the deadliest and craziest of felons. Pure punishment.

"How much you payin'? That hole shit don't scare me, so I need to hear a price offer," Izzo stated.

"Um, is that right? We will talk prices later, but I know you'll be home by the time her birthday comes. I'll keep my officers off your back so you could coast on up outta here. What do you say?"

Izzo paused for a short moment contemplating. "Whatever

man, I hear you. Just make sure I'm very comfortable for my stay." Izzo agreed.

"No problem. What is it? Prophet, right?"

Dro was in the infirmary getting his vitals read when pandemonium erupted. He jumped off the medical bed as the door busted open. "What da' fu—?" Dro pressed himself against the wall, trying to slide out of the way of the two inmates that fell through the door.

The doctor giving the exam jumped over them like it was an Olympic hurdle and ran, leaving Dro by himself in the middle of the fight. 'AIN'T THAT A BITCH,' he thought.

The inmates was fighting over a knife that both men had a firm grip of as they tussled. Dro was trying to find an opening to get out. Every time he had a chance, the window would close that fast. The one guy kneed the other in his groin. This forced him to lose his hold on the ten-inch ice pick to grab his jews.

Fatal mistake.

The attacker ceased the moment and plunged the knife repeatedly in the abdomen and neck of his assailant. The attacker looked at Dro who returned his stare. The guy gave Dro a head nod. That was all he needed to run. Blood was everywhere as he bolted through the door and down the hall.

The radio was blaring. 'CODE BLUE! CODE BLUE!' Multiple officers swarmed the infirmary as the call for lockdown was being announced. This was their attempt to get all involved locked down and to hopefully save a life.

Dro was back in the holding tank with a few other convicts. They silently watched the body get rolled down the hall. Blood leaked through the sheet. One of the detainees spoke to nobody in particular.

"Welcome to class gentlemen. First lesson of the day, get you banger."

❖   ❖   ❖

Black, a veteran on the block made a name for himself this past year. Many heard stories about him. Never did he confirm or deny any of the claims. He didn't trust anybody on the unit. Most people feared him and couldn't even hold eye contact and that's how he preferred it.

Black entered the unit. From the sally port he noticed another guy on 'his' phone. He was anxious for the door to slide open. It's a door that separates the unit from the outside hallways within the jail.

The door slid. Black entered and was doing a beeline to the guy on the phone. The unit seemed to get quiet. The interior included two tiers with two sides. It had eighty cells. In all, forty on each side, twenty on each tier. There were eight phones and three visiting screens. For recreation purposes there was two TVs, regular channels only and a basketball and handball court sharing the same area. It was one spot or the other and a command center in the middle of it nicknamed the bubble.

Two officers worked each unit, three, sometimes depending on the vibe of the unit. Vests were not optional. They were mandatory for their sake.

Most eyes were trained on Black. They knew what time it was. He was headed to the violator that had the heart to use his phone. In mid-stride an associate of Black's read his demeanor and intervened. "Slow down big guy, what's up? You a'ight?"

Black, a man of few words looked at the guy talking to him, then his phone and asked, "Fuck is dat?"

"Chill bruh'. He paid to use it. I got you, Slim."

"Ain't no got me, get me. I needs mine now or Slim coming up off dat joint like now," Black corrected.

Black went to approach the dude, but his homie pulled him in the other direction. "Come on bruh'. I got it in my cell."

"That's more like it. When that nigga done, I need to make a few calls. Don't put nobody else in line."

"Damn bruh', I already had a line set up. I didn't know you

would be back so—"

Black raised his hand. "Fuck all that shit, I'm next," he said, cutting dude's statements short.

❖ ❖ ❖

Izzo left Warden Marshall's office. He was escorted by the same racist correctional officer that didn't like American blacks. Most of the COs in the jail were from Africa. They felt like they were the 'real' Blacks and American Blacks weren't shit.

The CO led Izzo down the hallway, taking him back to the infirmary. Placing him back in the holding tank he reunited with Dro. "Where the fuck you just coming from?" Dro asked but continued to talk.

"I was in the doctor joint and deez two niggas fell in the room tryna kill each other. The shit was crazy, even the nurse bitch got up outta there leaving me in that bitch, on my mova."

"Oh yeah, that ain't shit compared to the shit I just went through. You know the dude I was sent to see . . ." Dro nodded. "That was the warden of this jail and basically told me that he could put me in the hole for my own protection because of my so-called super star statics," Izzo said, raising quotation gestures in the air.

"So, what happened?"

Izzo was shaking his head as he let out a sigh. "He basically bribed. Said he'll let me stay on population if I do a show for his daughter's 18th birthday and sign an autograph."

"That ain't so bad, but the nigga gonna pay, right?"

"He said he would, but I don't think he would play with me outside this building and think I'm sweet. Plus, I told him to put me and you on the same block so we could be comfortable."

"That's what's up, big boy."

The CO cut in on the conversation. "Come get your bed rolls

and face cards. Your unit is on the card, let's go!"

Dro and Izzo grabbed their belongings and headed to the unit on the card. Southwest II was their destination, another max block.

❖   ❖   ❖

Jroc

"Moe', this shit anything . . ." I paced the cell. ". . . got me in this cell with you. I feel wild ass shit, I ain't no P.C. (protective custody) type nigga," I said to the boy in my cell.

In a feminine voice Jazz responded. "Well, it's pretty much the same in population. We everywhere, but why you in P.C. anyway? It's obvious why I'm here." He struck a pose. "Nigga might try and get me."

"Wow." I shook my head. "I'd rather die than live this life. I did some messed up shit and looks like the joke was on me."

I sat in P.C. and pondered on my situation. It sucked. Here I thought about all this time I received, then to top it off they put me in da cell with a tranny. The guy had breasts and everything. I tried to buck the cell, but it would have been useless. There are so many of them on the unit. Then the officer threatened to put me on population, and I wasn't tryna run into Black.

I thought it was gonna be a 23 and 1 lockdown with the hour for recreation, but I was wrong. The unit was so packed that it was ran like a regular unit. Unlike the units upstairs, there wasn't a half and half set-up, everyone was out and about.

There was a few regular dudes that either got checked in or they told on somebody and couldn't leave this block; fear of retaliation from other convicts.

My ex-homies shouldn't even still be mad at me. At the end

of the day, I got tricked and received the end of the stick. They got a slap on the wrist while I got smoked' (a lot of time). Them peoples killed me. It's all good doe, I put my case in for appeal under insufficient counsel. I was unaware of the plea agreement and the case didn't make any sense.

I don't plan on being locked up too long. It's too many inconsistent things and loopholes in the case. I don't know law like that, but dudes been telling me this. I'll be home and I have a plan for they ass. I'ma shine and it's nothing they could do about it.

The unit was cool and laid back. Everything seemed new and worked properly. The staff was even decent. They treated you like humans, with respect, maybe because wasn't nobody on nothing.

The crazy part of this whole situation is that I tried to snitch on Black. I know I was wrong and wild for it, but I got jealous and had built up hatred from the past and some over a girl and ended up being the real joke. I think he still fuckin' her too.

Technically on paper, I didn't snitch. I could go on every block in their jail, my paperwork straight. I'm just not tryna see Black. That nigga crazy. I know he still tryna see me. I'ma run into him, just not in here.

"Did you hear me?" Jazz asked me.

"No, wasn't listening, but what time is rec'? I need to get on the phone."

"They should be poppin' our doors soon."

I patiently waited for the doors to be opened. This dude in the cell wouldn't stop talking and his voice was beginning to irritate me. This man really identified as a woman and it was throwing me off. I couldn't wait for the Feds to come and get me. All the females I had, money I blew, look at me now. I blew a sigh, shaking my head, tuning Jazz out as 'she' spoke.

CHAPTER 58

"Cordell Washington, Isaih Miller! Front and center!" the CO barked, calling Dro and Izzo. "Cell 65, bottom tier."

"That's us bruh'. I see you worked your magic and got us to be cellies," Dro said as he grabbed his bedroll.

Walking through the sally port and down the stairs they approached their cell as dudes hung over the tier watching all the new intakes. A couple of dudes noticed who Izzo was and gave a few respectful shout outs. This was regular. Others hung over making sure no rats or homosexuals entered the block. Southwest II another max block. It's just the way things worked.

"Pop 65!!" Izzo shouted to the CO. "Damn bruh', they got us." The realization of the jail was really starting to kick in.

"This shit ain't nothing. Time gonna fly once we leave this spot, trust me," Dro reasoned.

"Yeah, I hope so. This shit ain't where it's at."

The block seemed to be laid back. That was only a fool's imagination. The unit was too quiet, which only meant dudes was plotting and something was about to go down.

Dro and Izzo leaned on the wall at the back of the tier chopping it up (talking) and a random guy walked up and spoke.

"What's up, Slim? You like da hoods mayor bruh, ur' shit crank."

"That's what's up, homes', preciate it," Izzo said dapping the guy up.

"Listen, if you need anything, I know I don't know you personally, but I fucks wit' you. If I could help out, I got you."

Dro intervened. "Yeah, you could matter a fact. We need two joints. Could you get that?" Dro wasn't gonna get caught loafin', (slippin). He wasn't a jail buy, but he heard plenty of stories and everyone that told him their input instilled getting a knife before you even get soap.

"No question, that's easy. I'll be back."

After the encounter in the infirmary Dro wasn't taking any chances. That fight put him on point. He was determined. It was either be caught with it or butchered without it.

Dro and Izzo decided to go to the TV room. The CO made them move from the back of the tier. He thought something was brewing up as people kept going down there to the local star unbeknownst to them.

There were a couple dudes that were envious and wanted to make a name for themselves by touching Izzo. He wasn't trippin'. The inmate population knew Prophet, the rapper, not Izzo from uptown. "Aye Prophet!!" the random guy yelled from the bottom tier. "Come here bruh'. I got that."

Izzo looked at Dro and they both noticed the dude was callin' them to the shower area. There was two showers side by side on each tier, no cameras. It was the only spot besides the cell where you could possibly get away with anything or beat a shot if you get caught. "Walk with me bruh'," Izzo told Dro.

"No question, wouldn't be any other way."

Leaving the TV room, down the first flight of stairs, they were on the ground level where the command bubble was located. A few dudes were watching the intense 3 on 3 basketball game that went on in the small gym. That's the most that could fit on the court.

Making it down the second flight of stairs, they were on the ground level, the bottom rock. A couple guys were doing pull-ups on the back of the stairs while others had a workout car doing burpees. By passing them, the floor narrowed into a pathway leading to the shower area where the guy stood.

"What you think of these?" he asked, grinning. Izzo smiled as Dro looked around. "That's what I'm talkin' 'bout." Dro glanced at the makeshift shanks and was satisfied. "What we owe for these, Slim?"

Dude frowned and shook his head. He just wanted to be a part of the team, so no payment was accepted. His noble gesture was noted. Izzo acknowledged dude with a head nod. "Dats what's up, I got you baby boy."

Black collected his payment from the guy on the phone. He walked around the tier. He was on detail, a unit orderly. So much goes on on these units that rec' was on a half and half schedule. Top and bottom tiers come out a side at a time. Since he was detail, he had the privilege of being out all day, even after lockdown, depending on the officer that worked the shift. He been on the unit for a little over a year, but since he has been sentenced, he was now in transit, off to the next spot.

"Aye!" Black yelled across the tier. "Let me get that phone." He walked down the steps, headed to the phone. A guy was still on the phone and must have thought it was sweet. The 15 minutes for each call was up 5 minutes ago, and the guy decided to use it again, thinking Black wouldn't notice because he didn't see him go back.

Bad assumption.

Black walked straight to 'his' phoneline and pressed the dial, instantly disconnecting the conversation. "Times up, Slim," Black said with one hand inside his jumper.

The guy turned around. He was angry, but after noticing the eerie silence and the look on Black's face, he didn't say anything; only stood to leave the area with his head low. Black could tell almost instantly that the guy was new to the jail. The way he talked on the phone told it all. He had the phone to his ear with his head down, looking at the ground with his back to the unit. Any real convict know to put your back to the wall and eyes in front, so you could see everything moving.

In this environment you couldn't tell if a guy didn't like you until it was too late. The officers on the unit wasn't there to save you, they were there only to alert other officers to help. Black was on a mission. The first call on his mind to make was to Heather. At the sentencing he noticed her in the back of the courtroom with a baby. The part that had him stuck was when she mouthed the name, so he had to confirm what he saw.

His plate was already full in his opinion with his sisters and his newfound responsibility, Susan. Black wondered what Heather planned on doing. She sent money, pictures and letters, but never mentioned the baby until his sentencing. A lot was running through his mind as he dialed the 10 digits.

"You have a prepaid call from . . . Donte . . . Brown . . . from the Department of Corrections, press—"

"Hello? Black spoke first.

"Hey boo!!" Heather was excited.

"What's up with that baby you was carrying?" he asked, ignoring her excitement.

"What you mean? It's yours. If you going to deny our child, we could just end things now. You take a test if you like before you start saying some other nonsense. I'm not for the problems, Done," she said in a defeated tone as if she already lost the argument.

Black took a breath. "Where you been? Why you ain't been up here to see me?" Black asked, already knowing the answer.

"You know why. You know what I do and who I am. I can't be

caught anywhere near that place. I could lose my job. You know I'm here waiting."

"Yeah, I hear you, but I need to see my seed."

"I know Donte. We will make it work.

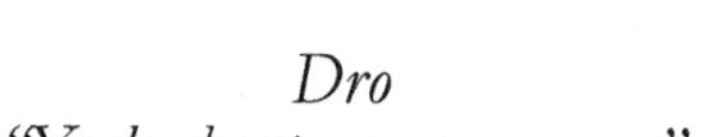

Dro
"Yeah about a year ago . . ."

Man, oh man, who would have ever thought I would be in an oversized orange one-z, tryna look sweet. I done popped my thin ass collar, cuffed my pants and even cut the elastic out the back of my jumper so my backside wouldn't be in a bunch, all hiked up.

The unit was tense. I could understand the feeling. Everyone here had a reason to feel this way. The fight for your life, some of these dudes didn't have a chance, this was it. Homicide, pistol offenses, home invasions, kidnapping and rapists are what made up this block. A few hustlers, not many.

On the street all the young dudes screaming thirty round extensions and Draco's. In here if you ain't got 8 inches or better cold steel or sharp plexy, you better tuck your tail and get out the way. I'm learning this from the few hours I've been here.

I know a few guys from the world in here. The world is what we call the streets now that we ain't there. I was most of their connect. Shid, the whole uptown knew me and other sections of the city.

My man Izzo was a city supastar and he just charted. Meaning his brand is not only in the city but is expanding. He was ranked #25, last, I seen. I know his statics about to rise now that he locked up, ain't that how it happens anyway.

Walking down the tier I was tryna find a line to get on, you know a phone. Luckily a few good men fucks wit' me which gave me a couple options. I made it to the top of the main floor, and I see Izzo already on the phone. I went to the phone beside him, it was hanging off the hook.

Usually when you see a phone like that the guy running it didn't expect anybody to grab it without permission. Since I already had the go ahead, I picked it up and made my call. The number I dialed wasn't even called in so long manually, I couldn't even remember it for a second. I used to just go to her name or face and push that. Not any more. It's different now I thought as I remembered the number as the operator spoke.

"Hey bae!" Charmine spoke after accepting my call.

"Sup' baby girl?"

"Missing you as you should know."

"Did you leave yet to make that trip?" I asked, my mind still on making money.

"Yeeeeeessss," she said dryly. "I'm just landing. Me and Tiara on the tarmac now hubby. I told you I'ma hold you down. You remember our first trip down here?"

"Yeah, about a year ago . . ." I reminisced.

❖   ❖   ❖

Reflection

"Baby I'm nervous," Charmine whined.

The crew drove in the limo headed to meet the connect. It was Dro, Izzo, Tiara, and Charmine. This was the introduction. Dro was putting everything into motion preparing for his absence.

"Don't trip boo, it's nothing," Dro said, pulling Charmine close.

❖   ❖   ❖

Miami. The city where the heat is on, palm trees and bright lights, the night life. Bikinis and shorts were considered casual wear. The ride was smooth. It felt more like a vacation than a business trip. Every establishment that was driven by Charmine and Tiara wanted to stop and shop. The streets were litter-free. If someone was to litter; a look of disgust would be cast their way.

Storefronts and different businesses quickly turned into luxury homes and mansions on the hills. Homes were surrounded by acres of land. The American dollar didn't go far in this part of town. You need 'mucho dinero', a lot of money.

"Bruh, I know you really don't need me for no intros and shit. You could drop me off at the spot," Izzo said, winking at Dro.

Tiara balled her face up and looked at Izzo with questioning eyes. "What spot?"

Dro chuckled. He knew what Izzo wanted to do and where he wanted to go. The strip club. The clubs down south were worth every dollar you would throw. Most women were considered exotic compared to the hood broads they were used to.

Miamians probably say the opposite. A lot of the families weren't even from the U.S. They were from different countries. Cartel families invaded Miami years ago and claimed their spot.

"Girl, chill out! Always on my line, I'm Prophet and I don't answer to nobody."

WHOP!

Tiara hit him in the back of his head. "Prophet shit! Boy, don't play wit' me."

Dro laughed, then said, "Nah bruh', I need your face to introduce Tiara as your better half."

"Better half?" Izzo questioned.

"Yeah fool, that's what I said."

Pulling up to the mansion would be an understatement. This was an estate. The girls looked on in awe. The property seemed to have a glow as the fiery inferno burned high in the sky forcing the trees to cast a shadow about 45 degrees. It had a 3:05 lean. Ironic, the zip code they were in . . . The 305.

Such a generous host the owner of the compound was. At the security gate they were greeted with tight faces and assault rifles. Welcome to the real Miami. A straight-faced guy walked up on the side of the vehicle.

"Que' 'Pasa hombre, a donde va?" he spoke, asking where they were goin'.

Dro spoke up. "Mira, I'm here to see Jose', comprende?"

"Si, si, un momento."

The security put a finger up telling them to hold on. After a second or two of waiting the gates opened, allowing them entry to the mega complex.

The scenery was colorful. It made them smile as they cruised the pathway leading to the main house.

"This ain't the same area," Dro said, noticing the scenery. Izzo looked around not really caring or paying attention. "And so, what. You know this slick head bamma got bacon out the ass, not tellin' how many cribs he got."

The tinted center window came down and the driver spoke. "Yes, you are correct my friend. Jose requested your arrival at this location in the Florida Keys."

"Damn, nosey!" Izzo rolled the center window back up.

Charmine's mouth dropped; memories flooded her mind. She always asked Dro to get some property in this area. She loved the Florida Keys. Her and Dro been on a few trips down here, but it was only in her dreams. As a child Charmine came down here once and remembered a great deal of tourist spots. One of her favorite places was located in the Upper Keys.

Charmine is a bird lover. It was only right for her to love the Florida Keys Wildlife Bird Center. It was dedicated to the rescue, rehabilitation, and release of ill, injured, and orphaned wild birds.

"Baby, can we go to some of the attractions down here while we're here?"

Dro smiled at Charmine. "Anything for you." He agreed.

They pulled in front of the main house after coming around a huge water statue. It was 10 feet tall, a molded frame of Jose, himself, making it rain, literally. His arms were spread wide with water descending from his palms.

The huge doors opened; 12 by 6 in diameter. Cherrywood with solid gold handles, not plates. "This nigga up, moe!" Izzo said as Jose came through the door with wide arms, looking just like his own statue.

"Oye, Hermano!" Jose spoke.

Fly? That would be another understatement. Jose looked and smelled like new money. Flawless designs, fashion forward would slightly give him justice. There he stood in all white linen by Yves Saint Laurent with some all white Salvortore Ferragamo loafers, no socks. Miamian for sure.

"What's up, hefe?" Dro extended his hand. "This here is my Queen that I've been telling you about." Charmine reached her hand out for a shake as well.

"Si, si bonita, I've heard nothing but sweet melodies about you." Jose kissed her hand, then released it. "And this must be Ms. Caliente . . .," Jose said, reaching for Tiara's hand. ". . . senorita Tiara, si?"

Tiara smiled, shocked that he remembered her name and accepted his hand. "Yes, this is me," she said, doing a ballerina squat.

Jose ushered them into his home. There were servants everywhere. They led them to a guest room that looked like a small retail store for clothes. Every designer was in the room.

"Take shower, get clean, pick something you like to wear. We go to eat in hour," Jose said with a snap of the finger.

Izzo never liked when Jose did things like this. Given the chance, Izzo would pull his card, but Dro always stopped him and talked logic to him.

Dro narrowed his eyes. Izzo let his shoulders relax and walked to the shower room with Tiara, biting his tongue yet again. Dro and Charmine headed to the other washroom to get a little fresher than they already were. Fully dressed and ready to depart, Jose and his guests headed to the transportation—a bulletproof stretch Hummer 1, the original one.

Inside was like a restaurant in itself. A mini bar, TVs and iPads ascended from hidden compartments along with a mini table that stretched the length of the truck.

Arriving at the restaurant, it was exquisitely nestled amid towering palms at the very edge of the Florida bay. Virtually every seat in the house affords a view of the water, be it from the elegant dining room or from a seat on the patio. Every section had linen cloths, napkins, fresh flowers and candlelight.

The food was finger licking good. This was the hype that circulated about the establishment. The meals ordered were signature fish; a yellow tail snapper seared in oregano with shrimp, tomato, almonds and Pernod. There was a seafood Dieppoise, a rich combination of shrimp, scallops, and mussels in a lobster cream sauce. A couple of Angus beef orders along with hazelnut chicken that was prepared with a delectable Frangelico Orange thyme sauce.

The meals were delivered. Jose cut straight to the chase, no interest in small talk. "So, bonita, you want to be head huncho for a while. Si?"

The question was directed to Charmine. She looked at Dro as he looked on silently, puffing an expensive cigar, courtesy of Jose. "Si, senor, Jose," she answered.

He smiled and waved his hand. "Just Jose would be fine."

Charmine and Tiara weren't your average hood chicks anymore. In all actuality, they were well seasoned with street smarts and very capable of firing a weapon. Their pretty faces and innocence that was portrayed was only deception to the naked eye. No one would suspect killers behind their smiles.

The food was devoured with minimal conversation in between

bites. Jose snapped his fingers. Izzo cringed, irritated. A couple waitresses rushed to clean the table as he stood. "Follow me."

A look of confusion plastered everyone's face. They followed and ended up in the back of the restaurant. Jose owned the place. No one knew but it was not a surprise, the service was too good for him not to be the reason why. Entering the kitchen area, it was business as usual, chefs were hard at work. Flames were high as the food was being prepared for the paying customers. They walked past them. None of the workers turned an eye.

Walking through the freezer curtain there was a man sitting in a chair. All types of meats hung around him as he shivered. He was restrained with zip ties around his ankles and wrist, duct tape on his mouth. Fear was etched on his face.

Jose slapped the man in the back of his head. "Eres medio tontito, no?" (You kinda stupid aren't you . . .). He taunted his victim as he paced the floor.

From his hip Jose pulled out a two-tone .40 caliber compact Glock. "He steal from me." Jose pointed, his voice calm and smooth. "Charmine . . . kill 'em."

Jose reached to give Charmine the pistol with the butt of the gun facing her. She looked at Dro. Tiara's eyes widened. This was unexpected and shocking. Dro had his game face on, trying to remain neutral. He had already warned her about the ruthlessness of Jose. Now it was do or die. Not in the literal sense, but as in lose the connect if that body didn't drop dead in a few seconds.

Two swell associates of Jose entered the freezer as Charmine grabbed the pistol. She pointed the pistol as the guy's heart, held it there for a while, then slowly lowered it.

"KILL HIM!!" Jose screamed.

Charmine looked back toward the door to see Jose's goons had pistols aimed at Dro and Izzo. The table has been turned. Charmine didn't like the scenery. Within milli-seconds, she raised the gun back up at the victim.

BOC! BOC!

One to the chest, another to the head. The chair flew back as

Charmine spun around quickly into a crouching position.

BOC! BOC!

Two more shots were fired at the goons, dropping them both. Now the gun was at her side as she looked at Jose. "Don't ever have weapons pointed at my man." Charmine narrowed her eyes. "Now what, boo?" She asked Dro for instruction.

Jose smiled and started clapping. Charmine and Tiara were confused but kept their game faces on. Then they noticed Dro and Izzo smiling as well. The two goons started getting up slowly. Charmine seen them out the corner of her eye. Instincts took over as she fired a couple more shots to finish them.

"Bae, those are blanks in your gun," Dro informed her as she was now completely lost.

Jose looked at Dro. "Yo puedo confiar en Charmine, es Buena gente." (I can trust Charmine, she good people.)

Dro smiled. "I told you my girl real as they come, cold blooded."

CHAPTER 59

Charmine

"Yes Hubby, I'm just landing. Me and Tiara on the tarmac now. I told you I'ma hold you down. You remember our first trip down here?" I quizzed.

"Yeah, about a year. You held it down. Jose loved you ever since that day," Dro responded.

"You dam right he did. If that gun was real, I would've blown his melon off."

"Yeah, he cool, but I'm 'about to get in the car with Lefty."

"A'ight, keep me in the loop." Dro ended the call.

I was in Miami. Me and Tiara was at the Miami International Airport on LeJeune Road. This was a regular trip now, my innocence left with my first body. I dropped that when my baby was home. My life is so sweet, only thing I'm missing is my king to hold his thrown, but until then I'm the HBIC, head bitch in charge. There was a limo outside of the airport waiting for us. I power strutted heading in its direction. Lefty and Tiara was trailing.

"Damn sis . . ." Lefty was fatigued. ". . . I guess your hands don't work, huh? You or Tiara . . ." He dragged four bags. "I'ma turn in my gun and start wearing a suit and white gloves. Fuck it, call me Jeffrey."

I laughed. I guess I did get a little spoiled over the last two years. A lot has changed. I wasn't playing with loose coins anymore. My boo made sure of that. We winning and losing ain't in the cards. "Shut up, stupid, always complaining." I threw a balled-up tourist guide at him. he tried to duck but ended up clipping himself up on one of the bags he was dragging. Tiara laughed hysterically like it was the funniest shit in the world. "What Black use to say to him?" she asked.

I smiled. I knew the saying oh so well. "That's why they call Lefty 'cause he can't do nothing right." We had a good laugh about that at Lefty's expense.

In the back of the limo, we sipped Merlot, an expensive brand. One thing I knew about Jose, nothing was cheap. This was a bi-monthly trip. Everything in place without him or me ever having to see each other, but he insists that we keep a line on each other, physically.

Surprisingly, he never tried anything when we were alone. We actually was never 'alone', but in each other's close vicinity. He liked meeting in water or secluded areas. His favorite line was that it was for our own protection, but I think he just like seeing me half-dressed.

We arrived at the YMCA. I didn't even know they still had these. I wanted to go to the hotel and get situated, but Jose had other plans. The driver informed us that all bags would be taken to the hotel and after the meeting with Jose a ride would be outside waiting for us. I guess this is why Jose been winning for so long in this dog-eat-dog world. Nothing he do or how he move is the same.

We entered the huge community center. Tiara and Lefty were led to a different area. Another worker asked me to follow her. She led me to a sauna. I smiled. 'THIS NIGGA ALWAYS TRYNA GET ME NAKED.'

I changed into a robe and entered the heated cube. It was smoking; literally steaming everywhere. I could barely see. There he was, Jose, Mr. Rico Suave himself. He sat on the bench with a towel around his waist. Even with just that on he still reeked of money. He made eye contact and spoke.

"Que Tal? Mi comay." (What's up my girl?")

I smiled. That accent gets me every time. "Hey Jose." I sat beside him.

We talked for a while but after I started sweating too much, I had to get up outta there. It got that hot. It didn't seem to bother him though, this was regular. It's always hot down here. Jose led me to the front of the sauna and wished me well. I didn't have to ask if he wanted me to drop the money somewhere because while we were conversing it was already taken by the driver. Then it hit me—a thought. I had a new driver and I decided to question him about it.

"Before I leave, what happened to Pedro?" He waved his hand in the air nonchalantly. "Esta que le sale!" (He's on fire) My eyes widened. 'THAT NIGGA DEAD,' I left it at that.

After reuniting with Tiara and Lefty, we headed for the hotel. We had two adjoining rooms and when we got there all our clothes were folded in different drawers, courtesy of Jose. All the money was gone that we left in the limo, which was expected. Dro never told me about that part the first time. I thought we got jacked until I received a text telling me all was well, and the birds were flying north as I read it.

Jose was always a step ahead. Business was good. The dope game and the record company kept me on top. Guys didn't want to respect my gangsta when Dro first began his bid, but after they heard about my work and how my pistol bang, shit stop coming up short.

Lefty really proud of himself in this last year and changed for the better. His name was already stamped from what Black and Izzo told me, but to see it is to believe it. I had him lay a few niggas down that played with my money. When my boo come back, he gonna come home to a fortune, not no petty change.

Tiara came in my room. "What's the move, bitch?" She was excited.

"We in Miami, trick!"

This was every time with this hefa. All she want to do is party and occasionally smoke' (kill) a dude. "Bitch, lower our voice. Why you so damn loud?" I asked her.

She shrugged her shoulders and responded, "You know how I get when I'm in Miami, da 305!"

Lefty walked past. "Hmph, sure do, like a straight slut."

"Fuck you nicca!" Tiara screamed on him as he walked on. She turned her attention back to me. "Soooooo?"

"It don't matter, let's roll."

The night life was always a plus in the city of Miami. Charmine, Lefty and Tiara was headed to the club. Business was done so this was their chance to let loose and enjoy a night of fun. Tiara was already drunk before she left the hotel. Lefty was livid. His plans of creeping off was now shattered. No late-night legs for him, he had to babysit.

Charmine didn't drink a lot. She had a wine cooler and a Martini. That put her on chill mode as she rotated her hips to the music. Tiara was enjoying herself, having flashbacks from her stripping days as she twerked and dry fucked the man behind her. The guy made an attempt to run his hand the length of her thigh and up her skirt. She was oblivious to the feeling and let it happen. Lefty peeped the move and wasn't having it.

He rushed to the area Tiara was in and pushed the guy off her. She didn't even stop dancing. She tried to dance on Lefty. Tiara was in her own world as she continued to rotate to the beat. Instead of dancing with her, Lefty grabbed her waist and started pulling her away.

The guy fell to the ground but quickly got back up. The club was crowded so it took him a few minutes to find out what happened. He noticed Lefty walking Tiara off the dance floor and followed.

Lefty laid her in a booth. She could barely hold the weight of her head. He was headed to grab Charmine from the bar. She was tossing back shots, getting on her level as well when he walked up on her. Lefty blew a sigh. "Lil Dro, time to roll." He grabbed Charmine's arm.

Little did Lefty know Charmine was all the way on point. She peeped the whole ordeal that happened on the dance floor and Lefty was the one loafin'. Charmin wasn't taking shots, that was a façade to throw everyone off.

Charmine fakes slurred. "Okay . . . okay . . . I'm comin'."

Lefty approached, leading her to the booth in attempt to grab Tiara and be on their way. Then the same guy that Lefty pushed moments earlier was now standing there talking to Tiara as she nodded in and out. Lefty frowned his face. "Yo, my man. She with me and we 'bout to rollout, Slim." He reached for Tiara's arm.

Tiara leaned in trying to accept the embrace but missed as the guy smacked Lefty's hand down. "Maybe she want to chill with a real nigga." The guy pumped his chest out in an attempt to put fear in Lefty. "Plus, ain't you da nigga dat pushed me on the dance floor, homes." He approached Lefty, now in his face.

Lefty was a slim guy, hand to hand combat was not his first choice, ever, especially with a guy this size. Tiara had her head in the booth as the guy pushed Lefty to the floor. Charmine side-stepped swiftly, getting out of the way.

The guy didn't even pay attention to Charmine as she slid her hand under her skirt, pulling out an 8-inch flip-out knife. The beat was so loud in the club no one ever head the screams of the would-be tough guy as Charmine quickly hit the guy with four rapid jabs of the knife. Two to his jugular and two to the kidneys as she portrayed the act of pulling him off Lefty as he tried to ground and pound him.

Lefty rolled him off of him. The dance floor just swallowed him up as the music continued to play. Charmine gathered Lefty from the floor and walked to Tiara as they both carried her out of the club.

Inside the limo they headed back to the hotel. Lefty had an ice pack on his cheek. "Damn TT, you always get drunk and put a nigga on babysit mode, you anything!" Lefty vented.

Tiara slurred. "No-body told you . . . look out fo me." She rolled from seat to seat. "You . . . a'ight, sssssuck it up, punk."

"Bitch! Look at my face!" Lefty pointed. "Talkin' 'bout suck it up, look at you, ass all out. You let that nigga touch you all over. If you wasn't my homie lil joint I would've let dude have his way, wit ur' rollin' ass," Lefty spat.

Charmine was on the other side letting the hash it out. Lefty was right, in her eyes. Every time Tiara got twisted it's no telling how she would end or where she would end up. Izzo left her with a vicious habit and any given night she would let a random guy explore her body and cry about it in the morning.

"Fuck you, Lefty! Yyyyou wouldn't talk . . . ttto me like dat if Izzo was home, you punk!" She was mad.

"You right, I wouldn't. You know why? Because you wouldn't be on every other niggas dick!"

The argument lasted the majority of the ride to the hotel. By the time they arrived, Tiara was passed out. Charmine tossed Lefty Tiara's card. She went and got her own room.

Lefty carried Tiara like she was a baby all the way to her suite with her head dangling as he walked. He opened her door and tossed her on the bed, but she bounced and hit the floor hard, and her skirt flew up.

"Owwww!" she moaned.

Lefty walked around the bed. 'DAMN, SHE PHAT AS SHIT, LIL HOE ASS.' He turned around to leave.

"Izzo! I mean Lefty . . . can you help me to the shower?" Tiara asked. Lefty shook his head but walked back to her. He picked her up and helped her to the shower. He leaned her against the sink as he went to turn on the showerhead. He adjusted the temperature. "Aye lil hooka, it's ready for you! I'm out." He turned around to see Tiara's ass naked.

DAMN.

Lefty tried to leave out after he examined her entire body, but Tiara grabbed him. he looked back trying to give her full eye contact, but his eyes continuously drifted to her naked flesh. Her body was tight and well sculptured.

'IS THAT A LANDING STRIP CUT,' he thought, looking at her silky center.

She spoke, breaking his glare. "Thanks Lefty. I know I can be a bit much as times."

He looked at her body again. "You think!"

She smiled and released his arm and entered the shower, slowly and seductively as she watched Lefty. "You better leave before you bust your zipper. Look like you getting excited."

Lefty looked at his pants. 'DAMN.' He shook his head, leaving the suite, headed to his own to get ready for their departure in the morning.

"Looks like it's me and you tonight," Left said aloud, talking to his hand.

CHAPTER 60

Lefty

'DAMN IT FEEL GOOD TO BE HOME.'

I walked down L.W., the name of my neighborhood, short for Lincoln Westmorland Projects. Since my big homie got locked up, I've been holding down all the traps in my hood. I put the streets on my back. You could say I'm carrying it like I'm moving a body. I heard that somewhere, maybe a rap song or some shit.

It's sad to say, but it ain't been much money coming through here, not since that bullshit with police. It's been super hot', them peoples' been rollin' like crazy, then Tiara, that's a whole other story. She be slow as shit on the re-ups. I wish I could deal straight with Charmine. One thing about her is that the 'bout dat dollar. Dro taught her well.

I was still a little tired from the flight. Shid, the trip period. I didn't even get to get no legs out there. No pussy for, that by itself had me tight anyway. Today was supposed to be a busy day. I had a shitload of things to do. Really, I didn't feel like doing shit.

Not a damn thing. This was a regular feeling of mines. I have to say, 'FUCK IT'. It's like a slogan to me.

I never thought I would be winning on this level. Thanks to Izzo and Black, they gave me a chance to shine and for that my loyalty lies with them. Dro always been the big homie 'round da way, but we didn't get close until Black started using me for his captors and trying to get his lil sisters back.

That was a crazy time. Matter fact, that's the last time I seen Black.

He got bagged after that. (Locked up) I walked into the court-yard of my complex and seen my roll dawg, Susan. This lil chick was like a silent assassin, in a sense. First off, the white, then she had a complete lifestyle change and been living in the hood for the past 2 years. My neighborhood rubbed off on her and she out here laying shit down with a purpose.

A few years back Black saved her from two pedophile twin brothers that kidnapped her from a school bus stop and was tak-ing advantage of her. After Black did what he did, Susan clung to him like he was her new purpose in life. Anything Black said was considered law and was to be done.

"Sup white girl?" I spoke.

"Hey L," Susan spoke in an innocent voice.

One thing I could say, the hood didn't take the suburban white girl out of her. This amazed me every time. I would listen to her talk and think of all the crazy shit she'd done and smile. Don't judge this book by its cover.

"Shit coolin'. How long you been out here?"

"Not long. Keisha just dropped me off. I don't understand what's goin' on with her though. She been actin' weird. I'm just going to stay out of her way for now before an accident happens to her," Susan said, nonchalantly.

That fraction of information she gave had me on edge. Some-thing had to be going on in the house. I know for a fact that Susan usually keeps household affairs quiet, so I decided to fish. Shid, why not. "Actin' weird how? She probably she stressing."

Susan looked at me like I just spit in her face. "Please . . ." She rolled her eyes. "That woman don't have any worries. My daddy made sure of that. He sends currency from the prison as well," she said, getting mad with every word. "I swear if she out of pocket, I'm going to handle her with pleasure."

I didn't respond for a second. I was lost for words. I noticed her heaving, then I spoke. "Calm yo' ass down snowflake. Don't jump to any conclusions." I pulled her close. "We just gotta investigate before we do anything if you think something's up, especially before you tell Black," I said.

She melted in my embrace and in almost a whisper she responded, "Okay."

Her head was resting on my chest. 'THIS CHICK CRAZY.' I rubbed her back as I released her and almost instantly she was back to her happy ditzy self. She smiled a big grin. "So, what we doing today?"

Her change of mood didn't shock me, but her question did. "Uh, we?" She didn't like that.

"What! So, you don't have time for me after you had sex with me, huh?" she said with much sass and a hand on her hip. The other hand balled up in a fist. "You got me fucked up!"

Every now and then when she was mad you couldn't tell. She just started cursing, rolling her neck and hips like a ghetto chick. This was new and I loved it, especially how she wore her hair. She was blond but wore cornrows. Some people call them braids. I don't know why, but I love that crazy shit. The best part of it was that it was unexpected, at least coming from her. She flipped like a switch. "Chill . . ." I covered my face. She liable to pop off.

". . . I didn't mean it like that, damn."

Now me and Susan wasn't a couple or nothing, but in the time we been around each other, we've grown close. I guess we fuck buddies in my eyes. I wouldn't mine making her mines, but she could be unpredictable, plus she won't kill me in my sleep. 'FUCK DAT.'

She narrowed her eyes. "Oh okay. So, what 'we' doing today?"

she asked again.

RING. RING.

'SAVED BY THE BELL.'

My phone range and I noticed it was a blocked call. It had to be a jail call, so I answered it. "Talk to me." I put a finger up to Susan who was still waiting on an answer.

"You have a prepaid call from . . . Donte . . . you will not be charged to this call . . . to accept press—"

I smiled as I pressed 5. It was my man Black calling from out the Feds. He been gone for almost 2 years. I knew he was getting short in time. "What up, blacker than me?"

"What it do, baby boy? I need a favor. I need you to drop some bread off to Heather for my Jr."

That was nothing. it was a usual thing I did over the last few months. He couldn't send money directly to his baby moms because of who she was, so he used me. Susan was all in my mouth as I talked.

"Ask him why he didn't call me?" She pouted.

I was about to relay the message, but Black heard her through the phone and responded. "I that my baby Susie . . ." She sighed. I had him on speaker now. Susan hated that nickname he had give her. "Tell her that she know I was gonna call her later but what y'all doing?"

"Shit. Round da way 'bouta check the trap, then go find something to get into," I told him.

"That's a bet. Have you seen Keisha lately . . .?" I turned the speakerphone off.

". . . She been acting a lil wild. I don't know what's goin' on, per you know who." I looked at Susan and put a fake smile on but didn't say nothing. She told me so I couldn't like to my mans. "Shid," he asked.

"Nah, I ain't seen her, but I could tell something up by the way sunshine been actin'. You need me to do anything?"

"Nah, don't trip. I'll get Susie on it. But what's up with you big boy, you a'ight? Did you complete that other task?"

I forgot to tell him about the latest mission he had me on. It's crazy he still had me on moves from the inside and they were big money ones at that. "Oh yeah, that shit was wild too Slim. This lil snow bunny that you molded, she the truth. She got you all in her. It's like she a clone, but listen, I remember it like it was yesterday . . .

❖   ❖   ❖

Reflection

"Stay in da car. I'ma go in, get this package. Just keep the car running," Lefty instructed.

Susan nodded her head in agreement but had other plans. Lefty still had the assumption that she was 'green' as when he found her tied up, defenseless. That girl died when Black took her under his wing years prior.

Lefty entered the house. It was supposed to be empty or with a maximum of three people in the spot. Black needed Lefty to grab some important documents and cargo boxes that Heather had informed him was there. The location was one of Fred's houses that he rarely used, but kept certain things there, incriminating things for his enemies.

Fred was a reason for Black's early incarceration. he was the man that kidnapped his sisters and during the exchange Black was arrested on weapon charges.

In the house was a couple guns that Black used when he was on a rampage and murdered endless people in search for his sisters that he wasn't to get out the possession of Fred.

Lefty crept through the house on his tippy toes, literally. As he crept through the living room, he seen a guy sitting on the sofa watching a soap opera, deeply invested.

'THIS NIGGA SWEET.'

Lefty pulled out his silver-plated Glock and swung it full force at the guy on the couch.

'BOC!'

The gun went off as it connected with the guys' temple, knocking him out. "Oh shit!" Lefty said as the bullet ricocheted and hit a chandelier making it fall, landing on a second assailant that was creeping from the hallway with a gun drawn.

'I MENT TO DO DAT, I'M JAMES BOND BITCH.'

Lefty was loafin', (bullshittin'). He approached the guy on the floor and started talking shit to him. "You thought you was just gonna walk up on me . . ." he paced the hall back and forth in front of the unconscious man. ". . . you thought I was a rookie in this shit nigga. I DO THIS SHIT!" he boasted, patting his own chest, extra animated.

'BOOM! BOOM! BOOM! BOOM!' Shots fired.

Lefty dived on the ground trying to locate the shooter as he checked his person for holes or blood. His breathing was heavy as he backed up against the wall. "What da fuck!!" Lefty crawled to the couch and peeked around the corner with his gun ready to fire. He was nervous.

Susan smiled at him as she stood over a third assailant. "You do this shit, huh?" she asked wit a smoking barrel about to blow it. Lefty jumped up.

"You dam right I do. I seen dat nigga. I just wanted to see what you was gonna do, feel me?" Lefty said as Susan gave him the face of disbelief. "I ain't gotta explain myself. Just hold it down for a minute. I'm 'bout to go get the package. It's time to bounce, okay, Ms. Rambo," Lefty said, climbing the steps, silently grateful for Susan.

'NIGGA ALMOST KILLED ME,' Lefty thought.

After grabbing what he came for he made it back downstairs incident free with a big duffle bag full of guns and ammo. "Let's go," he said, heading for the door. When he crossed the threshold of the door, more shots rang out.

'BOOM! BOOM! BOOM!'

"Shit!!" Lefty jumped and looked back, reaching for his gun to see Susan waling behind him. She just finished the other two dudes off for good measure.

"Back said no witnesses, never." Susan smiled walking past him out the door.

Lefty looked at her and shook his head. 'THIS GOT TO BE THE SPAWN OF BLACK. GOT ME JUMPIN' IN SHIT.'

Black laughed. "I see you still overconfident and sloppy. She saved your damn life."

"I wouldn't say all that, but yeah. I was happy she was there because it probably would've been a different storyline," I admitted.

"That's what's up. Aye, you ain't run into that nigga yet, huh?"

"Nah, bruh'. Dude be hard to catch up with. I'm still looking. I know you tryna get a dude," I said.

"A'ight I'm 'bout to get up off this horn. I'll be there soon. Look out for lil Susie for me and my lil sisters. I'm gone, Slim."

CLICK.

I looked at Susan who was clinging to our whole conversation but was giving me the mean mug. She finally spoke. "You stupid, you know that?" I was lost, didn't understand where this came from. ". . . them phones record dumbass. Just because you 'think' you talking codes, they decipher that mess," Susan said.

"I didn't say any names."

"Whatever . . . what's the move?"

"We gotta take some bread to Heather for lil Donte."

Susan frowned. I never knew why she didn't like Heather, but every time her name was mentioned it was the same result. First, I thought it was because she was Fed, but I know it's deeper than that.

CHAPTER 61

Federal Time

Time is the same in every location you arrive at. The only difference is the caliber of men and type of politics in your location. The rules are the same, universal. Coming into the Feds with only 36 months was a blessing for Dro and Izzo. Their educational background was also a savior in where they were placed. Their custody points weren't high, so they were sent to an FCI.

It wasn't nearly as rough as a penitentiary would have been. This made their time relatively easy, especially since they were sent to the same prison. It's been 30 months and time was moving. Their case was highly publicized, so most knew who they were. Some respected them, some hated and plotted.

Izzo and Dro were outside on the rec' yard chilling, spinnin' (walking) the track. This was daily. It was a way to free your mind and walk a few laps; either by yourself or with a friend.

"Aye bruh', this shit 'bout to be over. I can't wait til I'm knee deep in somebody's daughter," Izzo said, closing his eyes and pumping the air as if it was a girl in front of him.

Dro playfully pushed him. "Nigga, fuck pussy! That shit gonna be easy. I'm tryna get back to the money. I know you ain't forget the reason we do this shit."

"Hell, nah. I'm tryna go on tour and some mo shit. Get some of that Jay-z money. I'ma be da shit when I touch," Izzo boasted.

"Dats what I'm talkin' 'bout Prophet . . .," Dro said, calling him by his rap alter ego name. "But on another note, my new cellie been actin' kinda wild as shit. I might put his ass out if he don't tighten the fuck up."

"Shid, what's up wit em? You know that shit ain't 'bout nothin'," Izzo said, geeking to out in some work.

"I'ma wait. But Slim really pushing it."

"Is he a homie?" Izzo asked, tryna find out if he was from the city or not.

"Yeah, he say he from the west. I didn't even know dudes still claimin' that joint or that side of town."

They stopped spinning the track to chill on the bleachers. It was the weekend, and an A League basketball game was goin' on. This was serious, some of the best talent were behind the wall. The games would get so intense that if a referee made a bad call he might get touched during or after the game. Usually, cold-blooded men took these jobs because a sucker wouldn't last.

Dro had a bet on his unit for a certain team to win. The wages would be big in some circles. He bet 100 books on this particular game. In cash it transferred into $500 cash on your account. His team was winning by 15 points with 2 minutes left in the 4th quarter. Izzo noticed that the dude that made the bet was trying to ease off the yard, and activity move was coming soon.

"Don't trip, let 'em think shit sweet. We'll catch him in the dorm."

They sat and watched the duration of the game. The final score was 7-39, a blowout. Dro glanced at the gate when he heard the 7:00 move announced. The assumed bad pay-pal exited the yard quickly. This was common for suckers to do shit like this.

Izzo jumped off the bleachers, leading the way. He was following the dude as if it was his money at risk, with Dro close behind. Watching him enter the unit they noticed him do a beeline straight for his cell.

Dro wanted to give him the benefit of the doubt. "See, he probably in there counting the money." Izzo looked at him like he was crazy or stupid.

"Yeah, okay. I'll go help him count it then," Izzo said, goin' up the stairs to the top tier. Dro followed.

Opening the door Izzo smirked. "Unless he planned on leaving your money with someone else . . . I say he packing his shit up off some check-in type shit," Izzo said, catching the guy putting his property in laundry bags.

Dro shook his head. "Damn homie, just gonna roll on out, huh?" The guy was frozen and stuttered as he answered.

"Na-na-nah homie. I was gonna pay you . . . I-I was just—"
'SMACK!'

Izzo hit him with an open hand. "Stop wellin!" he screamed on him, tellin' him to stop lying.

Dude tried to plead his case, but Dro jumped on him instantly and started to ground and pound. Blood leaked from his face as Izzo pulled out his shank about to finish him. "Nooooo!" Dro yelled, stopping Izzo from stabbing the guy. "Nigga is your crazy? We tryna get out, not stay in."

"Fuck dat. He violated and he owe that bill," Izzo said furiously. The guy was barely conscience from the beating Dro put on him. Dro had to speak some sense into Izzo to calm him down.

"Nigga, we rich outside these walls. Fuck that lil bit-ass money. That shit don't mean nothing. It was just for the thrill of the gamble. Now that we bear this nigga, he could go ahead a check on in," Dro explained.

Izzo wanted badly to send the guy to the moon; stab him but calmed down after he listened to Dro. 'FUCK IT, I'LL GET HIS SHOES, I'MA TOSS THEM BITCHES ON THE WIRE,' Izzo thought as he reached for the guy's ankles.

❖   ❖   ❖

Black was another story. His history of violence and lack of education led him to a whole different type of situation. Is not much sunshine in these parts. In the mountains, snow from 3 to 6 feet covered the compound. Underground tunnels was how convicts moved from place to place. It was inclement weather on the highlands, so this was the only option. If it wasn't too much snow, it might be heavy fog, which would roll in at its own leisure. He was in the Pen.

This compound transforms boys into men. You could get your throat cut for making to much noise in the morning. A lot of guys in this condition usually aren't coming home. This is their new forever home.

Waking up, Black was happy as he stretched. A smile is a rare occasion. He slid off the bunk and began to run the water with a push of the button to wash his face. The officer walked past his cell and turned the key. The doors were finally opened from a two-month lockdown.

Shit happens. Investigations are concluded, then it's resumed, normal operations. This was a constant cycle; either someone gets severely beaten or somebody dies. This was a paperwork compound, meaning if you were on somebody's case and had loose lips, it's not the yard for you.

Black was getting short on time. His release was nearing. He walked down the tier and headed to the computer room. He had to check his e-mail. After receiving and responding to a few messages, it made his day. Susan always flooded his e-mails. He loved her more and more each day. Their bond was concrete and unbreakable over the course of the friendship. He realized that Keisha hasn't been responding to his message. This only irritated him. Walking through the unit he decided to get on the phone and give her a call to see what's up.

"What?!" Keisha answered after pressing 5.

'FUCK YOU MEAN WHAT, BITCH.'

"Damn. What I do to you?" Black asked, trying to remain neutral. He didn't want to give off her vibe. ". . . I'm just calling to check on you. You been acting real shitty lately, what's up?"

Keisha smacked her teeth. "Ain't shit up. What's you got goin' on is the question. Anything new in there or out here I need to know about?" Sarcasm heavy in her voice.

Black was silent. He didn't know what she could be talking about, so he changed the subject. "Where my sisters at?"

"Um . . . they think they grown. When I tell them to do something, that Shanae get to rolling her eyes, talking slick, then the other one just follow right along. I'ma drop dey' ass off wit' cho momma," she said with much attitude.

'CLICK.'

'I KNOW THIS BITCH DIDN'T HANG UP ON ME.'

Black hung up the phone after looking at it. He didn't like the way Keisha talked ill of his lil sisters. She been real snappy lately and he planned on getting to the bottom of it. A little heated, he had to wait 45 minutes to make another call. He decided to go to the sports TV and to check the scores on the games. He had a ticket in.

Jroc

ITS CRAZY. These niggas thought I was down for the count. Okay, they smoked my boots and gave me a shitload of time but I'm back bitches. I reached out to a few different lawyers but none of them responded. Out of the blue I received a letter from one of the best appeal lawyers in the city and she decided to take my case. The best part of the story is what she told me.

Listen, she told me that her services were already paid for, but she couldn't tell me who paid the balance. I know it was a hefty retainer. Even though I often wondered about it, I let is pass. Whoever it was, was about to get me out of prison. I had big plans if all this went through smoothly.

I think Black was on his way home with Dro and Izzo not too far behind. I was out the Feds for a minute now but just came back to the jail when I found out my case was in the courts under review.

Now I'm back at Gladiator school. Being though all my co-defendants are in the Feds I was able to go to a regular block. I damn sure wasn't going back to P.C. even though it was sweet there. The jail experience changed me for the better. Now I don't take anything for granted or leave anything to chance. I'm goin' home with vengeance and them niggas not gonna know what hit 'em.

I really was fighting a lot of demons and over my time being incarcerated I found religion. Islam saved my life and gave me a new outlook on the world, but I'm still damaged goods. I knew I was out of pocket when I just finished praying and evil thoughts flooded my brain right after I Tasleem out (end my prayer).

"Salaamu Alaikum!" the Imam spoke, breaking my train of thought.

"Wa' Alaikum Salaam, sup ock?" Really, I wasn't even trying to hear him kick no knowledge type shit, but Fisibililah I listen. I know it's always coming from a good place.

"Nothing brother, I've noticed your mind has been everywhere and it shows in your actions. Isha-Allah things will get better and work themselves out. If in need of help don't hesitate to ask or even offer dua', seek help," the Imam retorted.

"Alhamdulilah," was all I could say, giving praise to the highest, accepting the knowledge but then I stepped.

The unit I was on was real laid back, but don't get it twisted, shit goes down and it gets real, real quick. This was just a section of the jungle. If all went well, I was gonna be up outta this place in a few months, pending a court date.

I was called to the bubble. This is where the Cos are stationed. They informed me I had a pass of some sorts. It was a legal visit. I always love to see my lawyer these days, for one it means she's working wit' her sexy ass, and secondly, it's usually good news.

I walked down the hallway after leaving the unit. It seemed long as shit when you're the only one in it. There wasn't an officer in the sky bubble to open and close the doors that separate the east and west wings of the jail. They were just open both ways. That was suspicious to me. Instinctively I grabbed my banger' (knife) to make sure it was accessible if needed. Going through this system I learned to always have your defense even if you not beefing. Some niggas just don't like you.

I turned the corner and heard muffled screams of help. 'WHAT THE FUCK!' I seen a dude at the top of the escalator in a ball, curled up in a pool of his own blood. It looked like he was clinging to whatever life he had left. Whoever did this to him was way outta sight.

He reached for my arm in an attempt to get help. This shit was looking like a setup. I didn't want no part of this. If the Cos seen me helping, they would never believe me with this big ass knife I had tied around my waist. Plus, whoever did it I didn't want them thinking I was with it.

I ignored his hand. "Sorry Slim, I can't." I looked around and headed the other way. I had bigger problems and didn't need to be a part of anyone else's. 'I DON'T EVEN KNOW YOU, FOOL.'

I made it to the visiting hall and was happy to see my lawyer. Ms. Bishop was beautiful. 'DAMN THIS BITCH BAD,' I thought. She look like that sexy broad in the Avenger's movie. 'FUCK! WHAT'S HER NAME, OH YEAH.'

Scarlet Joanson, I think. And she was short, how I like my woman to be with a mesmerizing set of eyes. I put on my professional walk as I came through the door. I know she was on my line. Who wouldn't be. "Sup' Mz. Biishop?"

She giggled. "Hell James. Who do you think you are today? Over there walking in here with some type of purpose."

"Uh, nobody. I just know either you got some good news for me or you happy to see me. I don't remember requesting your beautiful presence in such a dark place." I talked that shit to her. I know she just got wet.

We sat in a little cubicle. The jail called it a conference room. The walls were off white with plexy glass surrounding us. Ms. Bishop just looked at me shaking her head. "James don't flatter yourself. Back to business. Your case will more than likely be overturned with the help of my employer." I raised my eyebrow. I was lost, but she continued. ". . . he told me to tell you if he get you off this case, he'll need yo when you touch down for business."

I looked to the sky and thought, 'BUSINESS?' But then I asked her, "Who is this employer you speak of?" I really wanted to know, but on the low didn't care. I was tryna get outta jail.

"Doesn't matter. All he needs is a verbal agreement from you through me.

'FUCK IT.'

"A'ight you got that. Now get me da fuck outta here!"

❖   ❖   ❖

Black

JUST WAKING UP IN THE MORNING, GOTTA THANK GOD I DON'T KNOW BUT TODAY SEEMS KINDA ODD NO BARKIN' FROM THE DOG, NO . . .

"Damn bruh, that shit loud as fuck of the amp'!" my cellie

said, pausing my music.

I was at my desk getting all my shit together listening to Ice Cub's song. It was my motivation for today. Release day. I could have left a few months ago, but with all the shit I did in the city streets of D.C. I would be a damn fool to take my black ass to anybody's halfway house. "You gonna miss a nigga blastin' this gangsta shit in the morning . . .," I said, pressing play on my MP3 player. ". . . plus, I'm leaving it with you, so enjoy needle dick."

"Fuck you lil hoe! Talking 'bout you leaving it to me. Nigga, that shit gonna be off in 14 days, then what I'ma do with it?"

"Buy you some deuce wit your clucka ass." I laughed. He didn't think I knew he was smokin' dat K2 heavy.

My day had finally came. It's time to reek havoc on the city streets. I got a few niggas I'm tryna get up on. The streets been quiet since I've been gone. I heard it's been a lot of suckers coming through. You know, friends of friends in shit like that out there tryna hustle without the dudes that brought them around. That's cool doe, the equalizer is about to touch any minute now.

After I gave all that institution shit away, only property I had was two photo albums, family pics. I was doing my final walk down the pound' giving my final goodbyes to a few good men on the way to R and D. It felt good to be on this side of the door. It led to a new and better beginning, freedom.

I was processed out. I was free. A couple of Cos tried to speak, but I didn't have any words for them, especially the ones that was speaking now.

'LET ME CATCH YOU IN THE CITY.' I smiled.

As soon as I felt the fresh air it was different. The institution wall was behind me. I inhaled. 'FREEDOM AIR.' I put my middle finger to the prison and screamed, "FUCK YOU< FBOP!" and started doing the nay-nay with my middle finger in the air, swaying to the imaginary beat.

BEEP BEEEEP!

A car horn blared stopping my celebration. It was an all-black Charger with smoked rims and looked to be armor plated.

"THAT'S MY FUCKIN CAR!'

The driver's door opened. I couldn't see inside the car but running around the door was my son. My face lit up as I kneeled to pick up my seed. I embraced him and he was happy as I was. Then the driver of the whip exited.

Heather, my baby moms. 'HOW DA FUCK SHE GET MY WHP?' She must have read my expression. "I'm D.E.A., remember, if you're wondering how I got your car." She smirked.

"I'm driving," was all I said after I kissed her cheek and gave her a half hug.

It felt good to be where I was at the moment. Squeezing the leather of my custom steering wheel, I knew I didn't have m permit on me, but I knew it was still valid and shid' I'm riding with the law. The bass of my system vibrated my seat, and my son bobbed his head, which brought a smile to my face.

'I'M OUT HERE!'

I took in my reality. The drive was lengthy as I arrived in the city. Heather sat comfortably in the passenger seat, hiding behind my 5% tints. Cruising, I finally made it to the city. I was in my girl's neighborhood, Keisha. She been on some bullshit lately. As I rode past what was supposed to be our home, I seen a nice car roll out of the driveway and coast past me. Heather noticed my slow creep and questioned me. "Boo, where are we and what are you looking for?"

'AT MY HOUSE, LOOKING FOR MY BITCH' I wanted to say. She never knew where I lived, not since me and Keisha moved. She was oblivious to her surrounding right now. "We in Wadolf, Maryland. I'm looking for this guy that suppose to give me a few dollars," I lied quick.

I wouldn't dare let her know the truth. She ain't got it all sometimes. She still act delusional to the fact Keisha been my girl, so I do too.

I still wondered who was in that car that slid off. I let the thought pass for the time being. I had other things on my agenda. Well, Heather had plans for us as we pulled onto the highway. She wanted to do this whole family type thing but me, I was on some other shit, vengeance.

It was embedded too deep in my heart. I'm gonna be out here on my nut shit tryna punish every foot soldier until I reach the General. But today, it's family day. I pulled around my way to see if my sisters were home at my mom's apartment. From previous phone calls and flicks I heard and seen that they aren't so little anymore. They were teenagers with their own way of life and personalities, but in my eyes, they were still my babies.

I walked through the door and the first person I seen was my mother. She still looked the same and didn't age much. She looked at me. "Well, look what the wind done blew in." She came in for a hug.

Me and my moms didn't have the best relationship, but I am her son, her only son and I've been gone for a while. I guess she miss a nigga presence. " 'Sup Ma, how you been?"

She waved me off and looked behind me. "Is that my grand-baby." Excitement could be heard all in her voice.

My son ran to her. I hope they have a better relationship than me and her had. After the commotion I was tackled from behind. Shaniyah, my sister was squeezing me so tight. 'SHE MISS ME.' It put a smile on my face as I reversed the hug and picked her up. It felt good to see her face and actions. She looked like she wasn't one of them fast girls and she didn't grow up too quickly. But Shanae, her twin sister was the complete opposite in every way. She was a reincarnation of me. The look she gave me as she leaned on the doorframe gave me worries. The eyes don't lie. I know she did some dirt since I left.

Shanae smirked. "Wut' it do, bruh?" she spoke. She had the whole swag of a young teenage goon rocking a fro-hawk as her choice of hairstyle.

I gave her my sinister smile and first thought. "You gay?" I really wanted to know. She looked like a nigga.

The hard expression she had disappeared, replaced by her natural soft features. "Would you be made at me?" she asked softly.

I chuckled. "Nah, for what?" I guess the way I asked her so bluntly it might have come off a little strong, but naturally I was shocked. I didn't want to turn our reunion into no Dr. Phil segment, so I changed the whole subject. "We 'bout to go out, y'all go and get ready."

Shaniyah put her hands on her hip. "How you know if I got plans or not?"

"Because I just changed them. Now go do what I said."

They turned on their heels rolling eyes and smackin teeth but did what I said. Heather sat quietly on the couch. I almost forgot she was there; how silent she was. She smiled at me, shaking her head when we made contact. I winked at her and grinned. "I'm da law round here!" I patted my chest. Heather waved me off.

I didn't know what or where we were going to do, but I knew I had to check my stash to see if I had any ends' (money) put up. I knew for a fact I had some at my house, but I couldn't get to it. Thinking of my house brought thoughts of Keisha back. In time I'll find all the pieces to this puzzle.

CHARMINE

LIFE has been lovely. I had my baby Dro's label still pushing out music. Him and Izzo were getting short in their sentence, so I decided to release a track from his unreleased mixtape to get his buzz back jumping. I even opened up a tattoo shop so IU could have a continuous frow of money. This was my way of chasing my own bag. I had some nice artist working for me. I named my shop 'VERSETILE INK.' I had so many different ethnic artists employed, you could have called it cultured.

My first idea was to open a beauty salon, but I didn't want to be around all the females all the time. My boo always told me how proud of me he was.

That was the legal side of things. The street life was always different and hardly ever went smoothly. Somebody almost always want to be who you are, and the game gets dirty. I'm still making plays in the streets for my bae until he returns. These new dudes think because I'm a woman that I'm not trained to go. My shit buss too. But quickly they got with the program when people started coming up missing.

I called one of the young boys that owed me some money, Boosie. He was about a week late and that was unusual, at least without a phone call or something. He always kept me in the loop. I did my homework and found out that baby boy wasn't locked up or in any hospitals. Now I felt like he saying fuck me as I waited for him to answer the phone.

"Talk to me," a voice answered. The person that was on the other end of the phone didn't sound like Boosie.

"May I speak to the owner of the phone?" I asked nicely.

"This is the new owner and I've been waiting on your call," the voice said blatantly.

"Is that right? Well, I have some unfinished business with the previous owner of that line so—"

"Yeah, yeah, I know all about it . . ." He cut me off. ". . . I have that lil change he owe, and I need another one. Come through the same spot, same time. My name Do-Dat when you come through."

I was kinda lost for words. This dude Do-Dat, he act like he me and he make some kind of rules. I'ma play the game for the time being over this phone. I'll check his ass when I get there. "I'll be there," I said hanging up, not giving him the chance to respond.

I was a little livid as I sat in the car replaying the whole conversation in my head. I decided to go home first, just to take my precious time. I fired up a blunt as I headed to the Beltway. I still had my vicious weed habit. I smoked like an ounce a week. It's not a lot for one person, right?

Pulling up to the house my nerves had calmed down a whole lot. Nice and mellow, the great feeling I was now enjoying. I entered my home and headed to the room to change my wardrobe. I had to put on something less revealing for this type of interaction.

My current attire was a short suit dress with long slits going down the side of my thighs. I wore this while at work at the Same Guy Label building. It was time to hit the streets, so I put on a pair of Joggers with my Space Jam Jordans and a fitted V-neck polo tee. Chill wear. Getting back to my car I headed to one of my stash houses to pick up what Do-Dat had requested. I can't lie, every time I thought of him an eerie feeling surfaced.

Our meeting spot been the same for the two and a half years I've been dealing with Boosie. Kenilworth Park, off Interstate 295. I felt that it was neutral as far as people chilled and mind their business. The hood that surrounded the park was no joke at all. Them guys weren't on no bullshit if you weren't. I felt safe in my own skin.

There was a youth football game goin' on when I pulled up. This made it a very public scene. I exited my car carrying my Michael Kors handbag. Inside it was a key of coke. I didn't like this dude at all, so I added a petty tax on the price to make a statement. 'SHIT, HE WAS ONLY BUYING ONE.' I hit him for 38,000.

The youth league football game was in full effect as I approached. Boosie, the young boy, didn't even move to greet me as I reached my hand out. I looked him up and down. "Damn Boosie, shade? You ain't fuckin' wit me no more, huh?" I smirked, really not caring.

Boosie put his head down. Usually he is all fun and games, but not today. I think he like 16 years old. I knew something was up when I noticed the change in demeanor. "I'm . . . chillin'," he said, never giving me an eye contact.

'FUCK IT. I GOT SHIT TO DO.'

"Aye, uh Two-Dat, Fat Dat, whatever your name is. Are you ready?" I asked, intentionally messing up his name.

"It's Do-Dat and I been ready." He eyed my bag.

I opened my bag to get the work out but was slapped by a dude that came from behind. I landed on the ground and immediately felt my purse leave my possession. I balled up, expecting more blows to come. Flickering my eyes was my attempt to get the stars to leave my vision as I noticed a car speeding in my direction. I was back on my feet now. I couldn't jump out the way, so instinctively I jumped forward. I was struck again. My body bounded once on the hood and then smacked the windshield. I tried my best to hang on.

"GET THAT BITCH OFF MY SHIT!!" I heard a voice say. "I can't drive with a dead bitch on my windshield."

When I heard the word 'dead' my senses heightened. It wasn't just a robbery; it was a potential homicide. I wasn't about to be another statistic and I damn sure wasn't about to get left in no park bleachers. I had to think fast as my face throbbed. I noticed a possible lifeline. It was a stretch but well worth the attempt. After rolling off the windshield I grabbed a metal screw that was supposed to hold the parking block in place. It was 8 inches in length.

One of the goons with him jumped out the car and tried to pick me up. I quickly jabbed the screw through his face. The screw was dull and rusty, but it still punctured his cheek.

"AHHHHH!!" he screamed, grabbing his face which now was leaking blood. I jumped up and started to run. I left my purse, and all thoughts of that coke came to mind. 'FUCK DAT COKE!' I told myself.

I looked back to see the distance I gained. 'SHIT!' Do-Dat was running behind me as well. The nigga was fast. I thought I was haul assin' but glancing again I noticed them gaining on me. Now on my trail was Boosie along with Do-Dat. I kept running, then heard a loud thump. It was Do-Dat rolling on the pavement with Boosie running in the opposite direction.

'WHEW! THANKS BABY BOY.' I was grateful for Boosie. He clipped ol' boy up so I could get away. I made it back to my war winded.

BOC! BOC! BOC!

I ducked. I heard multiple shots as I opened my car door. I jumped in not knowing where they were landing or coming from. I pushed my car to life and heard the growl of my engine. I burned rubber, leaving the parking lot with a storm of smoke in my rearview. The car rocked as I drifted from lane to lane trying to catch the car. A body vaulted on my hood. I didn't slow down. I hit him. He did a half-flip and landed facedown on the side of the road.

I smashed on the brakes and skidded to a stop on the shoulder. I sat there for a moment with my hands gripping the steering wheel unable to stop the shaking. I stared at the guy that slapped me through my rearview mirror. He was rolling around slowly trying to gain his composure from the force of the car. I opened my glove compartment and grabbed my pearl handle nine milly'. I exited my car cautiously, looking around as I walked up on him. I took aim at his head.

'BITCH ASS NIGGA,' I thought before I squeezed.

BOC!

CHAPTER 62

Charmine pulled up around the way. Angry would be an understatement. She was livid. Grabbing her phone, she called Lefty. He informed her to meet him at Izzo's building. He was in the trap', coolin'. She tried to open the door, but it was locked. The music was loud. No way could her futile knocks be heard was a thought that came to mind. The door was snatched open by a young boy with a tight face. When he noticed who was there, his features softened, but hers didn't. "Move!" Charmine pushed through the kid before he even had the chance to speak a word.

"Daaaaaaayyyummm!" Lefty sang after seeing her. "Somebody, please call 911. He continued to sing the Wyclef song, teasing her.

"Not right now, this is serious. I just got robbed by some nigga named Do-Dat. I'm tryna see him 'bout that. You ready to ride?"

Lefty seen the seriousness of the situation and got out of play mode. "Let's go. I got some throwaways in the next building."

They headed to the next building. In the midst of that a plan was developed. An agreement was put into motion. Lefty's phone rang and he answered it. "Hello?!" The call was private. "You have a pre-paid call from Cordell from the Department of Corrections. To accept the call press—"

Lefty was excited. "Dro pound! What it do, baby boy."

"Ain't nothing, slim, just touchin' base. What's goodie out there on the bricks?" Lefty looked at Charmine and lowered his voice.

"Bruh, a nigga played with the Mrs. and her face lookin' crazy. On my motha we 'bout to go handle and correct that shit doe."

There was a pause followed by a heavy sigh. "I need you to handle it. Don't care what you do or how you do it, but keep my wife away from it, feel me?"

Lefty agreed but didn't know how he was going to complete such a task. Charmine was staring directly in his mouth after he hung the phone up. "Was that my boo?"

He lied. "Nah, wit ur nosey ass. I have other homies behind the wall." Lefty opened the door to the trap, the other one. A bunch of his men were in there hustling, doing their own thing as they walked to the backroom.

Lefty had to think fast. Charmine was loading a gun, talking to herself, getting in the zone. She was still mad. Then an idea hit him. In the room they were in the door was just replaced. The genius that installed the lock put it on the wrong side of the door, which locked people in instead of out. "Aye lil Dro, give me five minutes. I gotta take a shit." Lefty lied. Charmine was in her own world and didn't even hear him.

"Huh?"

Lefty repeated himself. "I said I'll be back. I'm 'bout to sit on the throne and make King decisions." He smirked.

She frowned her face. "Ugh shitty! Hurry up."

Lefty left in a hurry with one hand holding his cheeks together like he really had to go to the toilet. He closed the room he just left and turned the lock on the door slowly and quietly. Charmine was now locked in the bedroom, unknowingly. Lefty left the trap in a hurry. He stood in the middle of the block with no real plan. All the guns were in the room with Charmine. Lefty remembered that Dro's grandmother lived on the next block over and in the backyard in a makeshift shed held a pistol. It was dirty' (used), but all he was going to do is make it dirtier.

Lefty jogged down the block smiling. He enjoyed being able to put in work. It was an instant high for him. He grabbed the pistol after jumping over the brick wall, quietly. Dro's grandmother liable to shoot first and figure it out later. Lefty's phone rang. He ignored it as he made his way back down the street getting in his car. He pulled off and turned some music on. At the stop sign he noticed Susan flagging him down. He pulled over. She hopped in the passenger seat. "What's up L?" she spoke, happy as usually when in his presence.

All he did was raise the window, but she took it upon herself to get all the way in. He looked at her crazy. "I'm on some ova' shit right now. You need to hop yo' happy ass on up outta my shit. I'm 'bout to go put some work in."

Her genuine smile evaporated and was replaced with a devilish grin. "Well, I'm going! I just recently purchased this new handgun. I've been anxiously trying to wield it," she stated.

Lefty couldn't help it. He burst out laughing and mocked her. "Anxiously trying to wield. Girl, just say you tryna buss your joint. You over there soundin' wild ass shit, moe." He giggled. She playfully punched him on his shoulder. "Forget you! Let's go."

Lefty explained the situation as they cruised. He had a plan to just pull up and go guns blazing in the honor of Dro's wife. Susan shook her head, not believing that was his plan. Susan had a better one and explained it to Lefty as they drove. They had to make a slight detour. Pulling in front of Keisha's house she got out to go get her gun and change outfits for her caper to come.

In the car Lefty's phone was goin' crazy. Charmine been calling him ever since she realized what he did. Finally, he answered. "Hey, boss lady?"

"Don't fuckin' hey me. Where my damn purse!" Charmine yelled. "I need my keys so I could go and see 'bout this nigga wit out cho' scared ass. If you ain't want smoke, YOU SHOULD HAVE SAID SO!!!"

"First of all, I want all the smoke. Don't trip. That's why I'm out about to take care of the problem. I'm already on my way. Remember, you a boss. Let me do you this solid." Lefty tried to stroke her ego.

"UGH! BYE!"

CLICK.

Lefty looked at his phone. 'HOW RUDE.' He tossed it in the back the center console, took a breath before lighting a cigarette and waited for Susan to return.

Susan exited the house with an attitude. She got into an argument with Keisha. In her opinion, something was up with her, and she planned to get to the bottom of it. Now was not the time. She had to push them thoughts in the rearview, for now.

'DAMN,' Lefty thought as he noticed Susan walking down the pathway leading to his car. She had on a leggings set by Fabletics and a fanny pack around her waist. "Pick up your tongue, boy." Susan smiled.

"You up I them joints shawty," he flirted. "But where in the fuck did you find a fanny pack?" He giggled.

"Whatever, boy you ready?"

The ride was smooth. Exiting the highway, they rode past a group of guys hanging out in Kenilworth Park, smoking. Lefty pointed to the guy that was described to him. Do-Dat. He sat on the bench as the group of friends kneeled, shooting craps in front of him.

Lefty parked. He walked back in the area of the crowd. His idea was to pose as a weed smoker in attempts to purchase some smoke. He walked. Step by step his nerves started to rattle as he neared.

Susan hung back. She was doing some stretches, getting her body loose in preparation for her slight jog. Lefty made it to the crowd. He spoke to nobody in particular, just anybody that would answer. "Wat' up, Slim? Any of that for sale?"

The crap game froze. Everybody looked at Lefty with the side eyes. "You know somebody right here, moe?" Do-Dat asked as he stood from the bench making his presence known as he mugged.

"Respect . . ." Lefty rose his arms in surrender. "Didn't know I needed to know a nigga for some punk ass pack, my bad, Slim. You got that."

"You got a smart-ass mouth, lil nigga," Do-Dat said as everybody stood from their kneeling positions waiting on the next call.

Lefty stood his ground. 'ANY MINUTE NOW,' he thought as he could foresee what was gonna happen next. Do-Dat and his men formed a semi-circle around Lefty. One of the guys noticed a white chick jogging their way. He gave a head nod in her direction and said, "Hol' up. Let this white bitch run on past."

Susan stopped right in front of the crowed. "Whew! It's hot . . ." She wiped the sweat from her forehead. Everyone stared at her trying to keep their cool. "You fellas wouldn't have the time, would you?" she asked, putting her hair in a ponytail as they admired her physique.

"6:00, beautiful," a young boy flirted.

"Thank you so much, but before I leave, I know it's old fashioned or what not, but I have this map in my pack . . ." She reached to unzip her fanny pack and dug in. "I just need direction to the nearest . . ." She pulled out an all-black Glock G30 S. It was the slim model built with the shorty polymer frame with dual recoil spring assembly. It had a white dot front sight with outlines in the rear. A .45 caliber automatic with 10 rounds, a baby cannon.

"Shit lady!" Do-Dat was shocked with bubbled eyes. Him and his team was caught slippin'. "Fuck is dis?" He looked around.

Susan didn't say a word. Lefty moved away from the crowd to stand beside Susan. "I'll answer that for ya' my man. Well, earlier right, today that is . . ." Lefty started to pace. "Your bitch ass, yup you . . ." He pointed at Do-Dat. "Had the nerve to rob my sister and put—"

BOOM! BOOM! BOOM!

"Damn girl . . ." Lefty flinched as Do-Dat's body hit the floor.

"You didn't even let me finish my speech." He grabbed his gun from the small of his back. "Okay, who's next?"

Susan and Lefty pointed their guns at the remaining so-called goons. The pleading was cut short with the sound of multiple gunshots. Five men laid sprawled out in front of them as they looked at each other.

Susan spoke. "You hungry?" Lefty looked at her and shook his head.

"You serious?"

She nodded. "Hell, nah ain't nobody hungry wit' cho crazy ass. Let's get the fuck outta here."

Dro

"Count time, count time gentlemen!" a correctional officer yelled through the unit.

I'M TIRED OF THIS SHIT. I blew a heavy sigh.

I walked to my cell. This shit done got old real quick. It's cool doe, this ride was nearing an end. I had a couple of weeks. In the cell I listened to my cellie rant. He just found out that his little brother got smoked in the city streets. This was regular in any hood. The only thing that threw me for a loop was the excessive line of questions he would randomly ask. He didn't care about that type of shit before.

The type of shit he would ask now was shit like, where I'm from, shit about my lil men and even who running my hood since I been in. He claim that he wanna 'fuck' with me when he touch but shid, the nigga still tryna get some play in court. He got forever and a day, 85 years. That's one of the reasons I'm real selective on what I be telling dudes around her. He won't use me to get a second chance in the world. Dude paperwork straight, but I don't put nothing past new niggas or niggas that back is against the wall.

His ranting lasted a whole hour and the count finally cleared, saving me from anymore of this conversation. Soon as they opened my door, I shot up outta there. I had to get on the phone.

Phones in the Feds was nothing like the jail. There wasn't no line or politics. After your 15 minutes up, you have to wait 45 minutes to use it again. I decided to call my wife. She been blowing my e-mail up, but I didn't have any tru-units to respond. It was system maintenance going on and I couldn't transfer money today. Luckily, I had some funds on the phone side. I picked up the receiver and dialed the memorized digits.

Izzo walked past. "Cuz, I'm gone out on the rec move. I'm bust these niggas ass in some b-ball."

I nodded my head, letting him know I heard him and then said, "I'll be out there."

The phone rang a couple times and was finally accepted. "Hey King!!" my wife answered.

"Sup' Queen, what's goin' on?"

"Nothing much. Our Tattoo Parlor doing well, and the 'other' business is boomin'. I had a situation a couple weeks ago, but Lefty stole my shine—"

"What?! What happened?" I cut her off, trying to give the illusion that was unaware.

"I'm trying to tell, dang. But listen, Lefty, dat fool think he have all the sense. I told him about the situation that I had just went through, right. Then the fool trick me into a room and locked me in there and left me. The fool took my keys and all. You should have seen me, I was heated. I didn't get to handle it, but it was taken care of."

I was laughing to myself. Lefty was funny as shit. He never told me this part of the story. I listened to my girl vent, then the conversation switched to some other shit.

"I'm mad at you, too," she randomly expressed.

"What I do?" I was truly lost.

"It's our anniversary and you forgot."

DAMN.

"Of course, I didn't forget," I lied. That shit truly slipped my mind. My head everywhere else. ". . . remember our wedding. It was the best day of my life." I tried to redirect.

It worked; I could see the smile through the phone. "Yes, I remember, boo! You made me the happiest woman in the world that day."

"You was mad at me too, but you played it off so well in front of our company. Remember when . . ."

Reflection

"Damn bruh, you 'bout to get married," Izzo said, blowing smoke throughout the car.

Dro, Izzo and Lefty drove in the car headed to the wedding. It was September, the autumn season. Charmine picked this set up so it would be right after her birthday. She loved the fall season, not the cold or the heat, but a nice blend with all the colors.

"Bruh, you gonna make me late. She already blowing up my pone asking me where I'm at," Dro said, declining the blunt.

The night before was crazy, and they had so much fun. No one made it home. As they drove, they all were getting dressed in the backseat of the limo. The wedding venue was set up nicely. It was outside on a national park. Family and friends were there awaiting the groom and the bride's arrival.

The limo pulled up and all eyes were on the vehicle. The doors were opened by the driver. Clouds of smoke left the car and floated with air. Tight faces and shakes of the head was what they received as a Lil Wayne track came through the speakers. Money on My Mind from The Carter had the younger youth bobbing their heads. "Fuck y'all staring at?" Izzo mumbled.

"Chill, fool. You can't talk to them ol' ass people like dat," Lefty chimed in, but Dro cut in.

"Both y'all fall back. Y'all got me high as shit right now. I really don't need any problems."

One of Charmine's uncles was whispering, talking about the groom and groomsmen. Lefty overheard them. "I hate when a nigga want problems but I love to give a nigga shells," Lefty said loud enough for the uncle to hear and see Lefty staring right at him.

The uncle raised his nose but didn't respond. Everyone was introduced as they waited on the bride. It was like clockwork. After the meet and greet, Charmine's limo pulled alongside the pavement. Two guns ran to the car to unroll a thin carpet leading to the alter so she wouldn't have to walk to the grass.

There wasn't no piano, just the sounds from the speakers playing as she walked down the rolled-out aisle. She was beautiful in her custom-made white gown. Everyone looked on in awe.

Charmine made it to the other side of Dro who stood at the alter. Her smile was big through the see-through material. She turned to lock eyes with her soon to be husband. There was silence, a deafening silence. Even the pastor felt the vibes.

In a shocking tone, Charmine snapped. "Oh, my fucking God . . ." The crowd gasped. ". . . the one day out the year I ask you not to fuck up, you arrive here high out your fuckin' mind!" It got silent . . .

"You was made at me too. But you played it off oh so well. Remember how high I was?" I smiled to myself.

"Hmph, how could I forget. You was at the moon." I heard Charmine giggling through the phone.

We talked and laughed for the duration of the call. By the time I finished my call they was calling my unit to chow. My stomach was empty and touching my back. Hot dogs and tater tots didn't sound too bad right now. I wasn't the only one that felt this way, because the unit got empty quick. NIGGAS ON TRAYS HARD AS SHIT. I shook my head.

Walking up the steps I head to my cell. I patted my pocket and noticed I forgot my ID. No ID no food until last call and I wasn't waiting for that. There were three of my cellies homeboys from around his way outside my cell. I figured they was waiting on him so they could go to chow together.

I made it to my door, their backs was toward me. "Excuse me, good men."

They looked back, but one of them spoke. "Oh, my bad, superstar."

I laughed a fake laugh. These bamma ass niggas be throwing me off. "Supastar huh, oh yeah." I walked past what seemed like his security. I noticed my cellie in his locker. I spoke to his back. "What's up, cellie?" As I spoke, something wasn't right.

AHHHH, SHIT! I felt cold steel puncture the backside of my neck along with a combination of punches as I hit the ground and curled up.

I heard a voice. It was my cellie's. "You thought your peoples could kill my peoples and not pay! That was my lil brother, bitch!"

The knife was hot. It burned each time I felt it pierce my skin. The room got smaller and smaller. I couldn't keep my eyes open. My throat felt clogged. Blood leaked everywhere. The room was empty. I looked to the light, then it went dark.

Jroc

Another day in the jungle. The jail been turned up so much that we stayed on lockdown. Today was different. I sat in my cell playing casino with my cellie. The sounds of the automatic doors unlocking turned my attention to the door as it slid open. Both me and my cellie stood up and put our backs to the wall. The unit was loud. I knew we was on lockdown, but everyone was biddin' (joking) through the slots from tier to tier.

Never slippin', to make sure nobody was tryna pull me a move, I pulled my knife out and crept to the entrance of my cell. Sometimes the Cos be on bullshit and would set you up quick. I peeked through my door with my knife on my side. I noticed a CO in the bubble waving a pass.

"What da fuck is that for?" I yelled.

"Taylor! You have a pass to go to R&D, pack your belongings."

I smiled. It sounded good but I headed to the bubbled, confusion heavy in my demeanor as I walked. The officer looked at me as I knocked on the bubble cause I could. He didn't like that. "I can see you! Don't bang. Are you deaf Taylor? Get your shit and get outta here. You fuckin' up my count!"

"Fuck I'm goin' at?" I hoped I wasn't goin' back to the Feds. If I was that meant my lawyer couldn't get me back in court or some shit happened.

"Home, now hurry up before count time."

The CO talkin' 'bout pack my shit. I ain't got shit but commissary and jail shit. They could keep all that shit. I didn't even tell my cellie or none of them niggas I was 'bout to roll. I grabbed my pass and got up outta there. "I'm ready, slid da door."

After the dragging process of getting released, I finally inhaled a breath of freedom. It felt good to breathe air. Words couldn't describe the feeling of being released from captivity. I opened my eyes and a Mercedes GLE63 AMG pulled up in front of me.

I read about this whip in the magazines and knew all the specs.

Its power comes from AMG's 5.5-liter twin turbo V8 developing 577 horsepower and a stout 561 lb.-ft of torque. Mercedes claims it get to 0-60 in 4.2 seconds.

'BREATHE,' I told myself.

The window came down in the back. It was my lawyer wearing a kodak smile. "Ms. Bishop?"

She looked at me. "James . . . you going to get in or what?" I looked in the truck to see nobody in there but her and the driver. I walked around to the other side to enter the vehicle.

"Damn it smell good in here. Smells edible." I smiled and licked my lips.

"In your dreams, Mr. Taylor . . ."

ALREADY DID IN MY DREAMS AND MUCH MORE.

". . . But if you remember when you were in there . . ." she nodded to the jail. ". . . you made an agreement, and my employer is ready to collect. Here." She passed me a sealed envelope.

I opened it. The first thing I noticed put a smile on my face. It was blue faces. It had to be at least twenty bands. WHAT THE FUCK! I was shocked.

I unfolded the letter and began to read:

> Jroc, congrats on your release back
> into the free world, must be nice. You
> and I have business and a common en-
> emy. You owe me, not for the money,
> that's mere change and a welcome home
> token. We also have friends in common
> and this is how I got in touch with you.
> I will see you soon. In 7 days meet me
> at Georgetown Mall at 5:00 p.m. by the
> old dirt road path. Stay safe and alive.

The last part of the letter gave me slight chills. It was kind of crazy reading it.

STAY ALIVE.

"What somebody tryna kill me?" I asked Ms. Bishop who was on the phone. She put a finger up to shush me.

I fingered through the money and that put a smile on my face. I didn't know too many niggas that was heavy like this who could just throw me twenty bands except Dro, but I haven't heard from him, and I know he ain't fuckin' with me right now. I looked out my window to see we were headed to Virginia. I just enjoyed the ride and watched the cars as they passed by.

Ms. Bishop finally got off the phone. "Okay, so my employer has a spot for you to stay, that is if you want it. It's a condo around the corner from Pentagon City. We're heading there now to go to the mall to grab you a few outfits and get you out of that sweatsuit." She pinched her own nose. "You need to hop in the shower to get that jail funk off you too . . ." I sniffed my armpits. I SMELL LIKE DEGREE BITCH. ". . . after that the rest up to you," she concluded.

"Lady, who is this employer of yours? This nigga doing all this shit for me, and I don't even know the dude. I hope he ain't gay."

She smirked a devilish grin. "Who told you it a guy." She opened her door. "Let's go."

I got out of the car. I still had on my blue decks, so I felt everything I walked on. First stop, I needed some sneaks, courtesy of the lawyer and her "employer." The mall didn't change much. I knew exactly what shoes I was gonna get. Walking in the store I had turned my swag all the way on high, at least in my mind.

Ms. Bishop was looking at me like I was crazy, especially how I wore my release clothes like it was the newest freshest shit ever. I noticed a sales associate and called her over. "Hey, excuse me!" The lady looked my way. "Can I get these in a size 10?"

She smiled. "Sure."

In my hand was a single shoe. The New I 990's. This was my first pick of the day. I also purchased a Lacoste Polo, and some Cardigan Vintage shorts by Bally. I was on my college boy look.

My outfit for the mall.

I shopped in a few more stores and ran the tab high. I shrugged my shoulders. 'SHID WHY NOT?' I had me a sponsor and I took advantage. Other purchases included Nautica, Hugo Boss, Purple Label Polo, and some Givenchy. Fly shit only.

Leaving the mall, I felt like a million bucks. I didn't spend a dime of the money the employer gave me or the money I had in my account. I sat in the whip hype. I'm free, money in my pocket and now wondering what the next move was.

"Where we going now?" I asked.

"To your condo, that is if you want it," she repeated.

'IF I WANT IT, FUCK YOU THINK.'

"Um, let me check it out and decide." I downplayed my excitement. Whoever this employer was he/she was looking out for the cookout, but for some reason it felt like I was selling my soul to the devil.

❖   ❖   ❖

Tiara

'My money stack, I just want my
percent
'She told me to hit the hoop, I use to
play running back
You niggas be fumbling don't u give
him no gun again
These bitches be flying out, cause
money be coming in.

I was on the highway crankin' Wale and Lil Wayne's song

'Runningback'. Today was a good day. My boo was getting out of prison today. I was excited as I drove. I knew I was speeding, but I was trying to get there ASAP. I pulled up at the facility and it was pandemonium. News crews and reporters were outside. I didn't expect this. I knew my boo was a rapper or what not but didn't think his wave was this lit'.

I'm glad I drove his car. Before he was arrested, he brought the newest Audi R-8. It was two years old now, but people still couldn't afford it. It was over a hundred-thousand-dollar purchase. As I rode up into the parking lot people rushed the car. I forgot this damn car had that stupid ass S&G logo on the license plate and it drew all the attention.

The flashes came rapidly. I honked the horn. "Back the fuck up off my shit!!" I yelled to the crowd as they snapped away. Random questions about different stuff was asked liked I had any answers. Izzo taught me a long time ago not to respond if the answer wasn't safe or could hurt him later. With that etched in my bran, I remained silent and kept pushin'.

I made it to the lobby and waited. About an hour or so passed and my boo made his exit looking sexy as ever. I had his outfit mailed to him. He stepped out in Versace all gold everything with a pair of loafers. He had his Fed glow and a toned body. Izzo walked to me with wide arms. "Did you miss me?"

I ran into his arms and jumped into his embrace. I was geeked. My boo been gone for a minute. I didn't have no dick in so long, well his. He put me down. "Dam bae, you ain't gotta squeeze a nigga so tight," he joked.

"Sorry boo. You know I miss you. You know it's endless reporters and shit out there." I hipped him.

He blew a sigh. "Damn, I can't even come home in peace." He shook his head. "Let's get it over with."

We walked through the crowds and the flashes went wild. I felt we were on the red carpet. Different magazine representatives were trying to ambush us and get an exclusive. I was surprised that he stopped and answered a few of the questions. There was one reporter that hit a nerve and asked the wrong question. He paused in deep thought as the question replayed in his mind, I guess because he kept repeating it lowly. He instantly got heated. I think the reporter asked: "Prophet, what kind of condition is your friend or manager is in? It's a lot of rumors of what has happened. Some say he is dead and gone, some say he is a vegetable. Can you shed some light on it? Either confirm or deny."

There was silence.

❖   ❖   ❖

Reflection

Izzo was in the middle of the softball game when he noticed multiple correctional officers running through the compound. They were headed to his unit. The compound was still open, movement ceased as the intercom blared. "ALL INMATES TAKE A KNEE.'

Izzo ran to the gate trying to see what was goin' on. An inmate was brung out on the stretcher then placed on a transport golf cart. As it rode through the compound heading to medical, Izzo noticed the shoe hanging off the back. It was a pair of all black Jordans, Dro's Jordans. He ran through the pound trying to catch up with the car but was tackled as he neared.

"Dro!!" he screamed. "Get the fuck off me, that's my brother, bitch, get the fuck off me!!"

Izzo tried to fight the officers off him but was restrained. From the ground he noticed Dro's cellie and a few of his men was being walked off in cuffs. Anger flooded his mind. He remembered Dro telling him about the problems him and his cellie were having. Now that Dro has been backed doored, he felt responsible.

Skeet. Dro's cellie smiled at Izzo and winked at him as they took him and the rest of them to the SHU, the secure housing unit, also known as the hole.

❖   ❖   ❖

"Bae, Bae!!" I called out to Izzo. He was lost in his own thoughts.

The reporter was persistent. "Prophet! Did you hear the question?"

Izzo shook his head, bringing himself back to reality. He blinked a few times. "Suck a dick, how 'bout that? Interview over . . ." He started pushing through the paparazzi. "TT get me the fuck outta here," he told me.

He was leading the way as he pulled me through the parking lot. He found his car, which I was driving and went straight to the passenger seat. He jumped in. "Come on, shawty!" He rushed me.

We drove for about an hour in silence before Izzo decided to speak. "I need you to make a pit stop when we hit the Maryland side. I have to holla at my man. He said he'll have something for me," he said, never giving me eye contact.

The tone in his voice had me leery, but I just kept my thoughts to myself. The reporter really changed the vibe of things. Izzo was supposed to be driving as I sucked him dry the whole way to the city, but nah, looks like he on some bullshit now.

First day out the Feds and I can't even get no dick. I was livid. I been doin' my keegles to tighten this pussy for him and he want to be on some gangsta shit. Seems like we have different plans now.

❖   ❖   ❖

Izzo

First day out of the Federal gates my mind as on murder. I had plans to deal with what happened to my man Dro anyway, but that damn reporter just put them plans on the top of my to-do list. Looked to the side and noticed my girl. She was sick'. When I say sick', I mean she was mad. I know she envisioned this romantic sexfest which really, I didn't mind, but them damn reporters and paparazzi rubbed me the wrong way and put me in kill mode.

I was off to see a big homie of mines. Big Purple. I called him Big Purp for short. He was the man out these parts when it came to artillery. Before I got backed doored and bagged, me and my homies use to always shop with him. I was just hoping he was still around and in business. Tiara pulled in front of the warehouse. It was one of his base operational spots. Still looked to be open. "Stay here, I'll be back," I told Tiara.

She smacked her teeth, but I didn't give any fucks 'bout that. I knew she was gonna do whatever I said. Closed the car door and headed to the steel doors and knocked. There was a slight pause before a small slit opened on the door.

"What you want?" All I seen was a set of eyes.

"I need to holla at Big Purp," I said through the slot.

"Password?"

'DEEZ NUTZ!' I wanted to say.

"I don't know no damn password nigga. Tell 'em it's Izzo from uptown."

A moment passed. The door opened. I walked in and was quickly surrounded by some security type goons. "Hands up!!!" one of them barked.

I mugged on them. I was tight'. "Nigga, I ain't got shit! I just came home, this the reason I'm here." I lifted my shirt. "Now please, if you don't mind could one of you topflight niggas go and get your boss."

In the distance I heard a giggle. It was childlike. I followed the sound and seen a "massive shadow appear coming around a dark corner. I recognized the laugh as the frame came into view. In a squeaky voice the massive man spoke. "Oh shit! It's mutha fuckin' Prophet y'all!" It was Purple. "You miss me baby?" His arms spread wide.

Naturally I smiled. I still couldn't get over the fact that this big ol' dude that stood over six feet tall and weighed in at least 280-320 lbs. easy and solid but sounded like a ten-year-old little girl.

"Sup blacker than me. I need you big guy," I informed him.

He smiled. Always on joke time. He started singing Erika Badu song. "Well, you better call on Tyrone," and then started laughing hysterically.

'BIG ASS NIGGA ALWAYS TRYNA BID.'

"For real bruh, I need some pistols, moe." He held his stomach trying to catch his breath. He looked at me. "Whew! That was funny." He put his arms around my shoulder. "But uh, what you tryna spend, playa?"

'NOT A DAMN THING!'

I'm tryna see you later for the bill. You know I'm good for it."

Purp led me to his arsenal of weapons. It was too many to name. Some of them I never even heard of. He had guns on the wall as if they were sneakers. Price tags and all hung from the trigger. I didn't want to get anything crazy or too big. Something slight would do me just fine for this situation.

My eyes stopped roaming and stopped on a small compact Glock. It was lightweight and two-tone, .40 caliber. Big Purp tried to give me a standard ten shot clip. I declined it and reached for the extended clip. Didn't really need all them shots, but I've been gone for a minute. I don't know what my aim looking like these days.

After getting all that I needed, I exited the warehouse. Sitting in the car, my girl had a pout on her face. I understood her frustration, but I know if it was me that got butchered and Dro was home in my position, he would be doing the same shit I'm doing.

I looked at her. "Come on, boo. I'ma drop you off for a while."

"No, you not! I'm goin' too."

'FUCK IT'

I pulled off and headed home. I had to change my clothes first. Cruising through the city streets was love. I missed the city. No better place to be. I wanted to go around the way and check in with a few dudes but blew off the thought. Blowing trees, I made it to my house. The house was cool as I looked around. While Tiara headed to the bathroom and relieved herself from the long ride, I jetted back out the door. Leaving out I didn't really get to take in the whole house. Did notice a lot of change. That only meant Tiara had a field day designing everything after I got bagged. I was gonna change some shit, but I put that on the back burner for now. I had an address on one of the dudes that was with the bullshit that happened to my man.

Come to find out they were from around the same area that the dude that got killed in Kenilworth Park. It made sense after the fact. It was one them, nah, a few of them that got crudded out that day. Now it was payback, again. I had a few good men in that neighborhood. One in particular, and I planned on touching base with him and see where his head at.

I drove in a bucket' (beat up car). If I would've drove in any of my cars I would've been spotted. I'm still shocked at how famous I became, it was surreal. Back when Dro decided to push me in this rap shit it was just something to hide the dope money, but now I ain't gotta hustle but I'm not stop. I'm a Hustler first. But now I see the other side to being known. I have to really be alias in all I do.

My phone was blowing up. It was Tiara. She was sick'. I knew she put in work or whateva when I was gone. I'm home now, but that don't mean we was gonna be off no Bonnie and Clyde type shit. Me and my men put in work, not me and my girl. I ignored the phone as I cruised. Thoughts to myself was tryna kill my vibe. I pushed that shit in the back of my mind when I pulled up to a used car lot my man owned. Me and this nigga did time

together and I knew him period from the world. He was introduced to me by Dro. He been in for a minute on a body beef but
got back in court and gave hid time back. Real nigga, now he out
on some chill shit. He was an official nigga from The Worth' and
well respected. He was under the hood of one of his cars as I
crept. I had to mess with him.

"Aye ol' nigga!!" I screamed on him. "Can I get some fuckin'
service?"

He rose up slowly, turning around talkin' shit. "Nigga I don't
know who da fu—" He recognized me. "Oh shit! Your ugly ass.
When you escape the zoo?" He tried to hug me.

'SKRRR!'

I gave his ass the Heisman trophy stance. "Whoa, Coka Moe."
That was his name. "I miss you too homie but you greasy ass
shit, Slim."

The nigga had on some oil-stained overalls, and some worn
out Nike boots lookin' like a real mechanic. "Go head, cuz." He
waved me off. "When you get out?"

"Today. But sad to say this ain't no social visit. You know what
happened to our man Dro. He still in the hospital fighting a coma
tryna come through. Word on the wire is that one of the niggas
live around your way." I paused to get some type of reaction, but
all he did was wait for me to continue, so I did. "The nigga name
Juicy J. You know him?"

Coka Moe blew cigarette smoke. "Yeah, I know the wild nigga, Jamal. He just came home too. I didn't know he was wit' that
shit."

"Yeah Slim, what's up wit em?" I asked.

"Fuck 'em! He ain't my man or he ain't original. It's a lot of
new niggas 'round there. I'm just in my own lane. They know
what's up with me. All my good men are dead or in prison."

"You down for a 187?" I smirked.

He laughed. "Your fake ass Menace to Society head ass boy,"
he said, always joning' (cracking jokes). "Fuck it, I'm wit it for my
man." He reached for the small of his back pulling out a HK45

and cocked it . . .

It was 4:00 p.m. as we cruised through the hood. People was outside chilling in different sections of the complex. We couldn't find the nigga for nothing. The address I had wasn't in the hood. Just figured to check around where he hang at first. It would have been better for me. His neighborhood would've offered a clean getaway. Interstate 295, I could literally go anywhere from southeast to uptown, even Maryland within a few short turns.

Jamal's house was one of the new homes built off Alabama Avenue. This area used to be one of the hardest neighborhoods in the southeast. Not it was renovated and gentrified. Driving through this area felt like the nicer parts of Maryland's suburbs. Just coming home, I was a little nervous. I can't lie. Coka Moe on the other hand was geeked. He couldn't put that pistol down. He was a fool with it and without it.

I told Coka Moe to put some music on then instantly regretted it. Wanted to listen to some gangsta shit to put me in the mood, but this fool plugged in his phone and started playing some old Linkin Park shit. I just laughed; my nigga never changed. He was bobbing to the music like it was some Wayne. I just drove.

We pulled down the block from Jamal's house. Coka Moe looked at the GPS and looked at me. "Why you so far away nigga? Go in the driveway, Coka Moe instructed.

I looked at him crazy right back. "What? The nigga know who I am, bruh."

"So, you smokin' him, right?"

"No question."

"A'ight den' pull. We invited guest. He should know we was on our way." He reached in his pocket to screw on his 'silencer,' a raw potato.

I looked at him and tried to smack the potato. "Nigga that shit don't work, and where the fuck you get a potato from?"

Coka Moe led the way. We walked the path that led to the front door. He looked at me with a devilish grin as he pressed the doorbell. "I promise you ain't never freak out til you had a freak out and see each and every freak out on freak out night."

"Wha-what?!" I was lost. He smiled like he said some scientif-ic shit. The nigga stay saying some wild shit that had you thinking then later it made sense. "It's a full moon tonight cuz," he said, looking up.

The moon was nowhere in sight. I just shook my head as the door opened. It seemed like I've been doing a lot today. A lady answered the door.

"Hi! Can I help you sweetie?"

Coka Moe was like that. He poured the charm on heavy. "Look at you. Ma, still beautiful as ever. You probably don't even remember me. I've been gone a little while. How you been? Is Jamal home?"

Just hearing her son's name and the tone he was using she assumed we were all friends. She smiled. "Come on in, I'll go get him for you."

Coka Moe followed her in. No sooner as she crossed the door-mat a semi-muffled shot was fired along with a loud one after the potato exploded. He turned around and smiled. "It worked, cuz!" He was excited.

"Moe!!" I was surprised as I closed the door.

I'ma take a wild guess and assume that was Jamal's mom. She laid face down on her own living room floor with two smokin' holes in her head. Coka Moe looked back to me, "Yeah, what's up, cuz?"

'FUCKIN' PSYCHOPATH'

"Nothing let's go find da nigga," I said looking around. I was sure that shot raised an alarm.

We moved through the house making it upstairs. I heard gun-fire and tried to scale the wall. The shots weren't real. It was coming from the amplified TV.

Jamal and a friend of his was playing Halo, deep into the game oblivious to us behind them. Coka Moe spoke. "Damn, cuz, you niggas like dat! Y'all both playin' online? Look, cuz!" He grabbed my arm. "Shit done changed from the PS2," he said really interested.

They paused the game looking back at the same time now staring down the barrel of two guns. "You thought shit was sweet after you left da Feds huh, fool?"

His friend tried to speak. "I ain't got shit to do with—"

BOC! BOC!

"Shut up cuz." Coka Moe shot 'em. "Ain't nobody even talking to you!" He looked at me. "As you saying, cuz."

I looked at Coke and smiled. "You right."

BOOM! BOOM! BOOM!

Coka Moe held his ears. "Damn cuz, that joint loud as shit," he said, walking toward the TV.

"Come on fool, time to go," I told him, but he continued to walk the wrong way. "Fuck you doing?"

This nigga really crazy. The Feds really fucked him up. He sat in the Lazy Boy and grabbed the controller and continued the game that was paused. "This the new joint, cuz." He looked excited. "I ain't play this one before. It look real ass shit." He was really getting into it. He looked back at me. "How you reset it?"

BOOM!

I shot a hole in the center of the TV, and he just dropped the controller. "You cheatin' like shit, cuz. That ain't cool. That's fine, I'm takin' it wit me." He stood up and began pulling the cord out of the wall. He looked at the corpse. "Homes, can I borrow this?"

We left the house. I was in a hurry, literally speed walking. I wasn't tryna go back to prison. I got in the car and seen Coka Moe out my side view with a water hose. He turned it on and began watering the grass and flowers that line the porch as he waved at a neighbor. "Hey Ms. Purely!" After a slight watering he wrapped the holes back up and waved to nobody in the window.

"Bye Auntie, see ya later!"

'YUP, THIS NIGGA BURNT TOAST'

He got in the car. "Cuz, you ain't tell Auntie and 'em bye?" I shook my head and put the car in gear, then pulled off.

'TIME TO DROP THIS NIGGA BAC OFF.'

Exposed
Three months later

Black sat in the basement playing Madden with Susan. For the last couple of months, he'd been keeping her close as they learned each other's way.

The vibes between them were always good and felt natural. It was platonic. If he wasn't molding Susan, he was working his magic with Heather. Heather had been looking out for him in so many aspects, legally and illegally. The child they shared made their bond tighter.

Smoke clouded the room along with music that kept the area mellow with chill vibes. Keisha and Black hadn't been on the best of terms. Something was up but Black just kept ill thoughts of her under the rug. The worst thing she could do to him was leave in his mind, or so he thought.

The door to the basement opened. "Black!!" Keisha screamed.

"Yeah, what's up!" Black yelled back, putting the game on pause.

Susan was pissed. "Come on. How are you going to pause the game in the middle of my pass?" she asked.

"Shhh . . .." He put a finger up to silence Susan. She smacked her teeth but listened. "Yeah, Keisha!"

Keisha came down the stairs. Her attitude could be felt with each step she made. She stood directly in front of Black after giving Susan a look. "I'm 'bout to go to the store. Give me a few dollars!" she demanded with her hand out.

Black chuckled as he peeled off a hundred-dollar bill and gave it to her. Susa rolled her eyes. They disliked each other for different reasons, but the tension could be felt between them.

Taking the money, Keisha didn't even thank him as she climbed the stairs. "You're welcome, Hooker!" Black said to her back as she kept on walking.

Keisha was heading to the store to meet up with her friend. There were plans she had to put into motion for the upcoming events. She pulled into a parking lot alongside another vehicle. It was a Ford GT supercharged Coupe. Metallic black with five percent tints.

Getting out of the car Keisha headed to the waiting car. She reached for the door handle, but it was absent. After a second, a hydraulic sound was heard as the suicide doors lifted.

A voice spoke, "What's goin' on sexy?"

She blushed as she sat on the leather seats. "Hey you. So what you got me meetin' you out here for?" she inquired.

"It's time to put shit into motion and make these introductions," the voice said. They sat and talked for a few minutes, then the conversation become vital. "You ready?" The voice needed confirmation.

Keisha wasn't ready. At least not at the moment. "Ready for what?! Is dude here right now?" she asked, looking around hoping not.

"Yeah, he is. Actually he inside the gym right in front of us." He used his head to point. "Time to get the ball rolling."

She inhaled a nervous breath. "Okay, here goes."

He smirked. "I'll be right here."

Keisha walked into the gym and looked around. The guy she was looking for was a person she hadn't seen in years. She spotted him instantly. He was hitting a punching bag as he rapped a "Shy Glizzy" track.

"Damn, he still fine," Keisha said to herself.

From behind him Keisha reached to tap his shoulder as he threw a jab at the bag. He turned around quickly. "Keisha?!" He was shocked first, then slightly nervous. "W-what da fuck you doin' here?" He frantically looked around.

She put her hand up. "I come in peace." She smiled. "Give me a hug, boy."

Jroc was confused. He didn't understand what was goin' on as he hugged her. He knew Keisha was Black's girl and from what he knew about her, she buss her gun. He felt naked, realizing his gun was in a locker out of reach.

"I'm a lil sweaty but what's up, shawty. How can I help yo? I see you ain't dressed to work out." He tried to play it cool, hoping his heart wasn't showing through his chest.

Keisha smiled. "Jroc, it's simple. It's time to pay the piper . . . to say the least."

Jroc frowned. "I thought you came in peace, so what piper do I owe that concerns you?"

"Ummm, let me think. Dem' lawyer fees, dat condo you laid up in . . . Am I ringing any bells niggah?"

Jroc's eyes got big. "That was you!?"

"Fuck no! You cut in all, but niggah pul-lease." She laughed. "The man of the hour is out front, so let's not keep him waiting. We've got shit to do."

Jroc gathered his things. He was skeptical but felt more secure now that his gun rested on his hip. He walked outside and noticed Keisha was on the phone, so he leaned against the wall and waited. After the brief conversation, Keisha turned her attention to Jroc. "He said meet him at your spot and I'll follow you to make sure you don't get lost and you feel safe."

"How da fuck do you following me suppose to make me feel more secure? You coming don't mean shit!"

"Boy, come on! You know what you owe."

Bumper to bumper they arrived at the parking garage of the high-rise that was gifted to Jroc. They caught the elevator to his floor and headed to the condo. Jroc went to unlock the door, but it was already opened. Instinctively he reached for his gun but was stopped by Keisha.

"You don't want to do that. I tol' you he rolyl' already here."

Jroc loosened his grip, letting his shirt cover the small of his back as he entered the apartment. A man sat in his Lazy Boy watching YouTube on his TV through the PlayStation system.

"Aye bruh! Bruh-bruh." Jroc tried to get the guy's attention. "Do I know you, Homes?"

The man stood up. "Nah, you don't know me, but you owe me. We have common enemies and I have a plan that I need you to execute."

Jroc folded his arms. "And who is this enemy of ours you speak of?"

"Black."

The name alone brought a lot of emotions to the surface from childhood to adulthood. Jroc wasn't the same person he was before the Feds. It transformed him into a cold-blooded man, but Black still held a small piece of his heart that he wanted back.

Jroc wanted badly for Black's heart to stop. "Okay, so I know I have an existing problem with him, but what dat got to do wit y'all, especially you?" He looked at Keisha, "And who the fuck is you?"

"My name is Fred Jr."

A slight recognition swept through Jroc's memory. When hew as hiding out at a friends' house waiting for court, he'd heard about the whole situation about Black's little sisters getting kidnapped. Fred was supposed to be the one who orchestrated the whole set-up.

"Oh shit! I heard of you." Jroc looked at Keisha. "But what the fuck you got to do with this?"

"Fuck Black!!" Keisha screamed. "First of all, he livin' this secret life with some bitch, like I'm stupid. Dis niggah even got a baby, plus he damn near adopted this crazy little white bitch! I wouldn't be surprised if he fuckin' her too. Then his demon sisters be testing my patience!" she fumed.

"Damn. You sound a bit jealous, maybe even overzealous." Jroc summarized the situation.

"Fuck you, Jroc!" She waved him off.

"So, let me get some understanding to this shit." Jroc turned his attention to Fred. "You da employer that got me that lawyer and dis condo. You must be the plug."

"Plug?" Fred didn't understand.

"Yeah bruh. You must be the plug. What you sellin' in these streets?"

He wave him off. "That's for another day."

They all sat and talked to build a plan to take down Black and whoever might be on his team. Fred still held a grudge. Black managed to touch someone dear to him. He felt like the streets were laughing at him and it needed to be corrected.

"Am I clear?" Fred asked after explaining what he wanted to be done.

Jroc rubbed his hands together. "No question. Dat nigga won't call me scary no more. Them days dead."

CHAPTER 63

Unexpected Victims

They done let a nigga on the streets
I'm home now
Bottles poppin', money blowin',
smokin' strong now
Think a nigga sweet til I blow ya top
All that lip jackin' gotcha stupid ass
popped.

Izzo was on the stage and the crowd was living him. he was giving a concert for Warden Marshall's daughter in the gym of her high school. Paying his debt came easy while collecting a nice lump sum of money in the process.

The city loved Prophet. He always rep' for his hood and the nation's capital. Currently, he had a few top names features on his album and was doing his thing. In attendance were Tiara, Black, Lefty, Susan, and Keisha. They were in the crowd swaying to the beats of Prophet, all except Lefty who was on the stage.

"This song right here is for the birthday girl! I hope you enjoy it." Prophet winked at the birthday girl as her friends went into a frenzy. "Matter fact, bring her on the stage."

As she made her way up, the beat dropped:

> I can't see nobody doubtin' you
> You da best! And I hope dat you know
> it's true
> All them bitches be hatin, let 'em do
> what dey do
> I gotcha back no question, you know
> dat I'am fool

After the song the crowd went crazy. Prophet wished her a final happy birthday with his gift. He gave her an autographed copy of his CD and keys to a new car. It was the latest Toyota Camry. She was geeked as she jumped into his arms, wrapping her legs around his waist trying to kiss him.

Security had to come get her off. He waved at the crowd and exited the stage. Leaving the school, Keisha had an idea for them to go to dinner on a couple's date to celebrate.

Lefty and Susan had other plans. They declined the gesture. Lefty had to make a few plays around the way while Susan just didn't want to be around Keisha any longer than she had to.

They were saying their goodbyes when Lefty's phone rang. "Sup Boss lady," he answered. It was Charmine.

"How did the concert go?"

"That shit was lit! Especially for it to be in a school gym. A lot of them didn't even attend that school. I seen a few broads I smashed. But uh, why you ain't come? Where was your antennas?"

"You know I'm not in no partying mood. I'm on my way to see my baby."

"Oh Ite. Is the big homie progress any better?"

"I'm hopeful. But tell everyone I send my love."

"No question. I got you Boss lady."

Lefty got everyone's attention and relayed the message. Him and Susan got in his car and was gone with the wind. Black and Keisha rode together and Izzo and Tiara rode in the Audi R8. The destination was unknown as Izzo followed Black's car as Keisha drove.

Keisha made reservations at an expensive restaurant. She was trying to "wow" Black and show him what he'd been taking for granted. The restaurant was nice. It was named Juniors. It had high ratings and great reviews. After only waiting five minutes the hostess escorted them to their seats.

The meals were good, and they enjoyed each others company. A few people spotted Prophet and he posed for a couple of pictures and signed a few autographs.

There was a commotion in the front of the restaurant but from their seating arrangement the problem wasn't visible. No one seemed to pay it any attention, but Black's radar went into overdrive as a leery feeling overwhelmed him.

Howard University

Charmine had just hung up the phone with Lefty. She wanted to be at the concert to show her support and do the manager thing in Dro's absence, but it was visiting hours and she never missed a visit.

There she sat in the room with Dro. His statics was still the same; not getting better but not getting worse either. Charmine talked to Dro as he peacefully laid.

She always heard from different people that victims in a coma could hear them and needed help getting back to the other side. Hearing this made her talk to him about the past and the future they'd planned to build when he awakes. She decided to tell her favorite story . . .

Charmine's voice:

I can tell you from the start. Your eyes are what drew me to you. There stood this young guy with caramel complexion aa of 5' with a muscular build, beautiful skin and a smile that melted my panties. It's like the earth knew exactly what the weather should have been that day so I could glance at your perfection.

So, I'm actually getting off the bus from work, so tired from a long day as I approached the bench to have a seat. I peeped you from across the buy way as I'm walking. As I sat and released an exhausted breath, I tried to take a second look. This time you're standing directly to my left. It's funny because from far away the perfection was as if it pierced through my soul as our eyes connected. It was like we were destined to meet.

Your demeanor came across as a bad boy from head to toe. Your body was draped in designer, both ears pierced with nice sized diamonds in them. You stood with a slight slouch, and I noticed your bowed legs. It was like my body began to go into hyper drive.

Had to turn back around quickly not to give off the thought I was staring you down like a hot summer ice cream cone, begging for me to lick you.

Mind you it's hot as hell outside. The temperature was all for ninety degrees and the sun was beaming. I closed my eyes and as I imagined my young Mr. Dreamy crept into my thoughts. My mind was still taking in all the sexiness your body was dripping.

Focused on your lips. They had the right amount of plumpness to keep my mind wanting more. The soft texture of them had me imagining them grace my neck, slowly approaching, you were down to be breast.

As the heat outside increased, so did the heat inside my body as it began to crave. My mind became open from the softness of your kisses. I began to become moist. It was as if you knew every area that begged to be touched.

Then I felt you hand brush upon my shoulder followed by your sexy voice. "Do you have the time?" I jumped. As my eyes opened there you stood, this beautiful black man. No words left me lips, so you repeated, "Do you have the time?" You took a step back and it was like I finally awoke from my dream as you continued. "My name, Dro. Sorry if I startled you."

I smiled and took a deep breath. "No, No, I'm just a little tired from work. I'm Charmine." I looked at my phone. "It's 5:30." You gave off a sly nod and walked back to the corner behind the bus stop. As I'm sitting there, I can't help but occasionally glance back and oh yeah! You're looking too, sitting there looking like a snack.

That day I wore a yellow sundress that hugged the curves of my nicely round ass. My breasts weren't that big as you know but are enough to add to the amazing stature I was given. Standing at 4'11 with hazel eyes didn't hurt.

Another five minutes goes by and finally the slow ass bus arrives. Happily, I jumped out of my seat at a chance to grab a good seat in the back of the bus where I can quietly catch a nap until I reached my destination.

As I made my way to get on the bus I heard your sexy voice again, "Aye, boo. No need for the bus today. I'll give you a lift if you want."

I glanced at you and giggled. "Thought you was waiting on the bus."

You laughed as well and gave a look that said you wouldn't dare be on a bus. "Nah, I was here waiting for my homeboy, but fuck him. I just met another friend." I smiled and walked toward you, then we . . .

❖ ❖ ❖

Charmine felt a presence in the room with her. "OH MY GOSH, Heather! Where the hell you been at and most important what you doing here?"

"Hey, Girly! That was a sweet story you was telling. I know it's been a while, but I wasn't sure if you still wanted to be my friend after . . . you know." Heather put her head down.

"Pick your head up, girl. Dro told me that you da police, but he also told me how you had helped out too, so you good. Oh yeah, congrats on the baby too, you slut." Charmine nudged Heather, smiling.

"Thank you, but Black told me earlier you'd be here and to tell you if I find out anything if I can't reach him."

"Find out what?!"

"Your girl, Keisha is in bed with the guy, Fred. I'm not sure what they're up to, but Jroc is involved as well. Last I heard he was out with T.T. and Izzo at a dinner. That's not the worse part. The restaurant they're in is owned by Fred."

"Oh shit! I gotta call them."

Charmine grabbed her phone, desperately dialing the different numbers to no avail. She called everybody and the only person that answered was Susan, but she wasn't with them. She kissed Dro on his forehead with promises to return.

She rushed to her car and headed to the restaurant. Heather was on her heels as she got into her own vehicle. "You don't think they would try anything in a public space, do you?" Heather asked.

Charmine gave her a crazed look. "This beef is personal. Ain't no restrictions.

❖ ❖ ❖

Back at the Restaurant

There was a commotion in front of the establishment. From the table they couldn't see. No one gave it a second thought, but Black had a leery feeling. His instincts came to life but a second too late.

Jroc came around a corner to make his presence known. "What's up wit' your wild ass, Black?" It was quiet as Black made an attempt to stand. "Whoa, whoa, whoa, big boy. Sit cho' ass down." Jroc whipped out his gun.

The section they were in was sectioned off. No one else in the restaurant knew what was going on. Izzo was irate. "What the fuck's up wit you waving a gun around in shit. I hope you know da rules to this shit," Izzo taunted.

Jroc smiled. "Oh, I've learned all the rules since I've been in and out of the pen. This ain't even for you. This for Black." Jroc winked at him. "But you could get it too, Prophet . . . it's Prophet, right?" He smiled.

"Nigga fuck you wit cho hot ass! Do what you gotta do because if you—"

BOOM! BOOM!

Izzo flew out the highchair with two big holes in his chest. Tiara dived on top of him. "Baby! Baby! No, no, no, please do be—"

"Shut that shit up, you rollin' ass bitch!!"

BOOM!!

Jroc shot her in the back of her head. He turned the gun on Black. "Fuck you too, nigga!" Then he fired two more shots but missed.

Black had a small .25 caliber pistol on his ankle that he pulled out after diving to the floor, then fired three quick shots. Two shots hit Jroc. One in his arm, the other in his shoulder that forced him to drop his gun. Jroc turned to run after throwing people in his path exiting the establishment.

Keisha ran to the aid of Black who was on the ground panting from his wounds. "Baby! You okay. Where did you get hit?!" she asked, hoping the shots were fatal. "I'ma go get help! Hold on." She got up and ran.

Outside was an awaiting car with Jroc behind the wheel. Keisha entered the car and they pulled off into the wind. Jroc looked at her breathing hard. "Is he dead?"

Keisha smiled. "He'll never make it. Let's go!"

To be continued . . .

Blue Face Dreams II
Love and Loyalty

Also By C.C. Spicer:

ABOUT THE AUTHOR

C. C. Spicer is crazy about writing. He has a wild imagination where he paints words and captures the reader's attention. He places you in the story. Writing wasn't always a passion of his growing up in the Nation's Capital. Life in the city wasn't an easy task. The pressures of urban conditions swayed him to the streets where he fell victim to one bad decision that changed his life. Twenty seconds instantly turned into twenty years. This is where he found the love for the pen and changed his life, dropping the sword. He'd love to hear from you. Send your questions or comments directly to him.

Mail:
Cedric Spicer 40847-007
F.C.C. Petersburg
P.O. Box 1000
Petersburg, VA 23804
E-mail:
spicer_cedric@yahoo.com
instagram@dro_pak2.0
Facebook: Cedric Spicer Dropak DaAuthor

www.ingramcontent.com/pod-product-compliance
Lightning Source LLC
Chambersburg PA
CBHW071524120726
47907CB00012B/267